What Others Are Saying...

"What would the Founders do? How many times have we asked that very question? What would the likes of Washington, Jefferson, Madison, Franklin, Hamilton, and the Adams cousins say to our current problems, challenges and crises? Joe Connor—my good friend and a true patriot—along with Mike Duncan, have taken a great stab at unraveling the mystery. In their novel, *The New Founders*, Joe and Mike bring them back to life in modern day America and record their reactions as they address the growth of the federal government, our overly partisan political environment, and massive national debt and our economic malaise."

—**Dick Morris**, *New York Times* Bestselling Author

"Sadly, our own Federal government systematically attacks our God-given natural rights of life, liberty, property and our pursuit of happiness as enumerated by the founders in the Declaration of Independence. Washington, Jefferson, Madison, Franklin, Hamilton and Adams are surely rolling over in their graves. And, if they happened to step into today, it would be most interesting to hear what they'd have to say about the sorry state of our union. Connor and Duncan lay out an interesting (although fictional) thesis for every American to consider."

—**Jerome (Jerry) Corsi**, *New York Times* Bestselling Author

"Connor and Duncan's *The New Founders* answers the question Americans have been asking themselves and each other recently: *What would Washington and the Founders do?* Joe and Mike's answer is delivered in a uniquely entertaining, exciting, thoughtful and surprisingly emotional modern day tale. Well-done, guys. What's next for the new founders?"

—**David Bossie**, Citizens United

"Connor and Duncan offer an imaginative and intriguing story that will help readers understand that many of the problems and challenges we are experiencing as a nation today were foreseen and addressed by our Founding Fathers over 200 years ago."

—**Joseph Farah**, CEO, WorldNetDaily.com

"*The New Founders* brings the ideas of o̶ of modern America. This is an exciting, that will help educate people on what th and Duncan put together a compelling with this book. Great work."

—**Brian Darling**, Senior Fellow for Government Studies, The Heritage Foundation

"*The New Founders* is a reminder of why the Revolution was fought, and a warning that a second one may become necessary."

—**Tim Sumner**, U.S. Army (ret.), 911FamiliesForAmerica.org

The New Founders

The New Founders

*What would George Washington think
of America if he were alive today?*

Joseph F. Connor and Michael S. Duncan

Foreword by Dick Morris

Dunham Books
63 Music Square East
Nashville, Tennessee 37203

Trade Paperback ISBN: 978-0-9855328-6-4
eBook ISBN: 978-0-9855328-7-1

www.TheNewFounders.net
www.WeWinAmerica.com

Printed in the United States of America

"Freedom is never more than one generation away from extinction. We didn't pass it to our children in the bloodstream. It must be fought for, protected, and handed on for them to do the same, or one day we will spend our sunset years telling our children and our children's children what it was once like in the United States where men were free."

—President Ronald Reagan

"America will never be destroyed from the outside. If we falter and lose our freedoms, it will be because we destroyed ourselves."

—President Abraham Lincoln

Foreword

What would the Founders do? How many times have we asked that very question? What would the likes of Washington, Jefferson, Madison, Franklin, Hamilton, and the Adams cousins say to our current problems, challenges and crises? Joe Connor, my good friend and a true patriot, along with Mike Duncan, have taken a great stab at unraveling the mystery. In their novel, *The New Founders*, Joe and Mike bring them back to life in 2012 and record their reactions as they address the growth of the federal government, our overly partisan political environment, our massive national debt, and our economic malaise. How do Joe and Mike know what they would say were they here? They asked them! Each of these magnificent men left a lengthy written record of their opinions on almost everything. By rummaging around original historical sources—their letters (often to one another), documents, speeches, and writings—they provide the answer to the key question: What would they say?

As he surveys the delicate web of international relations with the U.S. at the center, would Washington stand on his warning against "entangling alliances?" When Jefferson and Madison see what the political party they spawned is advocating, would they remain on board? How would Hamilton—the apostle of a strong central government—react to the modern American nation with its Washington-centric system? And what would the first Secretary of the Treasury say about our staggering debt and the freedom with which we print money, debasing our currency?

No need to wonder. Just check it out. That's what Connor and Duncan have done, and we all owe them a great debt for doing so.

I got to know Joe when terrorists who killed his father, Frank, in the Fraunces Tavern bombing were granted presidential clemency. Ever since,

Joe has been a staunch crusader against terrorism and a stand-up advocate for American values and ideals. But, as an historian, he may have found his true calling. Joe and Mike have not merely written history, they invented a new genre. By bringing these great men back to life and re-writing their own words in the modern context, they have done a real service to our understanding of democracy.

I can only hope that this is the beginning of a type of historical writing which will catch on.

The Founders have so very much to teach us. If we but listen to them.

—Dick Morris (July 2012)

Prologue

George Washington stared blankly into the computer screen, apparently overwhelmed by the information he was still digesting. He pulled himself together and replied.

"I see Mr. Jenson. How horrific that our generation left the next with such an insurmountable problem. We knew the injustice of slavery but could not abolish it in our time without tearing our infant nation apart. We established a time when the trade would end and believed it would result in the eventual demise of slavery itself. I even wrote in my own will that upon my death, slaves under my direction must be set free. Please assure me they were." Shaken, Mr. Washington turned to Mr. Anders.

"We did. Did we not? We believed slavery would fade away once the trade was removed. How shameful that we failed, but you must understand we were of a just mind."

For one of a handful of times in his life, Josh Anders was at a loss for words as he stared at the first president. The others remained silent while the father of our country endured a sudden moral crisis right before their eyes.

After a minute of solemn silence, a choked up Washington cleared his throat. "You all spoke of the president during this terrible war who would be assassinated. Please gentlemen, tell me about this extraordinary man."

Historian Jack Murray moved toward the microphone. The Civil War discussion couldn't wait. "Abraham Lincoln was the sixteenth president of the United States. He was born to a poor family in the state of Kentucky, became a lawyer and was eventually elected president of the United States in 1860 as the Civil War loomed."

Mr. Washington peered into the sunken eyes and deep lines of the face on the five-dollar bill in his hand.

Murray reiterated that like the founders, Lincoln had been torn between abolishing slavery and the threat of the country being destroyed by war; ultimately, Lincoln knew that the country could not survive divided.

Murray felt his throat tighten and voice quiver. As he spoke he thought about the horrors of slavery and the thousands of young men who were killed defending and opposing the terrible institution. He looked over at his boy Todd sitting innocently next to his mother and momentarily felt a twinge of resentment that the problem of slavery, like so many today, was "kicked" to another generation to solve....

———

Since learning of the Civil War earlier in the day, Mr. Washington had been thinking about Lincoln. He was haunted by Lincoln's weary and prematurely aged face. What kind of a man was he? Did Mr. Washington and his founding brothers fail? Lincoln was not a founder, but perhaps he was more of a founder than the revolutionaries themselves. Mr. Washington sensed Providence would reveal her intentions at the memorial to this great man.

Chapter 1

Congratulations Mr. Murray, you are our winner! You and your family have won our trip to Philadelphia. Now hold on a minute while Mr. Keaton here confirms your information. This is talk radio WJMD 1220am Charlottesville. You are listening to the *TJ Show* and I am your host, Tim Jenson. It's time to pay our sponsors but don't go away; during our last segment, right after the break, we'll be talking a little bit with Mr. Jack Murray the winner of our *What would the Founders do?* contest."

As an advertisement for the Great Harvest Bread Company began to play in the background, Tim Jenson slowly backed his swivel chair away from the microphone and getting the thumbs up from his producer Keaton, carefully removed his headphones, placing them on the table just to his right. "So tell me about Mr. Murray."

Jenson's young producer, sitting behind the glass in the control room, replied, "Here's the info. He's from out in Clover Hill. Says here, he's a high school American history teacher and teaches some classes over at James Madison University. He'll be coming with this wife and their teenage son. His information is on your computer screen right now."

Jenson, leaning back with his hands behind his head, turned toward the screen and did a quick read of the information. He bent his face toward the monitor. "Princeton, huh?" Jenson grinned. "Hope he's not another stuck up Ivy Leaguer." Jenson then tore off a couple of his familiar *Post-Its*, jotted down a few notes about Murray and slid the notes into his left sleeve for review after the show.

"He didn't sound that way," Keaton added with a smile. "I spoke to him a couple times already and he seemed like a pretty good guy. You can see from the contest that he has a lot of the same political views you do, maybe with more passion."

Spinning in his chair to face Keaton, Jenson raised his voice, asking "Quesque c'est? More passionate than *moi*? You'd better be joking." Keaton, arm outstretched holding the "on air" switch, spun his other hand and index finger in the air. Jenson looked up as the "on air" light illuminated.

"Hello, we're back and with us on the line is the winner of our *What would the Founders do*? contest, Mr. Jack Murray of Clover Hill. Mr. Murray, congratulations. You really know your American history and have an appreciation of this country."

"Thank you, Tim." Pacing the kitchen barefoot wearing shorts and a tee shirt Murray excitedly replied, "My wife and son and I are looking forward to meeting you and Skip, taking in the history, having a few cheesesteaks and celebrating our country's independence. Maybe we'll even learn a few things."

"We have quite an agenda planned Mr. Murray. It will be a great trip. You will get a 'back stage' tour of the Statehouse, we will visit the Franklin Institute and the Mint, and perhaps if time permits, the haunted Betsy Ross house. If we are lucky," Jenson joked, "maybe we will even see a ghost or two. I think we have all the details. We'll see you tomorrow. Stay on the line for my producer. "

With that the show went to its final commercial break of the day.

Now Jenson was even more enthused about the trip. He expected a broadcast from Independence Hall would boost his ratings but he was concerned that the winner, the person with whom he would be forced to spend the weekend and have on air may be a dolt.

Murray didn't seem that way at all. He was a born Virginian. Jenson could tell by Murray's accent. He displayed an intelligent, honest demeanor during those few minutes on the phone. He was obviously a knowledgeable patriot, shown in not only his thoughtful ideas on how the Founders would address today's issues, but also in his knowledge of historical details.

Murray knew for instance that the building commonly referred to as Independence Hall in Philadelphia was actually called the Pennsylvania Statehouse. Perhaps this was a minor detail, but to Tim a very telling one. Tim thought he might even forgive the fact that Murray went to an Ivy League school north of the Mason Dixon line.

But there was something else about Murray that Tim could not put his finger on. Maybe it was the inflection in Murray's voice that showed respect to him but also had a self-assuring quality. Whatever it was, Murray reminded Tim of someone. But who?

Jenson closed the show. "Just a reminder to the audience, we will be away from our regular schedule for the next couple of weeks. But don't fret; we will be in Philadelphia for the Independence Day weekend, broadcasting live from the Pennsylvania Statehouse in Philly tomorrow, July 3. We'll have some guests including our contest winner, Jack Murray, and hopefully the anchor of our little station and hundreds of others, the top dog, Josh Anders....So we will see you tomorrow from Philly."

With that, Tim switched off the air. Jenson and Keaton would arrive at the Murray home at 7:00am the following day in a large luxury conversion van for the five-hour drive to Philly. Tim thought the van perhaps a bit tacky, but it would be comfortable, and was a high-end expense for his, at times, chintzy little radio station.

Bottom line for Tim was that this *Founders* promotion needed to go well. It cost the station some bucks. He had pumped the idea up to management, and it was all his baby. Tim recalled that the idea for the promo came suddenly in the middle of the night. He thought it ironic because he'd always been kind of a dreamer.

Now fifty-two years old, the tall, slender Tim Jenson felt an urge from deep within to tackle a new dream. The contest would allow him to better connect with his listeners and broaden his exposure to a more national audience. He knew that larger than life Josh Anders, the most listened to man in America, would also be broadcasting on the third from Independence Hall. Jenson had sent Anders an invite to appear on his show, but as of yet, had not received a response. He really hoped to meet Anders (not in a confrontational sense) to possibly debate him on the air. His goal down the road was to one day whip the cocky Anders in the ratings. Anders of course was conservative talk show royalty and dominated the ratings even on Tim's local station. Since his wife died, Tim focused on his career with the goal of one day hosting a national show like Anders.

———

After hanging up the phone, Jack Murray smiled. He thought he had really clicked with his favorite talk show host. He laughed to himself recognizing that it was only a quick conversation, but he felt Jenson's respect for his knowledge and writing style in those brief moments on the phone. Jack deduced that this, combined with the content of the essay, was what won him and his family the trip to Philly.

This trip would be a great experience for the family but Jack knew it was mostly for himself. He had accomplished about all he could teaching high school and although he was well on his way to his goal of a full college professorship, he needed to "get out there" more.

Over the past several months, Jack had grown restless and impatient. His life was missing something but he did not know what. He didn't even have a clue where to begin looking. For the past few months, Jack Murray laid in bed, eyes wide, staring at the ceiling while the seconds crawled by on the clock on his night stand. Since he learned he had won the contest two days earlier, his anxiety had diminished, but the nights were still long. Murray joked to himself, "I'm going on a trip to a city whose football fans booed Santa Claus.

"If things are that bad that a trip to Philadelphia will cure what ails me, it's even worse than I thought."

Chapter 2

Although extremely focused during trading hours, Anthony Hahn tended to be drawn to debate toward the end of the workday. He loved a good argument and would spar with any person on any topic, at any time. It seemed the slightly built red haired young trader needed to continually prove that he was the smartest person in the room, despite no evidence to the contrary.

Possibly, it was because his position in the financial world started from such a humble and inauspicious beginning. But even being the head trader on one of the most prestigious currency trading desks in the world could not quench his desire to demonstrate, yet again, that he was superior. Or at least dislodge the chip on his shoulder that was so firmly set.

———

As he walked out of the elevator after another busy trading day, Hahn put his earphones over his head. He plugged the cord into his classic old am radio, and started toward Trinity Place restaurant for a quick drink and bite to eat before heading home. He fit right in with most Wall Street workers his age, in that once on the pavement, they seemed to be literally walking to the beat of their own drummer (or favorite band on their iPods).

Unlike most, Hahn's idea of winding down was listening to the fiery debate and heated arguments airing on any one of the conservative talk radio shows broadcast in the metropolitan area. But at four o'clock during the week in New York, there was only one show that kept his attention.

There was no radio talk show host more thought-provoking than Josh Anders.

Anders was the recognized, undeniable and self-proclaimed King of American conservative talk radio. He was bigger than life with a girth to match his ego. You did not get to be the king for nothing. Well-educated in law and politics, Anders used those tools to begin his burgeoning radio career, starting with a small popular station in Providence, Rhode Island, before being unleashed on the country. He knew the industry; friends and foes, competitors and novices. He kept tabs on them all throughout the country. Anders was a great judge of character and took many of these young talk show hosts under his wing, never refusing his advice and counsel when sought.

He also promoted many of these shows, some of which aired on the same regional station that syndicated his show. One of these shows was based in Charlottesville, Virginia with a host who seemed to echo much of his political beliefs. Tim Jenson's producer had called the Anders show asking for a few minutes on air while they both broadcasted from Philadelphia over the Fourth of July weekend.

Of course Anders agreed, but now the weekend was upon them and he jotted down Tim Jenson's name on his calendar, a reminder to google Jenson when he had a moment. As he looked at the calendar, he noticed Jenson's name was right next to the publisher's name to which he agreed to give an interview. Anders' son loved this guy's magazine and devotedly read it. Anders trusted his son's judgment so he happily agreed to the meeting. But at the moment, Anders could only think about getting through the next few days. He couldn't wait to get this weekend over with, so he could head to his retreat in the British Virgin Islands where he could kick back, relax, and vacation anonymously.

Anders scribbled in his calendar, packed it in his briefcase with his iPad and ledger book, closed the briefcase and told his staff that he would see them at the hotel in Philly later that night to go over Friday's schedule. How is it possible that the number one radio show in the country could be on tape delay in its biggest market, New York? A voice yelled that the show would be live within a month or two, to which Anders nodded. With that, he waved them goodbye and left the studio.

———

The main floor of the publisher's office was unusually quiet that Thursday afternoon. The buzz all week had been around the exclusive interview that the magazine's owner was able to land. A quiet, nervous energy permeated from cubicle to cubicle. Each desk was occupied by a young man or woman, none of whom looked a day over twenty-five. Some were writing while others were programming. One of the writers, a recent graduate of Villanova University, looked over about ten pages of his handwritten notes one last time before making his way to the boss's office.

The door was always open and upon entering, the writer noticed that though his boss was leaning in toward his computer monitor, his eyes were locked on the plasma flat screen television on the wall. He was transfixed on a political talk show on the World News Network. The young author shuffled his notes together one last time, fastened a paper clip on them, then dropped his notes on the desk, noting to his boss that everything he requested was in the clip, in chronological order. Brian Faulk looked down at the notes then back up at the young man and thanked him for his effort. The subordinate nodded, and exited Faulk's office with a look of contentment.

Faulk had planned to change the world when he founded the magazine, *The Impoverished Review* almost two decades before. Now all these years later, the seventy year old entrepreneur had not given up his quest. His magazine was the pulpit he always desired. Faulk hoped landing the exclusive interview with the one and only Josh Anders may be a way of bringing attention to some good men that might team up and fight the good fight. He almost felt guilty by the sheer luck of landing it. Anders' son was a big fan of the magazine. But while it may have been dumb luck, the good work done by Faulk and his staff resulted in the coveted interview. He smiled with satisfaction at the sight of Anders' background notes on his desk and began to sift through them in preparation of the next day's meeting.

But the sound emanating from the television on the wall kept diverting his attention. He couldn't pull his concentration away from the talk show host, William Fredericks, berating a US Republican Senator from Texas. Faulk recoiled at how over-the-top and personal Fredericks was getting as he directed his wrath at the politician. Faulk had no respect for this bombastic, pompous Brit, who never met a conservative American he did not despise. Faulk looked back at the notes, shaking his head and wondering how an individual could speak like that to another human being and live with himself, let alone sleep at night.

———

About sixteen hours later, Fredericks was awake again, alert and facing that horrible red light of his alarm clock. He had begun thinking of it as the red eyes of the devil mocking him as he suffered through yet another tormented night. He kept the stiff upper lip of a British Gentlemen, but how many more nights like this could he handle?

This time his bleary eyes and swimming brain registered 3:10am. It was going to be another bad one. The demons were back. Although he had been warned by his doctor to abstain, he continued to believe incorrectly that the nightly fifth of Beefeater would keep the demons away. Tonight they attacked with particular aggression, demanding Fredericks accuse his "enemies" of treason. These voices demanded the ruin of all opponents. The image of his enemies hanging from trees stuck in his alcohol-soaked brain as he stumbled out of bed heading to the loo for a few sleeping pills.

Fredericks did not understand why these nightmares had grown even more malicious recently. The voices had left him alone for the most part since he quietly began taking Xanax, but now they returned with a vengeance. Thank God they had not again interfered with his "day job."

Certainly, he had appeased the voices over the last couple of years by using his 8:00pm primetime political TV talk show, *Today's World* on the World News Network (WNN) to savage his conservative enemies. He had dutifully taken on every issue and every comer with all the dirt the research department could find and all the fervor a zealot could deliver.

But something else was troubling Fredericks this early July morning. Recently he began to question which side was evil, those against him or those with him. During these fleeting moments of clarity, before the sinister synapses of his brain kicked back in, he actually lamented his admiration for the American people. After all, it was the bravery, ingenuity and generosity of the Yanks that delivered England from the Nazis. He knew in his heart what they could and would achieve if the American people were to be left alone, free of interference and even free of his demagoguery. He was having his doubts about his overall view of the world.

But the numbing effects of the gin began to wear off and he could no longer hold at bay the demons that returned for the night.

Such was Fredericks' life. He imagined his death. Even Hell would be a welcome respite from these nights. But Hell would have to be put on hold. In a few hours, William Fredericks would once again begin preparation for another show.

Chapter 3

The red Chevy conversion van was in front of the Murray house promptly at 7:00am.

Jack was relieved. Dorothy was not sold on going to Philly during prime beach time so at least the trip was starting out right. The traffic to Virginia Beach or the Outer Banks was going to be murder anyway. The beach was always a zoo on Fourth of July and Jack knew that even Dorothy would concede that fact. She was putting the finishing touches on her makeup as Todd bounded out the front door in his favorite tee shirt, white emblazoned with a large red "USA" across the front, his blue Villanova lacrosse hat, black basketball shorts and red Nike basketball shoes with no socks, untied, and his black knapsack slung over his shoulder. There was no doubt he was excited, the all-American teenager looking forward to his first trip to Philadelphia.

As Todd jumped into the van to check it out, Jack followed. Neither he nor Dorothy, whom he called "Dot," knew how to dress for all this. And they were too embarrassed to ask. The diminutive contest winner decided on a pair of neatly pressed beige khakis, a white Lands End golf shirt and his trusty brown Sperry boat shoes with no socks. He carried two suitcases, over-packing as usual for what was anticipated to be a two night stay. Not knowing what to expect, he and Dot had packed some clothes for any occasion. Jack secretly hoped Jenson would take a liking to him. They were going to be travel companions for the next couple of days and Jack was anxious to meet some of the political types that Jenson's producer promised would be there. Hell, he may even get to meet Josh Anders.

Dot looked good in her light blue sun dress, low heels, sparkling blue eyes, and flowing shoulder length auburn hair. She locked up the house, turned and walked toward the van and Jenson. Jenson did a quick double-take as he introduced Skip Keaton and himself to Jack Murray. They then met his son, Todd. Jenson then righted himself, smiled, and reached his hand out to Mrs. Murray.

Keaton, looking at his watch said, "It's a good ride to Philly and we want to get there in enough time to set up. So I think we need to get moving."

With that, Keaton jumped in the driver's seat and started the van. Jenson took his place riding shotgun while the Murray family slid into their seats in the rear passenger area. Jack thought Dot looked impressed so far. Keaton and Jenson seemed like regular guys and the van was new and clean with plenty of room. It had a refrigerator, comfortable seats and Todd's favorite Xbox games to keep him busy. Everybody settled in as they pulled away from the curb.

Knowing the van's high tech navigational system would never recognize the area, Murray directed Keaton through the winding country roads toward Interstate 81 north. Todd dropped *Call of Duty* into the Xbox and began to wipe out a platoon of Russian Special Forces. Dottie put her headphones on, hit shuffle on the iPod, and drifted off blissfully to the sound of Alan Jackson (as only a busy mother granted a few hours of down time could do).

Keaton changed the radio station from his employer's talk radio, which was broadcasting a juvenile morning show, to classic rock station 106.3 WBOP, and began singing along to The Who's "Won't get Fooled Again." Amused, Murray noted to himself that Jenson just smiled at Keaton's abrupt behavior. Murray immediately liked the older Jenson and settled in for the long journey with familiar music, relaxed company, and the beautiful Virginia countryside as it passed by the window in a blur.

While baseball season was in full swing with the young, upstart Mets holding a four game lead on the high priced Marlins and Phillies, it was football that always ended up dominating any sports conversation in Murray's house. Murray was a born Redskin fan. One of his earliest memories was of his father sitting in front of the TV rooting on Billy Kilmer, Charlie Taylor, and the 1972 Skins against Bob Griese (and the undefeated Miami Dolphins in Super Bowl VII). They lost that day, but Murray was hooked on the Skins. Though not a gifted athlete, through playing sports, coaching and attending events, Murray developed a respect for people coming together to achieve a common goal.

Unfortunately for Jack, Todd inherited a love for all things Carolina from his mom, including the University of North Carolina Tar Heels basketball. This was a sore spot for her husband as Dottie and Todd enjoyed the friendly rivalry with Jack. Murray's one solace was that at least they weren't Eagle fans. After all, Dot was born in Philly, so it could have happened.

The radio show host and teacher began to jell as the upcoming football training camp became the subject of discussion. Jenson concurred with Murray that the Skins were going nowhere again and they both agreed that Mike Shanahan was a good coach if left alone by the meddling owner. If Dan Snyder sold the team or removed himself from the football operation, they could return to the glory days of Joe Gibbs and George Allen. Within thirty minutes, the wanna-be Redskin general managers had fixed the future of the team and now turned their attention to fixing America's future.

The next two hours were filled with lively political debate, ranging from the state of the union to which president was each man's favorite.

"Thomas Jefferson was by far the most accomplished of all the presidents. He wrote the Declaration of Independence, doubled the size of the country in one fell swoop with the Louisiana Purchase and invented products still used today like the dumbwaiter and the swivel chair," Jenson argued.

While Murray agreed that Jefferson was a great president, he countered that the man who was known as the Father of the Constitution, James Madison, was a greater thinker than Jefferson. Murray argued that Madison was underrated as a president and reminded Jenson of Madison's most important contribution, *The Federalist Papers*, which helped define the relationship between the States and the Federal Government.

"Madison made plain that the Rights of Americans are God-given and not subject to the whim of government or politicians," Murray admonished. While Jenson was not dissuaded from his opinion, he was deeply impressed with the depth of Murray's understanding and passion. At least both men could agree that no president or founder exceeded the talents and contributions of George Washington.

Dottie knew her Jack was on fire now, speaking of his beloved Constitution. She smiled as she thought, "That Mr. Jenson has no idea what he has gotten himself into," and quietly drifted off to sleep.

It was now ten in the morning and just in time to tune in to the *Josh Anders Show*. He too would be broadcasting from Independence Hall that morning, so Jenson focused on how Anders would kick off his show. Jenson's show followed and he did not want to copy anything the master would say out of the gate. But for Jenson, the best was yet to come.

Anders had agreed to appear at the beginning of Jenson's show today. The host from Charlottesville would be ready. Jenson and Keaton would be set up on "radio row" at the Statehouse before two, at least an hour before his spot with Anders and in time to begin his broadcast after the news update. Anders had only promised ten minutes, but Jenson was looking forward to it, keenly aware that even a few minutes with Josh Anders could potentially open doors for him nationally. It was exactly the kind of opportunity he wanted and hoped for when he originally planned the contest and trip. He liked the fact that he and Anders thought alike, both wanting to be in Philadelphia for the weekend. Jenson smiled as he turned his attention to Anders' voice roaring over the radio.

Anders opened with a fury, exclaiming that he was disgusted by the few remaining candidates sniping at each other rather than focusing on defeating the current president, who they all agreed was dismantling the fundamental principles of our nation. The attack on each other by way of negative ads, filled with lies and distortions, made him sick. He continued his rant that the candidates were engaging in the kind of class warfare usually confined to the Left, and using labels like "Vulture Capitalist" to describe one another.

As the van approached Philadelphia, Jenson added that it was unbelievable that these supposed capitalists would use terminology like that.

"I despise campaign catchphrases like 'Compassionate Conservatism.' If adhered to without intervention, there is no more compassionate, no more equitable a system as capitalism, and it need not be apologized for, nor should it be tinkered with."

Murray was on the same wavelength, following almost reflexively with a quote from Adam Smith.

"It is not from the benevolence of the butcher, the brewer or the baker that we expect our dinner, but from their regard to their own interest. We address ourselves, not to their humanity but to their self-love."

Murray could not contain himself.

"Unlike today's liberals, the founders understood human nature, you know, Smith's 'Invisible hand.' The founders designed the Constitution with this as a guiding principle. Human nature demands pursuit of one's own interest. The Invisible hand aligns self interest with societal interest through risk and reward, upper mobility, unfettered financial incentives and minimal government intrusion. As Smith said about man, by pursuing his own interest, 'He frequently promotes that of the society more effactually than when he really intends to promote it. I have never known much good done by those who affected to trade for the public good.'"

It was evident to him that he found in Murray a kindred spirit who understood that the only vultures in capitalism were those in the government who, through taxes and regulation, picked on the bones of once vibrant businesses.

"I knew I liked this guy, he's my kind of people!" Jenson yelled to Keaton, startling his producer and everybody else in the van.

Dottie, having woken up with about half an hour left in the ride, listened intently to the conversation as they pulled up to a red light in front of Independence Mall in Philadelphia. All heads were swinging back and forth taking in the immediate sights in the foreground and distance. With Independence Hall and the famed Liberty Bell to the left, Dottie happily noted to herself that Jack was really in his element now.

Jack needed this. She had sensed his recent restlessness and knowing her husband as she did, knew that he needed fellow conservatives with whom to discuss his frustrations; people who would listen, unlike many of his students who came to him already jaded by their liberal instructors. His words to them fell on deaf ears more often than not. Even the members of his local Tea Party were falling into the "all talk and no action" trap. Jack needed men of action who could affect a kind of real change that was not just words on a bumper sticker. Maybe Jack had found what he needed. Maybe he had won this contest for a reason other than an all expense paid weekend.

Chapter 4

W hat we need is a candidate this country can rally behind. I don't care what his political party is. I want a president that puts the good of the country first and not the good of himself, his wallet or his political cronies!" Josh Anders was in the latter part of his third hour on the air live from Independence Hall. It was the Fourth of July eve and he had spoken to just about every type of person that day. Even a handful of ninety-nine percenters who descended upon the City of Brotherly Love stuck around just to give their two cents to the radio behemoth.

His nerves were getting frayed and he consistently looked at the clock to see if it was time to wrap up. He glanced toward his producer, who signaled that they needed one more commercial break. Anders continued, "Well we have one more break before we wrap up, but stay tuned. We will take a few more calls before we finish with a reading from the nation's most cherished symbol of liberty and Thomas Jefferson's most enduring monument, The Declaration of Independence. So stay tuned."

As the show's jingle began, Anders leaned back in his chair and motioned to his producer to bring the section of the document to be read on the air. His assistant, Betty, a middle age brunette, pulled a chair next to him.

"We have time for two more calls before you read the passage and we pack up," said his producer.

Anders gave a quick nod and then turned to his assistant. "What do we have left on the agenda today?"

Betty handed him a folder and reminded him that he agreed to go on Jenson's show at one o'clock.

"Yeah yeah, I remember, we're giving him ten minutes right?" Anders asked.

"Yes," his assistant said. "We explained to his producer that we have a hard stop at ten minutes. When we finish with Mr. Jenson, we go back to the hotel for lunch, then up to the suite.

You can freshen up there and relax for a little bit before we come back here at four for the interview with that gentleman from *The Impoverished Review* and a private tour of Independence Hall for you and Steve."

Anders turned behind him where his cousin Steven was sitting and nodded to him.

"Steverino, five o'clock, you good with that?" Steve simply responded with a thumbs up. Anders turned back toward his assistant and with the radio console before him, asked what she had planned for the group for dinner later that evening. "We have arranged for a private room at the Philadelphia Art Museum where the chefs from Vetri, supposedly the best Italian restaurant in Philly, will prepare a great menu for us."

"Good, that sounds great. I'll eat light at lunch if that's the case. How many are we expecting?" inquired Anders.

His assistant was about to speak when Anders' producer motioned that they were about to go back on the air. Anders began, "Welcome back to the Josh Anders radio show!" Anders looked over to his assistant who put up eight fingers. Anders gave a puzzled look, but then continued "Bob from Raleigh, welcome to the show."

The caller from Raleigh began his rant by stating that the prior president of the United States did more damage to the economy than all previous presidents combined and that the current president was just trying to clean up his mess.

"Bob, how many times have we gone over this the last three and a half years? You sound like an intelligent fellow, so listen up...."

After explaining the president's policies of massive debt and tax increases, Anders turned to his producer while still on the air and asked if people were really that ignorant out there. He continued by saying that he knew a lot of smart and rational people from Raleigh but would hazard a guess that this gentleman is not one of them. "Who do we have next?"

"Joe from New Jersey will be our last caller of the day," the producer whispered in his ear. Anders jumped on it. "Joe, you're the final caller on this Fourth of July weekend, the pressure's on so make it a good call."

The caller gushed that he was excited to speak with Anders on the eve of our country's 236th birthday and cautioned that the Republican party candidates were in disarray. He wondered if Anders could forecast any candidate differentiating themselves in the two months leading up to the

Republican convention.

"Well Joe, as of right now, I cannot lend my support to any of them. Out of the four that remain, not one has distinguished himself among the voters and it seems like each new day brings a new front runner. None of the contenders have been able to gain even an iota of momentum and each state has a different favorite each week, day and hour. Just when you think one of these guys is ready to take the reins, he's bumped from the horse and has to scramble to get back on. So my opinion is that it's going to be a horserace right up to and into the convention in September. This should make for a lively get-together in Tampa, wouldn't you say?"

The caller then quickly added that maybe Anders should run as the Tea Party candidate because he would vote for him.

Anders let out a big laugh. "Well I'm flattered but I don't know if I'm the running type. To paraphrase Marx, Groucho that is; 'I wouldn't want to join any club that would have me as a member.' Thanks for the call Joe."

Anders then reached down to the table to get the passage he planned on reading as he finished up his Philadelphia remote show.

"As promised, given we are in Philadelphia broadcasting live from Independence Hall, what is a more fitting tribute to this great edifice before us than to conclude today's show by reading a passage from the Declaration of Independence. Here, in exalted and unforgettable phrases, Thomas Jefferson expressed the convictions in the minds and hearts of the American people. The political philosophy of the Declaration was not a new idea; its ideals of individual liberty had already been expressed by John Locke and the Continental philosophers."

Anders began reading the Declaration. "The unanimous Declaration of the thirteen United States of America; When in the course of human events, it becomes necessary for one people to dissolve the political bands which have connected them with another...."

Anders was halfway through the Declaration when he motioned to his producer. "Do we have enough time?"After his producer notified the audience that only a few minutes remained, Anders pushed onward, skipping the assertions and reciting the last three paragraphs. As he finished, he marveled at what he just shared with his audience. He could not help himself and decided to repeat the passage concerning Divine Providence before concluding how the founders mutually pledged to each other their Lives, Fortunes and sacred Honor.

Anders then turned to the crowd and said, "If that didn't give you goose bumps, then you might as well pack it in!"

The crowd in the foreground let out applause and started chanting Josh, Josh, Josh. Anders shouted over the din.

"My thanks to the audience and to everybody who made this remote broadcast possible, you did a terrific job. Have a great Fourth of July weekend and I will be back on the air live on Monday July twentieth. The best to you and your family and God bless this great country of ours."

Anders leaned back again, took his earphones out and spun in his chair to face his producer. The producer leaned in and said that Anders had about three minutes before being introduced on the Jenson show. He pointed Anders down the row of portable radio console tables to where Jenson was gathering papers in front of him.

Anders looked over his shoulder toward Jenson, then turned back and asked his producer what radio station was that again. The producer answered, "1220 WJMD out of Charlottesville. It's in a college town but it has a strong conservative following. And this guy Jenson is good, really well-read, up on his history. You'll like him."

Anders countered, "I read your notes and saw some of his writings, sounds intelligent. Make sure you signal me at nine minutes. I'm getting a little hungry."

On the other end of the row sat Jenson. He was going over some last second talking points before beginning the show. He was calm and composed, distinctly opposite of his frantic producer Keaton, who seemed to be having a minor nervous breakdown. "He's right over there, why isn't he moving yet?" yelled Keaton to the trees above.

The yelling startled Jenson for a moment, then looking toward the other end of the row, looked back at his frenzied colleague and told him to relax. A commercial for a local car dealer was playing in the background as Anders approached the chair next to Jenson.

Jenson stood, extending his hand to Anders. "Mr. Anders, thank you so much for giving us some time this afternoon." Anders shook Jenson's hand while sitting down.

"Don't mention it, the pleasure is all mine. Glad to do it. I've heard you've developed quite a little following in Virginia."

"Miniscule compared to you but we're trying," Jenson responded. "Hopefully today's broadcast will keep folks tuned in following you."

Anders, putting his headset on and lounging in his seat, replied that he was happy to help.

As the introduction song finished, Jenson commenced his show. "Welcome to a special Fourth of July weekend edition of the *TJ Show*. As always, I am your host, Tim Jenson, and we are sitting live outside of Independence Hall in Philadelphia as we celebrate the eve of our nation's birthday. We have a lot in store for you today as we discuss the historic significance of this great city and the role it played in our independence.

"We will also have a full slate of guests over the next three hours including our contest winner, Jack Murray, who traveled with our team to visit the sights. But our first guest here on the *TJ Show* needs no introduction. He is the host with the largest radio audience in the country and is heard live on WJMD 1220am weekdays from ten to one. It is my privilege to introduce Josh Anders to the show."

"Thank you, Tim," Anders boomed.

"You decided to broadcast your show today from Philly as did we," Jenson continued.

"What inspired you to come to the City of Brotherly Love on this particular day in this specific year? As you mentioned to us prior to coming on the air, this is the first time you've done a live remote show for the Fourth of July weekend in all the time you've been on the air."

Anders shuffled in his chair for a brief moment and then took over. "Tim, this country is at a dangerous crossroad. It's teetering on the brink; a cliff is a better description. And if we do not grab it by the neck right now, we are in jeopardy of losing it forever the way a lot of European and foreign countries have been lost. So we felt it was important to come to this great city and set foot on such hallowed ground with this great monument before us and try to inspire the masses to wake up and rouse their patriotism once again. We had this idea to come to Philly months ago because I was overcome with this feeling that I needed to be here, almost drawn to it. It may sound funny to the audience, but it was almost as if I was obligated to be here on this precise day. Although they didn't have to build anything, I just came."

Jenson laughed at Anders' long-winded response and told him he felt the same way.

Anders reiterated his feeling and began reading a passage from the Declaration aloud.

"That whenever any Form of Government becomes destructive of these ends, it is the Right of the People to alter or abolish it, and to institute new Government. Ain't that the truth, wouldn't you say?"

Jenson stunned Anders by completing the passage from memory.

"Laying its foundation on such principles and organizing its powers in such form, as to them shall seem most likely to affect their Safety and Happiness. Prudence, indeed, will dictate that Governments long established should not be changed for light and transient causes."

Anders sat silent, staring speechlessly at Jenson as an awkward quiet ensued.

Jenson apologized for interrupting but explained that he was caught up in the moment and felt it was important to finish that specific thought verbatim.

Anders stood, beamed a big grin and haughtily boomed, "Precisely! Mr. Jenson, I am quite impressed at your knowledge of this great document."

Jenson, looking satisfied but a bit embarrassed, said, "As most of my audience already knows, I am a self-proclaimed expert on the Declaration of Independence."

Anders, waving to the growing audience, confessed that he was no expert on the Declaration and asked Jenson if he could recite the names of the signers from Virginia.

Jenson rattled off in no time flat, "George Wythe, Richard Henry Lee, Benjamin Harrison, Thomas Nelson, Carter Braxton, Francis Lightfoot Lee, and Thomas Jefferson."

Anders turned to folks on the other side of the console table, clapped his hands and led a rhythmic applause that built to a stadium like roar.

"C'mon folks, let's give it up for this great patriot's impressive display. So Tim, to you, what is the most meaningful passage in the Declaration?"

Without hesitation, Jenson stood as if addressing the Virginia statehouse.

"Well, the most quoted part of it, and for good reason, is the strongest political text ever written, in my opinion, and that is, 'We hold these truths to be self evident, that all men are created equal, that they are endowed by their Creator with certain unalienable Rights, that among these are Life, Liberty and the pursuit of happiness.'"

"My contest winning guest sitting to my right, Jack Murray, may disagree, saying that the preamble to the Constitution is the most powerful of all. And he may have a point."

Anders repeated his question noting that Jenson gave him the most quoted words, not the words he found most meaningful.

"Josh," Jenson said. "The words I find most consequential come from the conclusion, which states, 'And for the support of this Declaration, with firm reliance on the protection of Divine Providence, we mutually pledge to each other our Lives, our Fortunes and our sacred Honor.'"

Jenson went on to explain that this was great foresight, how these special men knew they were doing something historic and realized the impact these words would have on generations to come. They knew full well that failure would mean facing the hangman's noose. They would live together in freedom or die together in honor.

Jenson, without realizing it, closed his eyes and spoke. "Finally, they understood that it was Divine Providence that brought them together, that by mutually pledging their lives, fortunes and honor, that the success of the group hinged on the success of the individuals. That was the only way they could declare their independence and survive as a new country."

Keaton gently tapped Jenson on his shoulder to break the spell, letting him know that they needed a commercial break. Jenson sat back down and leaned into the microphone.

"Mr. Anders, thanks again for spending a few minutes with our radio audience. Let's do it again if you make it down to Charlottesville."

Anders glanced toward his producer, then to his watch.

"Boy, ten minutes certainly goes by fast when you're having fun. Let's have our people talk so we can get you on my show sometime soon." Jenson smiled a big smile.

"It's a plan! We'll be right back."

Keaton quickly motioned to the group that they were in commercial. The gathered crowd broke into applause again. Anders, taking off his earphones, turned to Jenson and said, "Tim, what are you doing later on this evening. We have a dinner set up over at the art museum and we would love to have you. What do you say?"

Jenson looked toward his producer and Murray, and then back to Anders. He then replied that he would love to attend as long as it was okay to bring his guests along.

Anders smiled, "Bring them along. The more the merrier. I think we're on for seven-thirty, is that correct Betty?"

Betty shot him a stern glance as she nodded her head in disgust. She thought to herself that he had done it again.

Anders looked back at Jenson. "Listen," he said. "Go talk to my assistant Betty here. She's a darling and will give you all the details. Just give her the exact number of people because we're arranging an Italian feast. See you later."

As Anders and his cousin turned and walked through the autograph seekers, Keaton put his hand on Jenson's shoulder. "Mission accomplished, the guy loves you. National syndication, here we come!"

Chapter 5

The red light was on but this was a good light. It was again time for William Fredericks to shine again.

"Good evening all you colonists out there. My name is William Fredericks and like all Englishmen based here in our former outpost, this weekend is my least favorite time of the year. Tomorrow all you descendants of *émigrés* will be sweltering in the hot sunlight, grilling up your wieners, hamburgers and beans and drinking down that disgusting yellow colored concoction you refer to as the king of beers. Budweiser, a beverage that Americans worship and drink by the gallons. And what Brits call a specimen can. Calling it a lager is an insult to lagers."

Fredericks let go a hearty laugh.

"Well, I've digressed. What is on tap for today? During *The World Today* we will be focusing on the pathetic yet dangerous race for the Republican Presidential nomination and the future honor of being swept away by another historic Democratic Presidential victory."

William sat back in his chair.

"We will listen to some inane clips from the *Josh Anders Show*, which aired earlier today among many of his flag-waving, single digit IQ lapdogs making their yearly pilgrimage to Independence Hall in Philadelphia. It's getting bad out there for you red staters when even the water boy for your party, big Josh, and his monosyllabic callers are frustrated by the lack of quality in the GOP field and are calling for an uprising against society.

The manic host stood and began his trademark of pacing the studio as he spoke.

"I find it most amusing that these Conservatives, so-called Tea Partiers who quote their revered founders so often that they must wear powdered wigs to bed, have posters of Betsy Ross in a bikini on their walls and believe they are direct descendants of the sterile George Washington himself, cannot find a single soul even remotely suitable to become president."

Fredericks extended his hands out and continued.

"Am I right? You would think these over paid, trust fund leaching one-percenters could at least pool their considerable wealth and purchase a candidate. Or perhaps have mummy and daddy buy one for them. It's quite sad, really. My heart aches for them."

He began by sharing a few clips from that day's *Josh Anders Show*. He described Anders whining on and on about the horrible group that continued to spew hate onto the public and mainstream media. Disgusted by the patriotic passage, William played the first clip. He dripped of sarcasm and contempt as he mocked the conservative broadcast.

"Boo hoo, yes it is so sad, please bring me a box of Kleenex! My tears are flowing. First of all, Americans have been weaned on the medium of television for half a century. So what does old Anders expect, that sweet old grandma is going to change her routine after fifty years? To grandma, the voice coming out of the idiot box at six-thirty might as well be Walter Cronkite. She wouldn't know the difference. You can just see the scientists in the Pavlovian Institute in Moscow high-fiving each other as they listen to American television and talk radio."

Fredericks glanced up and asked for the next sound bite, which was an Anders' quote about needing a candidate who would excite the electorate and put country ahead of political party.

Fredericks, a big grin across his face, self-servingly interpreted the words for his audience.

"Even Anders is starting to see the light of social justice. It's about time. Jolly Josh is calling for a candidate who is inclusive, one that believes in fairness and social justice. Finally we can move away from those stale old dark ideas and into the light of progressivism. Even Josh Anders agrees! Somebody, get on the phone and give Hell a call to see if the ice skating rink is open."

He then asked his producer for the audio reading of the Declaration of Independence.

"I want you to hear for yourselves how pathetically reactionary and incendiary the party of Dumbo really is."

Anders reciting of the Declaration on the Tim Jenson show was the next excerpt. Fredericks ignored the fact that the audio originated from the Jenson show and forged on with his commentary.

"Who does this guy, Timmy Jetson, think he is, Thomas Jefferson? 'Governments long established should not be changed for light and transient causes?' He sounds like a dumb waiter if you ask me. They are quoting from a document over a hundred years old and finishing each other's sentences. How adorable. Two grown men slobbering to each other over an outdated piece of trivia like a duet in a bad country song. It seems so utterly precious until you listen closer and understand what they're really saying."

He accused the conservative movement of being dangerous subversives; racists openly calling for 'the citizens of the USA to take matters into their own hands.'

He shouted, "Mass anarchy! What they are really doing is calling for a violent overthrow of our president. Those founding fathers that these sheep quote over and over in their sleep used to refer to this type of aggressive action as treason, punishable by, a drum roll please… death!"

The host worked himself into a lather as he walked behind his desk and sat down once again.

"And I can tell you right now my dear audience these men who are quoting a document written by nothing more than racist slave owners hate our president because of the color of his skin. This is a fact. Anders and his ilk are bigoted dinosaurs and have no place in our modern society."

Flinging the notes off his desk, he alerted the viewers that he would be back in a moment.

His young engineer was immediately in his ear.

"Great segment boss. You really stuck it to them."

Fredericks winced and doubled over in pain. Even with his ongoing stomach issues, the blustery television personality managed a smile and a maniacal laugh.

"I did, didn't I? We have so much more to do with those tea-bagger types. We never have to do research to prepare for the show. We can just play daily audio clips and comments and we would have enough ammunition for three years worth of shows. As a matter of fact, I would love to get Anders or that other fellow, Tiny Tim, on the show. It would be great for ratings but I won't even bother asking. We know they would not accept. But you know what, ask anyway. Call their producer or agent or anybody that could give us a no answer. We can then use that with our allies in the press corps. Now be gone and do something I am actually paying you to do, whatever that is."

Fredericks still had over a minute until the show came back on. He sat silently in his chair as his earphone rang with praise from the WNN general manager. He had hit Anders right in the mouth this time. Who cared if he misrepresented what Anders and his colleague had said earlier? Fredericks was cunning enough to know that if repeated enough, the American people would start to believe that Anders and the Tea Party movement were actually heading left.

Fredericks did not doubt this for a second, convincing himself on a nightly basis that his rhetoric was reality and these citizens were pure putty in his hands. He felt they were so beneath him that he could mold them any way he wished. The recent ratings attested to that fact.

Just keep pouring it on, he thought. The current Administration would love the results, and in return, would most likely promise more access to the president and his advisors. On top of that, WNN would be their first stop for headline-grabbing leaks.

Clearly Anders had not called for a progressive candidate. Quite the opposite as the message he exuded was for a more conservative candidate to emerge. At this point, with all the turmoil brewing within the Republican ranks, William couldn't shake the notion that, while this group of GOP pretenders did not pose any kind of threat to the president, the real candidate had yet to show his face. Maybe he was lurking in the shadows, waiting to unveil himself at some time and place that remained to be seen. Sure it was late in the primary cycle process, but from where could a credible candidate like that emerge?

"He better show up soon, for the sake of the future of the Republican Party," Fredericks snickered to himself as he prepared his next television segment. "And maybe for the sake of the country."

Chapter 6

The clock on the bell tower of Independence Hall read 3:55pm. The sun, which had been burning bright overhead all afternoon, had ducked behind the high-rise buildings along Chestnut Street. Most of the tourists still mulling around the Hall put their sunglasses away as they checked their watches, blackberries and iPhones. The line of people for the four o'clock tour had swelled beyond the end of the rope and a number of tourists without tickets were being turned away.

The crowd had definitely thinned over the past two hours and now only a handful remained in front of Tim Jenson's radio post. Jenson was grateful for that. It had been a very successful day, but the heat was getting to him and he wanted to do the Hall tour, check into the hotel, and take a shower so he could look and feel his best when meeting the Anders team for dinner.

But one of those few remaining tourists piqued Jenson's interest. The older gentleman before him could not have been more than five foot ten, but he possessed a striking presence that made Jenson notice. His scholarly look was accentuated by the bifocal eyeglasses perched on the edge of his nose. He peered over them, almost studying Jenson. Keaton tried to get Jenson's attention. Jack Murray had taken a seat next to him and slipped on his earphones.

At once, the keen observer turned his head toward his younger companion. The glare off the bespectacled man's bald head shone in Jenson's eyes, immediately taking him back to the show.

As Jenson prepped Murray to go on the air, Brian Faulk and his assistant turned away from radio row and started toward Independence Hall. They had been standing on the brick walkway listening to the *TJ Show* for the last fifteen minutes and had come away impressed.

"That guy should be on television," said Faulk, glancing back one more time toward Jenson before focusing on the path in front of him. "He has a natural likeableness that would translate well on TV, especially when he talks about the U.S. political hierarchy. I like him."

The two men were greeted by a woman in a white golf shirt as they entered Independence Hall. "Hi, my name is Carolyn. I manage public relations here at Independence Hall. You must be Mr. Brian Faulk."

Brian, grinning, gave her a friendly wink, extended his hand to hers and introduced himself and his assistant Michael Lynne, who would accompany Faulk on the interview. The smiling thirty-five year old PR manager shook his hand, opened the door marked 'Employees Only' and asked both men to follow her. As they entered, all eyes in the room were on the two men for a brief second, and then back down to their desks. Carolyn told the two men that their small team was thrilled by Josh Anders' visit.

Faulk scanned the room and faced his host, "Yes, I know. Where will we be setting up for our interview?"

Carolyn, still smiling but a bit deflated from Faulk's lack of enthusiasm, motioned to follow her as she led them down a short hall into a room with a table and chairs set up. A couple pads of yellow lined paper and pens were set on top.

Carolyn informed the observant Faulk that there were five chairs because Mr. Anders would be accompanied by his cousin. She intended to sit in for the beginning of the interview and then act as guide for the Anders' private tour to follow. Pausing for a second, she continued, "It's ten after four. We're expecting Mr. Anders in about ten minutes. Please make yourself comfortable. Is there anything I can get you, maybe some coffee or bottled water?"

Mike moved to the table, oblivious to the offer, and put down his iPad. Faulk, standing with his left hand in his pocket, leaned into Carolyn and suggested that a cup of coffee would hit the spot. His polite "thank you" brought a wide smile back to her face. She quickly exited the room to fetch her guest a coffee.

Faulk watched her leave. "Let's get ready Mike. Josh will be here before we know it."

"Welcome back to the *TJ Show*. It's been one hell of a day here in beautiful, hot Philadelphia. The people of this great city have been nothing short of amazing, so accommodating and hospitable. No wonder the founders did their best work here. We could not have asked for anything more. Now in the remaining few minutes we have, it is my great pleasure to introduce the winner of the WJMD *What would the Founders do?* contest. This gentleman wrote an amazing piece on the timelessness of the U.S. Constitution and how it remains vibrant in modern American society."

Jenson raised the winning essay to his eyes to make sure he didn't miss a word.

"I'm quoting here, 'the rich remarks within this document are like swords and shields in their constant battle with the activist judges that try to rewrite this sacred text on an almost daily basis. The Founders foresaw the potential for an activist judiciary legislating from the bench and built in safeguards such as checks and balances, separation of powers and an unambiguous method for amending the Constitution.'"

The host finished the quotes as his guest took the seat beside him.

"Folks, let me introduce you to a man who grilled me on the ride up like my fifth grade history teacher and who I now consider a friend, Mr. Jack Murray."

"Thank you, Tim. It is great to sit with you for a few minutes in such a historic setting."

Tim informed his audience of Jack's educated views on the greatest presidents and the office of the president itself.

"In our last two minutes, I want you to explain to the listening audience your theories on these great presidents and where certain presidents should take their place among the greats."

Murray, excited for being asked to opine further, jumped right in. "Uh, well um, presidential greatness discussions have to begin and end with George Washington. If the founders were the gods on Mount Olympus, certainly Mr. Washington would be Zeus. He was the one founder that was irreplaceable. It wasn't so much that he was a great technical president, and he was, but he had the gravitas to keep our fledgling republic together as war, philosophical differences, power grabs, the unresolved question of slavery, and old-fashion politics swirled in chaos around the new nation. The people had an instinctual faith in and respect for General Washington and his ability to put the country first.

"And when you think about it Tim, aside from slavery, the issues I mentioned are very much the same as today. The big difference, and it is a difference of incalculable import, is the trust factor. The people over-whelmingly trusted President Washington to do the right thing in a directly inverse proportion to the trust they have in the current president which, frankly speaking, is almost non-existent."

Jenson was impressed.

"Spoken like a true professor. But you must get into more than a few debates with your liberal colleagues. By the way folks, Professor Murray teaches history at James Madison."

"Thanks Tim, I actually teach history at Turner Ashby High School in Bridgewater, Virginia. I've been fortunate enough, recently, to do some night classes at JMU. It's been great."

Murray emphasized that while Mr. Washington may have been Zeus, the group that founded this country was for the most part everyday people who somehow came together and achieved greatness. The founders knew what they were doing was exceptional and knew they would live in history for it.

"Of all the founders I am partial to, and it's funny because I teach there, is James Madison. Jefferson is well known as the writer of the Declaration of Independence, but Madison is kind of forgotten and even kind of underrated as the Father of the Constitution. He also wrote *The Federalist Papers* with John Jay, Alexander Hamilton, and some others. They were instrumental in the ratification of the Constitution. Sorry, I've talked so much."

"No by all means, please continue."

Jenson knew the day was coming to a close and decided to let Mr. Murray have his few minutes of fame. He hoped to wrap up the long day in the hot Philly sun. Jack took a sip of water before concluding.

"Thank you, Mr. Jenson. Do you realize he wrote the Bill of Rights by himself? Another thing people forget was that he was the president during the War of 1812. At the time, they even called it 'Mr. Madison's War.' He, Dolley, and their son had to flee Washington DC and rally the troops on horseback. Yet they managed to save important founding documents, artwork, and ultimately, the Republic itself. Do you know how close we came to reverting back to a British colony? Amazing, really. Didn't mean to ramble."

Jenson seconded Murray's statement that the US almost lost its sovereignty. He asked his guest if God may have intervened.

"Yes. They say Providence lent a hand. If it was not for a massive storm, probably a hurricane spawning a tornado that stopped the British in their tracks near DC in August 1814, we would not be celebrating this holiday. That's for sure."

"Fine job, Jack. We are out of time today, so I want to thank all the great folks that made this show possible this weekend. We will be on hiatus for the next two weeks, returning to the air live on Monday the twentieth. I am Tim Jenson and this has been the *TJ Show*. Have a great Fourth of July weekend and we'll talk to you soon. Be well."

As the closing music began, Jenson removed his earphones and looked up at the handful of folks around his table. He asked how he did. The small crowd responded with polite clapping that made Jenson respond with a thumbs up. He prompted Murray to take his earphones off since the show was over.

Murray responded that he had a good time as his wife ran over and gave him a big hug and kiss, almost falling into his lap. Todd followed with a high five.

Jenson viewed the scene and interrupted with a compliment and light apology. "You were terrific. Sorry I could not give you more time. Because of all the guests and calls into the show today, we were jammed at the end. When we get back to Charlottesville, I want to have you on for a full segment so you can give half of Virginia a well needed history lesson."

Dot asked Murray if they were really having dinner with Josh Anders that night.

"That's right," Jenson answered. "I have all the info on this itinerary that his assistant gave to me earlier."

Jenson began cleaning up the broadcast table and equipment, the price of a local radio host conducting a remote broadcast. The Murrays were about to walk away as Jenson called to them.

"Don't forget. We have tickets for the four-thirty tour of the Statehouse. It's the last tour of the day, so you don't want to miss it or be late."

Murray assured Jenson they would be there as they walked away from WJMD's broadcast spot.

While Jenson looked up to get an equipment box from his producer, a limousine came up the pedestrian walkway where cars normally did not pass.

"Gotta be Josh," Jenson mumbled under his breath. He thought only Josh Anders could make such a grandiose entrance into such an understated place. His eyes followed the car as it drove all the way up to the employee's only entrance. The white door opened and Josh and his cousin Steve, exited the car directly into the building. The door slammed behind them.

"Guess he wasn't in the mood for autographs," Jenson laughed to himself as he continued packing.

4:00 Independence Hall tour

"How did Independence Hall get its name if it was called the State-house in 1776? That's a good question that I promise to find out at the end of the tour," answered the tour guide.

"Marquis de Lafayette," interjected a gentleman in the back of the group.

"I'm sorry, what did you say?" the tour guide countered.

"Marquis de Lafayette," Anthony Hahn repeated. "He's the guy who coined the name. He came to Philly in 1824. The powers that be entertained him in the Assembly Room and he called the room the Hall of Independence. I guess the name stuck and they just started referring to the whole building as Independence Hall."

While the group shuffled along, another tourist asked if all the furniture and paintings on the walls were originals. Before the guide could respond, Hahn asked incredulously if he was kidding. "Nobody would come for a visit if that was the case." Then he asked the hapless guide if the Assembly Room was next on the tour.

The guide, again flustered but now angry, raised her voice to remind Hahn and the group that most of the furniture and paintings they were viewing were replicas or original pieces from the period.

"Four o'clock group, I ask that each of you respect all questions asked and let me answer what I can. And you, sir, in the back. The Assembly Room or signing room, is the last exhibit on the tour before you can head over to the document display. Please be patient, we will be there soon."

Hahn gave a quick nod and wave and continued with his tour group.

4:30 pm tour

Jenson stood in line with Jack, Todd, and Dot. Keaton had decided to pass on the tour and was probably headed to the hotel bar for a well deserved beer. Jenson was jealous but intent on capping off the afternoon with a tour of the Hall. He had never been inside and was looking forward to it.

He listened to Jack and Todd talking excitedly about what they were about to see. Jenson was distracted by the thought of having a private audience and late dinner with Anders. He was psyched, but nervous, and kept running the ideas he planned on talking about over and over in his head. He thought that the tour would last until about five before they made the short walk back to the hotel for a shower; plenty of time to meet at seven-thirty.

His train of thought was interrupted by a loud voice at the front of the line welcoming the last tour of the day. All eyes looked forward to the source of the voice. Before them stood an older gentleman dressed in colonial attire and bearing a striking resemblance to Benjamin Franklin. Jenson did a double take at first, thinking that his tour guide was the same man who had watched his radio show forty-five minutes earlier. As he walked closer, he realized that it was just a kindly old man making every effort to look and act like an eighteenth century relic.

"Boy that guy looks like Benjamin Franklin doesn't he?" asked Dorothy. "I'd like to buy him a kite."

The last line evoked a few laughs from the strangers around them, getting the group into a good mood, something for which the effervescent Dot had a knack.

"Hello everybody and welcome to Philadelphia, the home of Independence Hall and the Liberty Bell. My name is Ben and for you younger folks, Mr. Franklin will suit me just fine. I will be your tour guide for the next half an hour. And just looking around at all of you, it looks like we have an enthusiastic crowd, wouldn't you say?"

Most nodded in agreement just as Dot let out a loud "woo hoo" that made Murray shake his head and fondly remark the he could not take her anywhere.

"Okay, that's what I like to hear. So, let's start by following me through the doorway to the right." Then he opened the door and ushered the group inside the next room.

4:00 pm tour

"File in and gather around. Ladies and gentlemen, you are now standing in the Pennsylvania Assembly Room. Does anybody know the significance of this part of Independence Hall?"

Hahn, deciding to let someone else answer for a change, bit his lip and stayed quiet.

A tourist blurted out that it was the room in which the Declaration of Independence was signed. "That is correct," answered the tour guide.

Hahn, of course, could not hold his tongue anymore. "The Constitution was also drafted here, was it not?"

The tour guide, nodding her head slowly, informed the group that that piece of information was also correct. "Here the delegates from the original thirteen colonies gathered, and on July fourth, 1776, adopted the Declaration of Independence."

She reminded the group of the earlier question about original furniture and pointed to the exhibit before them.

"The Assembly Room does have two original pieces from colonial days. If you look closely behind the table, you will notice a brown chair with a hand carving at the top. This is known as the Rising Sun Chair. It is the chair that George Washington himself used for three months during the Constitutional Convention. It is widely believed that Ben Franklin coined the name Rising Sun. If you look on top of the table in front of the Rising Sun chair, you will also notice the silver inkstand that was used by the signers of both the Declaration of Independence and Constitution."

Hahn, standing to the right side of the group, stared intently at the engraved sun on the chair. He was so focused on the furniture and the aura of the room that he hardly noticed as his four o'clock tour group shuffled past him and through the door that led to the document room.

Thirty seconds later, Hahn stood alone in the Assembly Room. He leaned on the railing and tried to grasp the history that permeated through the air around him. He gazed upward, picturing George Washington surrounded by the founding fathers, as they took turns dipping their quill pens in the beautiful inkwell to sign the documents that turned out to be the foundations of The United States of America. He felt a chill run through him.

Hahn looked around and finally noticed that he was alone with the colonial ghosts. He wondered if anybody else had felt what he was feeling at that very moment.

———

4:30 pm tour

Tim Jenson stood behind Mr. and Mrs. Murray and noticed that they were holding hands. They listened to their guide explain how prisoners were escorted into the Philadelphia Supreme Court Chamber and made to stand in the prisoner's dock during court proceedings, hence the phrase "standing trial." He thought that this couple had to have something special to be married for as many years as they had, yet still held hands.

Murray turned his head and looked past Jenson's shoulder. Jenson followed Murray's line of sight and turned his head as well. Both men stared across the hallway into the Assembly Room. Murray, seeing a man hunched over the railing in a kneeling position, commented to Jenson that it looked as if that guy was praying to the flag mounted above the table and chair. Both men slowly detached themselves from their tour group and inched their way back toward the doorway. It was obvious that both men were not even aware of what they were doing.

They were slightly startled when Dot grabbed their arms and asked where they were going.

"Our tour's over here guys," Dot said loudly enough for most of the group to notice.

The men stayed in their respective spots in the courtroom until the tour guide made his way past them and led the group into the Assembly Room. Jenson and Murray entered the room and took their place along the railing next to the young man on one knee. They both looked at Hahn stooped before them and listened to the guide's description of the significance of the room and the artifacts that it housed. Hahn had no clue that the next tour group had just joined him.

After a few minutes, the guide led the group past Jenson, and Murray toward the exit leading to the document room and the completion of the four-thirty tour. The Assembly Room emptied, leaving Hahn, Jenson, and Murray to wonder why they remained drawn to the room. They had no intention of leaving. They looked at each other and their surroundings but, remained silent as if in church. They seemed to sense each other's thoughts and feelings without having to verbalize them.

Ten minutes passed before the serene silence of the great Hall was broken by a booming voice that left no doubt who was talking. All three men whipped their heads around just in time to see a small group turn the corner and enter the Assembly Room.

"No way!" exclaimed Hahn as he watched the rotund man with the distinctive voice lead his entourage into the Room. He was totally engaged in conversation with a balding gentleman holding a yellow pad with his pen at the ready. The three individuals with them listened closely as they walked in unison toward the trio.

"Hey guys, fancy running into you in here," bellowed Anders as he finally noticed Jenson and Murray a few feet from him.

Carolyn , her face turning from grin to frown, shouted at the three men.

"What are you doing in here? You're not supposed to be here, the last tour was at four-thirty." Turning to Anders, she apologized for the intrusion into their private tour.

"Don't worry about it doll. This here is my new friend Tim Jenson. Tim, let me introduce everybody."

Anders went on to introduce his following to him as Jenson introduced everybody to Murray. The history professor sized up the national radio show host and noted that he was shorter and a bit heavier than he expected. While excited to meet him, Murray was not in awe as a feeling of familiarity came over him. He could not put his finger on it and he knew that they had never met; but Jack was experiencing a déjà vu moment. He chalked it up to surprise and backed up to take it all in.

With introductions complete, everybody turned to the younger man with the backpack slung over his shoulder. "I'm Josh Anders. I didn't get your name."

Hahn, extending his hand, told the group his name and said he was a big fan of the *Josh Anders Show*. He exchanged pleasantries with everybody in the room before turning his attention back to the Rising Chair.

"This is where they signed the Declaration and the Constitution. And behind the table, there is the Rising Sun chair where George Washington sat during the Constitutional Convention."

Faulk explained that the name was given by Ben Franklin himself who, after looking at the back of the chair day after day and wondering if it was a rising or setting sun, determined with optimism that it was indeed a rising sun, symbolic of the new nation rising around them.

"That's fascinating, I did not know that," proclaimed Anders as he gazed upward and around the whole room, soaking in the atmosphere.

Carolyn stepped away from the group. She said she had to check on something back in the office before they shut down the Hall and needed to leave the group. She pointed to the exit and said she would catch up to everyone outside. She turned, walked out the door and was out of sight. Faulk then instructed his assistant to take his notes back to the office to start on the interview article. Mike closed his computer bag and thanked both Josh and Steve for their time. He nodded to the others and left through the document room.

Chapter 7

How did you guys like the tour?" Anders asked to the collective group. A smattering of comments such as fine, impressive, and pretty cool were the responses.

Faulk, standing with his arms behind him, shared that it was his first trip to this historical monument.

"Do you believe that? I'm seventy years old, have lived in Philadelphia for the last forty five years and this is the first time I've ever stepped foot in Independence Hall. My kids have been to school field trips here. I served as president of the damn Pennsylvania Historical Society and I never made it here. I'm standing here dumbfounded."

Jenson responded that he thought dumbfounded was an odd way of describing his feeling at that moment. "I'm dumbfounded because from the moment I set foot in the building I've had a sense of déjà vu. I saw everything today for the first time, yet somehow, I knew what was around every corner. And that chair with the rising sun carved in it, it's as if I am looking at it right this very moment and George Washington himself is sitting there before us."

The hair on Jack Murray's neck stood. He had the same feeling but kept it to himself, privately sensing that more odd occurrences were in store for the group. Anders, breaking the awkward moment, explained that it is probably a common feeling among many of the visitors that pass through these rooms.

"No Josh, I don't think so," Faulk replied rubbing his balding head.

"'There's something going on that I can't put my finger on right now," Faulk said. "And I think I am not alone in that feeling. I mean, look at Tony right here. I met him ten minutes ago, yet I feel that I know him better than my own sons. What do you think, Hahn?"

"Well, a room like this does bring out a special feeling in all of us, that's for sure. After all, this is where it all happened," Anders interjected. After a brief pause, the loquacious Anders continued, "Can't you just see all the founding fathers in their rightful place around that table there? With big George presiding over the historic meetings, I can picture them all. Jefferson to the left, Madison front and center during the ratification of the Constitution. Franklin, the wise old advisor too frail to walk. Then, up front and brown nosed Hamilton attached to Washington's ear, both men bantering back and forth. We could use that group today, wouldn't you say boys?"

All the men listened and nodded their heads in agreement as they surveyed the setting again. They moved in unison toward the center of the room.

Hahn threw in his two cents. "We don't have to reach as far back as the eighteenth century to get what we need today. We just need to go back to 1980 and bring back Ronald Reagan. That's who we need in today's world."

Faulk offered up an immediate response, stating that another Reagan would be nice but he would settle for an articulate leader who could stand up to the left, and at the very least, clearly explain conservative principles in a debate without backing down.

"We could use a Washington that doesn't have a DC hanging off the end of it!" Anders responded with a haughty laugh that broke some of the seriousness in the room. Everybody laughed at that comment and seemed to finally loosen up. "But seriously, I don't think we'll get another Reagan anytime soon. As I said on my show today, we cannot afford four more years of this Marxist dismantling the country that the gentlemen of this room dug the foundation for because, before you know it, there will be nothing left."

The overhead lights illuminating the Assembly Room shut off with a loud crack that startled everyone. They looked around and wondered if they had overstayed their welcome.

"You think old Carolyn is sending us a message?" Murray asked the group as each man smiled. The natural sunlight from the setting sun provided a dim light that was enough to keep the group out of the dark. After a few seconds, eyes in the room adjusted and the conversation continued.

"Reagan did warn us," Hahn began, "that America was and is the last great hope on Earth. Without us, the world would fall into a thousand years of darkness. Remember, the freedoms we live everyday as Americans should be cherished. Because that can change very quickly, in one generation, just as Reagan said."

Suddenly a sound of leather boots on the hardwood floor filled the air. While the sound was distant at first, it grew louder with each slow step. It was evident that someone was approaching the Assembly Room at a very deliberate pace.

"Sounds like security is coming to finally boot us out of here," joked Faulk.

"I don't think so," warned Murray. A long shadow appeared near the entrance way to the room. It stretched along the floor very slowly. The room fell eerily silent for a split second before Hahn asked the group if anybody smelled what he smelled.

The heavy sound of boots lasted only ten seconds but felt like an eternity.

"Is there somebody back there?" shouted Faulk while Jenson mentioned that maybe it was time to go.

Hahn said that he wasn't going anywhere. The words were barely out of his mouth when a tall, imposing figure appeared from the darkness of the doorway and walked toward the group. The impressive looking gentleman was clad in colonial period garb, from his leather boots and knickers, to an intimidating sword in its sheath. He wore a powdered wig with a ponytail, or in colonial language, a "queue," tied by a red ribbon at the back.

The stranger stood over six feet and walked erect and upright in a regal fashion, with long and purposeful strides, as if inspecting a regimen of troops for battle. He reminded Faulk of his childhood idol in Boston, baseball great Ted Williams, a larger than life presence.

Murray immediately focused on the stranger's distinct facial features and rather prominent nose that seemed to fit his large face rather well. All the men now got a whiff of the odor that Hahn mentioned a few seconds earlier, an odor that reminded both Anders and Faulk of the turf burned to warm homes in the Irish countryside.

"Good evening lads," the stranger offered, wearing a tempered smile that revealed a graying set of teeth. "Are you gentlemen enjoying yourselves on this fine day?"

Hahn was the first to speak, offering that they were all enjoying themselves and that the visit to the Statehouse was the highlight of the day. All the men nodded in agreement, except for Murray, who was transfixed on the figure; an image of the first president. Murray stepped forward and extended his hand to the stranger.

"Jack Murray, it is very nice to meet you, sir." A chill went up his spine as the tall man looked down on him and shook his hand.

"The pleasure is all mine, Mr. Murray."

Anders immediately jumped into the conversation. "We were all saying a few minutes ago that we could feel the presence of the founders in this very room. It's almost spooky. We thought you were a security guard coming to have us removed. I think I speak on behalf of our little group here when I say that we appreciate you and the rest of the guides and actors that are part of the tours for doing what you're doing. You really bring the roots of our country back to life for ordinary Americans like ourselves. We thank you, don't we gentlemen?"

Anders then looked to the collection of men who nodded, except for Murray, who shot Anders a look.

The tall stranger surveyed the group and smiled once again.

"Mr. Anders, what you do every day is of vital importance, too, and I thank you for your efforts."

He turned to Tim Jenson and paid the tall Virginian a compliment as well.

"You too, sir. As an old friend of mine once said, 'Interesting occupations are necessary to happiness: indeed the whole art of being happy consists in the art of finding employment. A good evening to you all.'

As he breathed that last word, the impressive man spun on one heel and strode toward the doorway, his left hand resting on the small of his back while his right hand paced his long and elegant stride. He turned the corner and disappeared out of sight. At once the group of men faced each other in a semi-circle and let out a collective, "What the Hell?"

"Wasn't that quote about occupations, a Jefferson quote?" asked Jenson.

"He is good and obviously he loves his job. I wish we all had that kind of attitude. Without a doubt, he is the most authentic tour guide we have seen today," blurted Anders.

"Wait a second, Hahn interrupted. "Do you hear that?"

The group leaned in and looked up and around.

"No, I don't hear anything now," said Jenson.

"Precisely! That's what I mean! What the hell happened to the clacking of that guy's shoes? He turned the corner and it was as if he tiptoed out of here!"

Murray broke from the group, ran to the doorway, peered around the corner and reported that he was gone.

Suddenly, the door at the end of the short hallway opened and their host reappeared, walking toward the Assembly Room carrying a large pocketbook.

Murray backed away and rejoined the group. "Did you hear what he said? Tim, you're right, that was a Thomas Jefferson quote. An obscure one though."

Faulk commented that the guy was definitely good.

"Too good," Murray exasperatedly replied.

Carolyn turned the corner and said that she was sorry but needed to escort the men to the exit as the building was now closed even to private tours.

Josh agreed and thanked Carolyn for her help and hospitality.

While she beamed a big grin and thanked Anders for his kind words, Faulk stepped forward, took her hand and kissed it, also thanking her for setting up the interview. This gesture made the host blush and look away as Faulk kept his gaze on her for an extra moment.

"Ready folks?" Anders asked as the group began filing out the exit door into the courtyard at the rear of the building. They walked around the Document section along Walnut and on to Chestnut Street.

"This has been one weird day that I won't forget anytime soon," Jenson said to Murray as they walked together onto the sidewalk.

Murray reminded Jenson that the day was not over yet, as they were going to dinner with Anders in a little bit. "I have to find Dottie and Todd. She's probably wondering what the hell happened to us. I hope she's not pissed."

Josh and Steve Anders, following right behind with Faulk and Hahn, let out a big laugh. "Mr. Murray, Josh said. "You have to learn to leave the wives at home like we did."

Hahn, needing to get the last word in, added that he should not have gotten married in the first place.

Five smiling faces continued walking toward their homes, hotels and cars, trying to digest what they had just experienced. They all agreed that they needed a drink and needed one now.

Chapter 8

Tim Jenson was not used to being up at six o'clock on a Saturday morning, especially after a night of great political conversation and debate between himself and a personality titan like Josh Anders. It wasn't every day that you had an audience with the great one himself. Jenson felt he made quite an impression. On top of everything, the food was great and the drink flowed.

But despite having just the right amount of wine over dinner, he had not slept well. Maybe it was because he had slept in a strange bed? What was it? He shook a few cobwebs from his brain and got himself out of bed. Tim looked in the mirror and realized it was the guys he had unexpectedly met yesterday that had his mind racing. Or more specifically, the tour guide that appeared out of nowhere at the end of the Statehouse tour, and who was a dead ringer for George Washington himself. He couldn't get the vision of that man, his voice, or his strong scent, out of his head.

After taking a quick shower, something told him to dress in his new khakis and a collared shirt, even though he expected another hot day in Philadelphia. Satisfied with his look, he took the elevator down to the lobby for a cup of coffee and decided to stroll to the statehouse through the quiet streets of center city Philadelphia. Jenson thought that the serene setting of an early Saturday morning would do wonders to clear his head and help him figure out why he felt compelled to return to Independence Hall.

Obviously, he was not the only one who could not sleep that morning. As Tim stepped off the elevator, the first person he saw was Jack Murray, standing in front of the lobby's complimentary coffee stand, adding a

Sweet 'n Low to his morning java.

"Hello, old friend," Jenson offered to Murray with a smile.

Murray turned around with a surprised look on his face.

"What are you doing up so early this morning, Mr. Jenson? Geez, after all that food and wine, I thought you would take a month to sleep it off."

"Couldn't sleep. And you?"

Murray replied that he couldn't sleep either, but for some reason, he actually felt energized. Jack relayed to Jenson that he had woken up earlier that morning and checked out a few things on the internet from his iPad. For some reason he felt like he had to check out Independence Hall again.

Sipping on his hot coffee as other hotel guests waited for the breakfast hostess to seat them, Murray went on.

"Yesterday was great, Tim. Just amazing. Beyond any of my original expectations when I entered that contest. Meeting you and the other guys, being on the radio show and having dinner with Josh Anders. Wow! Even seeing that General Washington guy, that blew me away with the way he dressed. And just his presence, I almost genuflected before him. You may think I'm crazy but...." Murray's voice trailed off as he brought the cup up to his lips for another sip. Jenson, waiting for Murray to finish his sentence, asked him to elaborate.

"Oh forget it. I'm going to take a walk back to where we were yesterday. Wanna join me?"

A wide grin came across Jenson's face as he grabbed his coffee to go, and reminded Murray that the Independence Hall would not be open at that early hour.

"That's ok. I just feel like going back there. You never know who you might meet. We can talk on the way over."

The fellow Virginians commenced their quick walk with a couple of jokes that nearly caused Jenson to spill his coffee. Murray thought he had a great sense of humor but always tested new jokes out on Dot. A smile from his wife meant he could tell the joke publicly.

As they approached the Mall with the asphalt evolving to green grass and trees, a white limousine drove past and pulled up a half a block in front of them.

"Guess who's coming to breakfast?" asked Jenson wryly as Murray's eyes followed the long car to a stop.

Josh Anders bounded out of the back of the limo, cigar in mouth, and without taking a breath, welcomed his new friends.

"I kinda thought I might find you gentlemen here. Going to the Hall? I gotta check in with the network and the wife. You heading over there? Meet you in the back."

Anders asked and answered the questions he posed to Tim and Jack without even eliciting a response. Murray just smiled and nodded while Anders began pounding on his cell phone. Steve Anders emerged from the car, looking at his watch.

"He made me come with him, but I have a plane to catch. I'm pushing it coming here this morning. You guys heading over there? I can join you for about ten minutes."

Jenson and Murray, along with cousin Steve, took the opportunity to loop around the back of the building only to find Brian Faulk and Anthony Hahn already there, sitting at a bench and engaged in an animated conversation. Hahn swung and splashed his Starbucks latte for emphasis as Faulk sat quietly staring at the younger man. Faulk's Dunkin Donuts black coffee remained still between his two hands.

"Hey, what are you doing here?" asked Hahn.

"I thought Brian and I were the only ones crazy enough to be here at this hour of the morning. Where's Anders? Buying Independence Hall? Looking at himself in the mirror somewhere?"

Steve let out a big laugh before Faulk interrupted by asking the newcomers to sit down. He shared with them that Hahn definitively believed they had seen the ghost of General Washington the previous evening.

Hahn, embarrassed, wiped the first sweat of a Philadelphia July morning off his brow.

"An apparition or something. The more I thought about that whole episode last night, the stranger it became. What else could he have been?"

"I don't know exactly," replied Faulk. "But I don't think it was a ghost.... You may think that I have Alzheimer's or something, but I think he was more than a ghost."

"You bet your ass he was not a ghost. I shook his hand and it wrapped around mine like a baseball mitt. That guy was real, no apparition," added Murray.

Josh Anders, flipping off his phone as he slipped it into the breast pocket of his sport coat, approached the bench. He listened to the discussion for a moment before asking what Murray and Faulk were discussing.

Before Faulk could reply, Murray blurted out the answer. "I think we met the real General Washington yesterday."

———

Jenson with a concerned look on his face, protested, saying that it was impossible. "The guy was a really good actor. What else could he have been?"

Not easily giving up, Murray quickly stood and countered his friend's statement. "Guys, there is a lot going on here and I don't pretend to understand it. After that guy left the room, I had this feeling about him. I think we all had a feeling about him. Anyway, I started racking my brain as to why we were all drawn here, as a group I mean. Like the movie *Close Encounters*."

"So you think he was an alien?" Jenson scoffed.

Ignoring the slap, Murray went on. "When I went back to the hotel before dinner, I went online, hoping I was wrong. I only had a few minutes to check some stuff, but instead of disproving what I suspected, the iPad seemed to confirm it. This morning I couldn't sleep so I went online again and reconfirmed."

"What are you talking about!?" Hahn inquired abruptly.

"I googled each of the founders and found similarities to us, similarities to all of us guys here as a group. Anders, you are from Boston. You are a lawyer and went to Harvard. Your cousin Steve founded the Tea Party in Boston. For crying out loud, he makes his own home brew."

Turning to Jenson, Murray continued his discovery.

"Tim, you are from Virginia, went to UVA, are over six feet tall, write like a poet, and quote the Declaration of Independence, ad nauseum, as if you wrote it."

Jenson stood in disbelief and walked a few paces from the bench as Murray continued on like a prosecuting attorney.

"You talked about your house designs, your love of wine, which you exhibited a few times last night, and your firm belief in state's rights. Tim, you were even right about that quote he made about jobs." Murray, now counting on his fingers, moved his attention to Hahn. "Anthony, you are from Barbados and work for The Bank of New York as a currency trader. A money trader! You are fiery, red headed and combative. You're the first one to tell anybody who will listen how brilliant you are. No offense."

Hahn responded with a shrug. Murray continued, "And you, Brian, you are from Philly by way of Boston, aren't you? You not only write, but you founded a magazine that, according to your website, was based on Poor Richard's Almanac. Your bio on the site says you own a couple of patents for things you invented and like to study philosophy in your spare time. Who the hell studies philosophy in their spare time? Jeez Brian, look at ya! You're Ben Franklin reincarnated. Or friggin' David Crosby for the pot smoking crowd."

Murray, now with both hands extended out, turned his thumbs inward and started to describe himself.

"Me, I'm a five foot four Virginian with an adopted son and I teach at JMU, James Madison University! I can recite the Constitution in my sleep. How many other people recite Locke and Hume? I even have a good looking wife whose initials are DM and she makes her own ice cream! All our initials match with the core group of founders."

Jack dropped his thumbs and scanned their reactions. He studied their faces as if he had just asked a tricky question to his high school seniors. But instead of calling on one of them, he decided to reach deep into each man's psyche.

"You think this all cannot be happening, but it is. Guys look inside each of you. What is your gut telling you? I rest my case."

The men were stunned and their faces showed it. Taking off his glasses, Brian Faulk agreed and rubbed his eyes. Josh Anders looked at his cousin, but Steve looked at his watch. Hahn stared into his Starbucks cup, not knowing what to make of the situation.

Jack Murray had built his theory to a crescendo and needed to finish his point.

"So yes, that was George Washington yesterday! That was the father of our country, the guy they named the city after, the guy who chopped down the cherry tree, the guy who led the army across the Delaware to defeat the British, the guy on the one dollar bill. If you don't think so, why not? Might as well be someone we know, because right now I don't think any of us knows who we are anymore."

After Murray's lecture, Steve Anders retorted, "I cannot believe any of you can believe any of this garbage. Do you realize what you are saying? That we are the founders themselves?"

Faulk jumping to Murray's defense explained that they were not exactly the founders themselves, but could be the spiritual embodiment of each of them.

Faulk expressed that while he found the whole notion disturbing, it did explain some passions, dreams and feelings he had had for years. He highlighted his fascination with the founders and the use of his magazine as a political platform in the same fashion as Ben Franklin. Faulk asked if they all felt the same compulsion. "My wife will love to hear this. It'll explain a lot," Said Faulk.

Hahn rubbed his eyes as he stood to face the group. "This is crazy but it feels like it's all coming together at once. The second we were all together in the signing room is when I felt like I had known you guys for years. And we only just met."

Looking down and leaning against the wall, he lit a cigarette and kept talking. "And then old George walks in and I was at a loss for words. And if you talk to anyone at the bank, they will swear that they have never seen me at a loss for words. So I get up all bright and early this morning with a yearning to come back to this very spot and just be. Nothing else. I just needed to be on this bench at this very moment in time and the world would be right."

The other men were drawn to the young man having an epiphany. They listened intently.

"I'm here no more than thirty seconds before I see old Brian strolling toward me and looking over those glasses at me. He sits down, we start talking, and five minutes later the rest of you join the party. I think we're still waiting for one more person. I felt like I didn't know him, but I knew him. Does that make any sense?"

Brian, calmly placed his coffee on the pavement, leaned back on the bench to reassure Hahn. "Yes young man, I think it does. Sometimes it takes a man to see into you to allow you to see into yourself."

"This is completely crazy, guys. I know who I am," laughed Jenson. "I am not Thomas Jefferson. It's impossible." Facing Josh Anders, he took a roundabout shot at the talk show behemoth. "Josh, I know you have a high opinion of yourself but even you are no John Adams!"

Josh rubbed his chin and looked skyward in a tongue in cheek manner. "Hmmmm, John Adams eh? I like that. Perhaps it is true."

Jenson's face, the definition of an agonized man, shook as he continued to plead his case.

"I still don't believe you guys. We are all intelligent and reasonable men here. Are you listening to yourselves? This is insane. It can't be true."

"Ah, but it is true, gentlemen," a now familiar voice came from the shadow of the Hall.

The men spun to face the direction of where the voice originated. Their faces froze.

Taking a final sip of his latte and leaning back on the bench with a wide grin, Hahn spoke first.

"We were expecting you!"

Chapter 9

The tall gentleman, dressed in the same eighteenth century clothing as the day before, strode purposefully toward the group of stunned men and stopped in front of Hahn.

"Young man, was that just a profound exclamation meant to be humorous or a keen observation that I know you are most capable of eliciting at this very instance?"

This quick retort from the imposing stranger instantly turned Hahn's relaxed demeanor to a serious one. He looked up from his place on the seat, in awe and intimidated. The man in the leather boots was again in their midst.

"Please do not be intimated by my presence. I am one of you. I believe all of you were to some degree expecting my return. That is why you have all been summoned here to celebrate this great July Fourth morning." Pausing for a second, he shuffled some gravel beneath his shoe while straightening his lapels. "Look deep into your hearts and souls. It is Divine Providence that planted the seed of curiosity and devout patriotism for these great United States, and made you travel great distances to share this moment with each other and me. You may not have even understood your compulsion to be here at this moment, but you see, there is a destiny which has the sovereign control of our actions, not to be resisted by the strongest efforts of human nature."

"We are sharing this moment with who? With George Washington? The George Washington?" exclaimed Jenson. "We are standing before the father of our country as he lectures us. I'm finding this all hard to believe."

"Ah, you question what your eyes show to be real. I would not have expected anything less from the man that penned some of the most important words in the history of liberty. It was your innate ability to question the political status quo that drove you to stir the echoes of the individual that you embody at this very moment, Thomas Jefferson."

His words agitated Mr. Jenson. "What? Are you crazy? I am not Thomas Jefferson! I am Tim Jenson, born and raised in Virginia! I'm a patriot, but not a great man. I'm just a local talk show host and former politician."

Tim looked to men for support but to no avail. The outsider would not be deterred.

"Sir, please look into the depths of your person. Close your eyes and open your mind. The vision you see before you will not deceive you. It is your destiny."

All the while, the stranger continued to peer at the men with a stern, yet soothing glance. He paced left and right before deciding once again to address his new friends.

"It is all of your destinies. Do not question why you made the journey because there are forces at work that cannot be explained, even by the most erudite chaps. Accept this invitation unequivocally and without question. You will be rewarded."

Hahn exploded to attention and extended his quivering hand. "General Washington, my name is Anthony Hahn. I cannot believe I am meeting you sir."

The colonial gentleman shook the young man's hand and nodded in approval.

"Mr. Hahn, I have had my eye on you for quite a while. Your intelligence and understanding of our financial system and others abroad has no bounds. You are only limited by your volatile and unpredictable outbursts. If you learn to temper your emotions, the heavens of opportunity will open wide for you. I had a protégé many years ago that was of brilliant mind and confidence but was only constrained by his tongue. This man was on the precipice of greatness before his words resulted in his demise. I believe you know of whom I speak."

Hahn could only nod as he stared at the imposing man. Pointing toward the group once again with a guarded smile, the mystery man addressed the group as a whole.

"I have before me some of my most trusted colleagues and perhaps my most difficult adversaries, some of whom reside in the same embodiment. We have known one another through our most difficult trials. We have not always agreed on the route to liberty yet we agreed on the destination and took heed of direction from all. My days on Earth have taught me to be intimate with few but to those few I pledge my confidence. You gentlemen are those few."

His focus moved from individual to individual as if to enter each man's mind and heart.

"Alexander Hamilton, John Adams, Samuel Adams, Thomas Jefferson, James Madison, Benjamin Franklin. All were outstanding men in their day, brave and forthright who understood the impact of their actions and their place in history. Praiseworthy men, who have come from another age and now stand before me."

The man who was the likeness of the first president, bowed to the semicircle of men and expressed his honor in making their acquaintances.

The men were taken aback by the humility of this great man and the ease at which he delivered this life altering message, a message confirming their earlier suspicions.

A simple, "Thank you Mr. President," was all Josh Anders could muster.

Anders spoke for the whole group when he said they all needed some time to digest it all.

"After all, the father of our country died in 1798."

"1799, my good friend. I expired in 1799. You were always a brilliant and deep thinker who gazed upon the larger view of history, yet you always left the smaller details to someone else."

The General stepped forward, placed his hand on Anders' shoulder and defined the king of radio as a modern day John Adams.

"You enlightened many individuals, including me, and were always a great judge of character, exemplified by the company you keep, the woman you asked to be your wife, and the outstanding young adult your son has grown up to be. The trials and tribulations you have encountered throughout your life have only strengthened your resolve immeasurably and allowed you stand up to your adversaries in a reverential manner. Your foes tend to walk away from a quarrel feeling inspired even though he or she may have been belittled. That is a rare gift Mr. Anders, one shared with your predecessor."

Turning toward Jenson and Murray, Mr. Washington continued his evaluation of the talent at hand.

"Mr. Murray, you are a gentleman with a keen intellect. Your grasp of American history and our founding principles is second to none. You work in a profession where you get to pass this great knowledge onto young and impressionable minds. Old Jemmy, you have never let your slight stature influence your ability to make an impression as weaker men may have. And you share abhorrence for excessive democracy and tyranny as do I. Your study of Locke, Hume, and Montesquieu inspired our great Constitution.

"Mr. Jenson, the Sage of Monticello, you are an interesting sort. You have always been a dreamer yet you strive to follow through on them as exhibited by your many published opinions and ascent as a voice of the people of Virginia, first a representative at the Statehouse then directly to the populous. Although you may not realize it, you are the nation's foremost expert on the Declaration of Independence. The knowledge and understanding of this great document housed in that brain of yours is unmatched in the modern day."

Tim Jenson, looking unsure, breathed a quiet thank you as Jack Murray leaned toward the General as if to study his five o'clock shadow. Murray raised his arm toward the man's face in an attempt to touch his skin to see if he was real. But Murray's action was interrupted by Mr. Washington's sudden focus on the group's elder statesman, Brian Faulk.

"Mr. Faulk, such a symbol of what this country is capable of producing, it is only fitting that a gentleman of your stature reside in Philadelphia; an individual who, if directed in a derogatory fashion to go fly a kite, would smile and welcome the suggestion with enthusiasm. Another voice of the people, delivering your political opinions as if it were gospel to a Sunday morning congregation. A pillar of this fine city, your antennae are always pointed toward betterment of this city, state, and country, and if left to your own devices, could possibly create magic out of thin air."

Faulk, sitting smugly on the bench with his legs crossed and his right arm hanging over the back rest, cracked a smile as he buried his chin into his chest. Steve Anders, glancing at his wristwatch for the seventieth time, grabbed his bag and saluted the congregation.

"Guys, it's been a lot of fun as well as the most bizarre morning of my life. I would love to stay but I have to catch a plane back to bean town. Mr. Washington, it was very nice to meet you and I hope to run into you again real soon, but I needed to go twenty minutes ago. Josh, I'll talk to you later."

Steve in full sprint, hailed a taxi on Chestnut Street. The rest of the men hardly noticed as their gazes stayed fixed on the first president.

The group may not have realized it, but the calendar read Saturday, July fourth, and the people of Philadelphia went about their business in preparation for the holiday celebration. Local merchants set up their storefronts for the potential surge of tourist traffic expected on the nation's birthday. The street sweepers went to and fro, cleaning up the city passageways as the sun peaked through the skyscrapers overhead. Employees and volunteers began to arrive for work at Independence Hall and the Liberty Bell museum. A number of these folks made their way through the tree-lined park, adjacent to the Hall.

As they approached the building, a handful of these men and women took notice of the tall man holding court near the tour entrance. Initially drawn by his presence, they were at once absorbed by the conversation. Within minutes, tourists mulling around the Statehouse joined the volunteers in their curiosity of the George Washington lookalike and the men gathered around him. The tall man's dialogue was direct and pointed while the men in the immediate foreground seemed to hang on his every word. Mr. Washington paused mid-sentence as he noticed the crowd forming.

"It looks as though we have company."

Anders, also realizing what was happening, drew the group into a football-like huddle and suggested they hop in his waiting limo and seek some privacy back at his hotel suite. Faulk interjected that he lived only two blocks away and they could walk there in a couple of minutes.

Mr. Washington broke the huddle by lifting his head up stating that Brian's suggestion was a splendid idea. The group of men as one unit was in motion immediately, parting from the crowd. The new founders were excited and energized as they approached the side street. The tour guide from the previous day, dressed again as Benjamin Franklin, stood on the sidewalk, perplexed at the oncoming General. Washington, stopping in front of the man, eyed him up and down.

"Very authentic, except for the knickers. Too long. Wouldn't you say Mr. Faulk?"

The Franklin impersonator looked down, and in doing so, spilled his morning coffee. Mr. Washington resumed his gait as his twenty-first century cabinet quickly followed with a few chuckles.

Murray excitedly moved with the group realizing he had not told Dottie where he was going so early in the morning. He made a mental note to text her when they got to Faulk's home, but didn't know what he would tell her. What would he say? That he was in a stranger's house with a bunch of guys he barely knew and an old guy who had convinced them all he was George Washington?

He would figure out what to tell Dottie later. Right now, he was caught up in an amazing moment and there was no time to explain.

The walk to Mr. Faulk's house coincidentally took the group across Sixth Street and through Washington Square Park, to the delight of the General. However, while he liked to see his name adorned on a park and the adjacent street, he did not mention this to the men. Always a humble leader, he appeared uncomfortable bringing attention to himself. This did not mean he was without ego. On the contrary, he had a very large sense of self, yet he led by the military belief that no one individual was superior to the collective unit.

Mr. Washington's head might as well have been on a swivel as he turned every degree (his neck would allow) to gaze at the miracles of the twenty-first century. While he had an idea of what they were, he still gawked in wonderment at each and every automobile that passed his way. He marveled at the sheer height of the structures around him and noted the intricacies of the masonry and architectural design. He stopped to examine a manhole cover in the street and asked what function it served. It took a few minutes to comprehend why one would dig a hole in the street on purpose, but less time to learn the dangers of examining it too closely.

But the one modern day addition to society that made him take note time and time again was the summertime fashions worn by the women of Philadelphia. He could not get over loose blouses and short skirts worn by the women of today. And he respectfully opined that he wished that attire was available in 1776, which elicited a chorus of laughter by the founders of today. Before long, the General just kept his thoughts on the topic to himself as he approached the Faulk residence.

———

Brian Faulk jumped to the head of the group and approached the front door, leaning down to pick up the Saturday editions of *The Philadelphia Inquirer* and the *Philadelphia Daily News*, publications of which he had written for earlier in his career. Instead of inserting a key into the door, he punched a numeric code into the keypad on the wall next to the door which unlocked the entranceway. As Faulk opened the door, Mr. Washington paused to inspect the keypad before entering the dwelling.

The smell of bacon permeated through the house and Faulk yelled to his wife that he was home and that he was accompanied by visitors. His wife Deborah, peering around the corner into the hallway, gave a quizzical look at the assemblage. Faulk walked down the hall ahead of the group to let her know that a number of strange men were about to assemble in the kitchen and dining area.

"I wish you would have at least called ahead. I look terrible," Deborah whispered irritably to her husband.

She looked over his shoulder as the men gathered in the vestibule, aware of the awkward intrusion. Faulk looked back down the hallway and motioned the group to take a seat in the living room. They filtered onto the couches and chairs in the room, which gave Deborah a chance to sneak upstairs to dress and apply makeup without being noticed. Brian turned to finish with the eggs and bacon on the stovetop, then turned the burners off. He opened the refrigerator and gathered more breakfast foods for the group. He left them on the counter to join his team in the next room.

"Lovely home you have here, Mr. Faulk. Am I correct in assuming your wife is to thank for the cleanliness and order of this room?"

Brian nodded in agreement, explaining that he was always the disorganized one, with papers and paraphernalia usually strewn about.

"I have a room in my basement where I write and tinker a bit. It's the one room my wife avoids because of the mess. She always tells me that she will find me dead under a pile of whatever I am doing at the present moment."

The men laughed. Mrs. Faulk, now neatly dressed with her dyed strawberry blonde hair, quickly coiffed, entered the room. At once, General Washington sprung up to introduce himself. The rest of the men followed his lead and rose in unison.

"This is my wife Deborah. Deb, let me introduce you to the fine gentlemen I told you about last night."

Mr. Washington was the first to step forward, shaking her hand while bowing his head. As each man stepped forward to introduce himself, Deb Faulk kept her curious gaze on the first president. Her attention was diverted at once when introduced to Josh Anders.

"Josh Anders? Wow, we listen to your show all the time. Welcome to our home. Welcome all of you to our house. Make yourselves comfortable. I am making breakfast for all of you, if that's okay."

The men nodded in thanks to the offer while Deb focused her gaze back on the tall man in the colonial outfit. Keeping her gaze on Mr. Washington, she whispered to her husband, "Is that the tour guide you met last night? He certainly is a dead ringer for George Washington. That's for sure." Mr. Washington, stepping forward with a concerned look on his face, inquired as to what the meaning of the phrase dead ringer was.

Hahn chimed that it meant an exact duplicate, allaying Mr. Washington's fears for the moment. Faulk then explained that there was nothing derogatory or harmful in using that particular description. Mr. Washington mentioned that he understood and took his seat. The group again followed the General's lead and sat down. Mrs. Faulk left the room to prepare the meal.

Anders then addressed the men.

"Guys, as you can see from the clock over the mantelpiece, it is eight-thirty in the morning. I am going to suggest something a little radical, so hear me out. We have with us the one and only father of our country, George Washington. Whether you want to believe it or not, he has come back and has gathered us together here in Philadelphia by some force we cannot explain. But it has happened, and we are here, so I think we should make the most of it."

Mr. Washington interjected that he was there for a reason. "Providence heard your plea for assistance and sent me as your servant. Gentlemen, you all know why you asked for my return and I believe you patriotic citizens know how I can help you. I am at your service. Understand only a twenty-first century man knows how to repair the problems of the current day."

Anders rudely lit up a cigar to the disgusted looks of the occupants of the room. "That's what I was getting at, sir. So here is what I would like to do. I would like to take Mr. Washington to the city he helped design, the nation's capital that bears his name. I have some time off now, so I'd take him later this afternoon."

He described how Mr. Washington could walk the mall and check out the monuments that had been erected in his honor as well as other great men. "We'll show him the monument named for him. What do you think?"

Mr. Washington surveyed the room before reacting. He agreed. "I believe we will find our inspiration in the city that bears my name. Please gentlemen if I may. I have entered a world that is in some ways very familiar to me; that is being in your presence. But in my few moments so far, I realize I have also entered a most alien environment. I ask that on our journey to the capital, you educate me on the vast changes that have occurred."

Anders took a long drag and let out a big puff of smoke. He pointed at the General with an index finger curled around his stogie. "Certainly, Mr. Washington. I have a fair amount of historical knowledge in this brain of mine to accommodate you. I'll do my best. And, Mr. Washington, you will be relieved to know that while you will see and hear things you could never have imagined, the basic nature of man has not changed; for good or for bad."

Murray glanced wide-eyed at Jenson sitting to his right. He noticed some odd facial reactions to Anders' idea. Murray thought the bigmouth radio personality had imposed himself into the center of the situation and Murray was not pleased with the turn of events.

For the first time in a long while, he did not think of anybody but himself and knew that if those two were going on a sightseeing tour of the Capital, he had to be a part of it. Fortunately, he wasn't the only one thinking that.

"Well if you're going, I'm going too!" said Hahn, looking for collaboration from his fellow founders.

"I'm on my two week vacation and had nothing planned. I was thinking of flying to Aruba from here. But I'd rather go to Washington, with Washington!"

Faulk, entering the living room with a tray of coffee cups and saucers, stopped short to see the waft of smoke in the air.

"C'mon Josh. Don't light up in here. It's too early for that crap."

Anders, a little startled by Brian's tone, lifted his hand in apology, went to the front door and threw the cigar onto the sidewalk. He came back in time to hear Faulk answer Hahn by saying he was up for the trip. He set the tray on the coffee table and passed the drinks to his colleagues. He glanced up over his spectacles to see the reactions to his statement. Anders made sure he was clear.

"I meant all of us when I suggested going to Washington. Just want to make sure you guys know that."

Jenson and Murray both reached for their coffee while looking at each other. Jenson mentioned how they would have to change their schedules.

"While we have an open agenda for the day, we were scheduled to stay over another night before heading back tomorrow morning."

As Jenson said this, he looked back at Murray who frowned as if to say there was no debating the decision.

"But as long as it's okay with Mr. and Mrs. Murray, I don't see any reason why we can't accompany you."

While keeping a calm exterior, Murray was alive inside with anticipation. Although he realized the whole situation was more than a little strange to say the least, he felt this Mr. Washington character was who he claimed to be. Murray had to be a part of the plan. He just wondered what Dottie would think of him for up and leaving from a family weekend and heading back toward Virginia. But what was he supposed to do?

Murray placed his coffee cup on the table, reached for his cell phone, hit a speed dial button and walked out to Faulk's small veranda overlooking the park.

Dottie Murray knew how smart her husband was and that he needed more intellectual stimulation. Teaching history to pimply faced, disinterested high school and college students just didn't cut it anymore. It didn't make it any easier when Jack called to ask her about heading to DC that very day with his new found acquaintances.

Dot did her best to understand as Jack tried to explain that something incredible was happening. Although he could not get into too much detail right then, he promised to explain everything when he got back to the hotel. Pacing the small deck, he sensed she was okay with the abrupt change of plans and asked her to pack up the room as soon as she could.

Her husband was the most level headed, logical person she had ever known. It was not like him to rush to conclusions or jump on any fly by night scheme. Something big was going on there and she trusted Jack completely.

"Ok, honey. If it's that important, Todd and I will be ready whenever you want to leave."

———

Josh Anders had been eavesdropping on Murray's conversation. He liked Jack and Dottie from the second he met them and thought they made a cute couple. He was pleased to hear Mr. Murray convince his wife to let him go.

"Then it is settled, we will all head down to DC today," Anders said. Mrs. Faulk appeared in the doorway of the living room. Anders noticed and made another suggestion. "But before we do anything, it looks as though Mrs. Faulk has gone to the trouble of making us breakfast. What do you say we try out her cooking?"

With that, the men stood up and followed their host into the dining area. As they approached the table, Mr. Washington instinctively took the chair at the head of the table and sat down. Brian Faulk took notice but did not object to the first president occupying his normal seat. As the men set their cups and saucers on the table and began to reach for the bacon, eggs and toast, Mr. Washington bowed his head and asked that the collective group say a prayer of thanks for the food they were about to eat. The suggestion silenced and halted the men, who all glanced toward the head of the table. Each man folded his hands and prayed with the president.

"Bless us, our Lord," Mr. Washington said, "for the food we are about to receive from thy bounty, through Christ our Lord, Amen." Mr. Washington then looked up at the group, nodded and breakfast commenced.

Mrs. Faulk cleared the dishes from the table as Mr. Faulk offered more coffee to the group. Hahn and Anders extended their cups. Small talk dominated the breakfast conversation and while Mr. Washington said very little, he listened intently as each man looked toward the president for positive acknowledgment as they spoke. When the table was completely devoid of dishes and utensils, the men leaned in and took a serious tone.

"If we are going to take Mr. Washington for a tour of DC and around the monuments, we need to get him some new threads," interjected Hahn.

Anders cautioned the group that it was of paramount importance that Mr. Washington's presence stays an ironclad secret, not to be shared with anyone else.

"Jack, obviously, your boy and Dottie will know, but we need to limit this just to us."

Jenson seconded the idea.

"Josh is right. If people found out about this, number one, they would think we were crazy and number two, imagine what kind of circus this would become. My God, gentlemen, think of the religious and scientific ramifications. I don't think we really appreciate what is happening here. This may be the largest event in world history since the resurrection."

Mr. Washington was momentarily jarred by this statement and responded in kind.

"Mr. Jenson, please do not compare my appearance with the Lord's resurrection. I am as insignificant as a grain of sand compared to that event."

Jenson didn't know how to interpret the comment from the father of their country, so he replied in words he thought Mr. Washington would relate to.

"I apologize. You are indeed correct, sir."

Anders jumped back in.

"Well, I am sure we all have a million questions for Mr. Washington along those lines, but he has asked us to educate him about our country and about us so I think we need to do that. There is a reason for all this guys. I'm not sure what it is yet, but I do know that Jerry Springer or the girls on *The View* are not going to figure it out."

He pointed at Mr. Washington and sized him up with both arms.

"Let's get Mr. Washington made over and go from there."

Anders swung his gaze to Faulk, asking the Philadelphian if he knew a good tailor nearby. Faulk suggested they possibly take him to the mall to get some walk around clothes that he would be comfortable in.

Upon hearing this, Mr. Washington looked down at the clothes he was wearing and pondered the thought of changing into a twenty-first century wardrobe.

"He's going to need new shoes, socks, probably underwear. What do you say, General, are you a boxer or briefs man?"

"Please, gentlemen," replied Mr. Washington. "I know not what boxer or briefs are but I must insist that my apparel be modest and endeavor to accommodate nature, rather than to procure admiration." The men laughed while Mr. Washington gave all a cautious look.

"Understood, sir," said Anders. "We were just joking. Your dress will be fully appropriate. First things first, we have to take care of that wig you have there."

Anders' innocent sounding suggestion was met with a vain response from the first president. "Wig? I do not wear a wig, my fine man. This is my own hair. A lot of the gentlemen of my time wore a wig but I never felt the need. Therefore, I would powder my hair to keep with the fashion of the day."

As Mr. Washington explained his grooming technique, the men's eyes were riveted to the top of the president's head. Faulk answered Mr. Washington by saying that he wished he had some of that on top of his own bald head, again eliciting a collective laugh among the men. Murray then asked Mr. Washington what the real color of his hair was.

"It was a reddish auburn," Mr. Washington answered. "Maybe a chestnut color. But that was years ago, in my younger days. I frankly do not remember what color my hair currently is. I know it is powdered and tied in a queue, by the very red ribbon given to me by Martha, so many years ago. And it has served as my connection to Providence. Perhaps if I cleansed it we would soon discover the answer."

Anders stood and walked around the table until he was directly in front of the six-foot-three Washington. "I'm guessing probably a 48 long, maybe a 50, don't you think?"

Anders looked at Faulk, who shook his head. "I think a size 50," replied Faulk. "He's pretty broad; definitely an extra-large for a shirt or sweatshirt."

Faulk put his foot alongside Mr. Washington's right foot and told the room that a size twelve shoe would fit fine. He motioned around his own waist and told the group that the General probably had a thirty-eight inch waist.

"You could always count on my husband," Mrs. Faulk added. "He may not show it, but he does know his clothes!" Everyone around the table erupted in laughter.

Faulk appeared with a tape measure and wrapped it around Mr. Washington's waist before the General knew what he was doing. "Thirty-eight, on the money," he exclaimed.

At once, Mr. Washington stepped back and told the men that they were proceeding a little too quickly. Anders stepped forward to assure him that if he was going to appear in public, he had to blend in and not be noticed as President George Washington. "With all due respect, sir, your face is everywhere. Your portrait is ingrained on our one dollar bill and twenty-five cent coin."

Anders affirmed his statement by reaching into his pocket and producing both pieces of currency. Mr. Washington took the dollar bill and quarter in his hand and studied and examined each. He was absorbed by the one dollar bill, inspecting the detail and artwork, continually flipping the bill from one side to the next and back again. His last flip of the currency was to his picture, which he brought up closer to his face for further examination.

"This is my portrait by Gilbert Stuart, a very talented man from a prominent Rhode Island family. This picture was referred to as The Athenaeum when it was painted. I do not believe it was ever finished. Well, it was not finished at the time of my death. But it must have been completed if the people felt it well-suited to appear on our nation's currency. Mr. Stuart completed other portraits as well; he was quite talented."

Once again, the new founders were awestruck of the man before them, describing his own picture, as if he was telling a story about a photograph taken at a family picnic. The silence was broken when Jenson blurted out that the whole scene was simply remarkable.

"There will be a lot more of that to come!" answered Hahn as he reached for the coffee pot to heat his cup.

Again, Anders took control of the room.

"Hahn, after you finish that coffee, you and Murray take a walk over to the mall and get the General some walking clothes and shoes or sneakers. You have the sizes we mentioned?"

Murray put up the palm of his hand to slow Anders down. The situation unfolding in front of him was unimaginable. But the control freak Anders was not the John Adams. Jack was still the same Jack Murray he was the night before. A reincarnate or not, he was not subservient to that Anders guy.

Mr. Washington, on the other hand, was a very different story. Murray found it hard to really believe, but he could come to no other conclusion than that his man was the George Washington. As Jenson had pointed out, this truly may have been the most significant event in the last 2,000 years.

This certainly was the event he had been searching for. So Murray decided to take a chance and go with it. Who knew what extraordinary fate Divine Providence had in store for them?

"Faulk, give Murray and Hahn the name of your tailor and you two go over and get a couple of size fifty suits with shirts and ties to match. Get some nice dress shoes too. Do you have a barber that you trust?"

Faulk smiled with a resounding yes, noting that she was in the kitchen, washing the dishes.

"Deb cuts your hair? That's great! We don't have to walk the General down the street nor worry about funny glances or questions. Can you ask her?"

Faulk said it was no problem. He thought it would be a good idea to wash his hair before cutting it, something that Deb was accustomed to doing anyway.

Anders was psyched. "Outstanding! If you get him started, I'll start to work on arrangements in Washington."

The team set in motion. Three men excused themselves from the room, gathered their belongings, and were on their way. Anders led Mr. Washington into the kitchen where Faulk was trying to explain the incredible and unfolding series of events to his wife. Deborah asked her husband for a word in private.

Mr. and Mrs. Faulk disappeared into the pantry. "Are you nuts?" she asked him. "This is a joke. It's bad enough that you bring an army of men into our house at this hour; accompanied by a guy you think is George Washington. He smells like a homeless man you would find at Thirtieth Street Station at one o'clock in the morning. And his hair, it has a smell all to its own and you want me to wash and cut it? Do we have turpentine hanging around in the basement?"

Faulk laughed and tried to explain that it was no big deal. Deb would have none of it.

"My God, Brian, did you happen to notice his teeth? Watching him eat eggs made me lose my appetite. Forget a barber; I think we should call a priest."

Faulk assured her that he was not a bum and gently coaxed her into agreeing to it. Deb was not sure she could believe another one of Brian's fantastic stories, but just in case he was right this time, she agreed to "hold her nose" and attend to the president's hair.

The couple reentered the kitchen and, to Brian and the others' delight, she cleared the sink of dishes and put on her trusty rubber gloves. Her husband grabbed a towel from the counter and placed it around Mr. Washington's shoulders and neck while Mrs. Faulk untied the ribbon and eased his head down into the sink. She started the water while her husband brought a bottle of shampoo from the bathroom. She held her hands up as if about to perform surgery and surveyed the room. With everything set in place, Deb began to wash and rinse the president's hair.

Now rinsed with a towel over his head, Mr. Washington was escorted to a chair placed in the middle of the kitchen. He glanced over his right shoulder as Mrs. Faulk gathered the scissors and comb and approached the subject. Everything was moving so fast that Mr. Washington did not have a chance to question the many decisions these familiar strangers had made.

He trusted these men but he recalled that even the original founding fathers did not agree on everything. On the contrary, they often fought like cats and dogs and worked for their own good, as well as the collective good—many times behind each other's backs. He wondered if everything they were doing was right and just. He was very excited to see the nation's capital, a city named after him, which he helped design some two hundred years earlier. He wanted to learn about the presidents that followed him and the advancements throughout the last two centuries that made this country great. Still, he had pangs of uncertainty as Mrs. Faulk commenced the makeover.

Chapter 10

Two open suitcases sat on the Faulk's bed, with newly purchased clothing, neatly folded. Shirts, pants, socks and underwear were all arranged in an orderly fashion. Next to the suitcases was a pair of loafers, a pair of Nike sneakers, and shiny black dress shoes, all size twelve. Mr. Washington and Faulk stood bed side, examining the new clothes and wondered if they were missing anything.

The General was fidgety as he got used to the clothes he adorned; a pair of blue Dockers pants, a white button-down dress shirt with blue stripes, and a blazer that fit his large frame very well. He pushed the red ribbon down into his right front pants pocket, no longer needing it (thanks to Mrs. Faulk's handiwork), but vowing to keep Providence with him in this strange new world. Mr. Washington looked as though he had just dressed for dinner at the country club.

Faulk commended the team on the clothing choices, noting that he would have chosen the same attire had he been instructed to shop. "I'll tell you what Mr. Washington, you look great. With the new clothes and new hairstyle, I don't think Martha would recognize you." Faulk noticed the mention of Martha caused a sad expression to pass quickly through Mr. Washington's eyes. Faulk leaned forward to zip the suitcases shut and motioned toward the open closet door from which Mr. Washington's new Armani suit hung in a garment bag. The first president strode to the door and unhooked the bag. He looked at the full-length mirror and studied his reflection from the bottom of his feet to the top of his newly cut hair. A look of satisfaction came over him.

As he turned back toward the bed, Faulk sized up the situation. "The boys dropped the clothes off while you were washing up and went back to get their things and check out of their hotels. Wait till they get a look at you, they may not know who you are... I think I hear Anders downstairs."

Mr. Washington looked around and asked if his host had packed a bag.

"Let's just say Deb and I had a bit of a talk while you were trying on your new clothes. It looks like I won't be leaving with you today."

The first president grinned with a familiar twinkle in his eye, noting that he fully understood the situation.

"Tomorrow is another day."

Faulk, smiling broadly, extended his hand to Mr. Washington, who shook it appreciatively.

"I have Anders' and Jenson's contact info, so don't be surprised if you see me again... and soon."

Both men descended the staircase. Mr. Washington stepped cautiously, his new suit draped over his arm. Faulk followed, lugging a suitcase filled with the rest of Mr. Washington's new clothes and toiletries. They placed the luggage on the floor in the vestibule and entered the living room to the sound of Anders' voice. With his cell phone still glued to his ear, Anders froze for a second as he faced the men. He took in the sight of the father of our country, looking as if he should be holding a golf club in his hand.

"You have all the details? Are we good? Okay, send them to me in an email and I'll pick everything up in the limo. Thanks for everything hon, I don't know what I would do without you... well yes, and without a paddle. Take care."

Anders hung up his mobile phone and examined the transformed General before him. As he did, Jenson, Murray, and Hahn walked into the house, also stopping to stare at the makeover in front of them.

Hahn approached Mr. Washington and tilted his body to one side as he circled the president, who at once stood at attention.

"Nice, real nice! You look like some of my friends' fathers. All you need is a pair of Ray-Bans and you're ready for the yacht!"

Mr. Washington, again confused by the young man's compliment, turned to Faulk. Faulk added that Ray-Bans were sunglasses, shades to protect your eyes from the glare of the sun.

"Ray-Bans sound like something you may have invented Mr. Faulk," replied Mr. Washington.

"Well it looks like we're all set to go. I must insist General Washington ride in the limo with me," Anders proclaimed as the group planned their ride to Washington.

"We can relax in comfort and Mr. Washington can enjoy the scenery as we get him up to speed on two hundred and thirteen years of America."

Jenson mentioned that the luxury van had more than enough room and suggested that Mr. Washington would be more comfortable with them. He thought the president would like the accoutrements it afforded. But after a few minutes of haggling, Jenson realized arguing with Josh Anders was pointless. Anders was a great debater and famously stubborn.

Jenson's famous Virginia statehouse saying was that he had never seen one of two disputants convince the other by arguments. Besides, he knew he would get ample face time with Mr. Washington upon arrival in DC. The king of talk radio agreed to connect the limo and van for the duration of the trip over the internet through Skype. Everybody was pleased to know that they would be part of the discussion down to the nation's capital.

As the men exited the Faulk home, they were met on the sidewalk by Mrs. Murray, Todd, and Skip Keaton. While the van idled in front of the Faulk home, Jack Murray introduced his family to Washington. Dorothy Murray giggled as she shook Mr. Washington's hand. As always, Mr. Washington bowed in the presence of a lady and kissed her hand, observing that Dottie Murray's charm was reminiscent of Mrs. Madison who he cared for very much.

Following the conversation inside the house, the General felt he needed to assure both parties.

"I will entertain Mr. Anders' offer and travel in his coach. I only require that Mr. Hahn join with me on the first leg of the journey. Certainly there will be adequate opportunity tonight as we rest. And on tomorrow's leg, I will visit with Mr. Murray and Mr. Jenson. And please refer to me by the familiar form of my name which I observe is the current custom. Please call me George."

As the whole group stood in awe of Mr. Washington, the young Todd Murray laughed out loud before righting himself. He reminded the tall man that the trip would only take three hours.

"We'll be down there before the sun sets."

Mr. Washington laughed and ruffled Todd's hair, noting that it took a young man of clear mind to alert him to the expediency of the trip.

He was about to approach the red van at the curb when, to Mr. Washington's surprise, Anders' white limo pulled up. Anthony Hahn stepped forward and swung the rear passenger door open for the General. After a brief examination of the long car, President George Washington hesitatingly slid into the back seat.

Hahn threw his overnight bag in the trunk of the limo and followed Mr. Washington into the car. Anders watched as the rest of the group filed into the van and shut the door. Keaton stayed with Anders on the sidewalk as they finalized directions for their trip south. When Anders was satisfied that Keaton understood the route, he turned and entered the limousine, closing the door behind him. As each excited group settled in for the ride, Mr. Washington looked above and around his head as the car lurched forward. A million questions swam in the president's head.

"Gentlemen, please excuse the inquiry, as I have so many, but in what kind of coach are we riding?"

Josh Anders asked that George not apologize for any question. "We understand. We have about three hours on our ride to Washington. Hahn and I will try to answer all your questions and bring you up to date on world history since 1799. And there is a lot to talk about, as you can imagine."

Both men took turns describing how automobiles come in different shapes and sizes and how they're commonly referred to as cars. Hahn defined the term limousine, explaining that it is a larger car that carries many people in luxury. George observed its spaciousness and noted that it was obviously a different breed of limousine than the limousin cattle herded in Europe.

"Yes, sir," Hahn said, smiling. "Though I understand the origin of both words came from the same region of France."

Mr. Washington saw cars everywhere he looked. He said aloud to himself that it was evident these autos were the preferred choice of transportation for twenty-first century Americans. He asked if they were made in Philadelphia.

"No, most of them are built in Detroit, which is a city in the state of Michigan."

George went on to mention that he was familiar with Detroit as it played a part in the French and Indian War. He also mentioned that the British surrendered Detroit to the United States through the Jay Treaty of 1796. But he said he was not familiar with the state of Michigan.

Anders was deep in a text message conversation but managed to say that if the British wanted Detroit back, they could have it. Hahn jokingly agreed before taking the floor again.

"Oh, we have 50 states now; three thousand miles across from sea to sea, plus Alaska and Hawaii. Most American-built cars come from Detroit, the center of the American auto-making industry. Sadly, however, many other cars are built in other countries such as Japan and Germany, or as you might have called it, Prussia."

Mr. Washington seemed astonished.

"Fascinating, just fascinating. I will remain quiet and at your disposal as I digest the marvels I am sure you will describe."

As the limousine negotiated Philadelphia traffic, Hahn's cell phone rang. He looked at the phone and realized it was Jack Murray from the van. He told Murray to wait about ten minutes until they reached the highway. Hahn hung up and told Mr. Washington to enjoy the city scenery before they reached the interstate.

Murray was as anxious to connect to the limo as the rest of his travel mates and showed his frustration as he looked at his phone. Dottie slid closer to him and put her hand on his.

"It's a three hour ride, babe. We're not going to miss anything. Just relax."

She brought her left hand up and began to massage Murray's neck and shoulder. Todd looked away, embarrassed at his parents' sign of public affection. Within an instant, Mr. Murray relaxed. He was always putty in her hands, and this time was no exception. He leaned his head back and nearly forgot where he was as the mobile phone fell to the carpeted floor.

The vehicles moved through the streets of Philadelphia as Mr. Washington continued to look near and far, trying to soak in everything he noticed. The last time he traveled these streets, it had been on a very bumpy carriage ride over a dirt road. He marveled at the way the automobile could move so smoothly at such high speeds. Hahn explained how the invention commonly referred to as the shock absorber allowed for a level and even transport. Upon hearing one of many explanations to come, Mr. Washington returned his nose to the window to take in more sights.

As the limo finally turned onto the entrance ramp leading to interstate 95, Hahn's phone rang once again. Contemplating not answering the call for a second, he picked up the phone.

"Hi Jack. Oh, I'm sorry. What did you say? Ok, I will get on now. Todd, what password should I use? Ok, thanks. See you in a minute."

The youthful Hahn leaned over to the keyboard built into the limo's console and typed in his ID and password. Skype connected the Anders' limo to Jenson's van with a crystal clear picture. On the other side of the connection, the men viewed the image of Todd Murray smiling as he adjusted the volume on the van's personal computer.

"George, you are looking into Mr. Jenson's automobile. Young Mr. Murray and the others can see and hear you just as we can see and hear them."

Even though the General was amazed at what he had seen so far, looking into the computer screen dazzled him. For the first time since he appeared, Mr. Washington seemed overwhelmed.

"I only just promised to remain quiet, but for this I cannot keep restraint. What is this looking glass that allows us to peer across space and privacy? How is it done? Did Mr. Franklin, or your Mr. Faulk create this miracle?"

Jenson's laugh was audible over the Skype connection while he peered into the camera, providing Mr. Washington the opportunity to see who was addressing him.

"No, I don't think so, although a former vice-president of the United States claims to have. That is another story for another day."

Centering himself in front of the camera mounted to the van's computer, Todd Murray contributed by describing Skype and the internet.

His father picked up on Todd's description. "These connections can be made anywhere in the world at any time. One can communicate with limitless numbers of people instantaneously. This internet and the technologies that drive it are extraordinarily powerful devices. Even for us, who have lived through the rise of these technologies, it is miraculous. For young Todd here, it is as mundane as a quill and parchment may have been for you."

Mr. Washington struggled as he slid down the limo's leather seat. He examined the computer and leaned forward to look left and right around the device. Perplexed, he tried to figure out how the contraption worked without asking yet another question. It was of no use.

"Forgive me if I ask a silly question, but back at the Faulk residence I noticed a number of what you called electronic devices and they were connected to the walls of the house by rubber wires. You explained that an electrical current ran from outside wires connected to the house and that electricity circulated throughout the dwelling, allowing twenty-first century man to power-up their devices. Well, I am looking at this device before me and I see wires protruding from the back into the car panel here, but the automobile is not connected to anything. On the contrary, we are mobile and in motion. So how is it possible that two automotive devices, moving simultaneously at a great speed, can be connected?"

Hahn stated that similar to the cell phone (that seemed to be an extension of Anders' hand), a computer sends a signal up to a satellite in space, then back down to another phone or computer, creating a link or a connection.

Mr. Washington, listening closely as he continued to study the device, turned to the two gentlemen in the back seat to explain that in his day, the word satellite was used to refer to a follower or attendant to a superior person.

Anders, taking a break from his cellular phone, blurted that if that were the case, the occupants of each car were his satellites.

Murray did not know what to make of Anders' statement. He looked around the van to find all of its passengers giving Anders the same odd look. He thought that maybe Anders had enough girth and gravitational pull to attract satellite objects, but Jack Murray was not one of them. As far as Murray was concerned, Anders could speak for himself. He may have been paid to talk, but there was no way Anders represented Jack.

Sensing his thoughts, Dottie squeezed his leg and smiled to her husband, causing Jack to bite his tongue. Soon everyone focused again on the computer screen as Mr. Washington cleared his throat.

"These wonders are most astounding and I am quite sure you learned gentlemen and the lovely Mrs. Murray will educate me further on their technical origins. However, what I find most astonishing, and I do hope it proves most gratifying about our society, is the mixture of races living among each other."

Jenson and the Murrays could see on the screen how the first president waved his arm toward the passing cars on the highway and pointed to each person within each car.

"In my very limited observations thus far, Negroes, yellow, white and brown inhabitants of Philadelphia appear as equals. Am I to believe that the question of holding such species as property has been addressed throughout the southern states? Perhaps wiser and braver men than us came together to remove the chains of bondage?"

From the van, Jenson beat the other new founders to the punch. "Mr. President, to your great satisfaction I am sure, the slave trade and ultimately slavery itself was abolished in these United States 150 years ago. We'll talk about it in more detail during our history discussion."

Mr. Washington agreed and thanked Tim for the quick answer. He was not prepared for the next question.

"Did you really chop down that cherry tree?"

George laughed at the blunt inquiry posed by Todd Murray. However, the only other sound audible in either car was the hum of the car engines as everybody in hearing distance waited for an answer. Mr. Washington went silent, surprised by the serious tones taken in the limo and van. He thought that these folks could not be serious.

"I hope you all realize that the story about the cherry tree is simply that, a story. I have taken many hatchets to many trees, including cherry trees in my gardens at Mount Vernon. And I had no reason to lie about any of them. In fact, my father would have been proud if I took one of our trees down as it would mean less work for him."

As Mr. Washington uttered those words, Dorothy Murray let out such a high pitched cackle that the limo driver tapped the brakes. Everybody followed with genuine laughter as they learned the truth about a centuries old legend.

As the laughter subsided, the navigation screen mounted in the dashboard directed the driver to turn on to I-95 South. Mr. Washington, hearing the artificial voice, looked around in every direction before sliding toward the front seat. He stared over the driver's right shoulder at the small colorful electronic map that moved in synchronization with the car. The curious electronic device continued to talk, directing the driver again and again as a map of the East Coast of the United States appeared on the screen.

"Please indulge me again my friends, to who did that disjoined voice belong? A mechanical navigator?"

Hahn slid down the seat next to the General and answered eagerly. "George, that device is a Global Positioning System, more commonly known as a GPS." Hahn went on to describe to George in detail how GPS works.

The first president was fascinated. He proudly told the group that he was a trained surveyor in the mid eighteenth century but he never imagined a device such as a GPS. He asked if the GPS was common in most automobiles.

"Yes sir, most cars have them now."

The van pulled up alongside the Anders limousine. Dottie patted her husband on his back and pointed to Mr. Washington in the window. She knocked on the glass and waved to the other car, expecting them to see her. Murray again shook his head, trying to direct her attention to the computer.

"You can see and talk to them right there. They're probably wondering what the hell you are doing."

All eyes in the limo at once looked at the screen, then out the window toward the van. Mr. Washington waved to Mrs. Murray. As he waved, he spoke. "During the next few hours, I am sure you will describe all the wonders of the country over the past couple of centuries. These states must have many problems now, which is why I believe Providence has called us together. But I expect as a nation we have overcome more challenges and achieved more in the last two hundred years than I could ever have imagined."

Hahn quoted Ronald Reagan, where he reminded everyone that America remained the last great hope on Earth.

Anders, noticing the driver's sudden interest in the conversation, used a remote button on his armrest to close the glass wall between the front seat and the rest of the car.

"Please relax if you can and listen to your legacy. It is truly a fantastic story."

But before Mr. Washington could settle in, a loud noise came from overhead that shook the car and the eardrums of the passengers. George leaned in toward the window and looked up as an American Airlines 757 roared over the highway and landed on the runway beyond the orange landing lights. George was wide-eyed as his gaze followed the plane down the tarmac to a stop. He whipped around to the men with yet another incredulous look.

"What, pray tell, was that? It looked like a giant silver phoenix. It had a long red and blue stripe and writing on it that I could not make out. Are we under attack from the sky?"

The group chortled and looked at each other as if to telepathically explain to each other that they had their work cut out for them.

Hahn explained the history of the airplane and its civilian and military uses.

Jenson picked up the conversation. "That area where it landed is called an airport, a port for air travel as New York was a port for ships in colonial days. Air travel is just one of the many advances we will be discussing over the next twenty-four hours. So, as I said before, please sit back and relax and enjoy yourself as we try our best to enlighten you on the history of this great country."

Mr. Washington took Jenson's suggestion to heart. He straightened his body out and faced his companions while staying in sight of the Skype camera. Jenson, Murray, and Anders took the cue from George and commenced a history lesson for the ages.

Not wanting to confuse Mr. Washington, they agreed to do their best to explain American history in chronological order. They began with the Louisiana Purchase as Jenson detailed all the facts and how with one stroke of the pen, the USA doubled in size. Murray took over the conversation by describing the War of 1812 and the crucial battles that saved the country from British rule.

Following Mr. Murray's account, Anders inserted himself into the conversation and, to the group's surprise, described the Age of Manifest Destiny between the War of 1812 and the Civil War, when presidents like James Polk and Andrew Jackson focused on the expansion of the country across the North American continent. He went into great detail on the occupation of the Oregon and Texas territories, again to the surprise of everybody listening. The blustery persona that the listeners heard on the radio was meant for ratings, while off the air Anders' erudition always came to the forefront. He described slavery and the Dred Scott case, but only briefly (to the General's disappointment).

With Anders' lesson on expansion and slavery complete, Hahn led the group in a discussion about the Civil War, providing a thirty thousand foot description of the historical points of the battles, speeches, and people associated with the war. They all agreed that the Civil War was a topic of such great importance and had such an impact and lasting effect on the country, that it would be better suited to discuss after they reached their destination in DC. But Jenson couldn't resist adding his two cents to the conversation. As the cars sped south down I-95 through Delaware and past the Mason Dixon Line, Jenson took a deep breath, righted himself, and took the floor once again.

"Please keep in mind the historical significance of the Civil War. This country was torn apart by an unimaginably bloody war between the northern and southern states to settle, among other things, the slave issue. Black, White, Asian, Latin, and everyone in between now live as equals in our country."

He emphasized how the impact of that event led to the first black president in American history.

"And it all started with the Civil War. It took decades for the country to recover, which included the assassination of one of our finest presidents. And believe it or not, even after all we have overcome, sadly race is still a very divisive issue today. The accusation of racism is often perpetuated as a weapon to smear the good names of those in opposition."

Mr. Washington stared blankly into the computer screen, apparently overwhelmed by the information he was still digesting. He pulled himself together and replied, "I see, Mr. Jenson. How horrific that our generation left the next with such an insurmountable problem. We knew the injustice of slavery but could not abolish it in our time without tearing our infant nation apart. We established a time when the trade would end and believed it would result in the eventual demise of slavery itself. I even wrote in my own will that upon my death, slaves under my direction must be set free. Please assure me they were."

Shaken, Mr. Washington turned to Anders.

"We did. Did we not? We believed slavery would fade away once the trade was removed. How shameful that we failed, but you must understand we were of a just mind."

For one of a handful of times in his life, Anders was at a loss for words as he stared at the first president. The others remained silent while the father of our country endured a sudden moral crisis right before their eyes. After a minute of solemn silence, a choked up Mr. Washington cleared his throat and spoke.

"Mr. Jefferson—pardon me—Mr. Jenson, you spoke of the president during this terrible war who would be assassinated. Please gentlemen, tell me about this extraordinary man."

Murray, the historian, sipped his bottled water and moved toward the microphone. The Civil War discussion couldn't wait.

"Abraham Lincoln was the sixteenth president of the United States. He was born to a poor family in the state of Kentucky, became a lawyer and was eventually elected president of the United States in 1860 as the Civil War loomed. We can fill in more details and get you materials to read when we get to DC."

Mr. Washington responded that the man was indeed interesting.

"Benjamin Lincoln was a good man, was my second in command. He accepted the surrender of British Forces. Could they have been related?"

Murray answered that no one was quite sure but they likely were distant relations going back to Norfolk England through Massachusetts.

George peered in the sunken eyes and deep lines of the face on the five dollar bill, which Hahn had quietly handed him.

Murray reiterated that like the founders, Lincoln had been torn between abolishing slavery and the threat of the country being destroyed by war; ultimately, Lincoln knew that the country could not survive divided.

Murray felt his throat tighten and voice quiver. As he spoke, he thought about the horrors of slavery and the thousands of young men who were killed defending and opposing the terrible institution. He looked over at Todd sitting innocently next to his mother and momentarily felt a twinge of resentment that the problem of slavery, like so many today, was "kicked" to another generation to solve.

Murray regained his voice and sounded like the history teacher he was.

"After several failed attempts at compromise on the slavery and states' rights issues, the south seceded from the Union in 1861. Lincoln would not allow the nation to break up, so when a southern force attacked the Union base at Fort Sumter, South Carolina in April 1861, the war began. Richmond was the capital of the Confederacy, and our Virginia was the site of many major battles during the war. Over half a million Americans died on both sides. Families were ripped apart and, like Tim said, it took decades for us to recover. But ultimately, the war solidified America as a nation."

"My Lord. And what of Mr. Lincoln?" asked Mr. Washington.

Hahn spoke almost in a whisper. "Lincoln suffered terribly during those four long years. He did what he had to do to deliver the equality promised in the Declaration of Independence. That included committing thousands of young lives to a barbaric war. He preserved the Union and has been recognized with you and one or two others as the greatest of our forty-four presidents.

Vocalizing what he already deduced, he asked if President Lincoln was in fact assassinated.

It was young Todd Murray's turn to enter the discussion and teach history. "Yes. Right after the war ended, he was shot while watching a play at Ford's Theater in Washington DC. The assassin was named John Wilkes Booth. He agreed with the confederates."

"I see," responded Mr. Washington. "Thank you, Master Murray. Obviously, Mr. Lincoln is remembered and revered to the degree that he is still the subject of lessons in schools?"

"You got it," replied Dottie.

"Washington DC has so many monuments and memorials to great Americans and events. There is a Washington Monument in the center of the city that I think is the tallest building in the city. There's a Lincoln Memorial with a huge statue of Abe sitting in obvious contemplation. We need to bring you to these memorials so you can get a look for yourself!"

"And we will, Mrs. Murray," interjected Anders through the computer screen as Jack gave his excited wife a wink and a thumbs up. In his mind, Anders had yielded to his counterparts long enough. "That is one of the purposes of this trip, to show General Washington the city and its monuments that bear his name. But we went off on a tangent there and we should get back to the timeline. We are through with the Civil War for now, is that correct?"

Mr. Washington wanted to hear more about Lincoln but stayed silent, respecting what the men were doing for him. It was not every day that one was asked to provide the history of the United States in a three hour drive. Plus, these gentlemen had rearranged their lives for him. So George made many mental notes, promising himself to come back to each topic once they were settled from their journey. He knew something that his companions did not; that time was not going to be an immediate restraint in pursuit of their ultimate goal.

The Industrial Revolution and Spanish American War were the next two topics touched upon. Hahn described the rise of the industrial infrastructure modeled on that of England, and followed with a very detailed description of the Spanish-American War and the legend of Teddy Roosevelt, which made Mr. Washington smile.

The whole group talked over each other in their description of the events of World War I and the rise of Communism. Small arguments arose over the facts. Murray noted that Mr. Washington, for the first time, demonstrated his authority and requested silence. "Gentlemen, I am forever in your debt for the information that continues to nourish my brain. But I ask that you respect each other and take turns speaking. I cannot comprehend everything if one is shouting over the other. Thank you."

George Washington was an exceptionally quick study, absorbing a great deal of the information the team threw at him. The men around him were impressed at the ease at which he understood everything.

As the information continued to flow in his direction, Mr. Washington still took the time to glance out the window and admire the beauty of the Pennsylvania, Delaware, and Maryland countryside. The sign on the side of the highway alerted traffic to the bridge ahead that crossed the Susquehanna River. "The Susquehanna River never looked so beautiful as it does from this magnificent bridge, spanning majestically over its soothing waters. Was the route to the West established through this river?"

Anders and Jenson both shook their heads at the same time and explained that despite what was believed during Mr. Washington's time, there was no single waterway leading to the continent's west coast.

The men enjoyed talking American history, learning from each other while trying to top one another with their knowledge.

Each took a turn providing a high level narrative of the events of the twentieth century—the advent of the Income Tax and Women's rights, the Roaring 20's and Great Depression. The rise of Adolf Hitler, Pearl Harbor, and WWII dominated the second full hour of the drive. This was closely followed by depictions of FDR and his New Deal, the Korean and Cold War, and technological advances such as television, radio, and cell phones.

JFK, Vietnam, LBJ, and the Great Society were described impressively by Tim Jenson. Hahn bridged the sixties and seventies by describing the space race, and the election and subsequent resignation of President Nixon over a scandal called Watergate, which became part of the American lexicon.

George began to yawn and fidget, so Jenson glossed over the Carter years to the delight of the assembled groups of both vehicles. He talked about Iran, the hostages, and the troubles that rose about in the Middle East. This was followed by a group discussion about President Reagan. They finished their chronological history of the USA by verbalizing the pros and cons of the Bush and Clinton years, wrapping up with a quick discussion of the last three and a half years under the current Commander-in-Chief.

Hahn described in personal detail the events of 9/11/01, which seemed to shake Mr. Washington to his core. He was sensitive to criticism in his day, wondering in his writings of how men could use their words as weapons to injure other men. Hearing of giant metal birds used as projectiles to kill Americans in the great city of New York was just too much to comprehend. He asked that they stop the conversation at that point and resume when they reached their destination. Sensing an air of uneasiness, the group agreed and responded with an awkward silence.

"It appears from the sound emanating from your GPS device that we will not be at our destination for at least thirty minutes," Mr. Washington said. "Please forgive my vulgarity Mrs. Murray, but might this limo contain an outhouse? Or perhaps there would be one at an eatery or tavern along the highway that might suffice?"

Todd Murray jumped in, "Yeah ma, I gotta pee."

As Mr. Washington let out a hearty laugh, Anders and Jenson asked their drivers to stop at the next rest stop, Chesapeake House, which was only four miles ahead.

As the limo and van stopped in front of the Roy Rogers sign at the Chesapeake House rest stop, Anders and Jenson jumped out first to talk. They walked around to the far side of the van in hope of not being noticed by curious travelers as Jack tended to his family.

"This may be a bit tricky," Anders began. "It's bad enough when I, the Head Honcho of Talk Radio, have to pee in crowds like this. But bringing a three hundred year old ex president, whose face is on every dollar bill in the place, to a urinal may be complicated. Here's what we gotta do."

Anders mapped out a strategy as if he was preparing for battle. He suggested that the group break up into smaller separate groups as to not draw attention. Anders would put on his big Navy baseball cap and sunglasses and walk alone into the rest stop and directly to the men's room. He explained that by going solo, if he were to be recognized, it would turn focus toward him and away from the president. He could then secure a stall and wait for George. He asked that Hahn and Jenson escort Mr. Washington straight to the bathroom while the rest of the group goes about their business. Dottie volunteered the Murrays to get lunch for the group and bring it back to the cars. Then, Anders made sure everybody was ready.

"I wasn't even thinking about that but now that you've said it, I'm pretty hungry myself. Okay, this is what we do. Get the kid's Villanova hat and make sure Mr. Big wears it in. You ready? Let's roll."

Both men went into their respective vehicles and shared the game plan with the team. Anders jumped out of the limousine with cap and glasses in place and started toward the door under the Roy Rogers sign. Tim walked to the limo and handed the hat to Mr. Washington, instructing him to place it on his head with the brim adjusted just above his eyes. The Murrays started toward the food court as Anders disappeared into the building, undetected.

As the others approached the door, Hahn and Jenson escorted Mr. Washington out of the car and started their walk to the men's room.

Murray was a bit concerned about his expense on this "all expense paid" weekend in Philly. Though Hahn paid for the Armani, Jack had already put several hundred dollars on his credit card for Mr. Washington's clothes. Now, he, Dottie, and Todd had offered to buy lunch for this group of strangers. Murray wasn't cheap but he was no currency trader or famous talk show host. He was a high school teacher and Dottie was a stay-at-home mom who loved to spend money on entertaining friends.

He didn't say anything to Dottie, especially in front of Todd, but Jack started to feel like a fool as if these guys were taking advantage of him. Intellectually, he thought he knew better but he was not sure of anything anymore.

As they returned to the cars with hamburgers, fries, coffee and cokes, Jack saw the excitement in Dottie's eyes. Ironically, she was having a great time. She seemed comfortable in the situation, gregariously talking with Tim and George as if they were neighbors. But that was always her way. Her cheery disposition was sometimes mistaken for flirtation. Even Todd felt important, having been part of the discussion himself.

Murray thought to himself that it was he who was having the reservations. To avoid conflict, he kept quiet, jumped back in the van with the food and waited for the others to return.

Mr. Washington's gait fell in line with the other two men as they found themselves breezing past strangers as they entered the restroom. Still in disguise, Anders drew a few stares from the men in the bathroom as he waved his colleagues to the far stall. Jenson mentioned under his breath that it was a good thing Josh had chosen a handicapped stall. Jenson and Mr. Washington entered the oversized stall as Hahn stood guard at the urinal closest to the stall door. Anders turned to the two men in an uncomfortably close proximity and asked a question that he never imagined he would be asking twenty four hours earlier.

"Ok George, you can stand here or sit down. Depends on what you need to do."

"I will stand."

"Thank God," Replied Jenson.

"Just one question, gentlemen."

"Yes?" answered Anders, warily.

"Where does it all go?"

Unable to contain himself with the madness of the situation, Anders replied, "I think General, it may go to Washington DC."

"I see. Just as I feared."

Jenson could not help but laugh to himself at the absurd exchange taking place between Anders and Mr. Washington. He and Anders looked at each other as if to ask what they were doing here. Jenson whispered that he had not been in a stall with another man since he was four, reiterating that the whole scene was too weird for him. So, he exited the stall with Anders in tow. Both men needed to take care of business themselves and were confident that the first president could handle the rest himself.

Fortunately, Mr. Washington completed his business as a proper eighteenth century gentleman would. He exited the stall and Anders lead him to the sink to wash his hands.

Mr. Washington and his men were pleased at the sight of the late lunch as they got back to the cars. They reached for the burgers as Mrs. Murray waited on the first president.

Mr. Washington climbed into one of the captain's chairs in the back of the van, keeping his promise to spend time with all, even if the last leg of the trip would last only another thirty minutes. He quickly got the hang of eating without proper silverware and even savored the newly found finger food. Much to Jack's amusement, he promptly downed the burgers and fries. Mr. Washington did not have a taste for the soda but thoroughly enjoyed the steaming hot black coffee that Murray suggested they buy.

Keaton gave a wave to his counterpart in the limousine, and both vehicles turned out of the parking lot to finish the last thirty miles of their trip.

Even though connected by internet through the Skype satellite connection, the occupants of both vehicles were unusually quiet, as if they had exhausted all of their energy during the three hour historical synopsis. After fifteen minutes, Mr. Washington, taking another sip of his coffee, broke the silence.

"Please forgive my self-absorption and selfishness, but I never asked you about yourselves. I would ask that you tell me a little about your backgrounds and who you are, including the Murray family. I have an idea of the makeup of each of you but I would like to hear from you, in your own words. You individuals have been so generous with your valuable time, fine people who have welcomed me into their homes and automobiles. Mr. Jenson, why don't you begin?"

Jenson was humbled as Mr. Washington listened intently to him describe his upbringing which, like Mr. Washington, took place in rural Virginia. He began his account in Albemarle County, a pastoral area in which young Tim lived in a fantasy world of books and daydreams. He portrayed a community where friends, neighbors, and family provided a great support network and encouraged a young boy to chase his dreams. He was about to continue when interrupted by a loud shriek.

"There it is. There's the Washington Monument!" Todd Murray's outburst resulted in attention being directed away from Jenson and toward the right side of the car. All eyes in both the van and limousine were now affixed upward in a southwest direction. Jack Murray managed a smile and glanced at Mr. Washington. "Fitting, wouldn't you say Mr. President?"

Mr. Washington looked in his direction and responded with a nod and a wide grin.

Chapter 11

"Mr. President, welcome home," came the voice of Anders through the van's Skype connection as both vehicles made their way down New York Avenue.

"Why don't we take a quick drive around and show Mr. Washington the city he helped design? Then we'll head over to the Willard Hotel on Pennsylvania Avenue, check in, and wash up for dinner. Hope you all don't mind, but while we were at Faulk's house, my assistant arranged for accommodations here in Washington. I've stayed at the Willard a number of times and I think everybody will find it comfortable."

"Hey Jenson, I even got you and the Murrays the Jefferson suite. Its 3,000 square feet; probably bigger than most houses and maybe more expensive."

Anders made sure everyone knew he also booked dinner in an exclusive private dining room of Café Du Parc in the hotel.

Murray politely nodded thank you and noticed Hahn roll his eyes through the computer screen. Anders was friendly, generous, intelligent, and politically brilliant, but at times a pushy and bossy windbag. Jack knew the type, and although Anders could be condescending and abrasive, he felt he was a good guy and certainly an ally worth fostering. Jack hoped his young new confidant thought the same, but could not be completely sure.

As the cars filled up at an Exxon station, Hahn stewed. Because of present company, he kept his growing irritation with Anders to himself. Although he enjoyed the Anders radio show every evening, Hahn was tiring of Anders "running the show" and felt the urge to give the pompous know-it-all a piece of his mind. As head trader at The Bank of New York, one of the most prestigious currency trading desks in the world, Hahn was used to being in charge and giving orders. He was out of his element and he did not like it. But for the time being, he agreed to keep his Caribbean blood at a simmer as he observed his new acquaintances following along.

Jenson, always one to keep the peace, simply smiled and interrupted Hahn's train of thought.

"Thanks, Anders, that's a great hotel. I think a ride around the city is a good idea. We can show George the memorials and drive by the Washington Monument."

Jenson suggested they park the cars while they got out and stretched their legs before dinner, noting the White House was only a few blocks from the Willard. Mr. Washington agreed, stating he enjoyed the comfort of the limo during the daylight heat, but would prefer an evening walk around the sights of DC while the sun set.

"Perhaps our inspiration will find us this evening, but more likely in the morn when we are better rested."

The group agreed to George's plan. After all, thought Jack, how could they not? Murray had noticed Mr. Washington was indeed a man of humility and of few words. But like other great leaders, his words had purpose, inspiring others. Jack thought of great athletes, such as Michael Jordan and Joe Montana, who quietly made those around them better. There was no doubt George had that affect on this little team.

George quietly observed as each driver monitored the nozzles attached to their vehicles.

Mr. Washington noticed Murray reaching over and taking the hand of his beautiful wife and placing his left hand on young Todd's curly hair as he sat on the floor of the van. Dottie squeezed Jack's hand and their eyes met briefly. In that moment, Dottie thought she saw in Jack the contentment of a man whose restless search may have finally been quenched. She had always been proud of her husband, but now the promise of greatness she had seen in him from the day they met was being brought to the forefront by a ghost from the past.

It was hard to comprehend. Dottie's little family woke up the day before, like millions of other so-called ordinary American families. Less than thirty-six hours later, she was no longer certain of anything. The absurdity and immensity of it all had not sunk in yet. But she was more than okay with it, embracing the phenomenon that brought the group together.

As the thought crossed her mind, Mr. Washington was deep in his own thoughts. He had been sitting quietly, watching the men connect the gasoline hoses to the respective tanks. Just another incredible technological advance he had witnessed, an occurrence that had become commonplace over the last seven hours. He tired of watching the dollar signs on the computer display add up, and now turned his attention to the Murrays. George knew Providence had plans for him and the men, but not knowing the grand plan gnawed at the General.

Seeing the Murrays holding hands and rubbing the head of their son, made George long for his old life, the sounds and smells of Mount Vernon, and his beloved Martha who made it her business to be with her "old man" as much as she could (even during the darkest days of the revolution). But she was not part of his new life now. Here, in the city that he helped design, in the country he founded, surrounded by his new confidants, he suddenly felt alone. He was snapped out of his thoughts as they exited the station and made their way back onto New York Ave. Anders' familiar voice once again permeated through the van, announcing that they would be passing the President's Mansion, now known as the White House. George was impressed at every turn. He recalled that eons ago he had laid the cornerstones for the ten by ten mile city. That was in another life, another age....

Sensing George's thoughts, Hahn broke the silence. "General Washington, as you may recall, the White House has been the home and office of the president since our second president, John Adams."

Looking over at Murray, Hahn continued by mentioning that it was burned during Madison's presidency and the War of 1812, but rebuilt after the war. "It's been remodeled a lot over the years but has remained the president's home ever since, even during the Civil War." Hahn reveled in George's undivided attention. "You may have noticed that DC is not the perfectly shaped 100 square mile city that you designed with L'Enfant. During the Civil War, when Virginia seceded, they took parts of the city, as well as Arlington and Alexandria."

Mr. Washington nodded as he gazed upon the White House.

Anders asked the drivers to stop in front of the manicured lawn before the Washington Monument. George watched through the tinted windows as tourists, equipped with maps, communications devices, and bottled water, stood in the long queue just to get the chance to reach the top of the imposing tower. George could not help but be profoundly humbled by the idea of these citizens, born hundreds of years after his death, remembering him, much less honoring him by visiting the city and monument that bore his name.

"Why is the stone of two shades?"

Murray enthusiastically answered, that at the time of the Civil War, the builders ran out of that kind of marble and granite and had to stop building it. "After the war, they started again, but had to use a slightly different color of stone."

"How appropriate," uttered Mr. Washington, "that these states, after the war, bore a more appropriate shade of liberty than they had before. So too should the monument. I would like to proceed to the Lincoln Memorial if we may. I think it will help me grasp the profound impact of this war between the states."

Since learning of the Civil War earlier in the day, George had been thinking about Lincoln. He was haunted by Lincoln's deeply lined and weary face. What kind of a man was he? Did George and his founding brothers fail? Lincoln was not a founder, but perhaps he was more of a founder than the revolutionaries themselves. George sensed Providence would reveal her intentions at the memorial to this great man.

Anders and Jenson asked the drivers to proceed west to the Lincoln Memorial. Parking was always problematic in DC, especially during the summer tourist season, so it was decided that the drivers would quickly drop off each carload and circle the National Mall while the new founders visited the memorial.

Old George was truly a quick study. He moved quickly from the van, pulled Todd's cap down over his eyes, and led the team up the marble steps. Looking around quickly, Josh scanned the crowd. He breathed a sigh of relief, confident the handful of tourists still mulling around would not disturb their visit.

Jenson had spent as much time as he could in DC over the years and was fluent in the history of most of the monuments and memorials. As a Virginia State Representative, he had participated in many DC events, including multiple CPAC conventions, seminars, and one inaugural ball for George W. Bush. He even broadcasted his radio show from these very steps once before.

As the group climbed the many steps toward the statue itself, Jenson, sounding like a tour guide, filled the group in on its history.

"The Lincoln Memorial stands as a neoclassical monument to the sixteenth president. It was designed by Henry Bacon, after ancient Greek temples, and stands 190 feet long, 119 feet wide, and almost 100 feet high. It is surrounded by a peristyle of thirty-eight fluted Doric columns, one for each of the thirty-six states in the Union at the time of Lincoln's death, and two columns in antis at the entrance behind the colonnade."

This initial description drew Mr. Washington's attention among others. His mind then drifted momentarily to his own death and wondered if he was interned with Martha at Mt. Vernon as he had requested. His mind now back to the matter at hand, the General looked to Jenson to continue.

"The north and south side chambers contain carved inscriptions of

Lincoln's Second Inaugural Address and his Gettysburg Address."

Jenson described these speeches as two of the finest pieces of oratory in American history. The Second Inaugural Address was given toward the end of the Civil War. The Gettysburg Address was a brief but wholly powerful message delivered during the war, November 19, 1863, on the very site of the most bloody of all battles, Gettysburg, Pennsylvania.

Jenson, too, enjoyed his moment before Mr. Washington, noting that Lincoln offered the speech to honor the dead and, as he said, "To consecrate that very battlefield in Pennsylvania to those who gave their lives that their country might live."

Mr. Washington, thinking the background was complete, turned toward the statue and started to make his way inside. The group turned and followed as Jenson concluded his illustration.

"This has been the site of many very large public protests and gatherings over the years, including one of the most famous speeches in American history—the "I have a dream" speech delivered here by a black man, Martin Luther King Jr. in 1963, one hundred years after Lincoln."

Tim was rolling and went on to explain how King, fighting for equal rights for blacks 100 years after the emancipation, delivered the famous words, "I have a dream that my four little children will one day live in a nation where they will not be judged by the color of their skin but by the content of their character."

The quote made Mr. Washington stop in his tracks. He did not turn back but only listened as he looked up at the stone face of the sixteenth president.

"Mr. President, I believe we have reached a point in this country where the dreams of you, Mr. Lincoln, and Dr. King have been realized."

The group now found themselves under the cover of the Memorial's ceiling. They mingled with the small group of tourists that remained in the late afternoon. Mr. Washington could not take his eyes off Lincoln. He noticed the inscription above the statue that read:

IN THIS TEMPLE
AS IN THE HEARTS OF THE PEOPLE
FOR WHOM HE SAVED THE UNION
THE MEMORY OF ABRAHAM LINCOLN
IS ENSHRINED FOREVER

Dottie saw the depth in Mr. Washington's character through his forlorn eyes as he studied the reflective sixteenth president who had the weight of the world on his shoulders.

Jack too saw the goodness in this great man watching George wince and wipe his eyes several times as he saw in Mr. Lincoln much of the same pain and uncertainty Mr. Washington himself had faced in those few quiet moments during the war and the establishment of the republic. Mr. Washington saw a man in Lincoln who probably understood him better than his closest friends, a man who, like himself, led millions, yet felt very alone. He saw a man who steadfastly stared ahead, knowing his decisions and actions to be not only difficult, but right and just. He focused on Lincoln's left hand clenched in a fist. He knew this man was strong enough in his beliefs to do what was right against all consequences.

George looked to the left wall facing Lincoln and read the surprisingly brief Gettysburg Address. He smiled proudly as he read the first sentence of the famous address, a sentence that was directed toward him and the original founders. He choked up as he mouthed the words, "Four score and seven years ago our fathers brought forth on this continent a new nation, conceived in liberty and dedicated to the proposition that all men are created equal."

He thought to himself that this president had summed up all the founders original ideas for a new nation in one glorious passage.

As Mr. Washington finished reading, he looked around. While the others went to and fro, the Murrays followed the father of our country. Jack noted that Mr. Washington read the powerful speech a second time. He stayed at Mr. Washington's side as the president moved unannounced to the opposite side of the memorial to read Mr. Lincoln's concise Second Inaugural address, delivered March 4, 1865:

Fellow Countrymen:

At this second appearing to take the oath of the presidential office, there is less occasion for an extended address than there was at the first....

With malice toward none; with charity for all; with firmness in the right, as God gives us to see the right, let us strive on to finish the work we are in, to bind up the nation's wounds; to care for him who shall have borne the battle, and for his widow, and his orphan—to do all which may achieve and cherish a just, and a lasting peace, among ourselves, and with all nations.

Mr. Washington read this speech a second time as well. He stayed on the final stanza, repeating this several times out loud to the delight of a few loiterers. He then asked that they return to the coach and go back to the inn to rest before dinner. Anders was immediately on the phone to the drivers, instructing them to pick up the team at the base of the steps. All started down, looking forward to checking in to the hotel for a respite, reflecting on these extraordinary events and hopefully enjoying a good dinner.

Chapter 12

Having finished washing and dressing, the group stood patiently outside the elevator door that serviced the two suites in which they were staying. However, Mr. Washington could not contain himself and carried on about the latest product that mankind invented in the time following his death: the shower.

Dottie couldn't squelch her laughter. He apologized profusely for being immodest but went on anyway about the delights of spraying warm water over one's whole body. Dottie had to look the other way as George talked about the great lather from twenty-first century soap. Jack read her mind, laughing at what a guy, who had been dead for over 200 years, might think of lathery soap in a shower.

George finished his fascinating theories on hygiene by saying if there were showers in the eighteenth century, he would have bathed nearly every day. Dottie whispered to Jack that she bet he would.

Todd Murray turned to his mother with a questionable look and mouthed the words, "Nearly every day?" Dot put her index finger up to her mouth to tell Todd to stay quiet for the time being. He looked down and shook his head as a bell rang and the elevator doors opened. The group moved as one into the elevator. Mr. Washington cautiously entered the metal enclosure.

"Mr. President," Hahn said, chuckling. "You rode the elevator up with us to get to the rooms. You did it once, there's nothing to be nervous about." Mr. Washington, looking around and toward the ceiling of the elevator, glanced back at Hahn and nodded.

George naturally denied he was scared but just not used to being with a group of people in such close confines supported by a single metal cable hundreds of feet above the earth's surface.

Mr. Washington then turned his glance straight ahead at the door as a hush came over the group. And when the elevator doors opened, Anders led them to a private room with a separate entrance from the main restaurant. Mr. Washington was the last to enter the dining room. Each looked around and soaked in the ambiance as Mr. Washington made his way to the head of the table and put his hand on the back of the chair. Jack noted that he stood as if to be posing for a portrait while Anders instructed everybody to take a seat at the table. A waiter appeared and asked which drinks they preferred, then went around the table, one person at a time, and took their drink orders. When he reached Mr. Washington, he asked for ale. When the waiter asked which brand, he shot a look at Hahn. A voice from the other side of the table answered the question.

"You can bring him a Sam Adams lager and make it a draught," ordered Anders, as the waiter scribbled the instruction and left the room. Mr. Washington looked at Anders with a big grin.

"So the famous Adams Ale survives."

A second waiter appeared and described the prix fixe menu selections. He went person to person taking orders, which went more smoothly than the drink orders. Once the second waiter left the room, Mr. Washington turned and addressed the troops.

"My dear friends, this gathering is very impressive, first class in its opulence. I look forward to the arrival of our meal. But while we wait, let's pass the time by telling me a little about yourselves. The charming Mrs. Murray, if you do not mind."

Mr. Washington leaned in, his chin resting on his arm and fist, as Dot described her early childhood in Philadelphia, adolescence in North Carolina, and college years at Chapel Hill. She skipped over her late first husband, Todd's birth father, and focused on the two most important events in her life—Todd's birth and meeting Jack. The mention of giving birth to her son raised a few eyebrows as most thought that Todd was adopted by the couple. But as Dottie moved on to describe her courtship with Jack, the men followed along.

Dottie finished her self-biography by describing her joy in entertaining and hosting parties at the Murray home. Mr. Washington attentively and respectfully listened to every word. With Dot's story complete, George turned to her son.

"Master Todd, if you please."

Todd was somewhat tongue-tied as he began, but told the group about his fourteen years, focusing on his love of sports and his plans for a sum-

The New Founders

mer filled with baseball and lacrosse. He was done within two minutes and Mr. Washington thanked him. He then turned to Jenson and asked him to begin again.

"Mr. Jenson, you spoke earlier about your upbringing and the splendid support group provided by your friends and family as you chased your dreams. Please continue."

Jenson was astonished that the President had actually listened in the car, let alone recalled the detail about his circle of friends. He recommenced the story of his life, talking in great detail about his interests in history, science, music, politics and sports. He explained how the Vietnam War and the Watergate hearings left an impression on him at a young age, an impression that remained with him throughout his teens and twenties. It also made teenaged Tim begin to question government and authority more and more, something that Mr. Washington duly took note of.

Jenson then moved onto more personal issues as he described the relationship he had with his father and how devastated Tim was by his death in 1975. Tim lightened the mood in the room by turning the conversation back to politics and his admiration for Ronald Reagan. President Reagan instilled confidence in the government and country and inspired Tim to write about conservative values and follow a career path in politics and public service. He ran for, and won, a seat in the Virginia Statehouse with the help of his wife, who unfortunately was killed shortly thereafter in a car accident. Dottie Murray, sitting to his right, put her hand on his shoulder and told him she was so sorry.

Mr. Washington leaned back in his chair as the waiter delivered the beverages. He reached out for his beer and thanked Tim.

"You have a lot of the same qualities as my friend and associate, Mr. Jefferson, especially the writing and the big ideas. Jefferson was a dreamer too, but he made his dreams come true. Thank you."

"Mr. Murray, what say you?"

Jack Murray was less than excited to spill his guts in front of strangers, living or dead, but in the spirit of the day, he explained that he had a normal upbringing growing up in a large family, with nothing unusual to report and no life altering events. He was always a student of history, fashioning himself as a self-proclaimed expert on the Constitution. Contrary to his often dour appearance, he developed a reputation at Princeton as a practical joker. This defense mechanism helped him deal with the barbs directed his way because of his short stature.

It was partly this unusual sense of humor that won over Dottie and helped him land the teaching position at the local high school. Not wanting to speak in front of his son, Jack also skipped over the fact that he adopted Todd as a stepchild. Mr. Washington showed interest in Murray's life story, but wanted to go back to the subject of the Constitution.

"My fine man, have you ever read the workings of John Locke or Edmund Burke?"

Murray responded that he was a big fan of both and that they had influenced Madison.

"They certainly did influence both Mr. Jefferson and Mr. Madison. Please continue."

Murray was also a political junkie who felt a need a need to serve his country in some fashion but was physically unable to join the military and didn't see himself as the political type. For the time being, his job was to try to mold young minds in his high school classroom as well as on campus at James Madison University.

Mr. Washington looked at him wide-eyed.

"James Madison University? How appropriate. Tell me, how did you and Mr. Jenson become friends?"

Tim and Jack looked at each other and shared a laugh. They explained that they had just met the day before through Jenson's radio show essay contest. Mr. Washington could not believe it.

"You are two peas in a pod. I find it hard to believe that you two gentlemen are not lifelong compatriots. Fascinating as I believe that each of you, one at a time, continue to fortify my belief that Providence brought us all together at this time for a reason. There is no doubt left in my mind of this fact."

As Mr. Washington spoke, the waiters entered the room with the main courses. The General stopped speaking as a waiter placed his coq au vin entrée in front of him. Mr. Washington took a deep breath, his olfactory senses enlightened by the pleasant aroma of the chef's creation. He surveyed the table to make sure everybody had their dinner before digging in to his own.

The next fifteen minutes were filled with small talk, most of it describing the gourmet dinners around the table. As George cut another piece of chicken, he looked up at Josh and asked him to tell the group a little bit about himself. Josh Anders relayed the fact that most of the group probably knew everything about him already, through his radio shows, his books, or the liberal media that loved to focus on him. Mr. Washington would not accept the answer.

"Then Mr. Anders, tell us something that we do not know about you, something that we would not find in the daily gazette."

Anders told everybody that at age nine he and his older cousin, Steve, campaigned door-to-door for Nixon in the 1960 presidential election, a fact that was not well received in Kennedy's home state. He also admitted that he wanted to drop out of Harvard to go to Vietnam, as he felt it was his duty as a citizen of the United States. He painfully explained that a lot of boys who worked at his father's produce market in south Boston had their number called and served, many of which never returned. Anders noted that this was the origin of his steadfast support of the military and why, while working at a prestigious law firm in Boston after Harvard Law School, he joined the Army Reserves.

He then told the story of being coaxed into stealing pieces of Bazooka bubble gum from a local delicatessen in Quincy by his deviant cousin. This evoked a roar of laughter from the audience, including Mr. Washington who added that Josh should beware as Steve was not there to defend himself and would most likely tell a different story. As the wait-staff reentered the room to begin clearing the dishes, Mr. Washington turned his attention to the youngest of the new founders.

"Last, but certainly not least, I ask that Mr. Hahn tell us a little bit about himself. Mr. Hahn, you have the floor."

Anthony Hahn enjoyed his moments in the spotlight and jumped right into it by telling Mr. Washington that he was not born in this country. He explained that even though he was born in Christiansted St. Croix, it was considered an American territory and that he was an American citizen.

"No need to be defensive, Anthony, you are among your brothers. Continue, please."

Mr. Washington reassured Hahn that he could tell the group anything and that he would not judge what was already stated.

Hahn loosened up and talked about his hometown, his job as an office clerk at the age of twelve at an import-export company, his mother's untimely death that same year, and how the local townspeople took an interest in his education, pooling their money to send him to the United States for college. He spoke of his days at Columbia and his love of New York City, especially Manhattan.

He described his internship and subsequent employment with The Bank of New York, initially in hedge fund finance, then in currency trading, where he currently worked. He talked fondly of his mentor at the bank, the former Marine who always looked out for him and once talked him out of joining the military. He then took on a serious tone when describing the effect that 9/11 had on his life, that with all of his financial success, he felt he needed to do something more with his life, maybe a higher calling that he had yet to find.

"Tell us something about yourself that your friends may not know," Mr. Washington asked Hahn. Anthony quickly responded that he hated

Princeton University because they would not give him a full scholarship.

Again, the room erupted into laughter, as Murray smiled and told the room that Princeton was his alma mater.

Hahn's smile turned serious as he addressed the table. "I thought I was going to die on September 11th, 2001. To this day, I still believe I should have died. I was not in the towers but I was in the shadow of the World Trade Center south tower when it collapsed. I had left my office and walked up Broadway to see what was going on after the second plane hit. I was standing there just like everybody else, hypnotized by the whole scene when the building started to fall. I turned and ran with the rest of the crowd. I ran back down Broadway, looking back as I did. I saw the dust cloud growing closer. As I got to Trinity Church, about five people were on the sidewalk taking pictures of the damn thing. So I ran into the courtyard of the church. When the cloud was on top of us, I dove on the grass and covered my head. I heard and felt debris falling around me."

Hahn's account froze the room. Todd Murray looked scared while his mother's eyes welled up with tears. Jenson and Murray were transfixed on him while Josh was rendered speechless. He had everybody's full attention at that moment. Hahn swallowed and went on.

"Everything went black, then grey. The roar of the building collapsing was followed by total silence. I felt alone and thought I must have died. After a few minutes, I heard some people crying and shuffling around, and the air around me started to lighten. It was then I knew I was still alive. It was also when I realized I was among the tombstones in the church cemetery and the smell of death was in the air. Those guys with the cameras were on the ground too. It was hell on earth. Only I was living it."

Anders reminded Hahn that he and thousands of New Yorkers experienced something similar that morning. Hahn's eyes were watery while he shared his experience. He asked the folks at the table if they knew anybody that died in the attack. Most shook their heads, while Anders mentioned that he was friends with Barbara Olsen, the political commentator, who was a passenger on one of the planes.

"Well, one of my best friends was a bond trader at Cantor Fitzgerald. His name was Steve Schlag and he worked on the 101st floor of World Trade Center One. He never got out, left a wife and three beautiful kids."

Hahn's voice tailed off as he was overcome with emotion. Mr. Washington decided to interrupt the 9/11 talk before it became the focus of the rest of the evening.

"Gentlemen, and lady, I sit here before you, and for the last sixty minutes I have had the pleasure of learning a little bit about each of you, specific stories that open up a window on your souls and describe the kind of individual each one of you was, is, and will be in the future. And my confidence in each and every one of you has been rewarded in the fact that we found each other at this moment in history. I must reiterate, our fates are now intertwined and we must go forward, working toward the good of this great nation."

George now stood at the head of the table and again surveyed the room. He addressed the new founders.

"I know I have your undivided attention. We do not know what fate has in store for us, but we do know that something extraordinary is occurring here. We can only imagine what grand plan Divine Providence will unveil to us. We each need to know that we are devoted to one another; that you are willing to give of yourself for the good of your country."

Murray looked around the table. Anders and Hahn nodded in agreement while Jenson looked unsure. Murray felt more like Jenson. He looked at Dottie, who seemed a bit horrified by George's demand of personal devotion. Perhaps Murray thought this kind of talk was the norm in the eighteenth century. But in the twenty-first century it made him uneasy.

"Mr. President, and I do believe I am speaking for everyone in the room. You are our leader and we will follow you to the ends of the earth. Tell us what you have in mind," Anders predictably announced as he stood to make his point. The statement received mixed reviews from his new colleagues, something that was not lost on the father of the country as he looked for feedback.

Mr. Washington gave one quick nod and sat down in his chair as the waiters commenced serving dessert and coffee. Anders followed his leader and sat down himself. George reached for his cup of black coffee and asked a question to anyone who could and would provide an answer.

"Tomorrow is Sunday. I would like to attend church services first thing in the morning. Is there a church nearby where we can honor the Almighty Lord? I would be extremely grateful if you could join me."

Jack and Dottie paused and looked at each other. They had spoken before dinner and agreed that she and Todd needed to get an early start back to Virginia since Todd was starting baseball camp on Monday.

She told the General that she had arranged a ride home with Skip Keaton before he went out to visit some friends in Georgetown. Keaton would be ready to leave with her and Todd at seven-thirty the following morning, but Jack would accompany him to church.

Jack agreed it was the right thing for Dottie and Todd to head home. He figured he would be in DC a few more days before returning home to spend the rest of the summer vacation at the beach and watch Todd play shortstop. Before he knew it, school would be starting and it would be back to the grind.

The General responded by saying that she and Todd would be missed, then shot a look in Jenson and Murray's direction to check if they were planning on leaving too.

With this settled, Jack responded, "Tim and I are in. We'll find a way home eventually, but for now, you've got us Mr. President."

Mr. Washington's stern nod in agreement let everybody know that he would not have expected anything less.

"How about the National Cathedral?"

The belated answer came from Tim Jenson who had visited this house of worship on a previous occasion.

Mr. Washington nodded in thanks as he tried his cheesecake. He had rejuvenated a regiment once again and he looked forward to a busy Sunday with his new cabinet.

Chapter 13

The sun, rising in the east over the US Capitol Building and the Washington Monument, shone its golden rays around the great obelisk and across the reflection pool as if to awaken the sixteenth president residing in his memorial.

The white limo's back driver side door swung open and out stepped an energized and purposeful General George Washington, followed one at a time by his new founders.

Each looked around and enjoyed the warm sunshine of this July 5th morning. Always mindful of the weather, Jenson thought to himself that it would be a hot one again today. But the sun felt just right.

Murray's exaltation was tempered by the fact that Dottie and Todd were on their way home. He knew they had to leave but was still saddened. Todd's camp began the next day. As an incoming high school freshman, he had to be at camp if he had any chance to make the team. And Murray had planned to hang around the ball fields during summer practices.

Now he felt selfish. He knew that Dottie would have liked to stay in the middle of all the excitement, but she also knew this was Jack's calling. Plus, someone still needed to tend to the responsibilities at home. So Mrs. Murray, as was her way, put on a brave face, smiled, and headed home to do what was best for her son and her husband.

Always effervescent, she still maintained a practical view of the world and an inner strength that came from life experiences. It was shortly after Todd's birth when Dot found the small jagged looking mole on her first husband's back. He was diagnosed with an aggressive melanoma and died only months later. She was devastated, but knew she had to be there to raise her son.

Only a year later she met a man who she knew would take care of Todd and her. Jack Murray was a contradiction of a man in a lot of ways. Though he suffered from asthma, she met him while he jogged in the local park. She liked to relay the story that he was not actually jogging but more like frantically sucking on his inhaler when she stopped her walk with baby Todd. She had to make sure this man didn't die right there in the park.

Dottie instantly loved Jack. What first attracted her to him was his affection for Todd and her feeling that he could be a wonderful husband and terrific father to her toddler son. She fell deeply in love with the smallish, somewhat quirky, brilliant man. Dottie wanted to spend the rest of her life with Jack Murray. But his insecurities, especially the unfounded feelings that she was too good for him, continued to perplex her.

She pondered these thoughts as she neared home. She had been away from her husband for less than an hour and missed him already. She wondered what he was doing at that precise moment.

———

The new founders had just experienced simultaneous epiphanies during the 7:15am services at the National Cathedral. George had asked to begin his Sunday in church and the men could not think of a more appropriate place for George to worship than in the exquisite house of worship. Using the minister's words as her vehicle, Providence found the men sitting quietly in the back of the old Cathedral.

The nation's recent birthday was the topic of the day's sermon and, accordingly, the minister discussed how our country was founded on Judeo-Christian values, documented in the Declaration of Independence, the Constitution and Bill of Rights, and reflected in the laws, customs, and mores of our everyday lives.

She preached that the founders knew that our civil society would only stand as long as the citizenry maintained such values. Without those values, our republican system would fail.

The minister seemed to be looking directly at the five men as she began quoting the founders themselves.

"John Adams wrote in the Massachusetts Bill of Rights that, 'The happiness of a people and the good order and preservation of civil government essentially depend upon piety, religion, and morality.'"

Josh Anders sat focused on the minister as she went on.

"Adams believed, 'One great advantage of the Christian religion is that it brings the great principle of the law of nature and nations; Love your neighbor as yourself, and do to others as you would that others should do to you, to the knowledge, belief and veneration of the whole people.'"

Mr. Washington looked fondly at Anders and the rest of the men as the minister continued stressing that America had lost its way; the United States of America was accelerating down a slope away from the values that made it what it was.

"We have allowed government to push itself into our lives and take responsibility for raising our children."

The minister continued, pointing to the recent examples of unwanted government intervention. She described agents, without parental consent, who confiscated school children's brown bag lunches they deemed not in accordance with federal guidelines. She touched on the healthcare mandates, laws passed without being read by the lawmakers. She was in a controlled rant, railing how society had marginalized religious groups, language and icons in favor of secular symbols.

The minister forcefully proclaimed that all of these godless policies must stop and be turned around immediately; that the country was in desperate need of a new leader, one who understood our country's founding, one who was one with our people, one who would lead us back to the principles that brought us greatness.

The four new founders were thunderstruck in their pews as the scattered congregation applauded. Each looked at the other, knowing that the minister addressed them and them alone. Each achieved inspiration as they focused on General Washington, his back straight, head slightly bowed, but eyes aimed forward in determination.

The minister closed by quoting George Washington who said that it was impossible to rightly govern a nation without God and the Bible and that reason and experience both forbid us to expect that national morality could prevail in exclusion of religious principle.

"Mr. Washington memorialized this feeling forever in his farewell address when he stated, 'Of all the dispositions and habits which lead to political prosperity, religion and morality are indispensable supports. In vain would that man claim the tribute of patriotism who should labor to subvert these great pillars of human happiness, these firmest props of the duties of men and citizens...'"

The men stood outside of Josh's limo at the bottom step of the Lincoln Memorial. They could not stop thinking of the sermon they had heard fifteen minutes earlier. They mulled around the sidewalk for a few moments while Mr. Washington studied each man, noting their expressions. The silence was broken by a smiling Anders.

"Gentlemen, Mr. President, I believe we all experienced an epiphany at the National Cathedral. All of us have been wondering since Friday afternoon why we were brought together in Philadelphia, the forces at work, and what they have in store for us. Well, I believe we received our answer this morning. Providence spoke to us and has led us to this brilliant morning. As President Reagan so optimistically stated, "It's morning in America."

With that said, General Washington looked up the steps of the memorial and led the men past a small number of early morning tourists to the summit. The father of our country was once again face-to-face with the larger than life President Lincoln.

Mr. Washington walked to his left and studied the inscribed Gettysburg address. He then turned right and focused on Lincoln's second inaugural. As George focused, he inched toward the middle of the rail and began speaking aloud, first directed toward the men and then for all within earshot.

"Indeed, anything is possible in this great land of ours. President Abraham Lincoln had uncommon strength, courage, and conviction. He took the sacred oath of office clear and forthright in his noble intentions, committed to relegating the shackles of slavery across these United States to, as President Reagan said in describing the demise of the Soviet Union, the scrapheap of history, while somehow bringing the nation together."

The men shot each other looks of astonishment. Hahn mouthed to the others, "What the hell?"

Anders shrugged, smiled and winked at Jenson, Hahn, and Murray.

"I guess he watched the History Channel in the hotel this morning."

The men looked down and chuckled as George resumed his lecture. "I see a man before me who knew that his ideals were supported by the majority, vehemently rejected by many and deemed worthy of war by all. I see a man who was viewed by more than a few as a tyrant, yet brought the country together. And yet with the threat of certain war looming, Mr. Lincoln steadfastly held his guiding principles."

Mr. Washington reviewed the growing audience that built around him. He started to walk slowly toward the top of the steps and into the morning sunshine. While his audience grew, so did his ideas and the strength in his voice. Mr. Washington said he could see the steadfastness in Lincoln's clinched fist and steely eyes. He described Lincoln as a man who may have bent during the horrific stresses of war but who refused to break.

George then quoted a founding father. "As Thomas Paine once wrote,

'Tis the business of little minds to shrink; but he whose heart is firm, and whose conscience approves his conduct, will pursue his principles unto death.'"

Mr. Washington was now on the top step of the Lincoln Memorial. He stood tall, erect and strong, as the crowd grew. Many cell phones were pointed in his direction, recording every word. One phone hoisted in the air to capture the moment belonged to Josh Anders. Even the park rangers moved in closer to listen. One even handed George his megaphone which he politely declined.

"The founders had not settled the question of slavery when the Constitution was adopted. It was left to the next generation to decide, but, like Mr. Lincoln, they truly believed in the individual's liberty and freedom in the Natural Rights of Man."

He spoke extemporaneously, something not lost on the new founders.

"Thomas Jefferson wrote in the Declaration of Independence, 'That all men are created equal, that they are endowed by their creator with certain unalienable rights.' Not all Caucasian men, but ALL MEN. Jefferson also wrote that the abomination of slavery must end, stating that there is a superior bench reserved in Heaven for those who hasten it."

Looking toward the turgid crowd, a more confident and passionate Mr. Washington began reciting some of the most famous words in American history. "'Four score and seven years ago....that we here highly resolve that these dead shall not have died in vain, that this nation under God shall have a new birth of freedom, and that government of the people, by the people, for the people shall not perish from the earth.'"

He paused as the waves of people soaked in one president's words delivered by another. He needed to connect these words and show relevance in today's world.

"Yes, the founders did bring forth a new nation dedicated to the proposition that all men are created equal. That founding principle is ingrained in our Declaration of Independence and Constitution, documents which lay out our principles as American citizens, inspired not from some legislature or monarch, but from God the Almighty Himself, stressing that our government is of, by, and for the people, not of, by, and for the government, nor of one man."

Mr. Washington chastised today's political class by pointing out that while DC had monuments to great men and women, there are too many monuments erected by government in honor of itself. He directly cited the colossal edifices erected for the Departments of Education and Agriculture. He questioned why anybody would have veritable monstrosities dedicated to bureaucracies called the Housing and Urban Development

Department and the Department of the Interior.

Looking right at Jack Murray, he asked if these leviathans were chartered in the United States Constitution.

Before Jack could even shake his head, a spontaneous, "No!" erupted from the fervent crowd.

The new founders looked at each other with nervous smiles. Jack's initial impulse was to try and stop a scene from developing, but all the men quickly realized that the assemblage was directed by Providence itself. They stood and listened, as enthralled by Mr. Washington's words as the mesmerized tourists surrounding him.

"In his second inaugural, Mr. Lincoln teaches us that ours is a just God. That the pain the country endured, indeed the pain that Lincoln himself endured, was as deep as the lashes from the whip of slavery. Lincoln was of one mind with the founders over four score years before."

He again quoted himself by explaining that the determinations of Providence were always wise, often inscrutable, and though its decrees appeared to bear hard upon us at times, was nevertheless meant for gracious purposes.

"Lincoln reminds us that even after enduring such pain, we will look to God's example to reconcile and come back together as a people. And that is a lesson for the ages."

As the unknown speaker paced the top step, the crowd followed, cell phones and video cameras trained on him. Mr. Washington slowly walked down the steps toward the reflection pool, pausing on a lower step to conclude his speech for the day.

"Political party allegiances have replaced the allegiance to the American people. President Washington predicted their danger over two hundred years ago, when he said that they serve always to distract the public councils and enfeeble the public administration. He said they agitate the community with ill-founded jealousies and false alarms. He believed they kindled the animosity of one party against another and opened the door to foreign influence and corruption."

George urged the crowd to look to Mr. Washington's and Lincoln's examples and reject party allegiances and put the good of the country above the wants of the party. He stressed that by doing so, the American people would once again be free to pursue the unalienable right of their happiness.

He warned that failure to do so would hasten our collapse.

The General paused for a moment, as if to gauge the reaction of the captivated multitude. He wanted to finish on a high note, and he would not be denied.

"Remember, these United States of America are exceptional in the history of human civilization. Do not let anyone or any law makers tell you what you or your family can or cannot have. Do not let them tell you what you or your family can or cannot achieve. Your life belongs to you. Your happiness is yours to define."

Hahn leaned toward Jenson and Murray and whispered that he felt like he was dreaming. The two men hardly acknowledged their colleague as they remained riveted on their new leader.

"Be sure that your public servants understand that they work for you. They are there to clear the way for your pursuit of happiness and not to limit it!"

By now, the crowd had surrounded Mr. Washington and the new founders. A number of well-wishers started to reach out and touch the first president, as if to ensure that he was not a mirage or a figment of their imagination. The General had whipped the mass into a near frenzy and his cabinet of gentlemen sensed it was time to depart.

To Jack's relief, Josh Anders took the initiative and quickly called his driver while motioning the men to surround Mr. Washington like secret service agents and lead him to the approaching limo.

The crowd followed with thunderous applause as their chant of "MORE" echoed throughout the mall and within the Lincoln Memorial itself. As the group of men hurried to the waiting car, Mr. Washington stopped and paused yet again. He placed one foot on the floorboard of the back seat, stood tall above the crowd, and surveyed the scene.

"Thank you for sharing this moment in history with me. God bless all of you and God bless the United States of America!"

The crowd, having drawn silent when Mr. Washington raised himself up, erupted into a deafening cheer, followed by a rousing "USA" chant. The father of our country gave one last look around, smiled, and disappeared into the idling limousine. At once, the people rushed the car to get a look at the most powerful and mesmerizing speaker they had ever laid eyes on. But their looks were fleeting as the car sped away toward the Jefferson Memorial.

Chapter 14

The new founding fathers had finally settled into the car as the crowd faded from view. As the car pulled up to the traffic light, the men pondered in silence what they had just experienced. But even though they were quiet, inside the men were as excited as kids on Christmas. Anders broke the silence with a clear proclamation.

"Now that was something else, wouldn't you say gentlemen? I'm going to go out on a limb here, but I don't care because I think it's important."

The new founders leaned in, eager to hear what their colleague was about to say, as if he didn't go out on a limb one hundred times a day on his show.

"I think we should put forth Mr. Washington as candidate for President of the United States."

Even though he was serious, Anders deliberately halted his words to see what the shock value would be in the car. The men knew from their collective experience in the National Cathedral that this was inevitable. Mr. Washington sat stoic, neither nodding nor changing his facial expression. However, Tim Jenson was enthusiastically nodding his head up and down in agreement. Noticing this, Anders immediately seized the moment.

"You agree, Jenson?"

"Absolutely. He is the perfect candidate. He's an eloquent speaker and there is no one more passionate about his country. He knows how to build a country. Damn, he built this country! If we bring him up to speed on world and US history and today's big issues, he would kick butt. Look what he did this morning. Twenty-four hours ago we were introducing him to the twenty-first century and giving him a crash course in US history. Throw in a few newspapers, a couple hours of the History Channel and cable news and you get what you saw this morning. Just imagine if we had some time. The people are starving for a candidate like George."

Anders noticed that Mr. Washington's expression never changed, hinting that maybe the General approved of his idea. The men took notice of this too. Their faces reflected mixed expressions as Jenson finished his thought.

"I agree with Anders. Why can't we run GW as a candidate? The Republicans seem to be going nowhere and can't get out of each other's way. Our current president has taken the country away from what made it great and his approval rating shows it. From socialized healthcare, to unsustainable deficits, to open borders, to an Attorney General who releases terrorists; this president is managing the ruin of our country."

Murray may not have physically shown it, but he emphatically concurred.

"Constitutionally, the most important job of the government is to protect our people and our rights under God. This administration does the exact opposite."

George sat up at Jack's interjection, as if waiting for Mr. Murray to enter the conversation. The history teacher from Virginia now had the first president's undivided attention.

He preached that those currently running the country spent trillions of tax dollars on some ridiculous 'stimulus' that did nothing to help the economy, on socialist programs like PresidentCare, and on new entitlement programs that did nothing more than cede the people's freedom to the government.

Murray, looked around expecting to be interrupted, but to his delight, the roomy rear of the car stayed quiet. It was lecture time as he expounded.

"Then they claim they have no money to protect our country, which is what they are mandated to do in the first place. Then they gut the military by hundreds of thousands of service men and women and reduce the number of warships to pre World War II levels. Hell, we decrease our nuclear arsenal by eighty percent while the most dangerous dictatorships in the world are developing and stockpiling nukes! My God, sorry Mr. President, our country is completely upside down."

Hahn jumped in, stating that he could not have said it better himself. It was rare that Anthony Hahn would ever breathe a compliment like he just had. But he liked Jack Murray from the moment they met at Independence Hall. Hahn didn't feel like he had to compete with Jack like he did with Anders. There was a quality about him that Hahn read as an intelligence that didn't need to prove it every second, something totally different from what the currency trader was. Now in the back seat, he thought that maybe opposites do attract.

"This country is craving a guy like George. We owe it to the people to do it. When will we ever get this chance again? Never."

Murray, playing devil's advocate for a moment, slowed the rally cry. He began by reminding the team that their new found colleague was not *like* George Washington. He *was* George Washington. He reiterated that it would be a tough sell to arrange for 'the' George Washington to run for office.

"We're already on that!" exclaimed Anders as the limousine pulled up to the hotel.

Anders described how he had made a call and sent text messages to some important people during Mr. Washington's speech at the memorial. Hahn, looking skeptical, let out a snort as he and Murray asked Anders who in the world he could have called to make that happen. Anders was all too eager to respond.

"I reached out to a cohort of mine; a very important person who you'll be meeting shortly."

Mr. Washington shot a look of concern in Anders' direction as the car door swung open and the sunlight lit up the interior. Murray and Hahn looked at each other as if to ask what this guy was up to now. Murray even whispered to Hahn that he didn't want to be a part of anything illegal. Hahn responded by alluding to the recent currency exchange scandal the bank had and that he was not about to embark on more legal troubles. It seemed like they were not the only ones with concerns.

George also did not seem comfortable with the pending introduction of another person into their tight group. He pulled Anders to the side of the front door at the hotel entrance. Jenson tagged along.

"Mr. Anders, do you think it is prudent that we allow a stranger into any grand plan of ours? I do not know if Mr. Jenson and I agree with this turn of events."

Mr. Washington guessed correctly that Tim, along with the other two men, had reservations of bringing in an extra political bigwig into the mix. Jenson nodded in agreement as they studied Anders.

Anders held his hand out, palm down as if to gesture that the men should calm down. He explained that the man they were about to meet had his unyielding trust and admiration. He reassured the two as he ushered them into the lobby and up the elevator.

The group assembled in the Anders suite. The men nervously loitered about the room as they waited for their new guest. Mr. Washington had again pulled both Anders and Jenson aside for a brief discussion. He described his trepidation at the initial thought of a candidacy. But in the last fifteen minutes, the ideas seemed to grow on him. He proudly proclaimed that he never actually campaigned for the office of president. The eighteenth century gentleman was asked to take a nomination and dutifully accept or decline.

———•———

Anders and Jenson assured him that they would handle his candidacy in the most gentlemanly way possible but warned that there was no tougher fight than a presidential election. They asked General George Washington if he was up for a good fight.

Mr. Washington stood tall and told the gentlemen that he trusted their opinion and valued their support. He smiled. "Gentlemen, the greater the chaos, the greater will be our merit in bringing forth order."

Sensing Anders' and Jenson's brief hesitation as they digested Mr. Washington's words, George removed all doubt as to his decision. He stated that if the two of them felt strongly about his run for the presidency, then he would agree to run.

Jenson and Anders responded with a resounding "Yes" and an awkward high five.

Mr. Washington moved away to seek out Anthony Hahn. Hahn stood with Murray in the corner of the room checking his iPhone. As the president approached, Murray turned and walked away, already dialing his bride to make sure she was home safe and sound. He was anxious to tell her about the mornings events, which he delivered to Dottie with the enthusiasm of a grade-schooler telling his mother he got straight A's. From what he overheard of the tone of the conversation, Mr. Washington surmised that Jack's wife approved of their plans.

He turned his focus on Anthony. Hahn looked up and the General asked if he could have a word with him. The duo moved toward the window.

"Mr. Hahn, I want to ask what your thoughts are on this whole idea of a candidacy for president. Do you think it possible?"

Hahn had hoped and waited for the opportunity to advise Mr. Washington. He felt the president valued his opinion and he knew of Mr. Washington's admiration for Alexander Hamilton and his reliance on Hamilton's viewpoints in colonial days. Hahn pounced.

"It can be done, it could work. I was thinking about it in the car and the main thing that needs to be taken care of right away is your identity. You need a foolproof identity that could not be questioned, especially if you're going to run as a conservative candidate. The liberal media will dig and have a field day if they could find anything detrimental. And secondly, in my opinion, you cannot run as a Republican. You need to be a third party candidate to buck the norm, to fly in the face of the establishment. I think you would be the perfect Tea Party candidate, but that is just my opinion."

Hahn said he was steadfast in his opinions and was ready to debate anyone that may disagree. He looked at Mr. Washington's face and realized that the leader agreed with his views. He decided to throw one more idea onto the table.

"Plus, you're going to need a lot of money. As a third party candidate, you won't have the Republican infrastructure backing you so we will need to raise a whole lot of money to see this thing through. I think having that guy over there involved can make it work."

Hahn was pointing to Josh Anders, the mouthpiece of the conservative movement. George took note of the reference as he glanced at Josh and Jenson in deep discussion. Again, Mr. Washington seemed to be in full agreement with his young adviser.

Hahn began to think out loud, verbalizing ideas about securing a new identity for Mr. Washington. He talked about a method called paper tripping, where an individual could assume the identity of a child that had died shortly after birth. He mentioned that questions had arisen concerning the current president and the question of his birth certificate and citizenship. Hahn told George of the possibility that the current Commander-in-Chief had used this method to secure an American identity. Mr. Washington was appalled at the thought that a man could catapult to the presidency using this method.

Another method Hahn was all too eager to describe involved building layers between the original identity and the person assuming it, in essence laundering an identity as if it was money. He said that he had read about this method and stressed that the keys to it included finding a person that died prior to 1988 with no social security number listed in the death file, with a name as generic and common as possible. Again, Mr. Washington cringed at the depths one would go to change an identity. He shook his head in amazement as the sound of a knock at the door overtook the room.

Anders walked to the entrance way, opened the door, and shook the hand of a distinguished looking gentleman as he entered the suite. He held a briefcase in his right hand as he surveyed the room and addressed Josh Anders by his first name. Hahn breathed the word "Wow" under his breath, which was audible enough for Mr. Washington to hear. He turned toward Hahn.

"Who is that man?"

Hahn looked back at George and stated that the man before them was William Pepper, the founder and man behind the new Tea Party. Mr. Washington did not change expression as Anders and Mr. Pepper approached the first president.

"Is this the man of the hour?" said a smiling Bill Pepper. He extended his hand toward Mr. Washington and offered a handshake. George stood tall and shook Pepper's hand.

Pepper, a cool customer in any situation, remained calm and all business despite just being introduced to a person who had apparently risen from the dead. He sized up the man they called Mr. Washington and immediately decided he was one to be reckoned with. He certainly looked like the paintings of Mr. Washington, except for his hair color. Pepper identified a rare elegant confidence in the physically imposing man. His handshake was purposeful and strong, his hands large and meaty. While he noticed the well manicured finger nails of a colonial gentleman, his palm had the leathery, calluses of a manual laborer.

Pepper had listened on the phone to Anders' story of how he met this man and trusted Anders' opinions, but was this guy really the father of the country Bill Pepper loved? If Bill determined he was *the* George Washington, then he had a job to do. There would be time to reflect on the moral, ethical, and spiritual ramifications later. Bill began the conversation by relaying that he had heard part of Mr. Washington's impromptu speech at the memorial through Josh's phone and it gave him goose bumps. He also said that a video of it already hit the web.

Mr. Washington's face revealed his uncertainty about the words being used, so Jack jumped in to explain that the web was synonymous with the Internet. George lightened as Pepper also described the YouTube video that had the full speech, start to finish, following the potential candidate from the Lincoln statue to the bottom step.

The billionaire businessman proclaimed that the speech was truly inspiring.

Mr. Washington thanked him for his kind words.

"The pleasure is all mine, Mr. Pepper. I trust you have joined us today to assist in our plan for a presidential candidacy? The men you see here have my undying trust and support for this endeavor. They have brought you forth as an important cog to the machine that will drive us over the coming months. Please share what you have in mind. But be patient. This is all happening quite fast and it is a lot to absorb for a bloke such as me."

If he had any doubts that this man was the real Mr. Washington, they were instantaneously dispelled when George opened his mouth. His voice was distinct, but unfortunately so were his teeth. Pepper gasped to himself that they were not only from another time but perhaps from another species or planet.

The businessman immediately pulled Anders aside and demanded that before they act on any plans, an appointment with a dentist was in order. He had the name of a doctor who worked with him on a few things before and would ask no questions. Bill whispered in Anders' ear.

"Try to keep his smiles to a minimum for the time being, will you?"

Anders told him to be serious. Bill Pepper smiled and asked everybody to take a seat. The men found spots around the room, settling on love seats and lounge chairs in the living area of the suite. Josh Anders decided to stand next to Pepper as he began his plan.

"First of all, I thank you for allowing me to enter your close circle. Josh explained to me what transpired over the last few days and I am excited to be involved. You have my full support and backing. Now, let's get down to brass tacks."

Pepper began by explaining the magnitude of financial backing Mr. Washington would have if he were to go all the way. He reassured the group that money was no object and that he would do everything in his power to get the Tea Party behind his candidacy. The men looked relieved at the mention of bottomless pockets of cash, but a couple founders spoke up simultaneously about the identity problem. Pepper then laid the plan for Mr. Washington going forward.

"As I mentioned just now, money is no object. We're going to spend some bucks. We are going to buy the identity of someone, a person similar in stature and age to our first president and, most importantly, someone who is near death. We will need an individual willing to sell his identity upon his death while securing his next of kin financially for the rest of their lives."

Anthony Hahn immediately spoke up, voicing his and everybody else's concern that it was impossible to do without any information getting out to the public.

Murray seconded this statement, referring to the plan as a pie in the sky scheme. He thought finding a donor who matched all of the needed criteria was nearly as impossible as Mr. Washington showing up in Philly. He caught himself and everybody noticed. He shrugged his shoulders at the sheer craziness of it all and told the smart man before him that he was interested in all the detail behind the grand plan.

Pepper took a sip of the bottled water which Josh had handed him thirty seconds earlier. As one of the top executives and a founding family member of the largest private company in the United States, he was used to pointed questions and, hostile, but intelligent discussions. He was neither intimidated nor knocked off point by Hahn and Murray's direct challenge. Bill was ready.

"Nobody said this was going to be easy, Mr. Murray. This is a daunting task, but I believe it can work. First off, we need to leave next to no paper trail ourselves. This means no written notes. And we need to limit all electronic written communication. Any leaks would be a disaster."

Bill had the full attention of the candidate and he could not believe it. One of his three favorite presidents was sitting before him, in the flesh, hanging on his every word. In all his years in the business world, Mr. Pepper had never had a more surreal moment. He took a deep breath and composed himself.

"Sorry. I digress. We need to find a man that is similar to Mr. Washington in age, height, and weight. Eye color is important too, although the colored contacts have made this a little easier."

The General looked in Jenson's direction as Tim studied his eye color, if only for a moment.

"Secondly, it would be preferable if the individual was self employed. Employees of big corporations have a paper trail a mile long so it is paramount that our donor be an entrepreneurial type, having started his own business, ideally an internet type entity. The man could be still active in the business or be recently retired, either way the plan can move forward."

Bill Pepper had everybody on the edge of their seats, fully engrossed in their lesson on identity purchasing. As they leaned toward the speaker, Murray, Jenson, and Hahn took mental notes. Even Anders stayed quiet understanding fully that the speaker was a man who knew what he was talking about. Pepper continued.

"Our donor needs to be an orphan. We want no parents and hopefully, no aunts and uncles too. Our guy would ideally be an only child as well with no siblings or step brothers. In addition, we would need a gentleman with a clean criminal record and, hopefully, a clean driving record although that could be a little tougher. Once we have a man with as many, if not all of these credentials in place, we can put the plan into hyper-drive. When we have our donor, and I think we have someone already, we move to the second phase of the identity mission."

Three of the men in the room mouthed the words, "Have someone already," all at once. Murray raised his hand like one of his high school students. Pepper pointed to him like a professor.

"You said you have someone in mind already? Seems to me Mr. Pepper that you may have done this kind of thing before."

Bill Pepper cryptically explained that this kind of identity change had been done before. George and the team were in the good hands of some serious men prepared for any eventuality. Feeling he had said enough, Pepper simply smiled and continued on with the plan. Jack's heart skipped a beat, understanding that he and his newfound colleagues had just been called up to the major leagues.

It was now evident that William had a plan and the motivation, the resources, and the know how to execute it to success. Pepper described the important actions that the donor would agree to upon payment. Their chosen man would agree to cremation upon death, with ashes scattered at some remote place and time. There could be no gravesite. The team would also ensure that the death could not be recorded anywhere. No hospital, coroner, newspaper or cemetery could be alerted to the individual's passing nor would the family be allowed communication with any official agency. Pepper's men would get a copy of the donor's credit report as soon as possible to ensure that all debts were settled and no credit issues lingered.

Anders leaned toward Jenson's ear and whispered that he knew introducing Pepper was a good idea. But he was concerned about Mr. Washington who remained stoic throughout the discussion. He was about to say something when his new found friend beat him to the punch.

"Mr. Washington, what do you think so far?" interjected Jenson, his voice also showing concern. Mr. Washington, seated at attention with perfect posture, turned toward Jenson and nodded.

"Mr. Pepper is very well prepared. I am impressed so far."

The General turned back toward Pepper and surprisingly asked that he continue. Murray and Hahn were shocked that Mr. Washington did not even flinch at the dark plan to get the candidate a new identity. They vowed the night before to follow this man through thick and thin but now the second thoughts were popping up. Did this man have as much integrity as the history books reported? While it mattered to Murray and Hahn, the man holding court didn't care.

Pepper was energized. Having been complimented by his hero from another century, he was more than happy to elaborate.

"I need to explain a couple more important steps to get this done. We would love our man to live in a college or university town. Towns like those have a lot of population turnover and normally do not have solid community bases or strong civic associations. His state of birth must be different than where he dies, even if we have to move this person to another state on his deathbed. This creates a new layer on the trail, which would at the very least dissuade a media type from digging further. Next, get hold of all of his bank and investment accounts and change the institutions where these monies and securities are housed. Do the same on 401k plans and any other account that may linger. Doing this is threefold. We put the additional layers down, get the monies under our control, and take away any personal relationships that may have been fostered over the years. Sounds abrupt but it has to be done."

Pepper was rolling and had every man in the room intrigued. Mr. Washington's mood softened as he leaned back in his chair, more impressed than earlier. He did not understand all the terminology used by Pepper but he did grasp the concepts. Like any good executive, George read the self-assurance and confidence in Pepper's body language and bought into the plan.

Pepper was not done as he paced the room explaining that they needed to settle any lingering accounts including all unclaimed property in the donor's name. Once they had those issues settled, they would bring Mr. Washington to the department of motor vehicles with all of the donor's paperwork and get him a new driver's license.

He further explained that creating the story of a lost license would not raise any red flags, and if there were any concerns, they would do a test run with one of the men in the room. Once he had a driver's license with his current picture, it would quell the identity issue among doubters.

The group realized that this plan was hardly some fly by night idea. It was well thought out, but the intricate detail involved continued to make most of them nervous and uneasy. They knew Pepper had obviously done this sort of thing, but after his reply to Murray earlier, none of the men wanted to know any specifics.

———

Faulk reported on the Lincoln Memorial speech in his magazine and had been trading texts with Murray since. Murray trusted the sage Faulk and although Pepper called for a written communication embargo, Murray provided updates to a skeptical Faulk. There seemed no stopping this steamroller now. Jack wasn't sure he liked Pepper, but he was sure the guy knew what he was doing. If anyone was going to pull this off, it would be him.

Then there was George. The president seemed more concerned about the risks of expanding the inner circle than about the ethics of the scheme. Murray found that disconcerting. However, he asked himself what George was supposed to do.

Somehow Providence brought him back and it wasn't to drive around in a limo. No, the logical side of Murray overruled the moralistic side. He was nervous in charting these unknown waters. Murray was on board, but needed some of his questions answered before he would have confidence in the plan's success.

The sight of their leader agreeing to the Pepper plan and backing it one hundred percent calmed the team's nerves a little. They may have come up with the plan to run for president but the new founders believed they had one leader. And his name was George Washington.

As Pepper finished his plan for an identity switch, Mr. Washington stood at attention and approached the speaker. He raised both hands and placed them on Bill's shoulders.

"Mr. Pepper is obviously a very prepared and capable individual which provides me great comfort."

Mr. Washington looked from man to man with a smile that eased their fears for the moment. He firmly stated that they had been brought together for a grand cause, old friends and new friends like Mr. Pepper.

"Fear not my brothers. I believe that Providence has guided us to this point and will see us through to bringing our ultimate success of restoring to America the principles that made us great."

The men now encircled Pepper and the first president. They fed off the positive energy Mr. Washington created. Murray was the last to join the semi-circle and, staring directly at his new leader while addressing Pepper, had to say his peace.

"I agree that George Washington should be president. I think we all do. Mr. Pepper, this scheme you presented is well detailed and a little bit extravagant. But once you have the donor, and it sounds like you do, what will you do about friends and extended family? How are you going to handle that? How are you going to ensure that in this day and age of cell phones, YouTube and the internet, that you're going to be able to keep all of this under wraps? Mr. President, I do not want to be disrespectful, but somebody here needs to play devil's advocate."

Pepper stepped forward and addressed Murray face-to-face.

"We have already put this plan in motion. We will secure the donor by tomorrow. And it will work."

The certitude with which Pepper spoke seemed to inspire the doubters and shocked Jack Murray. Mr. Washington took Murray aside in earshot of the rest of the men. He put his arm over Murray's shoulder and leaned in.

"My dear and trusted friend, the journey has begun. I need you to be part of the team. If you have faith and trust in me, we will reap the rewards and live to enjoy the fruits of our labor. Please trust in Providence."

As Murray and Mr. Washington stared at each other in silence, Anders once again decided to break it.

"Who's hungry? I'm hungry. How about we get room service and re-convene a little later. Don't want to start the president's candidacy on an empty stomach."

Murray, his glance momentarily distracted by Anders, looked back up at the father of our country. Mr. Washington's look was fatherly and Murray seemed to embrace his message. He meekly nodded and asked for a menu.

Chapter 15

As was his habit, William Fredericks sat in near darkness, the only light visible coming from his laptop. He listened to talk radio WMAL while he prepared material for an upcoming week of shows. Sunday afternoons and evenings were especially informative as back-up conservative talk show host wannabes generally regurgitated the ideas of their weekday counterparts. William learned he could tune in for a few hours each Sunday, listen to a summary of the enemy's talking points and prepare his venomous refutations.

While finishing his second drink of the afternoon, he scanned a story in the *New York Times* about one of the so-called conservative candidate's failure to pay his taxes. William quickly bored of the story and turned his ear toward the radio. The station's four o'clock news report grabbed his attention. An unidentified man caused quite a commotion earlier in the day on the steps of the Lincoln Memorial. The stranger recited Lincoln's Gettysburg Address and Second Inaugural Speech and followed that up with commentary describing each speech's relationship with the founding fathers and today's America.

———

"The audacity, please," said William out loud to nobody.

"How ridiculous for a cur like that to relate ancient history to our modern times."

Fredericks laughed at his own comment. He could not believe that this right wing station was so desperate for ratings that it would chose to air the mad rants of some random deranged man and try to pass it off as actual news. He thought that kind of reporting was limited to *The Daily Show* or *The Colbert Report,* comedy shows that the public mistook for real news. He thought this nut job's incoherent diatribe would make good copy for his Monday viewers, so he googled the story, hoping to find some video fodder for his show.

As the video buffered, WMAL played an audio clip.

"These United States were founded on individual liberty, the unequivocal principle that our rights are granted directly from God our creator and that we as Americans are free to attain individual property, the fruits of our labor and pursue our individual happiness."

Fredericks scoffed at the reference to God, yet continued to intently listen to the distinguished southern voice.

While clearly a Virginia or Maryland sound, William thought the voice had an air of elegance to it, something he was not accustomed to hearing from the right side of the political spectrum. The dignified man sounded as if he spoke the Queen's English as he described the framers' design of the United States Constitution to align individual success with the nation's success.

William figured this mystery man was destined to lose his audience when he quoted Adam Smith and the notion of the "Invisible Hand." The right wing fools were not intelligent enough to understand the passage, which stated that by perusing one's own interests, man frequently promotes that of the society more effectually than when he really intends to promote it.

William did a classic double take when the unknown orator expounded that in the parlance of today, that would mean the citizenry and (not the government) knew what was best for the people and the most efficient means to achieve their own happiness.

Then the stranger delivered a message that made Fredericks motionlessly take note.

"If the people were left alone to pursue their goals, the nation like a mighty ship would rise by the high tide of her elevated citizenry."

The blood drained from Fredericks' face. His stomach suddenly cramped and his head spun almost involuntarily toward the radio upon hearing these words. This unknown had actually coherently articulated conservative philosophy, misguided though it was, in a clear, direct language that might just resonate with the people.

It wasn't just the words spoken but the way they were delivered that sent chills up and down Fredericks' spine. His thought was immediately confirmed by the spontaneous cheering of the enthusiastic crowd and the return of this charismatic stranger's voice.

The voice emanating from the radio told how Lincoln understood the principles of the country's founding as explained in the Gettysburg address; Honest Abe sacrificed his own life fighting to keep the nation together and ensure the founding fathers' guarantee of equality.

Who was this man? Fredericks asked aloud. Who was this person that so eloquently connected the founders and Lincoln to modern times?

In Fredericks' mind, this dangerous man at the Lincoln Memorial clearly articulated that, as owners of those enslaved, the founders understood that their words were in competition with their actions. He made the case that absolute abolition would have meant no agreement among the individual states in Philadelphia, no United States of America, and therefore no foreseeable opportunity for emancipation.

The speaker had logically connected George Washington's words from his farewell address to the recent fervor over the president's unjustified warning to the Supreme Court about the constitutionality of his healthcare mandate.

The slightly built Fredericks wiggled in his chair and shook his head to himself as he turned up the volume dial.

"This guy is good. Who the hell is he?"

The stranger's voice rang clear when he said that if, in the opinion of the people, the distribution or modification of the constitutional powers be wrong, let it be corrected by an amendment in the way which the Constitution designates.

For the first time in a while, Fredericks was stunned. He had to see this guy. He finally downloaded the full YouTube video on his laptop and studied the grainy images of the impressive man. He was obviously tall, purposeful, confident, and blessed with a classical articulation. He was also not alone.

While the video showed hundreds of people up and down the steps, Fredericks noticed a small group of three or four men to the stranger's right side. Each hung on his every word like the rest of the crowd but something about them seemed different. If Fredericks didn't know better, he would have thought these well-dressed men were secret service agents. After all, they maintained serious and protective facial expressions throughout the speech.

As the camera panned the group, Fredericks paused and with a nervous smile focused on one of these men in particular. Though wearing dark sunglasses and a black baseball cap pulled low over his eyes, Fredericks was sure he knew who it was. But what was Anders doing there? How did he fit into this? And why didn't anybody notice him? He had to find out.

Fredericks paused and zoomed in on the speaker's face, frozen like a portrait. Fredericks studied the pronounced, somehow familiar features on the stranger's face and was drawn to his fixed, steely blue eyes. William Fredericks had a funny feeling that he would soon cross paths with this formidable adversary. He just wondered what the voices were going to want him to do about it.

Chapter 16

The afternoon consisted of continuous discussion and room service that was the equivalent of a banquet feast. Murray and Jenson sat on the couch in Josh Anders' suite, wondering to each other if there was a morsel of food on the menu that Pepper had not ordered. Jenson joined them in a semi food coma as they tried to prepare their next steps.

The late lunch even left Hahn speechless as he lounged across an easy chair and stared out the window toward the White House. Pepper quietly typed on his laptop at the dining room table while Anders excused himself to the bedroom, cell phone perpetually attached to his right ear, deep in conversation.

Mr. Washington, recovering from a long overdue trip to the dentist, devoured his daily requirement of ten newspapers while seated in front of the television, his right leg crossed over his left. He held an ice pack to his cheek as he tried to relax in front of a political talk show. However, the host of this particular program rubbed Mr. Washington wrong.

The Novocain had just worn off allowing Mr. Washington to speak coherently again.

"Who is this haughty man, so full of himself to speak in such a condescending manner?"

Mr. Washington had discovered *The World Today* and its blustery and pompous host, William Fredericks. The General was intrigued. George's question went unanswered and he looked to the trio on the couch and asked again. His Virginian brothers were about to nod off while Hahn continued to gaze out the window. He blurted only Fredericks' name to his new boss.

The New Founders

Mr. Washington was surprised at the indifference in his trusted advisor's voice and did not expand on his question. He instead focused on the program, anxious to listen to the host's next words. He watched the rest of the show alone with his thoughts. He understood that if he were to go through with these presidential aspirations, his path would cross Mr. Fredericks' at some point in the future. Unlike many of the candidates of the day, Mr. Washington looked forward to that encounter.

The rest of the late afternoon and early evening found the men scurrying about, going from suite to suite, making small talk, reading newspapers, and scanning the internet on their computers and iPads. Mr. Washington was fascinated by the remote control, the number of television programs, and only left the TV for a bathroom break. Bill Pepper warned the first president that the apparatus was commonly known as an idiot box and that one should not watch too much of it. Mr. Washington smiled.

"I am not worried about that, my good man. At my advanced age and my lack of exposure to this invention, I have a lot of catching up to do."

At once, the General turned back toward the screen to view himself in an unsteady video, taken the previous day during his Lincoln Memorial speech. He pointed toward the television as the rest of the group tilted their heads to get a better view. Mr. Washington grinned with satisfaction at the sound of his voice and his stature among his fellow citizens.

"I've never heard or seen myself speak. It is quite unusual and exhilarating at the same time."

Murray realized that was true. It dawned on all of them that they too had never seen George Washington himself speak on an audio or videotape. The elation of the moment was not limited to just the father of our country. The men looked pleased that he was already getting network coverage. Jenson let the room know that the first president had gone viral. George had never heard the word viral before, but recognizing the root of the word "virus" (which in his day was synonymous with poison), objected to its use. The men smiled as Jenson explained the twenty-first century meaning of viral, thus assuring George there was nothing poisonous about him, except perhaps to his political rivals.

Anders had reentered the dining area and sat at the table. He immediately delved into deep conversation with Pepper. Jenson hovered above them listening. Mr. Washington, his curiosity getting the best of him, rose and walked to the table. He asked if he could join them.

"Of course Mr. President, by all means," answered Anders as he pulled a chair out for the candidate. Anders mentioned that Bill had a good idea and wanted to share it with the team. Mr. Washington gave him the floor.

"Mr. President, we're pretty much cooped up in this hotel room. It's tough for us to go anywhere or do anything now that your speech is out there for all to see. Anders is getting calls from his friends and political buddies about the video, all of them asking who that stranger was. We have to be proactive now and seize the moment before George's fifteen minutes of fame run out. Besides, if we stay here, we're bound to be found out, by a maid or a busboy or a front desk girl with a big mouth."

"So what I suggested to Anders is that we get out of town and get a secluded house so we can have some privacy and come and go as we please. I have a business contact who agreed to let us use his fully furnished house for as long as we need it, no questions asked."

All eyes were on Mr. Washington as he pondered the thought. He slowly nodded his head in agreement.

"That is a paramount idea. The stale air of being indoors was starting to get to me. It will be good to get out in the fresh air again. Where is this house you speak of and how far a ride do you predict?"

The men at the table looked at each other with grins.

Jenson responded that the house was near Washington's Mount Vernon estate and that they would head there first thing in the morning.

Mr. Washington's eyes opened wide at the answer. He could not conceal his pleasure and beamed a grin once again.

"I was afraid to inquire. Are my land and home still in existence?"

Murray had wandered over to the table and replied in the affirmative, noting that his son's class had visited the estate on a trip this past spring.

"I got to go as a chaperone. I imagine it's as beautiful as you left it. Only a half an hour from here."

Mr. Washington excused himself. He was still not accustomed to the ease and speed of travel by automobile. He explained that it was a four hour trip by horse and carriage, not including the ferry ride across the Potomac River.

"Don't worry sir, I will pay the toll," joked Pepper as everybody let out a big laugh. Mr. Washington laughed along with the men as he stood up before them.

Walking to his bedroom to watch some more television, Mr. Washington thanked the men for their choice of destination and touchingly said that he would dream of his return to Mount Vernon. Before Mr. Washington could make his way into the bedroom, Pepper grabbed his forearm and asked for a word in private. The men made their way to the sitting area outside Mr. Washington's bedroom.

"Mr. President, we have an identity donor and he lives nearby. We would like to arrange for you to meet with him in the coming days. His name is Frank Walters and he is very sick."

The father of our country asked Pepper if this man was an honorable one. Pepper responded that he would not have been chosen if he were otherwise. Mr. Washington nodded his approval, saying that he looked forward to meeting him. Pepper continued. "Anders and I spoke about this a few minutes ago. As soon as you go to bed, I will inform the team. You may want to get used to referring to yourself as Frank or Mr. Walters."

Mr. Washington, agreeing with the last suggestion, marched to his bedroom. The rest of the men watched in silence as the bedroom door closed behind Mr. Washington. Murray offered a summation of what had just transpired.

"He's blessed? I think it's us that are blessed; should be an interesting morning."

Murray followed Mr. Washington's lead and went to his room to call home.

———

Tuesday morning was uneventful. Everybody was up early in anticipation of the trip to their new confines. Room service breakfast arrived early and they trickled into the Anders suite to partake in coffee, eggs, bacon and croissants. Mr. Washington was among the first to arrive and poured a tall cup of black coffee as he pondered the thought of possibly seeing his old estate on the river and the sprawling lawns that led to his home. He packed his belongings as soon as he woke and sat in quiet anticipation as he watched the men go to and fro. As usual, Anders was glued to his cell phone as the rest of the team picked at the buffet. Pepper entered the suite.

"Guys, just want to give you the plan for the morning. We have two limos waiting in the underground garage of hotel. I would like to leave in twenty minutes. We'll take the elevator down to the garage and go straight into the cars. This will ensure secrecy. Once we're in the cars, we'll be fine."

The new founders nodded as they noshed on their breakfast. Mr. Washington also nodded in agreement as he opened a copy of the *Washington Post* that Pepper handed to him upon entering the room. The silent okay was good enough for Pepper. He joined the team at the table and poured himself a cup of java.

The team was out the door and down the elevator in no time flat. As the elevator doors opened in the parking garage, the men made a beeline for the cars, threw their bags and suitcases in the trunk and piled in without hesitation. Unlike the trip from Philadelphia, Anders decided to ride with Pepper, leaving the other three men to accompany Mr. Washington home. Neither Anders nor Mr. Washington disputed the arrangement as the cars exited the hotel in haste.

As the cars made their way south past the Washington Monument toward the bridge to Virginia, the General took in the sights. It was early and the sun's rays peaked over and through the buildings. People hurried along to their destinations as rush hour commenced. The first president got a dose of this as the cars approached the river. The limos idled as traffic backed up through the intersection ahead.

Murray sat quietly next to Mr. Washington. He looked at Hahn and Jenson sitting across from him. He could not help but notice that Jenson had become one of Anders' newest confidants, almost a go-to guy for commentary. And there was no doubt that Hahn had the president's ear, a fact not lost on the rest of the group, either. In the short time together, Mr. Washington must have pulled Hahn off to the side for private conversations at least half a dozen times.

That left Murray. While he got along with everyone, he still tried to figure out where he stood in the grand scheme of things. Yes, he was the embodiment of James Madison and yes, he was told he had a lot of the same qualities and habits of the fourth president. But his role had yet to be defined and it gnawed at him. The car was quiet and he didn't want to just blurt his concerns out, since it may be taken as disrespectful or even as jealousy. His quick wit came through and he thought of a way to break the ice.

"Mr. President, should we call you Frank Walters now or continue to refer to you as George Washington?"

The men let out a quick laugh but leaned in, awaiting an answer. Mr. Washington, in his ever accommodating fashion, told Murray that he could call him whatever name he was comfortable using. But in front of others not in the inner circle, he was Mr. Walters or Frank. He gave Murray the opening he needed.

"You mind if I speak frankly? I'm concerned about where I stand in all of this, where I fit in to the grand plan Mr. Pepper has set out for us. I know it's only been a couple of days, but a lot has happened since Friday. And I realize you respect my opinions or else I wouldn't have been asked to accompany you. But I guess I need a little reassurance that I'm doing the right thing, leaving my wife and family for the time being, to play with a couple of strangers."

Mr. Washington adjusted himself in the seat to face Murray next to him. He assured him that he was vital to the team and that he was right, if he didn't need him, he would not be there.

"You are needed more than you could ever imagine. You may not see it now, but your presence will prove essential. Do not doubt yourself. You know in your gut what is true. And do not worry about your wife and child. Right now, you are home, with your brethren, and there is no other place you need be at this very moment. Remember Mr. Murray, it was neither Mr. Anders nor Mr. Pepper who planned this. We are but the vehicles of Providence."

Mr. Washington glanced to his right and noticed tourists lining up for a tour of a building with a sign in front. He read the sign aloud.

"Holocaust Museum? Gentlemen, what is the Holocaust Museum? What was the Holocaust and why is there a museum honoring it?"

Murray, understanding that the previous subject was now closed for discussion, described the horrors of World War II and how Adolf Hitler organized the mass murders of millions of Jews, Christians, and others in concentration and internment camps. The description of the atrocities horrified Mr. Washington. He cringed for the first time in front of his men as he soaked in the horrible facts. He motioned as if to speak, then remained silent, unable to find the words to express his feelings.

The car inched forward, and in a few minutes, the museum was behind them and the river ahead. The cars stopped at the traffic light before the bridge and Mr. Washington once again looked out the window. Standing before them, below their plane of sight, and next to the riverbank, was the George Mason Memorial. On cue, Mr. Washington turned to Murray.

"The George Mason Memorial. Mr. Murray, am I correct in assuming you are familiar with this great man?"

Murray assured the president that he knew just about everything there was to know about the man, given the fact that he co-authored the Bill of Rights with James Madison.

"I would have expected nothing less from you, Mr. Murray. Mr. Mason was a decent and honorable man. I am overjoyed to see that the men of modern times have so venerated him with a memorial."

The limousines now raced across the Potomac and into Virginia. Traffic had subsided going out of Washington, even though it remained bumper to bumper heading into the capital. Hahn mentioned that they were probably about twenty minutes from their destination. Mr. Washington asked Jenson about the book under his arm. Jenson told him that it was a condensed version of US history, which he picked up at the Lincoln Memorial gift shop. Mr. Washington asked if he could peruse it and the talk show host happily complied.

George flipped pages as the car approached Mount Vernon. Jenson tapped the president on the shoulder and pointed to the signs for the Washington estate. The General closed the book and took in the sights.

"Incredible," thought George as he was taken back to his childhood, almost 300 years earlier. The greenery of his beloved Northern Virginia blurred past the limo. He closed his eyes and remembered a younger version of himself roaming the countryside with his favorite hound, retrieving the rabbits and birds he shot with his trusty musket. What a beautiful country Virginia was. As he opened his eyes to the new twenty-first century world, he still pictured old Virginia.

George had the driver stop the car as he stepped out to gaze down upon the mighty Potomac. He breathed in the fresh air and realized that while America had changed in so many fantastic and sometimes dubious ways, his little part of the world retained some of its pristine charms. His three travel companions stepped out of the car with him.

As if on cue, George swung his head to the sound of hooves rumbling quickly toward the car. A man and women rode by; she on a brown mare and he on a fine white stallion. George froze as the riders disappeared into the wooded trail.

Noticing George's reaction, Jenson offered a reassuring word.

"Yes General, I am sure Anders or Pepper will find a fine horse for you to ride while we are here."

That promise brought a hearty smile to the General as he climbed back into the car for the remainder of the drive. Within minutes the car turned into a long, gated driveway.

Five hundred feet in front of them stood a house that could best be described as a mansion. The new founders muttered to each other that if Pepper and Anders were involved, it figured that their next destination would be a mansion.

The cars pulled up and the men exited. They stood in the circular driveway, looking up and around at the home and the grounds. The trunks popped open and they went for their bags. However, Mr. Washington did not.

Instead, the first president began walking in the direction of the Potomac River, which was situated across the expansive side lawn roughly 250 feet from the house. Hahn dropped his bag and jogged toward Mr. Washington, falling in stride with him.

"Where are you going, George?"

The General responded that the grounds reminded him of his home and he wanted to get a look at the river up close before he returned to join the team. Within a minute, the men stood on the dock at the river's edge.

"Beautiful, simply beautiful. This estate is quite similar to my homestead. It is almost as if this part of nature has been untouched by modern man." Pointing north, up the Potomac, the president continued. "If I had to hazard a guess, my plantation is only a mile or so, as the crow flies, along the river. Do you think we can walk the trail along the river one morning, Mr. Hahn?"

Anthony put a hand on Mr. Washington's broad shoulder and told him that it would be impossible as each tract of land between the spot they stood on and the Mt. Vernon Estate was privately owned. The last thing anybody needed was for George Washington to be arrested for trespassing.

"I think we should get back to the others, Mr. President."

Chapter 17

Anders waited at the back kitchen door, smoking his signature cigar, as the newest addition to the team parked his black BMW convertible on the gravel driveway behind the house. Anders had all but quit cigars in recent years, but given the remarkable turn of events and his desire to make a strong first impression, he thought the Cubans most appropriate.

He had known this man since the Reagan years when Anders was the young buck of talk radio and his guest made a name for himself advancing the career of an ex-CIA Director from Maine. Neither man believed in small talk in these situations, so after a quick business-like handshake and brief review of the circumstances, Anders led Mr. Ken "The Builder" Rader to the dining area.

While Anders had been around politics for most of the last forty years, a lot of what was transpiring was new to him. Neither he nor any members of the team had ever run a campaign, much less the presidential campaign of a three hundred year old man with a fake ID. He knew, even with Pepper now fully on board, that they needed a professional campaign manager. The good news was that Anders knew all the right people and had gotten a tip that the vaunted Rader, campaign manager for one of the Republican candidates, had resigned his post the day before. This news would not be public for a day or two, so Anders jumped on the opportunity and got his man.

Though Anders was a bit apprehensive that he had not discussed his new hire with Mr. Washington or the rest of the team, he knew he made the right decision and was excited to introduce "the Builder" to the men. Rader got his name from his reputation as an "Empire Builder." Corporate types, entertainers, senators, and even presidents had brought Rader in to see their ambitions through to the next level. Rader always delivered and Anders could take no chances using someone else.

———

This would be a very different assignment for Rader. Instead of leading the charge as the face to the campaign (as he was accustomed), he had been asked by Anders to keep a low profile, setting the strategies and working the candidate's message. What concerned Rader was that although he was on board, having been promised seven figures for only a few months work, he had yet to meet the client.

———

Since his spontaneous speech on the steps of the Lincoln Memorial, the whole country was consumed by the unknown orator. William Fredericks had even dubbed him the "Lincoln Continental." But he was still a stranger to the country and to the Builder. Ken understood that everybody knew of him, but no one knew his name. Rader looked forward to meeting the intriguing Continental that day.

Anders opened the door, to find the team seated at a large round table. Rader noticed the impressively large white board and the rather short balding man writing on it. A tallish looking gentleman sat at the table surrounded by four empty seats. Books, papers and coffee cups were spread around the table while scattered iPads, iPhones, and BlackBerrys buzzed with life. With the election moving quickly towards them, the men were in their element, negotiating and sniping at each other as they worked to put an agenda together, all fully energized by the massive task at hand. Mr. Washington and Hahn stood in an adjacent room discussing the campaign as Pepper, Anders, and the Builder entered together.

Jack Murray turned from the travel schedule he was drafting to face the three men. It took Murray all of two seconds to place the new face in the room, a man he had seen on television hundreds of times. Murray thought that if any more of these political big shots with giant egos entered the room, there would be no air for the rest of the team.

Murray looked to the seated Jenson who returned a silent look of shock and anger. They read each others' minds. What the hell was Anders doing now?

None of that mattered to Anders who in grandiose fashion introduced the familiar looking gentleman.

"I'd like to introduce you to our new campaign manager, none other than the Builder himself, Ken Rader."

Overhearing the introduction from the other room, Mr. Washington demanded of Hahn the name of the man just introduced. Hahn was caught flat footed by the Rader introduction and Mr. Washington's question. Hahn didn't like surprises, especially not in front of his new boss.

Murray and Jenson watched in silent satisfaction as Hahn excused himself from Mr. Washington, hurried into the dining room, and demanded to know why Anders would bring in an outsider without consulting with Hahn or the team first. Hahn didn't have to say it but he believed Anders was throwing his weight around.

Mr. Washington quickly read the situation and demanded Anders explain why he had brought in an outsider without talking to him and the rest of the team first. Mr. Washington understood the need for a professional campaign manager but would not accept being excluded from such important decisions.

Anders explained that Rader had just become available. He was the very best and had recently resigned from the former House Speaker's presidential campaign. Before he was scooped up by one of the other campaigns, Anders had to pounce and contacted him that very morning. Anders explained proudly that he had seized the moment.

"I understand Mr. Anders why you did what you did and I will not fault you for your efforts, for when a man does all he can, though it succeeds not well, blame not him that did it."

That being said, Mr. Washington needed to claim his authority right at that very moment. He insisted to Anders in no uncertain terms that while the decision may prove a good one, no one was to make any major decisions without Mr. Washington's direct approval. And if he were not available, they were to go through Hahn. To make his point perfectly clear, he ended his lecture by dressing down the most popular radio talk show host in the land.

"Do you understand me?"

Murray enjoyed the moment but was surprised to see Mr. Washington defer ideas to Hahn without mention of the rest of the team. It was only then that he noticed the General looking in his direction.

"Mr. Hahn, Jenson, Murray and Pepper, is that clear to you as well?"

Murray did not like being spoken to like a child. He cringed at the notion but also realized that the first president was in fact an assertive leader who let his actions speak for themselves. That was the first time they felt the full strength of George Washington's authority and it was clear that he was in control. No wonder we won the war, he thought.

While the men slowly took their seats, Mr. Washington approached Rader. He stood before the Builder and, looking down on him, extended his hand.

Though it was not directed at him, Rader felt the impact of Washington's reprimand. During his career, he had been through presidential elections. He had been in the epicenter of scandal and the object of CEO and presidential scorn before, but he had never felt as intimidated as he did at that moment. He was in the presence of a man, the likes of whom he had never known.

Rader extended his hand, looked into Mr. Walters' eyes and guaranteed his best efforts to the Walters team.

Mr. Washington noted Rader's firm handshake and clear, direct eye contact. He welcomed him to the team.

"Mr. Rader, I trust you will do a fine job."

Mr. Washington then left the room with Hahn. Murray and the rest of the team sat silently and digested the last few minutes. The remaining men in the room took a deep breath, fully aware why George Washington was the indispensable leader

---

It was time to build a platform.

Never one to remain silent for long, Rader immediately took the lead and described the Reaganesque belief that a presidential platform be built from multiple planks (rather than single issues within the overall platform). Murray and Jenson agreed with his philosophy of focusing on several but not too many intertwining issues. By not diluting the message, Rader believed they could present a cohesive overall strategy that would overwhelm and stifle the current administration. Murray thought in sports terms, whispering that the best defense is a good offense.

Jenson expanded on Rader's thoughts, reminding the new founders that during his Lincoln Memorial speech, George compared our society to a mighty ship being lifted by the rising tide of American success.

"A rising ship. That would be a perfect theme for the campaign."

Murray was excited. He transported himself to the summer of 1776 and imagined the voice of Thomas Jefferson next to him. Jenson practically finished his thought when he said that the planks Rader mentioned could build their symbolic ship which would be buoyed by the wave of the American voter. And of course, the ship would be piloted by George Washington.

Murray's inner Madison showed through. He said that anything was possible in this country if the government stepped out of the way and allowed its citizens to use their tools to build it.

Mr. Washington had just reentered the room and offered an elegant summary. "After the last four years of drifting in the shallows, we find the mighty ship of our nation being torn against the rocks of a low tide. But as we have proven as a people time and time again, anything is possible. So let us unleash the force of the American people to rebuild our great ship, plank by plank."

He emphasized that the greatness of America would rise again and sail triumphantly on the tide of the uplifting spirit and success of each American.

"In these United States, it is the strength and happiness of the individual that fills our sails, allowing our nation the safe navigation of these treacherous waters. Boys, I think we have our main themes. We each rise as individuals which elevates our society. We can refine them as we go. Now let's nail down the planks."

The men dug right in. Anders forcefully argued that the planks should focus on the dire financial and economic issues facing our nation. For once, Hahn agreed with Josh, stressing that the financial issues were the most pressing problems facing the country. But even though he agreed with Anders, he still smarted from the perceived snub earlier in the day and assertively reminded Anders that financial issues were under his domain.

"I, Anthony Hahn, will set the campaign's economic policy."

Anders, not one to back down, calmly reminded Hahn that the men had made a pledge to their country and each other. While they did not all have to get along, they did have to put personal animosities aside for the greater goal.

Mr. Washington allowed Anders and Hahn to complete their exchange before stepping in. Staring squarely at his young protégé Hahn, Mr. Washington chided the currency trader.

"Complaints ill become those who are found to be the first aggressors."

He then reminded the team that while he expected to receive advice, Mr. Washington alone would set all policy.

Both Hahn and Anders took this admonition to heart and while neither apologized, they stood down as Jenson filled the void by successfully arguing that the planks should consist of the principles most basic to our nation.

Murray allowed himself to let go of Dottie for now and seize the moment. He was finally making a difference. Sure, he was dealing with a bunch of egomaniacs, but he knew from history that he intellectually and politically fit in with these guys. Suddenly, he was less Jack the history teacher and more James Madison the founder. He admitted to himself that it felt great to openly express his opinions without hesitation.

"Our planks need to be simple," said Murray, "and composed only of our God given rights of Life, Liberty, Pursuit of Happiness, Property and Religion. Our planks will be joined as one to create our ship by the American people. Anything is possible in America if government steps aside and allows the people to use these tools for their own betterment."

Murray glanced in Mr. Washington's direction. The father of the country beamed from ear to ear as he realized that the man from Virginia with the pretty wife had finally channeled Mr. Madison.

After some debate, the new founders agreed on the following tools to connect the planks to the ship:

• Economy / Tax policy
• National Security / Foreign Policy
• Regulation / Health Care mandate
• Religion

Anders implored the others that the tools and planks were not enough. He urged that the new founders debate these issues amongst themselves to ensure that each item was fully vetted.

"Mr. Walters needs to put forth a clear and unambiguous message to each. The economy, the most important issue, has to be first."

After two full days of policy and political strategy sessions, the first president had survived his first crash course in building a campaign. George actually did better than survive; he thrived. Even his team marveled at the ease at which he had absorbed the information thrown at him. There was still a week and a half more of this to come. And this morning was finally the time for the first president to meet his identity donor.

Mr. Washington stood at attention in the foyer looking at his wristwatch. He studied the shape of the watch and admired the handcrafting that went into building such an elegant timepiece. He thought the name of the company, Tag Heuer, was rather odd. But in his experiences with foreign persons, he learned to not question foreign names.

However, it wasn't the model of the wristwatch that concerned Mr. Washington. The time on the watch read 7:05am and he was alone. He was sure the agreed upon time for departure was seven and the first president was perturbed. He simmered as he began to pace, wondering quietly what could delay his travel companions. Hahn, Murray and Pepper all agreed on an early departure at the designated time and now they were late. Mr. Washington prided himself for his strict punctuality (and this lapse in timeliness annoyed the General). As he turned to stride back to the front door, he heard footsteps coming down the staircase above.

"Good morning Mr. President!" exclaimed Hahn, smiling as he glided down the staircase. The smile disappeared as he descended the last step and noticed the glare from his new leader.

"Mr. Hahn, we did agree on seven o'clock, did we not?"

Hahn could do nothing but nod in agreement with the look of a scolded child. He realized the goodwill of the previous day's political conversation was long gone while he tried to explain that the eight minutes of tardiness was no big deal. Pepper and Murray entered from the doorway, already aware of the president's mood from the sound of Mr. Washington's impatient voice down the hall. The men were silent as they approached the heated candidate.

"Gentlemen, this is unacceptable. When we agree on a meeting time, we have to adhere to it. This is not a topic up for discussion or debate."

This time, Murray took the brunt of Mr. Washington's lecture on timeliness and discipline. Murray understood Mr. Washington's point as it related to a show of respect for those who took the time out of their schedule to meet with you. While being late for a meeting may be bad, it was especially disrespectful in the case of a man generous enough to hand over his identity for the good of his country.

Mr. Washington turned and opened the front door. The men fell in behind him, entered the limo and headed down the driveway.

The ride was a quiet one. Neither Pepper, Murray, or Hahn were about to speak after the tongue-lashing they received a few minutes before. They all sipped the coffee that Mr. Washington had brewed and poured into a thermos for their trip. The driver thanked him for the coffee as they met heavy traffic near our nation's capital. Their destination was Arnold, Maryland, a suburb of Washington, D.C., located near the US Naval Academy. Mr. Washington was anxious to see the campus following their visit and informed the driver, who assured him that he would be happy to bring him there.

The limousine pulled up to the address a few minutes before eight o'clock. The well to do neighborhood was still quiet, with a few people departing for work. Not one child was in sight. Mr. Washington exited the car and strode toward the front door of the two story colonial house. As he approached, the front door opened and a young man in his mid-twenties stepped toward him.

Connor Walters extended his right hand in introduction.

Mr. Washington greeted the young Connor Walters with his sincere appreciation. He then turned and introduced the members of his team to Connor. After the exchanged pleasantries, Mr. Washington addressed his colleagues.

"Men, I would like to meet with Mr. Walters alone. I ask that you please allow us approximately two hours. I think you should be able to keep yourself occupied during this timeframe, don't you agree?"

After the morning's scolding, none of the men were about to question the General. They all complied and turned back toward the car. Mr. Washington accompanied Connor into the dwelling and shut the door behind them.

As he led Mr. Washington down the hallway, Connor explained that they had converted the den into his father's bedroom since the elder Walters could no longer climb the steps. Mr. Walters lay in a hospital bed near the window of the makeshift bedroom. He held a remote control in his hand as he flipped through the cable television channels. Even though his face was gaunt, he was clean shaven and his hair was combed neatly in anticipation of his historic meeting. He also changed his pajamas and now wore a blue sweat suit and slippers. He was obviously weak, but proud, having exerted much of his strength to present himself in a respectable manner to his houseguest.

Mr. Walters looked up and saw the first president. Mr. Washington's frame filled the doorway. He smiled and walked to the bed. As Mr. Washington approached, Walters did his best to sit up. His son hurried around Mr. Washington to raise the back of the bed automatically, allowing his father some more comfort. He now sat erect and introduced himself. He told Mr. Washington it was an honor and pleasure to meet him. Mr. Washington grabbed a chair from the desk and pulled it to Walters' bedside.

"Mr. Walters, the pleasure is all mine. I am honored to make your acquaintance and humbled at your generous gesture."

Frank shook his head and stated that it was the least he could do. An old business acquaintance had reached out only a couple of days earlier and asked if he would like to meet Bill Pepper. He knew who Pepper was and thought they were soliciting monetary support for the Tea Party. Walters could not believe the fantastic story Pepper told upon his arrival and he agreed to today's meeting out of curiosity. His son Connor had made the arrangements and continued to tell his father that the men on the phone sounded very serious. Now that the one and only George Washington was before him, he was truly a believer.

Walters humbly placed his service before the first president, even quoting Nathan Hale when he stated that he regretted that he had but one life to give for his country.

Mr. Washington, leaned forward in his chair, and put his hands on the donor's hands.

"That is right Mr. Walters. Approximately 240 years ago a group of men pushed aside their egos and, for the most part, their identities, for their country. These were men of great character, foresight and patriotic devotion. And they are commonly known as our nation's founding fathers. You are one of us."

With tears in his eyes, Frank reminded the first president that he and his family had been paid handsomely for his patriotic gesture. Mr. Washington waved the statement off and said that the money was inconsequential when looking at the whole picture.

The conversation turned to personal issues as Mr. Washington asked the donor to tell him about his upbringing and background. As his father began talking, Connor entered the room with two big folders, filled with his dad's personal records. Mr. Washington took the folders in his arms, snuck a peek inside and placed them at his feet. He knew he had time later to sift through the paperwork enclosed. But at this moment, the General preferred to hear Walters tell his life story face-to-face.

The next hour was filled with great stories and laughter as the men hit it off. Mr. Washington felt very comfortable with his new friend and the feeling was mutual. Connor came into the room a couple times during the meeting to bring coffee, clean the nightstand and give his father medicine. Frank and George were so engrossed in conversation that they did not even notice him.

After ninety minutes, Walters was tired. His eyes were glassy and he struggled to keep his focus. He needed rest and Mr. Washington realized this. He stood up and pulled the covers up toward his friend's upper body. As Mr. Washington leaned over, Walters reached up and cupped his neck with his right hand. He mustered enough energy to pull himself toward the great man.

"The office of the president today has lost so much respect in the eyes of Americans. Whereas in your day, it was revered and held up to a higher standard. Bring that respect back."

Mr. Washington's eyes were now glassy, not from tiredness but from emotion. The man next to him was imploring him to bring the country back to where it once was. He put his right hand on the nape of Walters' neck. Mr. Washington said to him, "Remember always that the duty of our leaders was and is to follow the Constitution. The individual in the office of president is less important than the office itself."

Walters reached up with both arms and pulled Mr. Washington in for a hug.

"Mr. Washington, I will treasure this meeting always."

Mr. Washington tightened his hug, then pulled back from the embrace and looked the donor squarely in the eye. Mr. Washington spoke firmly. "Please call me Frank. My name is Frank Walters and I am honored to carry your name."

He gently helped Walters lie back down on the bed and made sure he was propped up and comfortable. Tears ran down Frank's cheeks as he let go of his grip on George's hand. Mr. Washington reached down and picked up the two folders as he backed away from the bed and walked toward the door. Each man gave a nod and a wave as the first president headed down the hallway and into the kitchen.

Connor sat in the living room as Mr. Washington entered. He stood at attention as George approached. He put his big hand on Connor's shoulder describing his respect for Connor's father and his pride in bearing his name.

The son welled up at this statement. He was visibly in awe of the father of our country standing before him in his own living room. He explained that his father had his doubts at first, but as soon as he realized the seriousness of the plan, he was in one hundred percent. He then asked if he could get the first president another cup of coffee or something to eat, to which Mr. Washington politely declined. He then moved to the credenza which had many framed pictures on top. As he gazed from one to another, he remarked at his uncanny resemblance to Walters.

"Mr. Pepper and his supporters do their job very well, don't you think?"

He turned back to face Connor. The young man was impressive himself, standing nearly six foot three and handsome. He was one person that could address the first president at eye level. Mr. Washington sensed that besides looks, he possessed many of the same character traits as his father. He now placed his hands on both of the young man's shoulders.

"Mr. Walters, I have agreed to take your father's name. In doing so, I now take you as my son. From this point on, I am Frank Walters and you are my son Connor Walters. If we are to accomplish all that we have set out to do, there will be no deviation from that, do you understand?"

Connor nodded in agreement. Mr. Washington cautioned about the tough road ahead filled with scrutinization in the press and on television. He explained that Providence has brought them together and they had to stay strong. The doorbell interrupted the pep talk. However, Mr. Washington kept his grip.

"I have always been a good judge of character. I look at you and I see your father, an honorable man. You have my full faith and trust, son."

While Connor was slightly taken aback by the "son" comment, he was overcome with a sense of comfort hearing the words. He was at ease and accepting of his new role and Mr. Washington sensed it. He released his hold and turned to open the front door.

Murray stood at the front door and asked if everything was okay. Mr. Washington looked to his side at Connor.

"Everything is fine. I'm ready. It would be prudent to get back home. We have a lot of work ahead of us. Connor, we will be in contact with you. Thank you for a most memorable morning."

The two men shook hands and embraced. Mr. Washington then walked past Murray and up the walkway to the waiting car. Pepper and Hahn were in the backseat talking amongst themselves. Mr. Washington took a seat, followed by Murray, and the door closed. He put the two folders on the seat next to him.

The street was almost desolate. Not a single person in sight. Pepper took notice of this and mentioned that he was pleased. He turned to Mr. Washington.

"Everything go smoothly, Mr. President?"

The General had been looking back at the house from which he had just emerged and turned his head toward Pepper.

"My name is now Frank Walters and you will address me as such. Frank Walters, candidate for President of these United States."

Hahn looked at his leader's expression and knew instantly that there was no turning back.

"Game on, gentlemen."

Chapter 18

Two weeks of platform and campaign preparation went by in a blur. The amount of effort and sweat spent building this campaign for president was well worth it. Even a seasoned veteran like Rader had to admit that these "novices" had put together one hell of a political platform. He felt as confident as he ever had with more experienced politicians. Rader deduced that it was the man himself that caused this effect. There was something special about this man that he could not put his finger on. But there was no doubt that Mr. Walters had that mythical "it" that people spoke about.

Murray watched as Rader quietly reviewed the updated events calendar. The team went about collecting their belongings and readied themselves for their trips home. The plan devised was to introduce their candidate on a local radio show in Charlottesville and follow it up with Josh Anders' national show a day later. The plan hinged on positive feedback on the local show, a prospect that gave everybody a hint of worry. Murray noted that the only person that did not seem nervous was Mr. Walters.

As he eavesdropped on Anders and Hahn's conversation from the kitchen, he noticed a focused Tim Jenson walk past the doorway and up the staircase toward his bedroom.

Jenson had just finished packing to go to Charlottesville. Like Murray, he had not been home in the two weeks since the July 4th weekend. Tim couldn't wait to get back to his familiar bed and day job. Still, he sat on the edge of his bed, staring wistfully at the lush lawn overlooking the Potomac. He realized that the most eventful, incredible fortnight of his life was coming to a close.

"Fortnight." Funny, Jenson thought. Now he was even thinking in "George Washington" language. It was very clear to all the men that the candidate, now referred to as Mr. Frank Walters, had rubbed off on them as much as the team had on him. Jenson could not help but notice how his confidence grew over these two short weeks. He realized it was his new mentor who had shown him how to "tell it like it is" and defend his beliefs. As a radio host, he knew how to stick to his guns while talking to strangers on the air. But the master instilled in the team the belief that their constitutional views were exactly right and that they would never need to apologize for their conservative opinions. He would never again back down to anyone in politics.

Neither would the other new founders. This was a big step for modern conservatives, who always appeared to be on the defensive, absurdly apologizing for what was right. Hell, thought Tim, we even had a former president who apologized for conservatism in his official campaign pitch; "Compassionate" Conservative. Those days were over.

While Murray was heading to Charlottesville with Walters and Jenson, he would not be going home. He hoped to at least see his wife and son while in town but it was not to be. Dottie had texted him that she was going to a tournament in Blacksburg with Todd's baseball team. Some of the parents rented a few hotel rooms and she thought it would be a good idea to stay with Todd for the few days there. She promised to call from the road.

Over the previous week, Murray had thrown himself headlong into the campaign with twenty hour days and had not talked much to Dottie or Todd. He felt detached but exhilarated by his new calling and surrogate family. Walters was at times an arrogant and a demanding task master who did not always appreciate Murray's contributions. But to Murray, the prize was so monumental that he willingly overlooked the thankless long hours and time away from his family, at least for now. He even applied for a leave of absence from school to stay with the campaign if need be.

He may have alienated his family, but Murray was in for the long haul. Besides, Dottie never had a problem speaking her mind. If she was not pleased, she had not said anything and he was not about to poke that bear.

His thoughts were interrupted by the dull thumping and a quick shout of a fast approaching horseman.

Smiling widely, Murray caught the image of a mythical hero on the back of beautiful white horse.

Murray couldn't contain his emotions. He choked back tears as General George Washington rode again in a full sprint past the secluded house. Murray looked on in awe as George, now "Frank Walters," disappeared around the far end of the house.

He kept telling himself that this was why he was here. The history teacher could not believe how privileged he was to be a part of all this. He did not dare ask where it would end, but he knew that as the twenty-first century Madison, fate would have great things in store for him. He couldn't look too far into the future however. The next few days and weeks were as far as he could venture.

Murray didn't know exactly where all this was heading, but he was going to see it through to whatever the end would be. He did know, however, that his next step would be monumental. Skip Keaton, Jenson's producer, was on his way to pick them up. The team had decided to test Walters' political savvy and erudition by unveiling him the following day on Tim Jenson's local radio show in Charlottesville.

Tim's station had begun promos for Monday's show touting his exclusive interview with the so-called Lincoln Continental during which his identity would be revealed. It was time the public got to meet Walters but they had to be sure his identity would be air tight. The General had devoured the personal life history of the former Frank Walters with the same zeal in which he studied the political topics of the day. They were ready.

If all went well as expected during the hour with Tim, Walters would board Pepper's' private jet to Boston for a national spot with Anders on Tuesday. The men hoped and expected Frank Walters' campaign to take off from there.

Murray watched Walters expertly dismount his fine horse. Keaton had just arrived. It was time to go.

Throughout the numerous internal debates and discussions with the new founders over the last two weeks, Walters had become an expert on matters of foreign and domestic policy. Understanding the nature of humanity as he did, he didn't have far to go. The last two weeks had confirmed to Walters, what the new founders innately knew and proved.

Times may change but people don't.

Aside from the catchy phrases the team agreed on, most of the education needed in preparing George for public discourse revolved around twenty-first century facts and, most importantly, twenty-first century dialect. At the team's urging, the candidate watched a lot of television and practiced his new words and phrases to master modern day English. However, he did revert to more classical speech at times, giving him a scholarly edge. But the team knew that would get old fast. Their new leader could get away with the Queen's English during a speech, but not an interview, something of which everybody involved was keenly aware.

But that wasn't the main concern this day. The biggest challenge for Walters was keeping to the script of his new identity. The General was now Frank Walters of Arnold, Maryland.

Chapter 19

Keaton had the studio ready when candidate Walters and new founder Murray arrived. Jenson had arrived a half hour earlier than normal to prepare for his show. He paced the studio as Walters walked in for the much anticipated interview. Murray stayed behind the glass with Keaton while Jenson prepped the father of our country. After a few minutes, it was show time.

"Hello, this is Tim Jenson, and welcome to the *TJ Show*. We've been away for a couple of weeks on vacation but I think you will agree, today's show will more than make up for it. We have an exclusive today. The so-called Lincoln Continental is here, in the studio live. For those of you who may have left the planet over the last couple of weeks, this gentleman created quite a political stir with his rousing speech on the steps of the Lincoln Memorial. He will reveal his identity and more for the first time. So let's get right into it."

Tim pulled his handwritten notes from his shirt sleeve. He began by asking Walters his name and to please tell the audience about himself.

"My name is Frank Walters and I am a patriot. Always have been...."

He kept to the script. He was a 63 year old from Maryland and owned his own very successful import/export business. Always keeping a keen eye on conservative politics, he felt the times were more dire than ever before and that the change promised was hollow. So he decided to enter the political fray. He thought coming out on the steps of the Lincoln Memorial most appropriate because he was emancipating himself, leaving the metaphoric shackles of his silence behind. He was a strict constructionist and a student of the founders. Walters explained that virtually all the issues facing today's United States had been foreseen and addressed by the founders.

Walters understood that our future would be secured by our past.

Jenson decided to get the conversation going.

"I place the economy as among the most important virtues of our republic and public debt as the greatest of dangers to be feared. How would you deal with the issue of the national debt and taxes?"

Mr. Walters explained without hesitation that Federal spending was out of control and needed to be reduced by the elimination of entire departments such as Energy, HUD, Education, EPA, and Agriculture.

He was highly concerned that the country's credit rating would be downgraded again, which would cause its debt to offer a much higher yield that may lead to default. Walters proposed the introduction of a consumption tax that would broaden the tax base, require the elimination of the IRS, and repeal the Sixteenth Amendment that created federal income tax.

He went on to explain that a consumption tax had been supported by Alexander Hamilton over 225 years before and by famed economist Arthur Laffer in the 1970s. He reminded the listeners that Laffer was the man to whom President Reagan based so much of his successful economic policy called Reaganomics.

Walters quoted Hamilton for effect:

"It is a signal advantage of taxes on articles of consumption that they contain in their own nature a security against excess. They prescribe their own limit; which cannot be exceeded without defeating the end proposed – that is an extension of the revenue…If duties are too high, they lessen the consumption; the collection is eluded; and the product to the treasury is not so great as when they are confined within proper and moderate bounds."

In other words, explained Walters, you had to keep the consumption tax low enough or it would stifle spending and actually reduce tax revenue.

Walters went on to say that James Madison agreed with Hamilton and thus Walters, when he wrote that taxes on consumption were always least burdensome, because they were least felt, and were borne too by those who were both willing and able to pay them.

Mr. Walters was on a roll and Jenson was more than happy to let the past and potential president explain to the greater Charlottesville area his economic plan: A proposed fifteen percent national sales tax but only under the condition that the Sixteenth Amendment, which authorized the federal income tax, be repealed.

"We would have to repeal the Sixteenth Amendment to avoid the double jeopardy of implementing a new source of tax revenue with the existing tax."

Jenson couldn't hide his pleasure and it was obvious the men behind the glass were having trouble doing the same. Murray was joined by Pepper and the surprise return of Steve Anders. Steve's appearance seemed to motivate Walters as he hammered away on the current administration's economic failures. Jenson noticed that each man smiled ear to ear like Cheshire cats. He began his next question.

"I often wish we could take the power of borrowing away from the federal government. Understanding that an amendment to the Constitution eliminating the power of the government to borrow is very unlikely, how would you deal with the catastrophic spending in Washington?"

Walters explained that the founders also struggled with this issue.

Like a storyteller, he told how Madison believed that a public debt was a public curse while Hamilton didn't quite agree, saying that a national debt, if not excessive, would be a national blessing.

Jenson interrupted Walters' reply, stating that they could not let the country's rulers load us with perpetual debt.

"Agreed, Tim. I am not saying that. Permanent funds are indispensable, but they ought to be of such a nature and so moderated in their amount as never to be inconvenient."

Jenson knew he was over the top in stating that government should not have the power to borrow. But he also understood that government knew no moderation and should behave like a private household.

Jenson channeled Jefferson by noting that the same prudence which in private life forbade paying our own money for unexplained projects also forbade it in the dispensation of public monies.

"Or in other words, spending for the sake of spending on these "shovel ready projects" is total BS and is destroying our economy, credit, ability to defend ourselves and our children's futures."

Walters recognized the passage and reflected for a moment before replying. He reiterated his belief in the fifteen percent consumption tax, coupled with the repeal of the Sixteenth Amendment. He also explained that America needed to eliminate unconstitutional spending by using federal credit as sparingly as possible.

"If we don't take control soon, we'll end up like some poor third world country without a currency to call our own."

The interview seemed to be going quite well as the phone lines lit up. It was time for the first commercial break. Jenson and Murray sat staring at each other through the glass in quiet awe of their new boss's command of the issues. But to Walters, these were not new issues. They were the same he had faced almost 240 years before, just with more zeroes.

Jenson wanted Walters to take a few calls. This would be the first time the General was directly exposed to the people and Tim thought the next few minutes may make or break their incredible experiment.

Walters seemed calm and ready as the host took his first call.

"Mr. Walters, this is Roy from Richmond. You seem like you know a lot but please tell me how you'd address the economy as it relates to national security. You know, illegal immigrants, nukes, and terrorists."

The candidate began by saying that our national security was inextricably connected to the economy. "Clearly these uncontrollable deficits must be halted and eliminated or we as a nation may not have the economic power to project our strength and battle our enemies."

Walters went on to say that these were dangerous times. Countries like Iran and North Korea continued to create and test nuclear weapons while threatening allies like Israel and South Korea with annihilation. He explained that now was not the time to weaken our military like the current president proposed.

Walters reminded the audience that the United States, during the Reagan presidency, defeated the Soviet Union by bankrupting them. He then warned that the same fate could await the United States if we were to allow government to control the economy and weaken our military while spending us into oblivion.

Jenson seconded Walters' argument, describing Reagan's doctrine of peace through strength as the way to avoid war instead of promoting it.

Walters added how that philosophy differed from that of our current president, who kicked off his presidency with an apology tour of the Middle East and most recently, his apology for an inadvertent burning of Korans by the US military in Afghanistan.

"As foretold by the founders, the request for forgiveness only increased the violence toward America, resulting in the murders of brave American service men. Like any predator, when our enemies smell blood, they attack."

Jenson and the new founders behind the glass realized that their man was certainly up to date on current events. They liked their candidate on the attack and pumped their fists in approval.

Walters concluded the thought with a quote. "Someone said many years ago that you should speak softly and carry a big stick. Peace through strength is one of the most effectual means of preserving peace."

As he waited for the next call, Walters remembered his discussions about illegal immigration with the team. They explained to him that there were millions of people in our country illegally taking jobs from the American people. He was stunned to hear they incredibly collect billions of dollars in benefits such as free health care, welfare, and other unimaginable freebies, all from a society going broke and supporting illegals at the expense of its citizenry.

More calls followed, leading up to the next commercial break. The flavor of each was purely basic political questions and local residences goading him to get in the race now. He deftly handled each with clarity and humbleness that seemed to endear him to Jenson's faithful following. As he fielded question after question, he continued gathering his thoughts on the immigration topic.

During the prep work, the team also explained to Walters that the country now had sanctuary cities where law enforcement could not question immigration status much less arrest illegal aliens. He could only look down and shake his head when he learned that certain states that began enforcing immigration laws along the Mexican border were actually being sued by the federal government to stop enforcing the law.

One of the Justice Departments arguments in the suit was that border control was the jurisdiction of the federal government and not the states. Washington could not believe his ears upon hearing this twisted argument. The federal government, who will NOT enforce the law, was suing those enforcing it because they (the federal government) would not fulfill their admitted obligation.

Washington was sick to his stomach as he wondered if he had returned to a different time or a completely different world than he had left over 200 years before; a world with different logic and values than his eighteenth century America. While those doubts filled his brain he also knew that this would be his one opportunity to make things right again. He was determined to make the most of his second chance.

He knew humanity and that while times may have changed, the nature of man did not. Therefore he knew there was something else at play here. He quickly inferred that his opposition was buying votes by using the security and rights of American Citizens as their currency.

The second caller following the commercial broached the immigration issue once again. On cue, Frank Walters climbed upon his soapbox.

"James Madison asked why immigration is desirable. He asked if it was merely to swell the catalogue of people? No. He concluded, 'Tis to increase the wealth and strength of the community, and those who acquire the rights of citizenship. Without adding to the strength or wealth of the community, are not the people we are in want of.'"

He decided to clarify the answer to his own question by detailing that the phrase "Not merely to swell the catalogue of people" was a prediction that the left wing establishment in the country would continue to push for amnesty and citizenship to illegal aliens, creating a larger liberal voting block.

Walters continued, hitting the point hard by saying that the United States was founded by those who immigrated in search of liberty, men and women who craved the freedom to succeed and even to fail based on their own abilities without government intrusion.

"That is my vision for America. The founders believed then as I believe now, that America would be open to receive not only the wealthy but the oppressed and persecuted of all nations and religions."

Walters paused for an instant and continued his thought by emphasizing they would only be welcome if their decency and conduct warranted it.

Pepper and Anders were gesturing through the glass, trying to get Jenson's attention to cut the interview short. They wanted to save some topics for the *Josh Anders Show*.

Walters took the sign and concluded by saying he would increase the border patrol presence and end so-called sanctuary cities. The "yes" emanating from Skip Keaton's mouth was audible to the radio audience. Jenson thought they had accomplished what they set out to do in an introductory interview and decided to end it here.

"I know you have to go Mr. Walters, so we will end here. Thank you for your time, your foresight, and your patriotism. We hope to have you back soon."

Washington replied that it was a pleasure, and that he would visit again as his schedule allowed. He wished the radio audience a good afternoon. As soon as the on air light went off, the candidate turned to his host.

"That was quite fun, Mr. Jenson. Can't wait to do that again."

Chapter 20

The General calmly removed his headset and placed it on the table next to the microphone before him. He was happy with the result of the interview. Though he would have liked to get into more topics and detail, he understood the wisdom in cutting off a few minutes too soon, which was better than a few minutes too late. Looking to his right through the studio glass, he observed Pepper, and was pleased to see Steve Anders talking away on his cell phone again.

Steve was back alright. He and his cousin only seemed to extract those devices from their ears long enough to stare into them and push keys. Walters wondered what could be so important for a man to talk in such a way all the time. His experience with non-stop talkers was normally limited to eighteenth century women and a few select politicians. But as long as things were moving ahead and on plan, the new Mr. Walters decided Steve and Josh could talk all they wanted.

Murray immediately entered the studio and congratulated Washington on a great interview. As they shook hands, Murray reminded him that given the feedback and success of the recently concluded show, they would be embarking on a trip to Boston to appear on the *Josh Anders Show* the next day. Walters appeared reassured after Murray told him Steve had returned to accompany them to Boston. The first president asked if the clouds and birds might get in the way of the "aeroplane" as he pronounced it. Murray provided Washington with some comfort by explaining that the flight would only take two hours and that the Pepper jet would feel very much like the drive in a limo, only more luxurious.

Jenson stood and, turning toward Mr. Walters, reiterated to Murray and the team that he would not make the trip to Boston due to the workload in the weeks ahead and some personal matters that needed his attention. He would assuredly be meeting the team over the next few weeks. After a hearty embrace and a most sincere thank you, Murray led Walters into the waiting area where Pepper and Anders reported a sizable crowd gathered outside the studio. Against his wishes, Pepper convinced Murray and the unnanounced candidate to exit into the limo waiting at the rear of the building.

Steve Anders kept an eye on his ever present iPad during the ten minute ride north up Route 29 to Charlottesville Albemarle Airport. He reported that the *TJ Show*'s website was alive with hundreds of comments about the interview. Murray commented wryly that he didn't think Jenson had that many listeners.

The vast majority of comments enthusiastically supported Walters for his principled views, remarking that Walters expressed conservative values in those few moments better than any politician since Reagan.

All signs pointed to the beginning of a groundswell and it seemed as if the listeners might finally have their candidate. Endless months of campaigning without a Republican candidate sealing the deal had the people starving for a direct, clear, and articulate man like Frank Walters. Now they had him and the excited comments proved that Walters' message resonated.

Ironically, even the negative reviews were positive. Steve smiled as he read one comment after another, accusing Walters of being racist and xenophobic. He knew that Walters struck a nerve in this college town and that meant that the liberal establishment took him very seriously. It was all good.

Washington blushed but wanted to hear everything as Anders playfully read him some of the very forward proposals from local women. Eighteenth century men were not accustomed to certain twenty-first century women.

Finally, the General leaned back and allowed himself a brief smile.

"My friends, Divine Providence is with us. People were drawn to us today and you must have faith that it will continue and the numbers will grow even greater. Please embrace it and do not dare doubt its power for there is a destiny which has control of our actions, not to be resisted by the strongest efforts of human nature."

The words had no sooner left his mouth than the limo pulled up next to the Gulf Stream and it finally hit Walters that he was about to take flight.

For the first time, Walters seemed nervous. Fidgeting with his pen and scribbling on his notes, he absently asked once again what the flight would be like, and obviously having done a calculation or two, how it felt for one's body to fly at over 300 miles per hour.

He boarded and was led to a plush window seat on the left side of the plane. The first president was seated no more than five seconds before Anders poured a brandy for the uncomfortable candidate to calm his nerves. Walters let out a thankful sigh as he sank into the luxurious leather chair.

The flight went without a hitch as Walters, relaxing with a second glass of brandy, peered out the window with breathless wonder; first for the miracle of flight that he never imagined he would experience, but mostly for the absolute beauty sliding beneath his 37,000 foot perch above the shoreline of the magnificent country's east coast.

Following a smooth landing at Logan Airport, the group quickly exited to a waiting limo and, like clockwork, was whisked away to Josh Anders's home studio in the Boston suburb of Weston.

Walters was a bit surprised to find Rader at the door as he stepped into the Anders mansion. After exchanging pleasantries, Hahn and Josh Anders pulled him to the side reiterating that Rader did not know and did not need to know Walters's true identity. They then moved to the parlor where the candidate was introduced to Josh's much better half. Gail Anders was fully engaged in the goings on and was enthralled to meet the General.

The team began prepping him for the nationally syndicated interview scheduled for noon the following day. Walters remained characteristically unfazed as Anders explained that he generally did not have guests on his show. Because of that, he wanted to make sure that his new mentor knew right away that it would be a special broadcast.

Anders followed his bravado by stating that because of the Lincoln Memorial sensation and the hype coming off the Jenson interview, tomorrow's show would likely generate the largest audience in the twenty five year history of the *Josh Anders Show*, well above the 15 to 20 million daily listeners.

Anders laid out the plan for the interview.

"The first thing we do is introduce him as Frank Walters, a self made, independently wealthy, successful entrepreneur and philanthropist."

They would start with foreign policy, move to regulation, including PresidentCare and wrap up with religion. The second hour's plan was more risky because they planned on taking phone calls from listeners. The old pro Josh Anders let them know that those calls just went with the territory. He was confident that if Walters could win over a college town, he would have a lot of friends in Josh's audience.

Walters commented that that was the best way to get the word out to the people, by addressing their direct concerns and questions. He added that he felt the need to touch on the economy once more, even briefly. The team concurred and relaxed for the rest of the evening with their hosts.

—•—

Murray was not sleeping well again. He was an habitual insomniac but chalked it up to impatience in bettering his station in life. He had needed something more, maybe something inspirational. But now that he found what he knew to be his true calling, he still stared at the dark ceiling. He didn't have Dottie by his side nor did he know where she and Todd were most of the past week.

Everybody else had made it home. Even the General got back to Mt. Vernon for a couple of weeks. Was it Murray's personality that compelled him to stay? Or was this providential set of events more important to him than the others, maybe even more important than Murray's own family? Dottie's texts and calls had become less frequent over the past week. What was she up to? And what was that personal business Jenson spoke about? His whole life was the radio show, so what could he need to attend to?

Murray tossed and turned as more thoughts raced through his head. He finally told himself he was tired and that his mind was playing tricks on him. Anyway, breakfast was in a few hours and then the final prep work for the show. He needed to get some rest for the busy day ahead.

During breakfast, Murray explained the concept of anchor babies and the Supreme Court's footnote in a 1982 ruling that children born in the United States, even borne of illegal aliens or visitors, were automatically United States Citizens.

"The 14th Amendment was adopted after the Civil War to overrule the Supreme Court's Dred Scott decision, that black slaves were not citizens of the United States. The amendment was designed to stop southern states from withholding citizenship from recently freed slaves."

He noted to an intrigued Mr. Walters that it provided that all persons born or naturalized in the United States, and subject to the jurisdiction thereof, were citizens of the United States and of the State wherein they resided.

—•—

"The drafter of the 14th Amendment had no intention of conferring citizenship on the children of aliens who happened to be born in the U.S.

'This will not, of course, include persons born in the United States who are foreigners, aliens, or those who belong to the families of ambassadors or foreign ministers.'"

Walters, nearly choking on his toast, replied that it was certainly not the intention of the framers either to confer citizenship on anyone who happened to be born here. A relieved Murray said he always suspected that was the case.

With prep work complete, the host and guest entered the home studio. Anders started the show by thanking Frank Walters for agreeing to the interview. He continued on, describing Frank's entrepreneurial background and finally the scene at the Lincoln Memorial and the subsequent internet sensation that propelled Frank to national prominence.

After Walters thanked him for the kind introduction, Anders asked the obvious first question.

"Why now, Mr. Walters? Why did you stand up at that moment in time? And why the Lincoln Memorial?"

Walters replied as he had done with Jenson the previous day. Like many Americans, he felt it was time to speak up, publicly express his love of America, and explain how he believed that the founding principles would show us the way back to prosperity.

He had long been a student of history and had been thinking along those lines for some time.

"On that particular morning, while on vacation in DC, I went to church and somehow felt drawn to the Lincoln Memorial. When I read the Second Inaugural and Gettysburg Address, this oratory came out of me in an 'inspired spontaneity.'"

Anders winked at the team behind the glass and smiled. It was time for the first foreign policy question.

"Over the last three plus years of this presidency, the United States seems to have embraced our adversaries and enemies through gimmicks like a "Reset Button" with the Russians, apologies to Islamo-Fascists, support of radical groups in places like Egypt and Libya, while at the same time, throwing an old ally like Mubarak to the wolves. We have insulted our British friends, and worse, have sided with Iran over Israel in its right to defend itself. If you were president, Mr. Walters, how would you conduct foreign policy?"

Walters began, framing the foreign policy of the United States since its independence by invoking President George Washington's famous warning to avoid foreign entanglements for good reason. He quoted the father of our country by stating that in revolutionary times as in present day, every nation was out for its best interest. And Washington, like the founders in general, believed that the United States should not join in any permanent alliances.

Walters wowed Anders and the audience by paraphrasing Thomas Jefferson's ardent desire to keep the United States free from political connections while maintaining peace, commerce, and honest friendship with all nations.

"Remember, at the end of the eighteenth century, the United States was still recovering from the Revolutionary War and could not afford to be dragged into another European War, so the powers that be, avoided these political entanglements."

Murray liked what he heard. He was especially pleased when Walters described that both Adams and Jefferson, following Washington's lead, continued the same neutrality policy with Britain and France, the two superpowers of the day. He loved that Walters had fastidiously studied American history since the revolution. But he sensed that his boss was about to expand upon his response in a twenty-first century way.

"We are in the second decade of the new century. The world is a much smaller place than it was in 1776. We need some alliances but we need to choose them wisely. I'm disgusted by the current administration's strange dismissal of our English brethren."

Walters was shocked upon hearing that his likely presidential adversary actually returned to England the bust of Winston Churchill, the man who set the tone of strength for the free world during World War II. Walters needed the pulpit at this moment.

Having framed the situation, he hit the point that with all due respect to the founders, today's world was much too threatening for the United States to retreat to its shores. Walters believed in continuing Reagan's policy of entering into temporary arrangements as necessary to promote our prosperity while keeping "permanent" allies in Britain, North America, and Israel.

Anders was so engrossed in the words coming from his guest that he did not realize that Mr. Walters had stood in the studio to address the millions of listeners.

"Alexander Hamilton had a great concept of rewarding friends and punishing enemies. His bottom line was to trade with friends and withhold trade from adversaries. If you want to trade with the United States, the rules have to be the same both ways, it's that simple."

Walters singled out China as being a poor trading partner for America because of their government protectionism and devaluation of the Yuan. This encouraged our government to devalue the dollar, leading to inflation, oil price increases, and a lack of confidence in the United States.

The New Founders

"If I was president, I would get tough with China and make sure we are on the same playing field."

Anders stood and interrupted. "But how? They hold so much of our debt. They own us."

Walters, always seeing the opportunity in a situation, explained that China owning our debt actually gave us leverage to some degree. He said that should America decide to continue the dilution of the dollar, we would erode the value of US debt China holds.

Anders referred back to Walters' comment on Russia and quoted Madison's observation over 200 years before that.

"Russia seems at present the great bugbear of the European politicians on the land. What is your view on the great bugbear as Madison so eloquently described?"

Understanding the history of the Russian Bear, Walters stressed that an administration should treat Russia very firmly and there could be no repeat of the pathetic "Reset" button gimmick this amateurish current administration employed in their early days. He would never have congratulated the Russian president on winning his recent election (as the current president did), but called for an investigation into many allegations of fraud.

Walters, seeing Josh's producer's continuous text messages on the screen before him, sensed the first commercial break was fast approaching. He once again fixed his eyes on Hahn outside the studio.

"There are universal truths at play here, Mr. Anders. Like Newton's laws of physics, they do not change. So therefore I quote the Isaac Newtons of American history when I say that no government could give us tranquility and happiness at home if they did not possess sufficient stability and strength to make us respectable abroad."

The guest paced the studio, entangling the cord on his headset around Josh's seat. Josh tried to straighten the wires but to no avail. Walters, not even noticing the disruption, got tough.

"Make no mistake, Mr. Anders. It has been our station since our founding, and that there is a rank due to the United States among nations which will be withheld, if not absolutely lost, by the reputation of weakness. And weakness, my friends, will not happen during my presidency."

During the commercial break, Walters stoically sipped on his water as Anders untangled the headset and checked his website for immediate feedback. Anders asked him if he realized he may have just inadvertently announced his candidacy, to which Walters replied that he used those words with great calculation.

The team was more pumped than ever. There was no turning back now.

It was time to take some calls. But before any calls, Anders had to ask the million dollar question and he had to ask it on the air. Anders began.

"Welcome back to the best show on the radio. My, we have quite a guest here and the switchboard is starting to smoke from all the calls. Before we take the first call, I want to clarify something you said Mr. Walters, before the break. "

"Yes?"

"Have you just announced your intention to run for President of the United States?"

"Yes, Mr. Anders and to your audience, I did. I plan to run for president and quite directly, I expect to win."

"You heard it here, ladies and gentleman. Mr. Frank Walters has announced on the *Josh Anders Show* that he is running for President of the United States!"

The first call came from Fred in Lynchburg, Virginia regarding the effect of regulation and PresidentCare on the businesses in the area.

Walters began his answer to Fred on the PresidentCare issue by first explaining that while it would certainly destroy private healthcare in this country, PresidentCare law was not about health at all. It was about the Federal Government dictating to the people what they could and could not purchase and could and could not do. It was a power grab directed at the rights and lives of the people.

The new candidate described his frustration that the PresidentCare mandate was one of the most transformative pieces of legislation in our history and was pushed through a lame duck session of congress and House of Representatives even though most if not all had not even read it.

Frank was outraged that that those who defended the legislation were falsely relying on the Commerce Clause in the Constitution.

"Had the founders intended for a government to attain the power to compel citizens to buy or sell goods, they certainly would have clearly defined so. However, it is abundantly clear that our government never intended to have that kind of power. That was the whole point. As Mr. Madison so clearly documented in the 10th Amendment, 'Powers not delegated to the United States by the Constitution, nor prohibited by it to the States, are reserved to the States respectively, or to the people.'"

Walters kept his train of thought by explaining that the government had already unconstitutionally mandated that citizens buy only certain items—for example, light bulbs, showers, and toilets. The federal C.A.F.E. standards had already compelled auto makers to build only cars meeting certain government standards.

Anders jumped in and told a story relayed to him by a friend in the financial services industry where his bank recently refurbished a new office. In order to receive financial favors from the government under a green certification, the federal government mandated the size and height of the desks, cubicles, and even the pantry.

"Can you imagine? Government bureaucrat regulators in Washington DC dictate at this level to private industry under threat of penalty?"

Anders relayed another story from that same friend about a recent regulation compelling financial institutions to record and transmit cost basis information from investor to investor and to the IRS. The law makers had little or no concern about the incompatibility of their new mandates, or the stresses and millions of dollars in financial impact these rules had on investors and the industries compelled to implement them.

Anders considered adding that the founders must be rolling in their graves, but after a quick glance at his guest, thought better of it.

As Anders explained these financial intricacies, Walters politely listened.

Like Madison, Walters understood that men were not perfect and because of that, there was a certain need for laws and regulation. He deduced correctly that reasonable men understood that if people were angels, no government would be necessary. And if angels were to govern them, neither external nor internal controls on government would be necessary.

"We must understand when it comes to regulation that it is the regulators who gain from the regulation, not their fellow citizens who suffer to live by them. Seems the old adage is true, that laws are made for the few, not for the many."

Walters shot up out of his seat once again. Anders followed suit and rose with the now official candidate for president. Walters wrapped up the point.

"A founding father once said, 'I own myself the friend to a very free system of commerce, and hold it as a truth, that commercial shackles are generally unjust, oppressive and impolitic—it is also a truth, that if industry and labor are left to take their own course, they will generally be directed to those objects which are the most productive, and this in a more certain and direct manner than the wisdom of the most enlightened legislature could point out.'"

Murray frowned from behind the glass, a bit perturbed that James Madison was not referred to by name. As he peered into the studio, Walters translated this passage into modern language, saying that while bureaucrats in government who pretend to be all knowing impose regulation on industry and people under some fantasy of fairness, the constraints of regulation were generally unjust and oppressive because they hit the most productive people the hardest.

The next call came from Jerry in California.

"Mr. Walters, do you have any original thoughts of your own or are you going to sit there and quote a bunch of dead guys all day? I mean come on, this is the twenty-first century, not the seventeen hundreds."

Josh's first instinct was to protect his guest and move on to the next call. But Walters would have none of that. He sat back down in his seat and, taking a more serious tone, pulled the microphone toward his face.

"Jerry, you have a point. This is the twenty-first century and times have changed. But a good idea then is a good idea now. Just as a bad idea then is a bad idea now. I quote the founders because they built a great country out of nothing. They put laws in place and put a Constitution in place that has stood the test of time and remains the cornerstone of the greatest country on earth."

Josh Anders reclined in his chair as the man to his right let loose.

"How about bad ideas, Jerry? Encouraging illegal aliens to come into our country and appeasing them, is that a good idea?

"Is pressing one for Spanish and two for English on your phone a good or bad idea?

"Is socialism a good idea, Jerry? Redistribution of wealth and the political policies of the current administration? How did that turn out in the Soviet Union?

"I quote the founders because they were men of character, men of dignity, who put their country before their own individual well being. Wouldn't you like to see a politician with those qualities in the twenty-first century Jerry?"

The caller had hung up during Walters' lecture. Anders said there was always at least one of them every day.

"We have time for one last call."

Kathleen in New Jersey wanted to know what Walters thought about recent demeaning remarks about women in our country. Frank cleared his throat and got ready to answer. But Kathleen added that in 1776, Abigail Adams wrote, in her most famous letter to her husband, John, in Philadelphia, the new code of laws (which the founders were in the process of creating), to remember the ladies and be more generous and favorable to them than their ancestors.

Frank knew of the letter and said that he hoped Jerry was still listening since he had not quoted a founder. His caller actually had. This elicited laughter behind the glass. He answered the caller by noting that he was troubled by recent events.

"I think you ladies are in the number of the best patriots America can boast. I will not allow such treatment of American Patriots. And by the way, I am very impressed by your knowledge of one of our founding women. Abigail Adams was a pioneer of her generation, much like the many patriotic women of today."

Walters smiled and offered a slight giggle, subconsciously, but openly flirting with the caller. He mouthed to Josh that she sounded attractive.

"At the risk of putting the entire male population in an unfavorable light, I'll add that I would never put such unlimited power in the hands of only husbands. Remember, all men would be tyrants if they could. And we cannot let that happen, now can we?"

At that point, both Frank and the lady caller laughed together.

Gail Anders quietly applauded to herself, listening to Walters use the words of her heroine, Abigail Adams.

Anders was mesmerized by Walters' mastery of history, policy and connection to the people as they went to another commercial break. While he was pleased with the show to that point, the General was not. He felt as if the last forty five minutes was a one on one conversation with Josh and he needed to talk to the people. Anders respectfully disagreed, but to no avail.

The remainder of the show would involve interaction between the father of the country and the populace which went by in a flash. Frank Walters was in his element and at his best in direct dialogue with the people. He loved every minute of it, even though Josh seemed uncomfortable ceding his show to the candidate. But Anders knew his audience had just been schooled by the most powerful figure in American history and sensed the excitement was building.

Knowing the interview was ending, Walters asked Josh if he could sum up his interview with a quote from a fellow Bostonian, President John Adams. The guest mentioned that it had been forty minutes since he last quoted a founder, so he thought it was as good a time as any.

"The safety and prosperity of nations ultimately and essentially depend on the protection and blessing of Almighty God; and the national acknowledgement of this truth is not only an indispensable duty, which the people owe to Him, but a duty whose natural influence is favorable to the promotion of that morality and piety, without which social happiness cannot exist, nor the blessings of a free government be enjoyed."

Anders announced that they were out of time and thanked Walters for his truly amazing interview and his blockbuster presidential announcement.

Mr. Walters asked for a few more seconds. Josh agreed and the candidate once again rose to his feet as if before a multitude of onlookers.

"I love this country. And understand by loving the country, by definition, I love its people. After all, what is a country if not the sum of its people? Americans have the same genetics as all other humans. So what has caused our country to become such a success while other countries failed?

Walters closed his eyes as if visualizing his words.

"The answer is that the civil society we established allows and expects the best from each of us. Each of us in turn offers our best, knowing that we as individuals and society as a whole will benefit. I see a current in America today that punishes, derides and deflates our tide of greatness; lowering our expectations and leaving the ship of our society stuck in a quagmire of rocks and mud.

"When we release the anchor of this current presidency, like a great ship, our society will once again elevate on the tide of our individual achievement. Individual achievement leads to societal greatness. That, my friends, is my American Message. Thank you and God bless."

Anders leaned in while reaching for the control panel.

"Ladies and gentlemen, I can add nothing more. Thanks for listening folks. Good day."

Chapter 21

As he became accustomed to doing on the talk show circuit, Mr. Walters removed his headphones and placed them gently on the control panel. He leaned toward Josh to shake his hand, complimenting him on a job well done. They both felt the interview went well. The candidate was about to find out how well.

"I believe we touched the American people today. Men and women were calling from sea to shining sea."

Steve Anders laughed and quietly whispered to Murray that Walters did resemble Kate Smith when the light hit him just right. Looking straight ahead, Murray mentioned that Ms. Smith had a smaller nose.

"Your radio signal is far stronger than Mr. Jenson's, wouldn't you say, Mr. Anders?"

Josh quickly explained how radio simulcasting worked; that his show aired across the nation by way of individual radio stations that signed an agreement with the Josh Anders Network. Josh's words were abruptly interrupted by his producer's voice through the studio intercom. He informed Josh that the switchboard blew a fuse toward the end of the segment from the overload of callers.

He also relayed that everybody at the Boston flagship station, including upper management, was looking for Walters.

"I think a couple of big wigs may be on their way out to your house!"

He then yielded the phone to the president of the radio station in Boston, who repeated the news that the circuits had overloaded, and added that every top advertiser and many new prospects had called to ask for time on the next show with Walters. The station head then asked if he could speak to Frank directly. Josh told him he was already on the intercom.

By now, the rest of the team had entered the studio with Josh's wife, Gail. All congratulated the guest as Walters tried to focus on the words emanating from the speaker overhead.

Murray stood off to the side, impressed by Frank's poise and confidence, given Frank was in the middle of one personality trying to talk over the other. He asked for quiet as he tried to listen to the head honcho's words to Walters.

"Mr. Walters, you are the real deal, the candidate for president we've all been waiting for."

The first president thanked him for his kind words and support. He said it was always good to know that he had such support in the great city of Boston. He ended the conversation to the applause of the team. As he put his hands up, showing his humility, Pepper entered the studio holding his cell phone up.

"Mr. Walters, I have a phone call for you. It is Connor Walters."

The General immediately took the call and turned his back on the team. He only spoke for a few minutes outside of earshot of the other men. He deliberately spoke softly to keep the conversation as private as possible. When he finished, he flipped the phone closed like any twenty-first century man would do. He insured that the microphones in the room were dead before addressing the team.

"Mr. Walters' son and I spoke. His father tried to listen to the show but has taken a turn for the worse and may not survive the night. He was lucid enough to listen to the beginning, and told his son that he could die a happy man, knowing that he contributed a small part to the betterment of our country."

Murray noticed for the first time since their encounter in Philadelphia, that a small tear appeared at the edge of the General's left cheek. Murray was relieved to find out that the General was at least partly human, but was still not sure if Washington was real flesh and blood. He had seen sorrowful emotion, but he had yet to see any outward sign of physical injury or pain.

Washington asked the group to offer a prayer for Connor's father. The people in the room bowed their heads in silent prayer.

Amen still hung in the air as Steve Anders interrupted the touching moment with some good news from his ubiquitous iPad.

The blogs on Josh's website were already hundreds strong and growing. The response was overwhelming. For every negative comment, there were a hundred vowing support and their votes. People were already asking how they can donate to the campaign!

The team was fired up as the phones rang off the hook. Even the *Drudge Report* instantaneously linked to the story about the man who intended on challenging the Republican candidates and the incumbent president. But the one man who remained stoic was the General.

He sat back in his chair, contemplating the news just told to him. Josh Anders mentioned it to him. Pepper brought it up. Steve Anders all but confirmed it but now it was reality. The first president, a man who served two terms running this great nation, and the first modern leader to voluntarily abdicate power, rather than seek an additional term , had begun his campaign for a third term. And there was no turning back.

The General thought to himself once again that he had never originally campaigned for the job. He was virtually appointed president the first time and was unanimously elected for the second term without much of a fuss. But now he was in for a fight. And not the fight he was accustomed to, with cannons and gunpowder, wartime strategy and taking hills and bluffs. This would be a battle of words, ideas, policy, and desire.

Once he realized this, his apprehension eased and his confidence grew once more. His core values were second to none and he feared no man when it came to a debate geared toward the good of the country. He again stood at attention and addressed his cabinet of the minute.

"Guys, we've had a very successful day today. You've all done great so far, but there is a lot of work ahead and only a little time in which to accomplish it. But right now while we have the rest of the day free, I would like to travel to Boston and see this great city again. I read in one of Mr. Jenson's books that there is such a thing as the Freedom Trail tour, a walking tour of some of the historic sights of the city? Might we partake in that?"

Murray smiled noting that Walters reverted back at times, but sounded more like a twenty-first century man since he assumed the Frank Walters identity. Josh thought the tour of Boston was a great idea and asked Murray and Hahn if they could take Mr. Walters to see the sights. He would supply them with the limousine and a credit card. Hahn scoffed at the credit card, stating emphatically that money was no object to him and that he would handle all expenses.

Murray was actually fine with going to Boston on Josh's dime, not wanting to shell out anything for expenses if he didn't have to. He thought back to his days in junior high school when he tried to fit in with the popular rich kids, pretending to keep up with their spending habits.

Josh was not up for another debate with Hahn. He gave them a wave of his hand, saying Steve and Pepper would stay back and plan the candidate's week ahead. This statement pushed Murray and Hahn's buttons, but they both felt time alone with Walters would ease the tension. So they gave each other a look and left without further comment.

The car pulled up to Boston Common within sixty minutes of the show's end. Few people noticed the three men leaving the luxury car. Walters leaned in and told the driver to meet the group in Charlestown near Bunker Hill in two hours. Murray and Hahn were surprised at the order, given that each man had never walked the tour themselves. As they looked at their leader, he addressed them.

"The book said that the tour can be completed in two hours if briskly walking. Let's get going."

The asthmatic Murray and younger Hahn had trouble keeping up with the General's long strides and fast gait. Hahn thought that Walters must have worked out the last two days in the hotel gym as he watched his older and smaller colleague try to keep pace. Given his stature and short legs, the Virginian needed to double time his walk just to keep up with the candidate.

Having covered the Boston Common and Statehouse as they received a personal history lesson from the man most qualified to give it, the men halted at the Granary Burial Ground cemetery. Walters paused at the entrance.

"This is the final resting place of some great men. Let's pay them their due respect."

Walters pointed out the gravesites of John Hancock, Thomas Paine and none other than Samuel Adams himself.

He described Sam Adams as a great man, a deeply religious man who came from a family of maltsters. He portrayed the less famous Adams as a man who fought endlessly against taxation without representation.

Murray thought he knew everything about the founders. Hahn thought he knew everything about everything. But in only a few minutes, Walters taught them that long before anybody poured tea in the harbor, Sam Adams was the driving force behind protesting the Stamp Act and the Townshend Acts, movements which opposed British taxation of both printed material in the colonies and imported goods from the British Empire.

"The latter led to the British occupation of Boston and along with the Tea Party, a precursor to the Revolutionary War. Onward, men."

Murray and Hahn were floored. Each knew about the Boston Tea Party but was less informed regarding the other acts. Murray leaned in to whisper to his younger teammate. "Can't wait to see what's next."

"When's he gonna show us where Cheers is so we could meet Sam Adams and Sam Malone? I could use a beer."

Hahn got a laugh from Murray but Walters continued on as if he said nothing.

After traversing through a few of the less notable highlights of the tour, they came upon the site of the Boston Massacre, now State Street. It was time for the two new founders' next history lesson.

"Tensions were high during the British occupation. It came to a head right here, the exact spot where the Boston Massacre took place."

Again both men knew of the massacre but not of the detail as the General did. Murray asked Walters to elaborate.

"Redcoats stood guard in the wake of the Stamp Act, trying to quell any potential riots. It came to a head and shots were fired. Five men lost their lives and Sam Adams arranged for funerals in their honor. Let's move on."

Faneuil Hall and Paul Revere's house followed and the men came upon the Old North Church. Again, Washington paused to pay umbrage. "This is the Christ Church, the tallest church steeple of its day. The Sons of Liberty warned the citizenry about the British invasion. Paul Revere told Robert Newman to hang two lanterns in the steeple to alert the populace that the British were approaching by sea. Then Revere and William Dawes rode the countryside warning all of the impending British invasion and start of the revolution. We continue."

This history professor was all business. Murray and Hahn looked at each other and shrugged.

"You ever hear of Robert Newman or William Dawes?"

Hahn shook his head again joking that the only Newman he knew was a mailman in New York City.

The tour had become a lesson beyond their wildest imagination. The three men continued on across the bridge spanning the Charlestown River. A small group of tourists had fallen in line behind them, listening in on the stranger's description of each site. He might as well have been a tour guide for all they knew.

The men paused for a brief moment. Walters looked up at the obelisk, memorializing the battle of Bunker Hill. He took a deep breath and then continued on his march up the hill. His quick stride caught the new founders off guard and they hurried to catch up.

Upon reaching the statue, Walters decided it was a good time to address the small crowd of approximately twenty people that stood within earshot.

"We could have won this battle. We should have won this battle. We exhausted our armaments and had no choice but to surrender. It was a defeat —but a victory in the long run. The British lost a thousand soldiers and many officers. The battle gave the American war effort resolve and proved we could stand toe to toe with the supposedly superior British army."

One spectator in the crowd yelled the famous quote that is long remembered from the battle. Walters responded with vigor.

"Yes, Yes! As Colonial William Prescott ordered, 'Do not fire until you see the whites of their eyes!' The men knew their firepower was depleted, yet they fought on. This was America at its very best and we were only in our infancy.

"General Nathanael Greene put it best when he wrote that he wished he could sell them another hill at the same price! This is the message we have to get out right now. We may have lost this early battle, but we ended up winning the war!"

Another voice cried out from the right side of the growing crowd, recognizing the speaker as Mr. Walters from the *Josh Anders Show*.

Walters looked directly at the young lady and decided to make the most of the opening.

"Yes. I am Frank Walters and I seek the presidency of these United States."

The crowd erupted in spontaneous applause. Murray looked at Hahn as if to say, "Here we go again." Neither expected the Freedom Trail Tour to turn into a campaign rally but forces were at work and they went with the flow.

"This country is in the midst of a modern day Battle of Bunker Hill, against an opponent who out-number us in resources, out-number us in influence in the press, and out-number us in influence in the media. But they do not out-number us in resolve or intellect or the truth. They will not out-number us in patriotism and love of this country and they will surely not out-number us in the will to fight for what is right and just!"

The crowd had grown to nearly a hundred and the candidate purposely whipped them into a frenzy.

"June 17, 1775 was a dangerous time in our young country. Well, our country is still young, my friends, and it is still a dangerous time. Government is not reason, it is not eloquence, it is a force! Like fire, it is a dangerous servant and a fearful master. Never for a moment should it be left to the irresponsible action of the administration in charge at this very moment, men who do not have the interests of you fine Americans in its heart. Government is not the solution. Government is the problem."

Murray again looked at Hahn. Hahn looked back and mouthed that they were witnessing history in the making.

"We are one with the original Continental Army. Discipline is the soul of an army. It makes small numbers formidable as the British found out during the Revolutionary War!

"As your president, in executing the duties of the office, I can promise nothing but purity of intentions, and, in carrying these into effect, fidelity and diligence. I thank you and God bless you all."

The crowd lurched forward and rushed toward the candidate. Murray and Hahn tried to shield Walters from the oncoming throng, but to no avail. Within seconds, he was surrounded by well-wishers and people touched by his words. A chant of "Walters!" began and delighted the General.

Hahn whispered in Walters' ear that it was time to go. He had trouble getting the first president to move as Walters quickly became accustomed to signing autographs and posing for pictures.

The limo sat at the bottom of Bunker Hill and the two men used all their power to clear a path toward it. Mr. Walters was now outside of the friendly mob when he turned to face the people applauding on higher ground.

"My fellow Americans, do not forget that every post is honorable in which a man can serve his country. I compel each of you to spread the word and join with me in our fight for independence from our current administration. My fellow patriots, I thank you all!"

With a friendly wave, Walters walked to the waiting car. Hahn and Murray followed. The three men disappeared behind the tinted glass as the car sped away.

Chapter 22

The inner voices had been relatively merciful on William Fredericks since the Lincoln Continental emerged on the steps of the Memorial. They ordered Fredericks to confront, expose, and publicly humiliate this political interloper, tasks that were nothing new to Fredericks. He had made his bones and a handsome living doing these exact kinds of things.

Now he simply had to have Mr. Frank Walters as a guest on his show. He wanted the first shot at delving into this newcomer to expose him as the unqualified bloviator he knew him to be. Josh Anders was the first to have the man on a national radio show but Fredericks had to be the first to get him on national television. The problem, it seemed, was that Fredericks would have to go through Anders himself to get him. The talk show host always made William Fredericks nervous. But this time would be different. In Fredericks' eyes, he was as qualified as anybody to grill the new candidate.

Fredericks prided himself on being the privileged son to an upper crust London family. He claimed his ancestry directly to the eighteenth century British Royal family. The roots of such a claim were dubious. And given his confidence that the American media would never question this assertion, he proudly stuck to it.

Will suffered from a hereditary disease that caused, among other things, blisters, severe stomach cramps, and periodic mental disturbances. He was loathe to admit the existence of the late night voices—"Them" as he privately referred to the demons. But it was clear from a young age that Fredericks had issues. His father, a respected barrister, and his mother, the daughter of a member of the House of Lords, recognized Fredericks' problems and like any good upper class English family, dealt with them by sending Fredericks to the finest boarding schools in Switzerland. He was popular in school for all the wrong reasons. Considered too spindly to compete in his favorite sport rugby, Fredericks turned to fencing, making the college club's first team. Even so, he had no real friends until he met fellow fencer Sophia during his third year at Oxford.

Fredericks was immediately taken by Sophia's piercing violet eyes that seemed to see into him, see what others could not, to understand him. She didn't glimpse the madness, but instead the goodness in his soul. When he was around her, the demons retreated. She kept him from those dreadful nights of screams, orders and howls in his mind.

Knowing he could not survive without her, Fredericks married Sophia immediately upon his return from his mission on the destroyer HMS Sheffield during the Falklands War. Fredericks nearly lost his life along with twenty of his shipmates when the Sheffield sunk after being hit with a French made Argentine missile. Fredericks spent several terrifying days in the Atlantic and developed, among other things, an irrational fear of the water.

Through a family contact, Fredericks landed a job reporting politics with the WNN London affiliate. Within the year, he applied for a stint in America, hoping to escape his demons.

Fredericks and Sophia arrived in Los Angeles in September of 1984, the proud parents of a little boy. Fredericks' first assignment was covering the Reagan reelection from the president's ranch in Santa Barbara. As with many of his life experiences, he felt the assignment was beneath him.

Fredericks eventually moved the family back East to host WNN's day-time political talk show out of New York. He built his reputation by lambasting conservatives and Republicans. Soon thereafter, Fredericks was named host of WNN's New York City based morning show in 2000. This assignment lasted only three years as his erratic behavior and disheveled appearance in the studio, set off alarm bells within WNN.

He was live on the air the morning of 9/11/01 when the planes hit the World Trade Center and Pentagon. He reported the facts that day and for months after in a strangely detached, almost robotic fashion, displaying no outrage. It was as if he felt the attacks were somehow justified. Even through the many memorial services he attended, his disturbed colleagues at WNN only saw him shed a tear or show emotion once, when he described the youngest of the 9/11 victims, beautiful two and a half year old Christine Lee Hanson.

A move back to the west coast and a new assignment calmed his life. His personal life and career benefitted as the ratings showed. But he wanted a higher profile job and pushed management until WNN finally relented, naming Fredericks the new host of their flagship political talk show based in Washington DC.

Fredericks knew the move to DC without Sophia was wrought with landmines but his never ending ambition made him go. Unfortunately, the voices in his head also demanded he go and while she stayed behind in LA with the kids, the demons accompanied him to DC.

Fredericks excelled in the nation's capital. He was on his game and managed to book the cream of the crop within Washington political circles, finance, entertainment, and even the sports world. It was evident that the more contentious he became, the more the audience grew and paradoxically, the easier it became to book his guests. Everyone wanted to be heard and seen by as many people as they could. No such thing as bad publicity.

But something else was troubling Fredericks this July morning. Recently, he began to question which side was evil, those with him or those against. During these fleeting moments of clear self-reflection, before the sinister synapses of his brain kicked back in, he actually lamented his admiration for the American people. After all, it was the bravery, ingenuity, and generosity of the Yanks that helped deliver England from the Nazis. He knew in his heart what they could and would achieve if they were left free of demagoguery and government interference. He had reservations about his overall view of the world.

There was no time for self-doubt now. Fredericks had just finished listening to Frank Walters for a third time; this time on the Anders show, and he knew his moment of truth had arrived. The Anders' appearance topped both his speech at the Memorial and his spot on that local Virginia radio show. Fredericks' clever Lincoln Continental nickname was even obsolete now that the world knew the man's name.

Walters used founding principles as his candidacy platform, becoming the darling of conservative blogs and pundits everywhere. Fredericks was repulsed by the thought, telling himself he had to take this man down. He had never come across a man like this before. Unlike most conservatives who immediately fell into apology mode when pressed on the issues, an unapologetic Walters seemed astonishingly comfortable with his positions.

Walters differed from other candidates in that he had a deep understanding of the Constitution and a grasp of the day's issues. His verbatim recall of the American Founders' positions and an uncannily clear ability to articulate each was impressive. To top it off, he also had Josh Anders and the Tea Party on his side. All those factors made Fredericks uncharacteristically cautious about confronting Mr. Walters.

The voices compelled Fredericks to confront and destroy this enemy. He sensed a moral clarity in Walters that he had yet to confront in the politics of the day. Recent skepticism about his life-long statist positions, brought on by the reality of the current government, caused Fredericks concern that he may not be able to take down Mr. Walters head on. But he must and there was only one way to do it.

Fredericks smiled. "I would love to have him on my show," he thought. Fredericks quickly called his "people" who had undoubtedly already begun extensive "background checks" on Mr. Walters. His next call went to his producer. He directed him to invite this mysterious candidate to make his television debut the following night on *The World Today*.

Fredericks' blood went cold once again when his producer informed him that not ten minutes before, Ken Rader of the Walters' campaign had called Fredericks requesting he do his first television interview on *The World Today*.

He couldn't believe a guy as well-known as Rader would take up with this virtual unknown. Fredericks scratched his head, muttering to himself that this Walters guy was certainly not your run of the mill conservative. Anyone requesting a confrontation in the lion's den must plan to bring along a weapon or two. Fredericks was nervous. He certainly needed to prepare for this formidable foe.

Chapter 23

Frank Walters sat on the oversized brown leather sofa in Josh Anders' study, reflecting on the day's events. It was a successful day by any measure. The interview with Anders was getting plenty of "airplay" and "positive tweets." Walters was not sure what those were. He could ask, but decided not to bother since he understood what positive reaction meant. And that was good enough. Plus his team seemed to be pleased.

There was no stopping him now. Providence had seen to that. Still, he wondered why he continued to feel a bit uneasy. He loved his second chance at life, but seeing the tombstones of old friends in Boston made him wonder again if he really belonged here. The obvious answer was that he did not. He knew how America used to be and he knew how America should be in the future. But he did not know her in the present day. Sure he learned quickly and understood the issues, but George Washington did not share the same life experiences as today's Americans. Hell, he thought, he had never been alone with a twenty-first century woman or even driven a car.

But he was here now, had a job to do, and was determined to see it through. He knew this second life could not last forever, but he just didn't know how or when it would end. Soldier that he was, he decided that if he was going to be in the fight, fight he would.

After a few tumultuous moments earlier with Rader, the candidate had convinced his campaign manager to set up his interview on *The World Today* with that Fredericks fellow. Rader preferred Frank's first TV spot be in a friendlier setting, but Walters, in his words, insisted he first vanquish the serpent in its own lair and be done with it. Besides, the General saw something in Fredericks' eyes that reminded him of someone from his past; someone he vowed to defeat.

Josh Anders was apoplectic. He was on the phone with Jenson as the new candidate confidently walked into Josh's kitchen with Ken Rader at his side. Jenson had just seen a promo for Walters' interview on cable and called Anders to find out what was going on.

Josh could not control himself. Putting his iPhone on speaker, he demanded of Rader an explanation as to why he booked Mr. Walters on *The World Today*. Josh was careful to conceal Walters' true identity as he decried to Ken that he may have jeopardized the entire candidacy by being so irresponsible.

Mr. Walters smiled and, putting his left arm around Anders' shoulder, calmly explained his reasoning. Murray and Hahn had entered the room, curious to see what all the fighting was about. Their leader quickly calmed the situation.

"Josh, it was not Mr. Rader who insisted on the interview, it was me. Gentlemen, will you excuse us for a moment?"

Walters quietly led Anders away from Rader and the other men and into the backyard. He kept his left arm on Anders' shoulder the entire time.

"Josh, with your volcanic temper you are so much like your predecessor, Mr. Adams. It brings me reassurance that Providence remains with us. In you I see its wondrous works and the uncertainty of things human…. In today's language, don't worry, Josh. Have some faith."

Anders smiled and looked sheepishly at Walters. He nodded his head in agreement, his internal fire extinguished for now.

"We've come this far George. I know I shouldn't doubt you, but this is different. You do not know William Fredericks like I know him. The guy is an anti-American mouthpiece for the Democratic Party that spews nothing but hate. Are you sure you know what you are doing?"

Murray and Hahn joined Walters and Anders on the back lawn as the first president answered Josh's question.

"There is nothing so likely to produce peace as to be well prepared to meet an enemy. I feel well prepared to meet this enemy and intend to slay this dragon first."

As was his custom, Washington let his words sink in for full effect on his men.

"And besides, my dear Mr. Anders, I believe I know Mr. Fredericks a lot better than you could ever imagine. May we leave tomorrow morning on that fantastic airplane for the interview with Mr. Fredericks in our nation's capital?"

So it was decided. Candidate for president, Frank Walters would enter the lion's den the following evening on national television.

Like heavyweight contenders, Fredericks and Walters prepared for their duel. Walters went over last minute notes with his most trusted advisor, Hahn. Both saw the irony in considering the interview a "duel." Deemed illegal in the eighteenth century, armed duels were euphemistically termed "interviews" to avoid attention from authorities. The most famous of these types of interviews was the duel in which Vice-President Aaron Burr shot and killed Alexander Hamilton on the cliffs of Weehawken, NJ. Hahn vowed not to let history repeat itself this night.

Walters was ushered to the set where the host was already seated. As he took his seat, the guest extended his hand to Fredericks for a salutary greeting. The host shook his hand quickly without uttering a word. He reviewed his notes on the desk before him as Walters sat calmly under the bright lights. The candidate made a mental note that the host's hand was soft and layered with perspiration. He looked toward Hahn in the wings and mouthed a few words to him.

"We got him."

After welcoming his audience to the show and describing the lineup, Fredericks decided that raising questions about Walters' background would be a good start. The interview began.

"So Mr. Walters, you have come out of nowhere to become the Tea Party candidate for President of the United States and have chosen to make your national television debut on *The World Today*."

"Yes. Thank you for having me, Mr. Fredericks. I must admit the advice of my team was to sit down with another host, but I felt drawn to your show."

Walters leaned in toward Fredericks and focused his eyes into William's. Fredericks was unnerved for that moment. Random thoughts coursed feverously though his brain. Pleasant visions of a fox hunt through the pristine rolling hills of rural England jumped at once to dire feelings of pain and dread. Uncertainty swirled in the pit of his stomach. He had these kinds of flashbacks before, but always in the dead of night when They showed up.

He could feel a drip of sweat on his brow as the stoic man next to him seemed to peer into his soul. Fredericks appeared to accept his guest's compliment and settled himself by adjusting his glasses and taking a sip of his Evian water.

"Candidate Walters, who are you?"

"I am Frank Walters, a man who believes in our great America, its people, its traditions and institutions."

"No, Mr. Walters. Who are you? A few weeks ago, no one ever heard of Frank Walters. Now you are a household name, running for president with the so-called Tea Party. According to an overnight poll, right now you would win over twenty-five percent of the Republican vote, sixty percent of the conservatives and astonishingly close to fifty percent of the vote against our seated president."

Almost frothing from the mouth, Fredericks went on. "How is this happening? We really know nothing about your background?"

Walters smiled easily. He turned, looking in earnest into the camera.

"I suppose I am a man who says what I mean and that just happens to be what the people feel in their hearts and minds. It's really rather simple in words, but much more extreme in deeds."

Fredericks came right back at him. "But a higher percentage of the general population would vote for you over any single Republican candidate out there. The polls even say you would get a higher vote total from minorities and women. How do you factor that?"

Walters wanted to scold his host right there but took the high road. He smiled, like a father to his son. "Mr. Fredericks, I suggest you stop categorizing Americans as you do. The results of your precious survey reveal that Americans are not groups, but individuals, with their own individual views and values. They should not be thought of as blocks, but blokes if you will. I believe sir that you answered your first question with your latter one."

Fredericks visibly recoiled. Sensing he was losing his edge as the conductor of the interview, he immediately upped the rhetoric.

"Mr. Walters, you have a resume of running your own businesses, including one that imported dangerous chemicals and high tech surveying equipment that has subsequently been banned by the EPA for fouling our environment. You have become a wealthy man on the backs of non-union labor and have attempted to keep union workers out of your businesses. On top of that you have a very sketchy public record, virtually no political record, aside from four years on your local school board. How do you expect to become President of the United States and further, how do you expect to be an effective Chief Executive with such a light resume and public record?"

Walters once again maintained his cool.

"Thank you, Mr. Fredericks. You flatter me by pointing out so many virtues." Walters halted his statement and smiled. He looked for physical feedback from his host and William did not disappoint as he appeared confused. "You have revealed much about yourself, Mr. Fredericks. As

Thomas Jefferson pointed out, 'Let those flatter who fear. It is not an American art.'"

Hahn, who had joined Rader in the "green room," burst out laughing. "Holy cow, Ken, can you believe him? I hope he is not being too aggressive."

Rader thought the same thing and prayed Frank would get back to his message and not be taken off his game by the slick Fredericks. Mr. Walters did indeed return to his message describing his strong record as a Chief Executive in the private sector where he created jobs and pushed for innovation. He followed by detailing his two tours in Vietnam and remarking that he was proud of his service to family, country, employees, and his Creator. "It is the service to my family and my God that I most cherish. For when we raise the level of our families, so do we raise the level of our society. And to raise the level of our society is to honor our Creator—the source of our natural rights."

William was visibly frustrated, but composed himself as he called for a commercial break.

Walters quickly exited the studio as the break began. Josh's crash course in television presentation proved invaluable, especially the warning about the odd powder that would most likely be applied to his nose and forehead. He had advised Walters to think before speaking and address his adversary in a clear voice.

He also gave Walters two old tricks taught to him years before; to look into the camera when addressing the people and avoid any small talk with Fredericks. Live microphones were dangerous and Mr. Walters was taking no chances.

As the second segment began, Fredericks looked for a one punch knockout.

"Mr. Walters, you are obviously a very skilled politician. You have managed to avoid the questions, so I will put it to you most clearly. There are people who say you are not who you claim to be. You came from nowhere. There are even precious few photos of you during the last few years. Once again, Mr. Walters, who are you? Are you a fraud?"

Hahn shot a look of shock at Rader who didn't comprehend the reason for the alarm in Hahn's face. If he was bothered by the question, Mr. Walters did not show it.

"William, let's be frank. We agreed to participate on your show and were told by your producer that we would discuss my policy ideas as candidate for president. But you have ignored politics altogether and directed your line of questioning toward my person. If you feel more comfortable doing so, so be it."

He knew that addressing his host as William was disrespectful and he made a mental note to try to avoid that in the future except under special circumstances. Walters had been tested by far more confrontational and direct questioners before, most of which had been in his own administration. The host before him offered no such challenge.

Once again, Walters penetrated William's familiar eyes, eyes that offered a window into who this gentleman really was. Walters felt he knew this hostile and terse individual from many years earlier. But after a few minutes of back and forth dialogue, he finally understood that his initial impression of William Fredericks was correct. He had gazed on an image of those eyes before. Putting his revelation aside, he continued.

"I understand your thoughts, Mr. Fredericks. I would find it most disconcerting as well to swear in a president who may not be of the identity he claims; where little proof of his lineage exists. Such a fellow would be a danger to these states and the people. Even a hint of impropriety would be worthy of further intensive investigation, especially with all the resources you and your media colleagues have at your disposal. I am sure you would agree, William."

He had called him William again but by this point it was inconsequential. Walters was now in charge, and his subordinate on the studio set was going to listen to him. It was at this moment that the first president had his own epiphany that members of his new inner circle may have already suspected.

"Fortunately, Mr. Fredericks you and the people of this great land need not have any such concerns about my intentions."

Though William didn't understand why, he felt an odd connection to Mr. Walters. While he continued the direct questioning for the remainder of the half hour segment, sprinkling in political issues, Fredericks backed off his snarling intensity.

As the segment concluded, the host thanked his guest for appearing on the show. Fredericks and Walters offered one another a respectful handshake and Walters stood, looked down upon his still seated counterpart, and marched off set.

As Frank moved toward Murray, Hahn, and Rader, they noticed something slightly different in their leader. Maybe, Rader thought, it was a sense of relief from getting through the interview. But the perceptive Murray was not so sure and had his suspicions as the four men exited toward the elevator.

Chapter 24

Ken Rader, Bill Pepper, and Steve Anders were back at their Potomac headquarters near Mount Vernon planning their candidate's barnstorming tour around the United States. The whirlwind ahead would span the month leading up to the Republican convention. Rader's goal was to build Walters' popularity so that it would crescendo with the opening of the convention in Tampa.

Rader presented the plan to their leader. But Frank Walters had his own ideas.

Walters outlined his vision of an overall strategy in which they would plan their attack in week by week intervals. He explained that every general had a plan going into battle, but once shots were fired, most plans needed nimble revisions. The team devised a seven city, six day insurgency in which Walters would focus on Democratic strongholds. He knew that for the most part, conservative America would enthusiastically back him.

"Men, we need to go to the urban areas and to constituencies who do not know my message. We must focus on areas where misinformation and propaganda has thrived. There will be time for Tea Party meetings and rallies in the heartland from coast to coast. But right now, our focus needs to be on the less enlightened population."

A couple of the men looked down at their toes and chuckled as Steve Anders sheepishly mentioned that the first stop they planned was a Tea Party rally on the Boston Common. Walters paused, and then nodded his head.

"Boston is fine, a traditional Federalist, Democratic stronghold. But can we change the venue to one of the poorer sections, possibly South

The New Founders

Boston? Josh has told me much about his father's produce business in that neighborhood and the men and women that frequented his establishment. We need to be there."

Steve Anders was frustrated but assured the first president that he would do all he could to comply with his request. Within seconds, Anders was on his phone and out the door.

Rader quickly got Walters' attention when he laid out his new plan-for the trip, starting with Detroit, Chicago, and Madison, Wisconsin, three union centric cities that were virtual locks to carry any Democratic vote for president. Walters took note as the Builder's itinerary showed Las Vegas, San Francisco, and Los Angeles as the next stops. Rader explained that the trip could be taxing and the team would be short on sleep because of the cross country journey. Mr. Walters dismissed his concern. He looked forward to seeing the western expanse of the nation and meeting its people.

"I've slept long enough in my life. Where to next after the city of angels?"

Rader outlined a return flight cross country to Atlanta, then to Baltimore. He explained that the day after Baltimore, the group would rest and map out their next plan of attack. Walters again rebutted the idea of rest.

"Gentlemen, Baltimore is still close to the capital is it not?" Mr. Walters asked with a touch of sarcasm. "I would like to go back to Washington DC and speak there; not only among the great monuments, but in the urban areas among the people. We can plan the following week while we stand on our soapbox, don't you agree?"

——— —

Neither Ken Rader nor the rest of the team was about to disagree with the assertive candidate. He had exhibited the energy of a twenty year old on the Freedom Trail tour and the team was not about to doubt the man's drive at this point. Rader instructed the team to pack their things and head to the waiting cars outside their headquarters in Mount Vernon.

——— —

Though relatively lightly attended, the Boston Tea Party rally went off without a hitch. A small platform and dais had been set up in front of the elder Anders' produce market in South Boston. Candidate Walters addressed the assembly of well wishers and skeptics and held them glued to his every word for just short of an hour.

Joseph F. Connor & Michael S. Duncan

He spoke about the origins of the Tea Party and the events leading up to it. He hammered home the tyranny of taxation without representation, translating the rallying cry of 1773 into the modern day equivalent by noting that the people of South Boston saw their taxes increased as unemployment rose, hope diminished, cynicism grew, and public services declined. He stressed how the city of Boston was integral in the fight for freedom during the revolutionary times and how it could be integral now in the fight against government oppression.

Walters concluded with a story of how the Vietnam War had such a profound effect on the South Boston area. He spoke of the young men who were called to duty during the war, only to return to the neighborhood with missing arms, legs, and souls, if they were fortunate enough to make it back at all.

Instead of coming home to a hero's welcome, they were confronted with war protesters that shouted obscenities to their faces. Frank described an incident in which police tried to quell a protest, only to be attacked and provoked. He told how the protesters had pre-meditated the scene and had cameras at the ready as the police force used night sticks in their defense.

He again translated this story into modern day current events, outlining the left wing's use of war protesters like Patty Sheehan and schemes to buy votes in general elections. He reiterated that the people of Boston were too smart to fall for this once again, sparking the crowd into applause.

Walters finished by telling them that the police in the Vietnam incident had a guardian angel in a young lawyer that took the case when nobody wanted it, and ultimately exonerated the officers involved.

"And that lawyer was none other than the son of the man who owns this very establishment. And I know you know who he is!"

A chant of "Josh" rained down as the men left the dais.

The campaign was invigorated as the team took off for Detroit. There they visited an automobile factory which the candidate found fascinating, judging by the fact that the team went over their originally planned time schedule. The union workers were impressed by the quick witted and genuinely interested candidate. He then went directly into the heart of the city and gave a short speech in front of an abandoned building near downtown. He was disheartened by the lack of feedback and came down from his perch to talk with people one by one. This gesture won him favor with some of the Detroiters, although Walters left feeling unsure.

The New Founders

Next stop was the belly of the beast where Frank quickly snapped back with a successful visit to the Chicago Board of Trade and the Cabrini-Green projects. He warned residents of the Hog Butcher to the World that the current administration will not end its goal of controlling the people with PresidentCare, cautioning that it was only the beginning. He advised that in a second term they would set their sights on the food we eat and begin regulating production and distribution of the very sustenance of Americans.

"If you think they have power grabbed now, wait until they get a second term and go after your food."

The campaign continued in search of the illusive blue dog Democrats in Madison and managed to find a few during his speech in Veterans Memorial Park. Frank addressed the very public sector unions that had protested the current governor and his budget. Walters hoped to win over some of these Reagan Democrats who identified themselves as Americans first and Democratic Union labor second.

He emphasized the notion that public sector jobs, particularly teachers, police, and firefighters, were extraordinarily important to the betterment of our society, yet municipalities could no longer afford to pay for certain benefits and under-performing workers. He explained that public sector workers would be compensated appropriately according to market forces. Public servants would continue to enjoy long and meaningful careers serving society so long as the public could afford to pay them. The candidate concluded by emphasizing that if society suffered, so too would the workforce.

The team thought Walters presented a strong argument. It was, however, received with protests and less enthusiasm than the new founders would have liked. Still Frank was pleased with the message presented and expected he would win over some of those detractors.

Despite the mixed results in Madison, the team was energized for the long trip west. Frank was inspired by the breathtaking views of the beautiful country passing beneath the jet. He beamed with pride as he sang to himself the words to a song he had recently heard: "From the mountains, to the prairies, to the oceans white with foam, God Bless America, our home, sweet home." Then, the jet touched down at Las Vegas McCarran International Airport.

— ◆ —

Now they were rolling.

The team had just pulled off a major coup having their "rock star" candidate deliver a rousing version of his rising tide stump speech to an after-noon teamsters union convention in Vegas. Mr. Walters knocked it out of the park, yet again. Murray was beginning to think that it was Babe Ruth that had come back from the dead, not George Washington.

Murray was blown away thinking they now had members of the country's largest labor union aboard the SS Walters. Who would come on board next, the Wisconsin teachers union?

The Cafe Bellagio bar was rocking this early evening. Even though it was crowded, Murray and Hahn secured seats of honor at the corner of the bar facing the TV. The sights and activities of Vegas were famous and Murray enjoyed some of those leggy sights as they walked past the bar-stools.

Murray was relieved that Walters was back in the hotel room now, probably watching the History Channel or reruns of *American Idol*, his other favorite show. As a candidate for president, their boss was now under full secret service protection or professional sitters, as Murray called them.

"That one secret service agent Michelle, she's not bad. I saw the big guy eyeing her this morning. You think he's finally getting acquainted with a twenty-first century woman? You know how those secret service folks are these days."

The men smiled at Murray's comment and toasted the image of Walters' wicked ways.

Murray was just grateful the old man was not at the bar with them. He would most likely spoil the fun by barking orders and demanding every-one cater to his every whim.

Murray felt his BlackBerry vibrate again as he reached for his second Tanqueray and Tonic. Instinctively, he reached down and hit the off but-ton to stop the annoying vibration. He'd get to the call or text after another drink or two. It was probably Walters busting his chops or Dottie telling him where she'd been while he was away. Maybe it was Todd calling from one of his summer baseball tournaments. Regardless of what the message was, Murray told himself it could wait until he was done with a drink or two. Relaxation was the word of the moment.

Murray smiled and joked with Hahn while they ordered another round. It was the first time they had a chance to let down their hair since the first day at Mt. Vernon. And they took full advantage of it. The next set of drinks had just arrived when the Virginian pointed to the television over the bar tender's right shoulder. The TV might have been muted but there was no missing William Fredericks' familiar face.

As the cool hint of lime passed his lips and added to his pleasant buzz,

Murray noticed Fredericks was not wearing his usual arrogant smirk but instead a look of genuine grief. On the flat screen just to Fredericks' right was a video insert from a helicopter showing an overturned school bus that had obviously plunged over an embankment.

Murray asked the bartender to turn up the volume. Fredericks' voice revealed genuine horror as he talked about the tragic accident and possible fatalities of the teenagers aboard. He spoke of his own kids back in California and the pain he felt for the kids and families involved.

"Is that a tear I see on his cheek? The guy is human after all!" Hahn's comment got a good number of laughs.

Fredericks announced that he would personally spearhead the collection of donations and organize the volunteer corps in the Central Virginia area. He asked for his audience to pray for the families as he went to commercial.

The scroll across the screen read, "Live, HS baseball team school bus accident near Harrisonburg, Virginia."

Murray had his glass to his lips when the caption finally caught his attention. His heart stopped as he froze for what seemed like an eternity. He could not remember the schedule Dottie told him. Wasn't Todd headed to Washington, DC for a baseball tournament? He thought it was this week but could it have been today? Murray hated himself for not being able to think clearly. He just did not know.

Rader approached the duo as Hahn chatted with two women at the bar. Rader asked Murray if he was all right.

Suddenly, his phone vibrated again. Rader slapped Hahn on the shoulder, interrupting his romantic overtures. Both men saw the panic in Murray's face as he read Dottie's name on the display. He ran toward the door while he hit the green answer button.

"Hello Dottie. He was in the bus, wasn't he?"

Murray froze again. As he digested his wife's words, a million thoughts instantly passed through his mind.

"Oh my God, Dottie. Where are you? Yes, I'll talk to him and try to get there as soon as I can."

———

The Walters tour continued with his arrival in the Golden State, where Mr. Walters marveled at the beauty of the San Francisco terrain, the bay and the majestic bridges. He concluded that the people of northern California were very nice but a little odd. They did not seem to have the same level of intensity nor sense of urgency exuded by their East Coast brethren.

The tour continued to Los Angeles where Walters addressed a Baptist congregation in East LA. They finished the campaign stop with a tour of Universal Studios before a red-eye flight back across the country to Atlanta.

The flight back gave Washington time to ponder the campaign and evaluate the events to that point.

The trip lived up to expectations and had been deemed an overall success. But the news from Virginia had put a damper over the tail end of the journey. Walters was distressed over Todd Murray's accident. Murray had taken the news hard and Walters was sympathetic. Todd had been in a coma now for almost seventy-two hours since his head hit the side of the bus as it flipped over the highway guardrail. The baseball tournament at George Washington University was cancelled in light of the accident.

The first president stared out the airplane window, thinking back to how Jack Murray had burst into his hotel room that night, demanding to leave the campaign for his son's hospital bedside in Virginia. Walters reacted to Murray's demands with his typical stoicism, which angered the distraught father. Walters agreed that Murray should be with his family but still coerced Jack into completing the west coast trip.

The father of the country knew that in his day and age, over thirty five percent of children never made it to adulthood. He just didn't understand how twenty-first century medicine in America had changed that grim eighteenth century reality. As a result, he didn't really appreciate why a twenty-first century father would react as Jack Murray did; why he would want to leave the excitement of the campaign to lay vigil over his son's hospital bed. Walters decided wisely it was best to not verbalize his thoughts. Walters told Jack to continue on to LA and fly back to DC separately while the rest of the team headed for Atlanta.

Now, seventy-two hours later, Walters reflected on the way he manipulated Murray. The grieving father looked deflated the rest of the west coast swing as he constantly checked in with his wife. Walters was also perceptive enough to observe the fact that Murray was drained by the barrage of apologies and excuses he continued to give his wife. Each hourly call resulted in a frustrated man mumbling and venting to himself.

Walters knew Jack felt awful, yet he still pressured him into agreeing to rejoin the campaign within a couple of weeks, regardless of whether Todd was in or out of the hospital. The candidate deduced that he needed Murray and therefore had no qualms about his expectations.

He turned his attention back to the campaign trail. Crowds had grown larger and more enthusiastic with each day and the media continued its fascination with the Walters' campaign. The voracious reader that he was, the candidate read every newspaper and magazine that he could get his hands on. He also borrowed Hahn's iPad, something that had become habit over the previous weeks. Walters was somewhat embarrassed to discuss it with anyone and certainly not in front of Rader (who still did not know his true identity). But he believed the iPad must have been magic.

This was certainly a wondrous country. As flawed as it had become, it still infinitely exceeded his wildest expectations from the eighteenth century. Perhaps what was most fantastic to Walters was that, in this age of miracles, there were still so many Americans who valued freedom and would dedicate their lives to the liberty of others the way his generation did. Walters was grateful to Providence for providing him a second opportunity at this time in history.

Intrigued by the electronic media since his exposure to the wonders of Skype that very first day in Philadelphia, Walters focused on using the modern mediums to reach the populous. Even though he was not a fan of the policies he had read about from the 1930s and '40s, Walters borrowed an idea from FDR and recorded a library of "fireside chats" based on current issues. He and the team created five minute video briefs on issues from spending to defense, immigration to healthcare, and overall liberty. The videos posted on a new website, www.WeWinAmerica.com, which Rader created for the campaign. The series of chats went viral and donations poured in from across the country.

As the jet winged toward Atlanta, Hahn made his way to the seat next to Walters. He looked behind him to make sure the two men were alone.

"Mr. President, you should try to get some rest. Rader has a hell of an agenda for you tomorrow, morning to night. The room in the back of the plane is all yours."

Walters thanked him for his concern and assured him he was fine. He then asked his trusted adviser what he thought about the whole series of events to date.

"It's been a wild ride, that's for sure. You're getting to the people. Virtually every news report is carrying the same theme, that you are different. It doesn't matter if they're left or right, they all say that this candidate is different. They love that you don't pound your own chest. The conservative media is eating it up. And don't worry about Murray. You did the right thing."

The General leaned in close to Hahn and asked for more assurance that the team was going about all of this the right way. Hahn, always an opinion at the ready, gave it to his leader.

"You should just challenge the president to a debate and end all of this right now. No more campaigning, no more rhetoric, no more red-eye flights. I'm just venting. You're in the best hands possible with Rader and the team we've assembled. You have a lot of smart guys here and we're devoted to seeing this through, but I think it's time we end this thing. Let's beat this guy now."

Walters put his arm on Hahn's forearm, a gesture of thanks without saying a word. He handed the iPad back to Hahn and made his way for the bedroom at the rear of the aircraft, setting his sights on Atlanta.

The reports in the local Georgia newspapers focused on Walters' unwavering values. The slant of the mainstream liberal media viewed this as dangerous, a step backwards. They derided Walters and his followers and asked how America could move forward by taking the quotes, ideas and values of men that died two hundred years before.

In contrast, the more conservative television and radio talk show outlets relayed how a quickly growing populous now understood the founding principles that built Walters' platform. And the populous identified them as timeless values that would eventually lead us out of the dark ages of the current administration.

It was in Atlanta that the team got a welcome surprise. The current president finally acknowledged the Walters phenomenon by attacking Walters' platform in public. He scoffed at the notion that scrapping vast regulations such as PresidentCare in favor of the basic liberty expressed in our founding documents would help the people and the economy.

The team knew they had now reached critical mass and would soon be in the daily crosshairs of the president's attack machine. Rader assured the team and the candidate that coming to the attention of the White House was a positive. It meant they were gaining legitimacy and traction.

Upon arrival in Baltimore, Walters pulled Rader aside. "See if you could get me on the Fredericks' show tomorrow. We'll be in DC in the morning and I would like to speak with that charming fellow once again. Please see what you could do. Thank you."

Rader was not used to taking instruction from a candidate, but he liked the fact that he didn't have to play wet nurse to the usual spoiled and inconsiderate politicians. His client was always engaging and always concerned with his well being, even to the point that he made sure Ken called his wife each night from the road. He immediately dialed the producer of *The World Today*.

———

"No way, not so soon after the last one! Who the hell does this guy think he is?" Fredericks barked.

His producer reminded him that Walters was the leading candidate for president in the polls and it may be a good idea to have Walters on again. He also reminded him that the last show was his highest rated show ever. Still, William Fredericks balked at the idea and stormed back to his office.

Within minutes, the general manager of WNN was on the phone with Fredericks. One minute later, candidate Frank Walters was scheduled for his second appearance on the most popular liberal television talk show in the country. Everybody at the station was excited except the host himself. He was visibly nervous and called his wife in Los Angeles.

He arranged for her to fly to Washington DC later that morning because he missed her and needed her support as work had become taxing. When she agreed, he turned his attention to the interview preparation and focused back on his work. The voices in his head that chastised him for originally taking it easy on Walters cheered his resolve and goaded him to attack the candidate. William Fredericks readied himself for round two.

Chapter 25

Walters stepped out of the car first and looked around at the growing audience. How ironic he thought, it seemed like a lifetime ago that he made his first public appearance on these very steps. But whose lifetime? George Washington's or Frank Walters'? It didn't matter now. Rader had set up another impromptu gathering on the steps of the Lincoln Memorial, and the Tea Party candidate had a job to do.

As he moved to the podium he thought to himself how politics had not changed in over two hundred years. In what other world, except maybe show business, did someone "set up" an "impromptu gathering?"

He had to put those thoughts out of his mind. Once again, he was resolved to do his job. He would unseat this most treacherous of monarchs; of that, he had never a doubt. But unlike the last time he was on these hallowed steps as this miraculous adventure was just beginning, this time he understood his own endgame. As he stepped up to the podium, his eyes met the massive crowd. As he scanned the friendly faces, he wondered who else knew of Destiny's plan.

Young and old, boys and girls, thousands of people of all races had played hooky this warm August day to be a part of growing legend of Frank Walters. They came to hear his direct no-nonsense style and unbridled optimism.

One of the DC papers described the Walters phenomenon in baseball terms. Frank Walters' no-nonsense style was like a strikeout pitcher in baseball blowing fastball after fastball by his opponents. He did not try to trick anybody as the current president was accustomed to do. He just brought old-fashioned heat and people loved it. After all, fans loved strikeouts. The other candidates, including the president, kept trying to fool the American people with their curveballs and changeups. The editorial even called one of the candidates a screwball.

Frank Walters stepped to the podium.

"Hello, my fellow Americans. It is truly my privilege to speak with you again from this historic site and before one of the great men of American history. I am humbled to stand in his shadow."

The crowd cheered and began chanting, "Walters, Walters, Walters."

Frank put his massive hands up, asking the crowd to quiet for a moment. "In deference to Mr. Lincoln, whose two most important speeches were engraved in this magnificent memorial, I will endeavor to remain succinct." Mr. Walters surveyed the audience and smiled broadly. "As you know, I am a man of few words, having held my tongue for a considerable part of my life. Unlike my opponents, I am not a lifelong campaigner. This, as a matter of record, is my first campaign. I seek the presidency with all humility as I understand the position to be that of a temporary steward of our great society. My goal as president is far different than that of our current resident, who believes he is larger than the office he holds. Indeed, he believes himself greater than the millions of electorates who provided him with this position."

Walters pointed to several examples of the current president's flouting of the Constitution on the way to tyranny. He held up three fingers to emphasize his point and started to count each down one at a time. They included:

The PresidentCare monstrosity that mandated the people make a purchase they do not want to make.

The pressing of government appointments while the Senate was in recess.

The strong-arming of private industry and religious institutions to provide free goods and services and pay for devises and procedures that violate religious tenants.

"This man has become a tyrant! Actions speak louder than words. Don't listen to his words. Observe his actions—carefully."

The crowd erupted in cheers.

He explained that he saw the president's role much differently, believing that as steward of this society, the president's role was to allow the people to choose for themselves. He pointed at the citizens in the first few rows and asked them if they knew what was best for them.

"Of course you know what's best for yourself. The role of the president is to make sure people have the ability to bring happiness to their lives."

The candidate looked to his left to see Rader and Pepper one step down from his own perch. Walters took a sip of water and winked to the two trusted advisers.

"We only live once. So government's job is to provide the framework that allows us to meet our God given individual potential. That job includes protecting our people, protecting our borders, protecting our property, protecting our thoughts, our religion, and our families."

The crowd grew larger and even more impassioned. Like most Tea Party rallies, the throng of well wishers was well mannered, behaved, and enjoying themselves in the mid morning sunshine. They had their man and were delighted by the majesty of his vision for America.

"Dr. King stood on these very steps almost fifty years ago. He echoed the words of Jefferson, Madison, Jay, Hamilton, Franklin, Adams, and Washington, when he said that he had a dream for America where people were judged on their character and not the color of their skin. The founders agreed when they wrote the immortal words, "All men are created equal" and created a Constitution that would guarantee that promise. Mr. Lincoln agreed when he fought a war to remove the curse of slavery from these shores. All of you here agree?"

The pitch grew louder and more intense. Mr. Walters seemed to be very much enjoying the moment. "I will promise nothing if I am elected as your president, except that I will do what I know is right in my heart to protect America. I am not so arrogant to think that a group of politicians or advisors, or even I myself, could ever know what is right for you as individuals."

Chants and cheers rose again across the mall. And one more time, Walters raised both hands asking for silence. A hush came over the crowd instantaneously. The sound of birds chirping in the trees was all that was audible. Frank took note as the peaceful sound was interrupted by a plane approaching the Potomac River. The jets engines would not deter him from delivering the last few words of his speech.

"Please allow us to pull the anchor of government intrusion off you. Allow the rising tide of individual liberty to raise the ship of our society, enabling it to sail into the open waters of prosperity. You, the American people, are the captain. I would be honored to be your first mate. Thank you, and may God bless these United States of America."

Chapter 26

L adies and gentlemen, welcome to *The World Today*. As always, I am your host William Fredericks. Our guest this evening, for the second time, is none other than the Lincoln Continental himself, Frank Walters. Good day Mr. Walters. Another fine show you put on today on the steps of the Lincoln Memorial. Don't you think it's getting a little stale, maybe, 'Been there, done that?' But I digress. My real question is, why did you want to come on our show so shortly after your first appearance? Are you here today to reveal your true identity?"

Murray's attention was glued to the nineteen inch old style Cathode Ray Tube television hanging from the ceiling, facing Todd's hospital bed. Dottie had been keeping vigil at the hospital since the accident in which Todd sustained severe head trauma. He was put into a medically induced coma to allow his brain to heal. The fourteen year old boy had not regained consciousness since the accident.

In some odd way, Dottie thought that may be for the best for now. Two of his closest friends were dead and another was paralyzed from the waist down. She knew she would eventually have to tell Todd when he woke up, but that wasn't her first concern right now. She just wanted him to get well. The doctors were very hopeful that Todd would recover, at least to a reasonable degree. She had great hopes for her only child.

Those hopes did not translate to their marriage. Even before the horror of the accident, things were not going well. Murray was jet setting around the country with American Royalty and God knows who else. Meanwhile the rest of the Murrays felt as if they were relegated to second class citizens in Jack's eyes. She did her best over the last few weeks, going on overnight trips with Todd's team and his teammates' parents. An outgoing and vivacious woman, Dottie made new friends with ease.

She glanced from her son to her husband as he watched the television. She sensed a cold, distant vibe she never felt before from Jack. If Jack didn't want to be around her, why should she care about being around him? Dottie could not believe she felt that way. She also could not believe how at peace she was with that scenario.

While he was away, the frequency of phone calls and texts had diminished and the more the couple stayed apart, the easier to it was to remain apart. Even now, Jack was in the room but his mind was in some studio in Washington DC. All she had was the back of his head as he stared at the boob tube while a 300 year old boob debated a fifty something year old twit.

She took a deep breath and tried to stay calm. She knew this was not all Jack's fault. She urged him to go on this crazy adventure but resented him when he did. Dot knew that deep down he was a good person and a great father to Todd. But he didn't come home right away when he heard about Todd's accident and that cut her deep. She felt like she didn't know Jack anymore. Maybe a step child was not the same as your own flesh and blood.

Jack watched the silent pause between Washington and Fredericks as he felt his wife's glare of tension burn on the back of his head like a laser. But he steadfastly refused to turn away from the TV, knowing that if he did, another fight would erupt. He had no more words to explain his actions of the past four days, and he wasn't about to try to find new ones.

He did love Todd and he adored Dottie. She had to know that, but he was literally and figuratively not himself right now. This was not all his fault and she knew it. She encouraged him and then hated him for it. Besides, he had heard a few disturbing stories about goings on in the motels at the baseball tournaments after the kids went to bed. The phone bill he reviewed online revealed some long phone calls and texts to Tim Jenson and a 202 area code phone number he did not recognize in DC.

So the adult Murrays sat quietly around Todd's bed. Jack focused on the picture on the screen while Dottie held young Todd's hand. She listened to the show too, but feigned non-interest, not wanting to let her husband know at that moment that she still cared about his cause.

Walters was not amused by Fredericks' opening salvo, but decided in that instant to take the high road, figuring it would take William off his game.

The New Founders

The candidate peered down toward his questioner and startled the host by replying with a sincere thank you from the Walters' campaign. Fredericks had helped raise money and found volunteers to help the injured and all the families involved in the deadly bus crash. Mr. Walters explained that the son of one of his campaign members was still in the hospital recovering.

"Your money has helped ease a few burdens through this terrible time. As for the member of our immediate family, we hope to see a full recovery, thanks to your audience's faith and prayers, as well as a few good doctors."

Fredericks was not aware of a connection to the Walters' campaign. He immediately turned to one of his people off stage and mouthed the words "get on it." As he turned back to his guest, the names of the grief stricken families started to race through his head.

What he could not remember was what Dottie knew all along. The voice of the liberal establishment had personally called Dottie and the other affected family members to offer his condolences and prayers for their boys' recoveries. He even offered additional money if she needed it. Fredericks may be a twit, but he was there for her and the community, raising significant donations for medical and funeral expenses. It was a lot more than her history professor husband had done so far.

But what moved Dottie the most was when Fredericks shared the story of his own loss several years earlier. Fredericks had never spoken about it publicly, but one of his sons, Harry, had drowned in a neighbor's pool at the age of three. It still affected him deeply and he never got over his loss.

Mrs. Murray saw goodness in the heart of the man that her husband despised. She wanted to say something to Jack, but a hospital room was not the right place for a conversation of that nature. She continued to keep an eye on the television.

Walters saw that his gracious thank you may have taken Fredericks away from his initial focus. But his answer would surely get Fredericks back on track. The guest addressed his host in a purposeful condescending tone.

"We went through this once before William. You and your attack hounds have tried to dig things up on me but to no avail. And that is because I have nothing to hide. What you see is what you get. What you hear is what you get. Now stop this nonsense."

Murray clenched his fist in delight to the reply while Dottie thought Mr. Walters was unnecessarily nasty to the William she knew.

The tone and last comment got William's blood boiling. He started in on Walters' lack of experience and public record. He then turned toward Walters' family history. The host described that Walters' son had been arrested in college for DUI, criminal mischief and disorderly conduct. He asked how Frank could leave his business in the hands of a person of questionable character.

When he intimated rumors of an inappropriate relationship involving the wife of a member of Walters' team, Murray cursed audibly and popped out of his chair. He shot Dottie a quick glare and then looked away. He didn't want to fight but the voice in the room had just turned his thoughts upside down.

Dottie's face froze as she looked at her husband. He continued to stare at the TV, but she could read his mind. She knew in her heart that she hadn't done anything wrong over the past few weeks. But the guy she had recently found a new admiration for had just said something to a national audience to intentionally hurt her.

A gloating Fredericks glanced in the direction of his wife for approval. Sophia, who had recently arrived, stood just off the set as the guest pondered the question.

Frank Walters' composure was being tested on the air once again. But he was not about to let his adversary get away with this one.

"Mr. Fredericks, to speak evil of anyone, unless there are unequivocal proofs of their deserving it, is an injury for which there is no adequate reparation. My son is an honorable man as are all members of my team and their families. Not all of us were born with a silver spoon in our mouths. I am running for the office of the presidency. My son is not. The fact that you have stooped so low as to bring a good man such as my son into the conversation and then attack my staff based on nothing but gossip shows you to be a man of very weak character. I'll remind you and your audience that good moral character is the first essential in a man."

Walters finished his thought by explaining that he came on the show a second time to discuss the policies needed to right the ship that was the USA.

"Why don't we begin?"

Fredericks pushed harder as he felt the candidate's defenses rising. "Mr. Walters, if you are going to call the show and beg us to put you on, you have to face the issues and answer the questions. I ask you again, how can you entrust your family business to a person with a criminal record?"

Walters understood that the battle was now joined. He looked at the smirk on the host's face as he gloated again at the redirect. But nobody was better at obtaining genuine insider information than Ken Rader. He had provided a set of notes that Walters memorized prior to the show. The candidate counter punched.

"We asked to come on your show because we felt the left side of the aisle needed to be educated about what America is all about, something they do not get from the carousel of uninformed and anti-American guests you parade here on a daily basis. So you see, Mr. Fredericks, I am not going to cower under your attacks and innuendo."

Murray blurted out, "Go get him, George!" which won him an odd look from the nurse changing the IV drip.

"Two can play at this game. I ask you Mr. Fredericks, why did you fly your wife into town last night? I see her standing over there. Why is she all of the sudden here? And why did your children not accompany her? Did you need the support of your spouse today knowing that you were entering the battlefield with an adversary such as me?"

Fredericks was alarmed at the turn of events. Most of his adversaries allowed him to discuss their families but never replied in kind. Walters stared at him, creating dead air and a very uncomfortable set. The teacher had scolded his pupil but he was not finished.

"Tell me this, young man. Was it I who begged to be on the show? Or was it your producer who begged you to put me on the air? Or was it your boss who called you and insisted you interview me or you be fired?"

Fredericks looked toward the camera and said that they would be right back. The show went to commercial and Fredericks made a beeline for Sophia. The candidate followed his every step, never taking his eyes off the host. Rader tried to get his client to step from the set but Walters waved him off, leaning back in his chair with his hands clasped behind his head. Rader turned to Hahn next to him and said what everybody already knew. "Welcome back to the *Frank Walters Show!*"

Both men let out a big laugh that echoed through the studio as Fredericks made his way back to his chair behind the desk.

Excited, Murray asked Dottie if she had heard all that. Dottie replied in a subdued tone that it was impossible not to with all his yelling. She went back to tending to Todd, bathing his face with a warm compress.

As the red light reappeared, the sullen host welcomed the audience back with a question about the candidate's health situation.

"Yes. As you have repeated over and over, I am a cancer survivor" said Walters. "A number of years ago I went for a routine colonoscopy, which revealed a blockage. I had the tumor removed but unfortunately, the cancer metastasized to my liver. However, we were lucky enough to catch it early. I had a small concentration of cancer on my liver that the surgeons were able to cut out and remove. The liver is an amazing organ in that it can regenerate itself and that is what my liver has done. I am happy to say that at the moment, I am cancer free."

Fredericks nodded and quietly said that it was good news that the popular candidate had one less thing to worry about on the campaign trail. But before he could utter another question, Frank Walters interrupted. "But William, I did not come here today to talk about spouses or children, closed door conversations or abdominal CT scans and X-rays. I am here today to challenge the President of these United States to a debate, one on one, just he and I, next week on the steps of the Federal Hall building in lower Manhattan."

Fredericks laughed before looking at the candidate's serious expression. He stated that he could not be serious.

"I am serious, very serious. Man on man, an old-fashion debate based solely on the issues. If the president is a man of honor like he consistently portrays himself to be, he will accept my challenge and make arrangements to leave the golf course behind for a day and show up in New York. He can choose the topics, prepare the questions in advance, and even decide what issues are forbidden. I will even agree to allow him a teleprompter on the dais."

"What the hell is he doing?" asked Murray to no one.

Audible laughs in the background could be heard on the air, undoubtedly belonging to Hahn and Ken Rader. Fredericks was now wide-eyed and he immediately changed his persona to that of PT Barnum.

"Well, ladies and gentlemen, you heard it here first on *The World Today*. Frank Walters, the candidate of no political party, has challenged the president of the United States of America to a political debate in New York next week. Whether the president accepts or not will be seen. But the gauntlet has been thrown down on our show by the gentleman from Virginia. More newsworthy events brought to you courtesy of William Fredericks."

They went to commercial once again. Walters stood and walked the few steps to the host seat. He extended his hand to Fredericks, thanking him for the time. Fredericks stayed seated and shook his hand, uttering neither a thank you nor a good luck. The guest had struck a nerve in the host by mentioning Sophia.

Fredericks wondered how much more this Walters bloke knew about him. Did he know about Them? Fredericks was shaken both inside and out and had to compose himself for the remainder of the show. He gathered his notes for the next segment as Frank Walters exited the studio to congratulations and well deserved handshakes. Even Sophia Fredericks, outside of William's line of sight, introduced herself and shook Walters' hand. Hahn pulled Walters to the side.

"I knew you would do it, I just knew. That was awesome. Did you see the look on his face? Priceless."

Mr. Walters cautioned Hahn not to get ahead of himself as Rader appeared at his side.

"I guess I have a lot of work to do over the next week. Federal Hall? Do you think it's safe? You couldn't have picked Madison Square Garden, some place we can rent out that doesn't have high rise buildings with open windows all around?"

The man who would not be king put both his hands on Rader's shoulders as he addressed him.

"I wanted to be in a familiar environment and among some old friends. Mr. Rader, I have every confidence in your ability to pull this off. Now, let's go back to the hotel for some libations."

Murray just stared at the commercial on TV and continued to shake his head.

"What on earth is this guy doing?"

Chapter 27

Jack Murray felt the pressure coming from all sides.

He was summoned back to the Mount Vernon estate by the boss himself for an important summit of all the new founders.

As if his life was not already in a crisis, Murray would once again be apart from his family. The doctors remained hopeful, but his son still lay in coma, now at Rockingham Memorial Hospital (having been transported closer to home at Dottie's insistence). Dottie had become just plain hostile, continuing to project her fear and anger about Todd. Jack knew her patience was at its end, but he had to be with the team. There was nothing he could do to make his son wake up from his coma. That was up to the doctors. There was nothing that could make Dottie feel better about their time apart.

He understood how traumatic situations could quickly rip even the closest families apart. Jack feared he could easily lose his son and his wife, but he suppressed his doubts as he fled the hospital and entered the livery car waiting for him.

The ride was uneventful, leaving Murray to his own thoughts. He had to put his wife out of his mind for the next few hours and deal with the tasks at hand. He had been away from the campaign for a week, which made Jack feel like an outsider. He needed to catch up and fast. He had to figure out how he would deal with Fredericks' attack on George's identity and his unfounded remarks about infidelity within the team.

Murray had seen movies in which people came back from the dead, only to encounter physical or psychological problems. He wondered if life was now imitating art with George's half-cocked challenge to debate the president one on one at Federal Hall in New York. Did he realize that there were four other candidates in the Republican tent that were vying for the office as well? Or that nobody would take him seriously? It sounded like something Hahn would think up.

Of course the president snidely derided the founding movement as he tried to put the Walters' team on the defensive. Even the Republican establishment quietly set out to undermine the Walters' campaign by questioning his qualifications. The Tea Party base had started to voice persistent fears that Walters would "sell out" to the Republican establishment. Even infighting among the team had arisen when Walters snubbed Josh to go on Fredericks' show for second time.

And now Walters decided to disrupt Murray's life yet again.

Not a man comfortable with conflict of this sort, Murray didn't know where to turn. He would normally confide in Dottie, but that was out the window as she was suddenly one of his major concerns. He had felt a closeness and connection to Tim Jenson, but that was before he left the campaign to go home and do his radio show.

Murray kept telling himself that he was just imagining things, but he wasn't even sure if he could trust Jenson after hearing the infidelity allegations and seeing his phone number appear on her cell phone bill. Dottie explained that Jenson had been there to talk with her while Murray was on the road. Even if it wasn't physical infidelity, Murray's feeling that she was emotionally cheating on him hurt him just as deeply. With everything in his life turned upside down, Murray actually looked forward to reconnecting with the other new founders.

He figured something big had to be brewing if the General asked for the entire team to be present.

All the new founders would be back together that evening as Faulk had concluded a business and diplomatic visit on behalf of Walters to London, Paris, and Tel Aviv. Though he was turned down for face-to-face meetings by the heads of state due to diplomatic protocols, he did meet with their senior advisors and the heads of the conservative movements in each country. Faulk achieved his goal by making sure they understood that Walters was a serious contender. The influential publisher convinced his European counterparts that their candidate was a trusted ally in the global fight for freedom.

It had been several weeks since the New Founders had assembled in the same room and there was a feeling of anticipation as the men, accompanied by Rader and Pepper, sat down over dinner to discuss the future of the campaign and what lay ahead.

Mr. Walters got right to the point as he surveyed the table and watched his men dine on his twenty-first century favorite meal of hamburgers, corn on the cob, and french fries. He informed them that Rader had received feelers from the Republican Party about designating him the vice-presidential running mate to whomever won the nomination at the Republican convention. Frank explained that he was not interested in the offer but he wanted to get the team's thoughts on the idea. A resounding "No" followed as the new founders collectively let their leader know how they felt. Walters was pleased with the response as he sipped his red wine.

Pepper took an additional sip of wine and then reached behind his chair for his briefcase. He placed it in front of him on the table and opened it. He pulled out a stack of envelopes and proceeded to pass them to each person at the table. As Pepper went founder to founder around the oak table, Walters explained that the men were receiving paychecks for their work on the campaign. The checks would be the first in a series of payments to be made to each person through Election Day.

Murray opened his envelope and gasped. His eyes were wide as he viewed the six figure dollar check. He took a deep breath as he pocketed his newfound wealth. It took a few seconds to dawn on him that he had just earned his yearly teaching salary and more for just over a month's work. He looked around to see the looks of satisfaction on the faces of his fellow patriots.

Murray could get used to working in politics. He looked up to see Walters smiling with satisfaction. Then Walters tapped his glass with a fork.

"Gentlemen, let's get back to business. Now that the idea of the second spot is off the table, let me elaborate on what I have in mind."

He then asked Josh Anders to take a leave from his radio show and hit the campaign trail with the team. Anders protested that this would spur rumors of Anders as the VP candidate, something that was already being spoken about in certain circles.

"Besides, it would mean the end of my radio show and the public disclosure of my finances."

Walters agreed but said that if he was going to be the presidential candidate, Anders was destined to be his running mate. Anders was unsure.

"Vice-President has to be the worst job in government. I would not be able to speak my mind publicly. I would be the president of the senate, but with no vote. As John Adams wrote to Thomas Jefferson upon becoming George's VP in 1787, 'My country has in its wisdom contrived for me the most insignificant office that ever the invention of man contrived or his imagination conceived. And as I can do neither good nor evil, I must be borne way by others, and meet the common fate."'

Walters let Anders think about the words he just stated. He waited for clarity in Anders' reasoning as the number one radio talk show host mulled over the idea. The rest of the table sat silently. Anders took a deep breath and turned to the head of the table.

"But then again, like Adams before me, how could I turn it down?"

Perhaps he would learn to like being vice-president as he had learned to love being a radio host. Anders recalled early in his tenure on the *Josh Anders Show* what he penned to an old friend.

"I said I hated speeches, messages, addresses. I told him that I couldn't stand speaking to one thousand people or ten million people, listening to them blather on and on about anything political. Yet all of this I can do. In the end, it became my second true love after my family. We said that we would do anything to achieve the goals we set out to accomplish at the outset of this journey. So the answer is yes. I accept wholeheartedly the position of your vice-presidential running mate."

The New Founders had come full circle with their original counterparts. Anders and most of the men felt there was elegance in all of this.

However, this elegance didn't sit very well with Hahn. Although he was not eligible to be president or vice-president due to his youth and place of birth outside the United States, the ambitious Hahn still felt slighted that he should have been at least part of the discussion.

Walters turned to Hahn to reassure him and everybody in the room that there would be a place for all in the new administration if elected. To ease his fears, he offered Hahn the post of Treasury Secretary in his potential cabinet. He stressed that there was still work to be done as his senior policy advisor on the campaign trail before any White House appointments could be officially designated. Hahn dutifully and graciously accepted Walters' words and took them to heart. He even seemed slightly embarrassed at his behavior and directed his attention back to his dinner.

Anders again focused on his radio show. He asked the men if they had any thoughts on his replacement since a decision needed to be made soon. As names were bandied about around the table, Walters sat back in his chair and interjected.

"Anders, you know who the perfect candidate to replace you is and you won't have to look far."

As if Anders read his leader's mind, he turned and looked directly at Jenson. A big grin on his face appeared and he nodded in agreement. Anders, as majority owner and president of the Josh Anders Network (JAN), offered Jenson the permanent replacement slot on the spot.

Funny, Jenson thought, that when all this began, his ambition was exactly the job Anders just offered. But somehow, with all that had transpired, this incredible opportunity seemed almost trivial. He wondered if the candidate had a position in the administration in mind for him too. After all, wasn't he the embodiment or reincarnation of one of the greatest minds in American history, Thomas Jefferson?

Still, Walters was the one who suggested Jenson as Anders' replacement so it had to be part of the overall master plan. The men saw the thought process in Jenson's eyes as he hesitated briefly before gladly accepting Anders' offer. A slight weight lifted off Murray's head, knowing that one of the main concerns in his personal life looked to be headed 400 miles north to Boston.

The next item on his agenda was Walters' debate challenge to the president. In his most recent press conference, the president had offhandedly dismissed the challenge chuckling that he had no time for a debate with a nobody, like what's his name? Washington or something.

The president and his loyalists in the press had all gotten a good laugh at the candidate's expense. Mainstream news reports and articles called the challenge nothing more than a stunt by a desperate amateur. Walters chalked up this disrespect to old-fashion politics.

"In all free governments, contentions in elections will take place, and while it is confined to our own citizens, is not to be regretted."

Anders and Jenson had taken it more to heart as it seemed to be the continuous topic of discussion on their respective shows. Ironically in his most recent show, Anders unleashed a direct verbal attack on the president, deeming him a coward for ducking Walters. Anders went on, saying the president was afraid to take on a man that did not need rehearsed lines or a teleprompter to get his message across. Jenson echoed Anders' sentiment as he explained that Walters' strength of character exuded conviction, constitutional principles, and core values which would trump the teleprompter's stale rhetoric, no matter how flowery the president dressed it up.

Rader had arranged for Mr. Walters to call into Anders' show, where the candidate announced he would be on the steps of Federal Hall on the corner of Broad and Wall Street in New York City the following Monday evening, regardless of whether the president showed or not. He outlined the premise, half joking that the president had repeated the same old clichés, rhetoric, and catch phrases for so long that Walters could debate his previous quotes to the point that the audience would not be able to tell if the president was actually there or not. Anders jumped right on it, saying the JAN network would be there to cover this unique debate.

Jenson, having heard the exchange live, now put two and two together.

"I guess my first assignment as permanent replacement for Anders will be to cover this unique event for the network. Now I'm excited!"

The serious nature of the discussion lifted with Jenson's exuberant exclamation. As dinner plates were cleared and dessert served, Faulk reported his successful mission in Europe and the Middle East, saying that he believed our closest allies would welcome the change in leadership in the US.

"I believe they will wholeheartedly endorse a Walters' administration policy of 'temporary alliances for extraordinary emergencies' and ongoing support for our staunchest allies. Assuming, of course, the majority of their goals coincide with those of the United States and none conflict to the point of injury to our nation."

Walters nodded his agreement. Faulk concluded his summary by providing the team with a rallying cry for the rest of the campaign.

"It will not be easy, but you must see it through. Without pain, Mr. Walters, there is no gain. No pain, no gain."

The dinner adjourned with Walters, Anders, Hahn, Rader, and Murray in preparation for a campaign stop on the Green in Morristown, New Jersey. Then, a visit to George Washington's headquarters. The team would conclude their New Jersey swing with a visit to nearby Jockey Hollow, where the Continental Army spent the most severe winter, 1779 -1780, of the revolution.

"Why is it that the history books go on and on about Valley Forge but hardly mentions Jockey Hollow?" Mr. Walters continued his lament to Hahn. "Over six feet of snow fell that year as the soldiers nearly starved in the frozen meadows and forests of New Jersey. It was just as bad as the winter at Valley Forge, maybe worse."

Walters leaned in to whisper in Jack's ear. "Mr. Murray, in our travels near Morristown, maybe we could visit the old oak tree that I rested under with my troops. It was on the basking ridge of those low lying mountains, if I remember correctly."

Then it would be on to New York City, scenes of some of the general's greatest victories and worst defeats. Rader scheduled morning visits to Ellis Island and the Statue of Liberty, concluding with Walters paying his respects at the World Trade Center site in the early afternoon. The team would then retire back to their hotel to complete Walters' preparation for the Monday night debate, with or without the president.

Chapter 28

The light from the setting sun still shone bright over the New York Stock Exchange. The scene had taken on a carnival atmosphere, a crowd of wall to wall people stretching from the police barricades in front of the Federal Hall steps, down Broad Street toward the Staten Island ferry depot. The west end of Wall Street had become a pedestrian walkway after 9/11 but right now there was no place to walk. The mass of humanity swelled past the entrance to the Exchange and onto Broadway in front of old Trinity Church, temporarily closing the lower part of Broadway in the downtown financial district. The throng stretched in the opposite direction as well, as smiling faces could be seen as far as Water Street, practically in the East River.

The streets behind Federal Hall and Chase Plaza were cordoned off for security. The expected route of the debaters resembled a ghost town as the line of limousines made their way through. The NYPD received word from the secret service earlier in the day that the president would not attend. That was the good news. The bad news was that they did not anticipate the tens or hundreds of thousands who did attend. The crowd affected many downtown workers' commutes home and officials did their best to accommodate local businesses. Many workers decided to stay and witness the debate from office windows.

While the mainstream media announced early on that they would not waste their time or money covering the so-called debate, they had a change of heart. Every cable news network and local television station had coverage. Their platforms lined down the sidewalk along the stock exchange on Broad Street. As expected, analysts and television personalities mocked the candidate while in agreement it was newsworthy enough to be there. One reporter in the crowd compared the scene to Times Square on New Year's Eve, with thousands of people crammed together in anticipation of a transformative event.

One media personality who would not miss this was William Fredericks. He was on the air telling his audience of the sheer absurdity of a candidate debating his own shadow and how the conservatives were lapping it up like dogs. While deep into his pre-debate diatribe, his wife Sophia sat nearby on the platform, just off camera, offering encouragement for her excited husband. They exchanged winks as the eight o'clock hour approached.

—●—

"I don't believe it. Man, you see this? There must be half a million people out there! You sure you're ready for this, Frank?"

Anders watched the limousine television in amazement. Hahn was to his right and Faulk was to his left. Rader and Murray were opposite him but leaning forward to watch the screen. Walters sat between them, leaning back while examining the downtown skyscrapers. The driver was given a pre-determined route by the police that he followed to a T. As the car weaved in and out of the maze of narrow streets of lower Manhattan, the new founders began to question their leader. Walters' calm in the face of the craziness actually unnerved rather than calmed the men.

Faulk turned to Walters. "How can you be so composed right now? I've traveled the world but have never seen anything like this."

Walters, turning his attention back to the inside of the car, ignored Faulk's comment and addressed Ken the Builder.

"Mr. Rader, I commend you on the fine job you did in preparing this event. I tip my cap to you, sir."

Rader didn't know whether to thank him or jump out of the moving car. He was afraid if he didn't bail, Walters' cabinet members may throw him out for arranging the insane setting. Instantaneously, the columns of the rear entrance of Federal Hall were ahead of them. So was a living and breathing wave of humanity that made the expanse of Broad Street ahead look alive. The sun had now set over the buildings, yet the television lights ensured the street was as bright as midday.

The car pulled to the curb and the team exited to a military-like police escort. They were ushered through a covered walkway along the side of the Hall. As they approached the debate lecterns set on the top step, Walters paused. The new founders halted with him, expecting a prayer.

Instead, the candidate motioned for secret service agent Michelle. He wrapped his hand around her waist and pulled her close. He looked like he was about to kiss her but instead, whispered in her ear and pulled a piece of paper from his pocket. He handed her the folded paper, which she promptly put in her jacket. Murray turned to Hahn.

"I'm glad we're out of camera range. Who knows how that exchange might have been construed?"

Walters looked out at the crowd. His team silently wondered if the candidate was having second thoughts.

"Men, before we begin, I would like to say a quick prayer of thanks for allowing us this opportunity to address the nation in this setting."

Walters led the prayer. Amen was hardly out of their mouths before their leader spun on one heel and strode onto the debate stage to a thunderous roar from the crowd. The team followed, taking their places to the side. Walters walked across the set to his podium. Even though everybody involved knew his debate opponent was not coming, a second podium sat empty across from him. The irony of the situation was not lost on the new founders. Faulk said that he figured someone would have been smart enough to get rid of the second podium. Rader leaned in, smiled and slyly responded.

"I wouldn't let them. I kept telling city officials that the secret service had heard the president had reconsidered. They may not have really believed me, but they didn't want to take the chance and remove it and then have him show up."

Walters stood behind the podium and looked over his shoulder at the massive statue behind him. It was the first time he had ever seen this particular depiction of himself and he liked what he saw. Turning back to the crowd, he introduced himself and stated that he was running for President of the United States. The crowd erupted again, a foreshadowing of things to come.

However, a small group along the front barricade heckled loudly causing a stir. The candidate noticed them right away. He removed the microphone from the stand and walked to the far end of the platform where the cement steps began. He descended the steps until he was within a few feet of the spectators, out of sight from the left side of the scaffold. He towered over them and looked down upon the protesters, who were shocked into silence.

"My dear ladies and gentlemen, I ask that you have the common decency and respect to allow me to say a few words this evening. You must have been here for hours to attain such a fine vantage point. Please show my opponent and me a modicum of courtesy. Thank you."

As the General climbed the steps back to the stage, the once vocal protesters stood in silence, humbled by the personal lecture.

Faulk put his hand to his forehead. "He's going to give me a heart attack before it's all done."

Mr. Walters stood at the podium. He looked directly at Jenson. The new national talk show host sat at a desk in the first platform to the right. Each man exchanged a nod as the candidate began.

"My fellow Americans, in 2009 our president infamously said that 'We do not consider ourselves a Christian nation, or a Muslim nation, but rather, a nation of citizens who are bound by a set of values.'

This is nonsense, Mr. President. Our country was founded on Judeo-Christian values and morals and a belief in God the Almighty. Our founding fathers understood the potential we had as a new country to achieve greatness in the face of adversity. It was their faith in God and the abilities bestowed upon them that allowed them to overcome the obstacles they encountered. Ladies and gentlemen, this sentiment still bodes true today. It is alive and well in each and every one of you."

The crowd cheered as Walters' eyes panned the masses.

"If my opponent, the current president, was here tonight, he would probably tell you that you could only overcome the obstacles in your life with the assistance of the government. All you have to do is look at his monstrous health care mandate where the government has attempted to compel the citizenry to purchase a product that they deem necessary for your happiness."

He asked everybody to look at the billions of hard earned tax dollars invested in green energy automobiles and called the idea nonsense.

He paced back toward the middle of the stage as the mass applauded loudly. He stopped mid dais and looked to the far reaches of the audience.

"American. You, me, all of you are Americans. What are the four most important letters within that word? Is it 'Yes we can?' No, it is 'I can!' I can make for a better future for myself and my family! I can overcome the obstacles that are thrust in front of me! I can better my situation without government intervention! I can!"

Walters looked down as he stood at the right side podium. He had the crowd in his hands now and he was not about to let them go.

"You folks, the ones that heckled me, do you agree that an individual, who is possessed of the spirit of commerce, who is focused on success and betterment of his or her life, who will pursue the advantages they created themselves, can achieve almost anything? Do you?"

The rhetorical question was again met with silence from the front row crowd.

"This president does not believe that. Under his administration, the number of Americans on welfare and food stamps has grown exponentially. By extending the unemployment benefit to ninety-nine weeks, this president has not helped the people but has hindered them. He has discouraged many Americans from looking for work. Many of our able bodied countrymen are living off the government and their fellow citizens and it is because of this president's abuse of the system. He believes that if he keeps this population dependent on him and the federal government, he can control you. Well we are Americans and nobody in government should control how we earn a living or live our lives."

He paced back and forth while delivering his messages. Hahn turned to Anders and asked how much the big guy had left in him. Murray beat Anders to the answer.

"He's just getting warmed up."

Walters looked up at his statue and pointed. He explained that this man had great men around him, men that put their country before their own well being by creating a militia that went to war against a superior fighting force, the British. He went on to explain that many of these men lost their lives for their country.

"From the time of the Revolutionary War, through the War of 1812 and the wars of the twentieth century, World War I and II, the Korean War, the Vietnam War, the Gulf War and the current battles in the Middle East, our fighting American soldiers have continued to be the model for military forces around the world. And you know why? Because we are a free society. We are free because these fighting men and women keep us free, allow us to sleep well at night knowing they are sitting guard. But does our president believe this? Just ask him."

The candidate pointed to the empty podium, eliciting a roar of laughter from the audience. Walters went on to list the current administration's efforts to weaken the US military, from budget cuts and thinning personnel to fostering bad morale through the scourge of political correction and lack of support.

"Our captured enemies are treated better than our own soldiers. And that will not happen in my administration! Our fighting men and women are so mistrusted by this administration that they were forced to put down their arms when the Secretary of Defense recently visited them in Afghanistan. And that was for a morale boost!"

The sound of cheers shook the microphone and reverberated down the concrete canyons. Cheering came from the windows above and George acknowledged them with his favorite newfound gesture: a thumbs up.

"See this guy behind me?"

He asked the question rhetorically for effect. He pointed to the statue of General Washington and held his pose.

"He once said that being diligent in preparation for war is the most effectual means for preserving peace. You know who followed those words perfectly? Some guy named Ronald Reagan."

He once again stepped toward the other podium and other microphone. For effect, he put his microphone in his jacket pocket and stepped behind the president's podium. He held his hands out.

"What, no teleprompter?"

The crowd erupted into a roar that rivaled a rock concert. Walters used the president's own words.

"When this man campaigned four years ago, he questioned our military presence in the Middle East on a daily basis. He ridiculed his opponent's political party for starting the wars and overstaying our welcome. He even said that we should avoid any foreign entanglements. Well, Mr. President, what are we doing in Afghanistan and Syria and Libya? You have been more of an aggressor than any of the recent presidents."

Walters went on to talk about discipline, describing it as the soul of any army or any group for that matter.

"Whether it is a military force, a kindergarten class or a Freemason meeting, you cannot be successful unless you take a disciplined and organized approach. If you are undisciplined, you will lose the battle and your kids will be out of control. An undisciplined administration and White House is a disaster waiting to happen. And that is what we have right now. The president's message changes like the wind, by the hour. He does not listen to his cabinet and he does what he pleases, without regard for the American people or American industry. And that is unacceptable."

He looked across the stage for what seemed like the hundredth time. He asked the ghost of the president's podium if he needed a commercial break, which drew more laughs from the hundreds of thousands of people in attendance. He decided to change the tone a bit and become more serious.

"We are back to the malaise of the Carter administration."

Walters detailed how the late 1970's was a time of low morale because of the economy, troubles with Iran, and skyrocketing gasoline prices. He said that anti-Americanism and lack of patriotism had also risen in a similar fashion under the current president.

"Just imagine, almost eleven years to the day, the people of this country and, more specifically, this city, watched in horror as the great towers fell only a few hundred yards from where I stand right now. Do you remember the American pride that each and every one of us exuded that day and the weeks and years that followed? If that happened today, I would shudder to think how this apologetic president would react."

He went on to say that the whole world has turned upside down and what was right is now wrong and what was up is now down. And he had no explanation.

"Even respectable men and women, elected officials and individuals responsible for delivering our daily news on television and in print, now speak of our monarchial form of government without horror or question. They sit idly by while the president continues to circumvent that great foundation this country was built upon. The U.S. Constitution. Anybody know what the meaning of the word Czar is?"

A few yeahs could be heard over the inaudible din of the people.

"The word Czar is derived from the Latin word Caesar, meaning monarch, emperor or supreme ruler. Anybody know how many czars have been appointed in the past four years? Don't look over there because you won't get an answer. Over forty czars. How many have been confirmed by the Senate? You can count them on one hand. If you remember anything from this debate, remember that arbitrary power is most easily established on the ruins of liberty abused to licentiousness or lacking moral restraint."

Calmer applause followed as the crowd fed off Walters' serious tone. It was time to turn up the dial once again and hit the nerve of the people. He walked to where his new founders were seated.

"How about the First Amendment, freedom of speech? How about that great medium in our great country called talk radio. If the president was standing up there, he would tell you that the hosts of conservative talk shows were hate mongers, trying to scare the populace into voting Republican. He said a fairness doctrine should be put back in place. Equal time. The problem with that ladies and gentlemen is that nobody listens to liberal and left-wing talk radio. Americans at their core are conservative and do not like hearing the bile being spewed about everything that is wrong with America."

He stood directly in front of Anders.

"See this man in front of me? His name is Josh Anders and he is public enemy number one to this current administration. They will stop at nothing until he is silenced. Well I can promise one thing, this great man is not about to be silenced, not in the least!"

The throng let out a deafening cheer at the mention of Anders' name. Simultaneous chants of Josh and VP wafted toward the building tops. It took a few moments before Walters could continue.

"If freedom of speech is taken away, we may and will be taken away and, like the dumb and silent, we will be led like sheep to slaughter. A man who cannot call his tongue his own can scarce call anything his own. As president, I promise that will never happen."

He shook Anders' hand and headed back toward center stage.

"This president continues to be an advocate of despotism. As I stated earlier, he believes that we are incapable of governing ourselves and that the system this country was founded on is merely fallacious. A system founded by the likes of men named Jefferson and Adams and Madison and Hamilton. Who would you trust at the helm of this great country, one of these men or the fallacious man who currently holds the office?"

Cheers echoed as the man called Frank Walters went behind the podium and placed his microphone back in the stand. He knew he spoke enough and decided it was a good time to wrap up the conversation.

"I remind all Americans that every post is honorable in which a man can serve his country, not serve himself nor his personal egotistical needs. Unfortunately, that cannot be said of the current administration or its Commander-in-Chief. It is said that few men have the virtue to withstand the highest bidder, as we see every day in the politics of this country. Well I can tell you I am not one of those individuals. I am not even a career politician.

I am just an American who served his country and served his family in an honorable manner; a so-called ordinary American with a plan to bring this country back to its original glory. So that when we meet our God and our founding fathers, we can stand proudly before them."

"In executing the duties of president of this great nation, I can promise nothing but purity of intentions and, in carrying these into effect, fidelity and diligence. My main goals as president will be to remove government from your lives, preserve and defend the Constitution, and protect America and our citizens from enemies foreign and domestic.

"I thank you for joining me this evening and may God bless America."

Washington walked to center stage and stood at attention, as if to invite a potential assassin to take a shot at him. He beamed as the masses surged toward him, only to be detained by the NYPD. He humbly received the adoration; if there were any boos or protests, they were drowned out by the fervor amongst the supporters.

Within seconds, studio lights on the network platforms fired on the air. After what seemed like an eternity, the candidate bowed and turned toward the walkway and exited the Federal Hall stage. The new founders followed him into the covered walkway and to the waiting limousine that whisked them away.

The initial reaction from the media in general was positive. Even the liberal outlets reported that the one man debate was a clever idea executed powerfully. The conservative networks were unanimous in their opinion that Frank Walters not only locked up the conservative vote, but may have won the election right there and then.

——— —

However, one liberal talking head had not bought in.

"Do you believe that guy? He thinks he's a combination of George Washington and Elvis."

William Fredericks stood, arms crossed, watching the crowd below wave and sing praises of the candidate. He shook his head as The Who's "Won't Get Fooled Again" blared in the background. He turned back to the set, not expecting what he saw behind him.

"What are you doing?"

Sophia Fredericks was standing among the WNN technical folks applauding and swaying to the music. She was laughing and singing along with the conservative revelers on Broad Street. Fredericks' initial shock wore off and he exploded.

"Bollocks, Sophia, what the hell? Are you one of them now? I can't believe my bloody eyes!"

The set went silent. Sophia was the one with the shocked look. She saw Fredericks' outbursts from time to time but this was the first time he ever directed it at her. His high piercing voice cut through the roar below and even Jenson on the next platform turned his attention toward Fredericks.

Sophia stood in disbelief as Fredericks let out another string of expletives in her direction. She started to well up, more out of embarrassment than being yelled at by her husband. She sulked into her chair as WNN personnel pretended to be busy. Fredericks' producer reminded him that he was about to go on the air but it did not seem to sink in.

Fredericks' eyes were fire red and the veins stuck out of his neck as he fumed. Fredericks' wife turned away, not wanting to see the optical daggers being hurled her way. As she turned, Fredericks, still enraged, sat down at the desk and adjusted his remote microphone. His producer whispered in his ear that he needed to calm down. Fredericks took a deep breath but could not shake the internal inferno. He went on the air with a verbal tirade, this time directed at his nemesis Frank Walters, which pushed the boundaries of FCC guidelines.

As he wrapped up his analysis ten minutes later, he saw that Sophia had disappeared. But unlike previous instances where they quarreled, Fredericks felt nothing. Watching his wife support his foe had flipped a switch in Fredericks' head that cemented his persona, possibly forever. It looked as though They had finally won.

The New Founders

Chapter 29

Since his one man debate, the Walters' team had not only drawn the attention of the liberal national media and the president, but of the Republican Establishment as well. It was now only two weeks before the convention in Tampa and the Republicans had yet to produce a legitimate frontrunner. Each candidate continued to conduct himself as if they were marksmen in a circular firing squad.

While they were hell bent on destroying one another, Frank Walters rocketed in the polls. The RNC was nervous, having no answer for the one man show that the entire country witnessed just a few days earlier. Rader and the Walters' team figured the entire primary process was destined to be decided in a brokered convention only eight weeks before the general election. Under Republican rules, if neither candidate won the majority of delegates, those delegates were free to vote for any candidate of their choosing.

In other words, everything seemed to be breaking nicely for the Walters' campaign. Perhaps they would have the opportunity to win over the Republican establishment prior to the convention. Rader just hoped that the RNC was smart enough to realize that Mr. Frank Walters was their only shot to beat the president.

Walters found evidence that Providence had planned his rise several months before he met the New Founders in Philadelphia. While researching on Hahn's iPad, he came across a *New York Post* Op/Ed piece from March of that year describing the Republican nomination process. Washington had to read the quote aloud.

"Guys, listen to this. 'So what then? A magical figure descends from the heavens, one of the people who took a look at the election and decided he (or she) couldn't actually win and therefore didn't run?'"

Hahn blurted out laughing, "The heavens? Is that where you are from?"

Walters ignored the quip and finished his thought. "That's kind of eerie, wouldn't you say, my friends?"

Tongue firmly in his cheek, Hahn took the iPad and stood up. He scratched his head, put his fist up to his chin, and put on a regal sounding voice as he read another passage to the ceiling.

"Hmmm? 'But where would such a person find a ready-made campaign organization to take on the president in the seven weeks until Election Day—with local organizations county by county and neighborhood by neighborhood, SuperPACs at the ready. Oh, and a vetted vice-presidential nominee as well?'"

He handed the computer back to Walters who finished the point by reading that any such scenario involving an unprepared candidate and running mate would likely be a world-historical disaster, far worse for the GOP than even a weak nominee. The consequences further down the ticket would be parlous, as well.

"Anders, read this. Seems Providence has been at this longer than we thought. Our circumstances are not exactly what the writer describes but fantastically similar."

Anders just smiled.

"You know, sir, now that you mention it, I think I had seen that piece and maybe even quoted it on my show." Showing the iPad to Steve, he asked what his cousin thought.

"Hey, maybe in eight years when your term is up, you can help us summon Abe Lincoln."

Rader entered the room and paused. The jovial mood abruptly stopped and he wondered what the discussion was about. A split second later, he snapped back and informed the campaign hierarchy that he was there to deliver some big news.

"You guys ready for this? I just got a call from the head of the Republican National Committee. He wants to meet us in secret, tomorrow morning outside of Pittsburgh. Six o'clock in the morning in some retreat house, and he said representatives of each Republican candidate will be there."

The men pondered the news for a second while they looked at each other. Faulk had joined the men and asked Rader what he thought.

"I think they want to make a deal. And not for the VP slot. I think they see the giant snowball rolling down the hill and they can't stop it. The only thing that they would call a meeting for would be to ask Frank to be the Republican nominee."

All eyes in the room turned to Mr. Walters. He nodded with a small smile as he reached for the iPad yet again.

"Providence, gentlemen, Providence. Tell them we will take the meeting."

———

The morning came quickly. Rader devised a plan to exit Walters from the mansion through the woods, thus avoiding the media camped at the entrance to the estate. The plan worked perfectly and the new founders boarded Pepper's private jet. They left the non-descript airport in Manassas, Virginia at fifteen minutes to five without fanfare.

Wheels touched down in Pittsburgh within an hour and the team left in the waiting cars, heading to the town of McKees Rocks. As they entered the large dwelling, they were met at the door by the head of the RNC. He escorted the gentlemen into a spacious conference room where four sets of bloodshot eyes sat motionless around an oak conference table. The men stood as the new founders approached.

All exchanged handshakes and pleasantries. But the four men around the table looked as if they did not want to be there, as if they were little children in timeout.

Anders scanned the room and was delighted. He believed from the beginning of the candidacy that Walters should have insinuated himself into the wide open Republican field. Anders subscribed to Reagan's mantra that third party candidates would only split the conservative vote and guarantee the Democrat nominee's election.

RNC chairman Dudek introduced the campaign managers for the four Republican candidates. Rader knew each man intimately and took the responsibility of introducing the new founders, concluding with Tea Party candidate for president, Frank Walters. Dudek commented that it was a sincere pleasure to meet him. Walters thanked him.

"The pleasure is all mine. Please take a seat, gentlemen. You have asked us here at this early hour under the cover of secrecy so as not to alert the media sorts. So my friends, what can we do for you?"

Walters knew exactly why they were called to the meeting but he ceded the floor to the chairman.

"Mr. Walters, we've asked you, Mr. Rader and the rest of your team to Pittsburgh because we have a proposition for you. The Republican National Committee would like to ask you if you are interested in becoming the Republican candidate for the president of the United States."

Frank Walters sat at the head of the table in silence. He studied the

RNC chairman and the four campaign managers among them. He felt their mistrust and quiet hostility directed toward him. But it was neither the time nor the place for petty jealousies. The time had come to rise above the fray. Chairman Dudek felt uncomfortable in silence and continued his thought. "We all believe that with you as the nominee, we can unite the conservative movement, Republicans and Tea Partiers alike, and defeat this president and take back our country."

The General now felt it was time to speak. He rose to his feet.

"Mr. Dudek, I am flattered at your offer. But the men who accompany you do not share the same sentiments as you and the Republican National Committee. Am I correct in making this observation?"

The chairman told the group that Walters' assumption was correct. The advisors for the party's four candidates were not happy and did not take kindly to being shoved aside. But the party's financial backers and boosters instructed Dudek to make the offer. The only thing that mattered now was for Walters to take the helm and steer the ship to victory.

Walters listened and walked to the other side of the table. Standing behind the disgruntled managers, he began. "Everyone on the team, including myself, Mr. Rader and the rest of the team, agree that if the current president was reelected, it would mean the end of the constitutional republic the forebearers worked so hard to create. We discussed various ways to unite the Tea Party and Republican Party in order to win the conservative vote. Our pollsters and supporters informed the team that the Tea Party was fragmented and mistrustful of mainstream Republicans. They also believe the GOP establishment had become too arrogant and proud to even acknowledge the Tea Party. We had to unite forces."

Candidate Walters went on to explain that he appreciated the deep pitfalls of party politics saying that that these political parties needed to come together or face disastrous defeat. Walters reminded everybody of the 1992 election in which third party candidate Ross Perot took enough conservative votes to hand Bill Clinton the presidency. Murray and Jenson smiled knowing that the history lessons with their boss had paid off.

"My team believes, as do your bosses with the deep pockets and heavy wallets, that I am the candidate to bring all factions of the conservative movement together. In light of this, I accept your proposal and will humbly accept the Republican Party nominee for the office of President of the United States."

Chairman Dudek offered immediate thanks and breathed a sigh of relief. Frank Walters led all current polls and seemed to be just getting started. Dudek pulled a folder of papers from his briefcase and passed them to the men at the table. He announced that the document in each man's hands was a multiple point strategy of how to win the election. He was about to begin when Anders interrupted the presentation.

"Bullet point number three states that Walters will choose a running mate from the four candidates currently in the race."

The chairman told him he was getting ahead of the plan but yes, he was correct. Mr. Walters immediately placed the paper on the table.

"That is not negotiable. I will choose the vice-presidential candidate of my liking."

This stopped the chairman in his tracks. Instead of confronting the issue head on, he asked the teams to start with the first topic on the agenda, which was the transfer of delegates to Walters and then they would get back to Anders' point.

"This would take place on the third day of the convention. The candidates will instruct their constituents, prior to the convention, to announce all of their delegate votes to you during the roll call. Election rules allow us to do this. But we want to do this quietly. We do not want word getting out to the media so everything to be done under the cloud of the convention has to be done in stealth secrecy. We think that keeping everybody guessing until Alabama announces their delegates to Walters will maximize the drama. It's easily worth five to ten points in the polls."

Walters nodded in agreement. He liked the idea of secrecy and was confident that his team was up for the challenge. But upon further inspection, he noticed that point two in the strategy agenda did not meet his expectations, either.

"Your second point states that the RNC will choose the keynote speaker to open the convention. Is that correct?"

Dudek explained that having the party choose the speaking lineups was always convention protocol. He asked how that could offend the new candidate.

"I trust you men know what you're doing when it comes to setting up a gala such as this. But I ask that you allow me the honor of choosing the keynote speaker. Anything else you do within those four days is perfectly acceptable to me."

The head of the RNC scribbled notes on his legal pad. In all his years in politics and now, in his second term as chairman, he had never encountered a politician barking orders and making demands in the framework of the Republican Convention. He, however, muttered meekly that there should be no problem accommodating the candidate's wishes.

They moved onto post-convention events and policies going forward. The chairman decided to skip the vice-president issue and circle back to it. He described how bringing two conservative teams and philosophies together would mean a little compromise from both sides. He stressed flexibility in dealing with the hot topics of the day. He listed two to start.

"Our polling has shown that illegal immigration and the economy are on every American's mind right now. The Tea Party has pounded away on the illegals saying they should all be sent home. Many people consider the Tea Party's economic approach to the spending issue 'draconian.' And taxes, well, they are a whole chapter by themselves."

Walters now seemed concerned. He looked up at Dudek without moving his head and asked the party chairman to elaborate on his concerns.

"You need to lighten up on the illegal immigration hot button. It's not going away any time soon. Think of it as the crazy aunt that you can't get rid of so you just deal with it. And with the economy, we can't cut spending all together nor can we eliminate tax increases entirely. But if we promise to manage each properly, we can secure the votes to win the election. What do you say?"

Walters placed the paper back on the table and answered with a resounding *no* that took the room by surprise. He sat expressionless, waiting for a response from anybody. Rader broke the uncomfortable aura by asking the candidate for a word in private. The two men excused themselves into an adjacent hallway.

Murray, who had been silently obsessing over his personal issues (while keeping an ear on the conversation), stared into Mr. Walters' face. Murray couldn't shake the questions that had surfaced back in Vegas when Walters convinced him to continue on to California despite his son being in a coma back in Virginia.

What was this guy? Was he from another time or from another planet? What did he really care about? Himself? His men? His country?

On the other hand, he had never met anyone as strong willed and sure of himself. There was no wishy-washy political correctness to the General. He was hard core, literally old school and willing to stand or fall on his principles.

"My God," thought Murray. "We have gotten so soft as a people and have accepted such mediocre leadership in this country that we don't even recognize greatness when we see it."

Hahn leaned toward Murray and whispered that Rader's idea was not a smart one.

"The General is going to take him out to the woodshed for an old-fashioned ass whuppin,' wouldn't you say?"

The comment broke Murray's seriousness and he let out a laugh that drew attention around the table. His fellow new founders seemed to read his mind as they too smiled while the strangers looked puzzled. Concurrent with Murray's personal revelation, Rader led the candidate into the adjacent hallway. Once out of earshot of the conference room, the two men huddled.

"Mr. Walters, politics is tricky this way. I know you're steadfast in your opinions and ideas, but we have to be flexible in matters of the American people. That is the only way we can win this thing. These guys want you to be their candidate. You have to give a little."

Walters listened respectfully. Then as what had become a custom of his, Mr. Walters placed his hands on Rader's shoulders and shook his head.

"Ken, please take off your figurative political hat for a second. This is our ship and we are steering the rudder, not them. They came to us. It was foretold and inevitable that they would eventually seek us out to join forces. What they have suggested will just make our ship weaker; make our wooden planks leak until our ship ends up sinking. I will not allow this to happen and we will not waiver. Do you understand?"

Rader hoped to influence his candidate but to no avail. He saw determination in Walters' steely eyes, which told him Walters would not budge. He said okay as both men reentered the conference room.

The adviser's head hung low as both men reappeared. Hahn slapped Murray across the shoulder and nodded a big grin as if to say I told you so. Murray responded with a thumb up below tabletop level so as to keep the gesture secret.

The chairman expected Rader to influence the candidate's position and grew frustrated when he learned that Rader had not been successful. He implored Walters to reconsider his positions. This clearly agitated the candidate and he took a tone even the new founders had yet to see.

"Mr. Dudek, you asked us here this morning because you need us. We do not need you. The most recent polling of likely voters shows us holding a 56-39 point lead on the top GOP candidate and a 51-47 lead on the incumbent president. We will easily defeat any of your four candidates. And a Tea Party victory will be the beginning of the end for the Republican Party as you and I know. We did not come here to listen to demands. We came here to win this election. We will stop this nonsense of compromising our values or dictating our choice of vice-president."

Chairman Dudek was not used to being dressed down in any setting and he asked that Walters look at the big picture and be reasonable. In Mr. Walters' view, he could not have been more reasonable.

"You are losing this race. It is now time to attack. And attack we will. Get on board the SS Walters now before we leave you at the dock. Conservative America and its media counterparts are behind us one hundred percent. If the people had their way, guys like Bill O'Reilly and Sean

Hannity and Dennis Miller would have us on twenty-four hours a day."

Walters felt his blood at a boil and decided to take pause; if he had his sword he may have drawn it. He did not want to lose his temper in front of these new acquaintances. He stepped back and took a deep breath before continuing.

"We will look at the rest of your strategic endeavors and let you know what we think. Mr. Rader will be reaching out to you over the next day. And remember, in politics, the middle way is no way at all. Good day, Mr. Dudek."

The new Republican nominee shook the hands of each man at the table. He informed his team that their business was done and they exited the room behind him. On the walk to the front door, Hahn could not contain himself.

"You really did a number on him in there."

Mr. Walters, not breaking stride, reached for the front door.

"Pleasant man, but very naïve. He thinks sticking to a stale formula that does not work anymore is going to win an election. We will educate him."

The Republican candidate for president and his campaign management drove toward the rising sun, eager to get on the plane back to Virginia and plan their campaign's next adventure.

Chapter 30

Jack Murray sat at the bar in the 360 Steakhouse at the top of the Harrah's Hotel and Casino in Council Bluffs, Iowa. He had just finished a big filet mignon dinner with his fellow campaign staff and finally got a free moment to himself as his colleagues departed for the casino downstairs. It had been a long day of barnstorming throughout the heartland, culminating with a rousing rally in Omaha, Nebraska's Rosenblatt Stadium. The crowd was larger than expected, revealing the Midwest's enthusiasm for the Tea Party and Republican Party candidate for president.

Rader's suggestion that the team stay at the hotel casino across the river from Omaha was met with excitement. Even Frank Walters himself agreed with the decision, understanding that the men needed to unwind after another grueling stretch. It was not lost on him that after the stay in the Las Vegas casino a couple of weeks before, the men seemed re-energized and focused; all the men except Murray.

The Virginian history professor sat quietly, sipping his gin and tonic as he stared at the lights of Omaha across the Mississippi River. Murray stared at their reflection on the river as he thought of the events of the past month. He needed the time alone. His boss was a few floors down in a suite, probably with his favorite secret service agent, while his colleagues were most likely at the blackjack tables. Faulk fancied himself an expert card counter and Murray really wanted to see if he was on par with Rain Man.

But there was time for that a little later. Right now he had to absorb what had transpired since the festivities at Federal Hall in New York. Murray thought that challenging the president to a debate was crazy, knowing that he would never show. But the gamble paid off when the polls skyrocketed in their favor. It showed Walters really understood people.

Even the liberal media acknowledged the success of the showing. Murray mumbled that if it was Walters' intention to drive William Fredericks crazy, he had succeeded. Fredericks' daily television show had provided the comic relief their campaign needed as each day brought a new allegation of stolen identity and sordid accusations that made even his bosses at the network tire of the rants.

Murray and his fellow founders knew the truth but still took pleasure in the left leaning talking heads "eating their young." As he took the last gulp of his drink, he motioned for the bartender and stated aloud that the nut on WNN was worth two percentage points by himself.

The bartender shot him an odd look as he poured Murray another drink.

"What do you think of that guy, Walters?" Murray asked. "You see him today?"

Murray had to get some feedback, and who better to ask than a local bartender. He responded by telling Murray that he hated all politicians.

"But this guy seems alright. He doesn't sound like a politician and there's no BS."

Murray recalled the trip from New Jersey to New York before the Federal Hall debate. The men kept pointing out landmarks and notable towns but Walters downplayed it. He certainly was not as impressed as he had been on that Fourth of July weekend in Philadelphia that seemed like eons ago. As they approached the toll booth to go into Manhattan, the George Washington Bridge was in full view before them. The candidate took note but Murray noticed that he was not impressed. When Faulk asked him about crossing the Hudson to escape the British during the Revolutionary War, he shrugged, stating that the river was a lot wider back then without the landfill and bridge. Then, Walters refocused on his debate preparation.

Murray turned on his stool to face the diners. He watched the patrons enjoy their steaks over lively conversation. He wondered how many discussions revolved around his boss and the rally earlier in the day. The overriding thought in his head was, "If these people only knew who he really was. If they only knew what had gone down in that small conference room outside of Pittsburgh."

He could not believe how Walters had dressed down a high powered political professional like Chairman Dudek in front of the whole room. He was astounded at how disrespectful the nominee was to the man who was charged with bringing forth a candidate to win the presidency. But even through all of that, Murray could not help but be impressed with the RNC chairman's professionalism and maturity. After that morning, Dudek deferred to the Walters campaign team and accommodated the men at every step.

His lineup of speakers at the convention and the arrangement of the talent were crucial to building the excitement in Tampa. He embraced Walters' suggestion to have Tim Jenson deliver the keynote address, a decision that wowed the crowd and ultimately made Mr. Jenson a future candidate for national office himself. Murray could not believe how good his speech was, even intimating a bit of jealousy.

His thoughts jumped back to Dudek's plan to throw all delegates to Walters during the roll call. It stayed a secret and was carried out to perfection. When Alabama announced their contingent to Walters, the media was stunned. As each state followed in kind, the reaction could not have been more favorable for the campaign. The media did not know how to react. Their hesitation and confusion just added to the positive fervor in the domed stadium.

Even Dudek's prediction of negative feedback over the selection of Anders for vice-president was correct. But to his credit, the nimble chairman soothed over the hard feelings in the Republican establishment without once apologizing for the Anders pick. Dudek might not have fallen on his sword all the way for the new nominee, but Murray respected his political acumen and knew him to be an asset for the rest of the campaign.

Walters seemed to realize this as well, as he relied on Dudek more and more in the days leading up to the first debate with the incumbent president. He brought the chairman into debate preparatory sessions and asked his opinions regularly. He blended in well with the rest of the team, even though he clashed a few times with Ken Rader, who felt threatened by the outsider. And Hahn, who seemed to clash with everybody before long.

Jack slowed his drinking now, understanding that tomorrow was another busy day. He nursed his gin and tonic as he watched the baseball game on the television over the bar. As he did, he reviewed in his head the main points of the debate for which they prepped Walters. They wanted their candidate to stress the economy and to use the president's own words and promises against him. He recalled Walters sitting quietly in those brainstorming sessions, soaking in the content.

Of course, the General did not disappoint. The one debate with the president went about as well as it could have. Walters figuratively took the president to school, talking about high taxes and gasoline prices and redistribution of wealth. He described the Laffer curve and how it applied to the current economy, following the script the team had laid out for him. He then moved to illegal immigration, citing the Supreme Court case against Arizona, and ridiculed the Commander-in-Chief when he asked how the federal government could sue one of its own states for enforcing laws that the federal government deputized the states to enforce (and refused to enforce themselves).

When he showed the absurdity of PresidentCare, the traditionally stoic cadets in the audience at West Point couldn't hide their amusement and erupted in laughter so boisterous, their Tactical Officers had to ask for quiet and respect.

But neither the economy nor the border issue were what won the night for nominee Walters. It was his closing statement that had the greatest impact, an idea that he had not shared with his team previously. As a matter of fact when he started his summation, Murray and the team let out an audible gasp. Dudek looked at Rader, who looked at the others as if to say, "Here we go again." The newest additions to the campaign were about to get another lesson in unorthodox politics.

Walters started by scolding his opponent for starting an era of class warfare and creating jealousies between fellow Americans. He called the idea of redistribution of wealth in the name of fairness an anathema to our society, benefitting chosen constituents and many of the forty-seven percent of Americans who did not pay federal income tax at all. He exclaimed that fairness was not defined by one American giving more of his hard earned dollars to a government that would take its cut and then use the balance to attempt to buy a vote from another American.

He asked who was qualified to judge what was fair.

Walters rhetorically asked if any political leaders, founding fathers or even Supreme Court Justices could be entrusted as the arbiters of fairness. Murray chewed on a lime as he recalled a nervous president peering down at his podium, not having the courage to look his opponent in the eye. Murray knew Walters had the eye of the tiger, but on that night, it was more like the eye of Godzilla.

Walters turned his head toward the camera and announced to the world that God was the judge of fairness; the Almighty deemed what was fair in the world when He delivered the Ten Commandments to Moses. Walters listed the commandments, stressing those related to honesty and envy. Murray thought Walters made a mistake of biblical proportions. The rest of the new founders agreed with Murray, understanding religious references to be the suicidal powder keg in presidential politics.

But Walters did not care. He understood what people wanted, needed, and believed. Had they known what he was going to say in advance, Murray knew the team would have done everything to dissuade their candidate from raising this taboo subject. The candidate knew that too, which was why he had kept it from them until he used it during the debate.

Once again, it worked.

Walters seemed to be addressing each American one on one when he said with reverence that nothing but harmony, honesty, industry, and frugality were necessary to make us a great and happy people.

He concluded by challenging his opponent, pronouncing that in his four years, the president offered America exactly none of those essential elements. Walters took the president to task on each of his four points, detailing the fostering of class warfare, the misrepresentation of President-Care, the attack on vibrant and successful industries, and the spending that brought the country to the brink of oblivion.

The civilian part of the audience shot to attention with the military contingent and let out a roar of approval that rivaled any C-17 on takeoff.

The president's closing statement was rendered moot. Murray noted that it was as if the Rolling Stones had opened for Don Ho. It seemed that Frank Walters had all but secured the White House that night.

Murray settled his bar tab and headed toward the elevator. He wanted to go to the casino and join his friends. He felt lucky and was eager to test that luck at the roulette wheel or the blackjack tables. As he waited to go down, his thoughts wandered back to his wife and son. He wanted to call Dottie. In a moment of immaturity, he told himself that it was her turn to call as he put his cell phone back in his pocket.

The last time he called, she told him that Todd had shown improvement. He was still in a coma, but his body responded well to treatment and the doctors thought that a full recovery was very possible. He was thrilled and relieved to hear that, but uneasy with the tone in which Dottie delivered the news. She was still very cold to him, which made him feel angry and sick to his stomach. Murray's wife had taken on the persona of a criminal attorney in cross examination and it made him cringe.

As the doors opened and the lights and sounds of the casino filled the elevator, Jack Murray soberly gave his marriage a 50/50 chance of survival.

———— • ————

Dottie was thinking the same thing. She was in the same spot she had been in for the past month. She sat at the bedside of her son, holding his hand and stroking his now long and unkempt hair. Dottie looked at her boy, thinking that he looked pretty good for a kid that had been in a coma as long as he had. He had not lost much weight and his face had good color. She looked at her reflection in the window and realized she could not say the same for herself.

She looked tired, almost frail, and had circles under her eyes that could not be hidden by makeup anymore. Even though the doctors had given Todd a good prognosis, she still worried as he had still yet to respond.

Those worries were not just limited to her son's condition. The status of her marriage weighed heavily on her mind. She had cheered Mr. Walters during his debate win over the president and had watched the evening news report of the rally from Omaha. Her husband was in his normal spot during the speech, three men to the candidate's right on stage.

A little jealousy seeped into her thoughts as she wished she could trade places with her husband for just one night. Dottie started to rattle off different scenarios for the future, telling herself that if Walters won and Murray was to be part of his administration, she and Todd would not move to Washington. She knew an election win would all but solidify Jack joining the Walters' administration. She did not know what election outcome would be better, a Walters' win or loss.

Dottie took a deep breath and realized she was getting ahead of herself. She squeezed Todd's hand and told her comatose son that a politician's paycheck was a lot better than a high school teacher's.

Dottie started to think of Jack's good qualities. As always, she told herself that Jack was a good person, the type that always wanted to please everyone. He probably struggled with his decision to stay with the campaign. He told Dottie over and over to look at the big picture and the importance of the world-changing events to which he was now an integral part. She understood, but could not bring herself to give him the satisfaction of agreeing. The hurt caused by Jack's delay in coming home had yet to go away.

Still, she could not shake the feeling that the schism between the Murrays was partially her fault. She pushed him toward this, but had she pushed him too far? And over the last month, had she pushed him far enough away where it was impossible to reconcile? The thought of a life without Jack would devastate Dottie.

These thoughts consumed her so much that she did not notice her son's subtle squeeze of her hand.

She told herself that if Todd recovered in the next week, she would join her husband for the remainder of the campaign. After all, who was Dottie Murray to judge anybody? Walters' words from the debate left an impression. Whatever was going to happen was God's will and as she told herself this, a quiet calm came over her. She felt at peace and reminded herself to call Jack in the morning.

Murray had been at the blackjack table for an hour, but his mind was elsewhere. He was only down twenty dollars, but he was just going through the motions. He could not get his mind off his wife and son. The campaign was scheduled to be in New York and then back to Virginia in the days leading up to Election Day. He hoped to see Dottie and, if Todd was on the mend, possibly have her join him on election night.

Jack pushed his chips toward the dealer, asking to be cashed out. He spied Faulk and Hahn at the next table. Sure enough, the two card sharks had huge piles of chips in front of them. The dealer gave him his chips back as he informed him that the cashier would pay him the money he was owed. He thanked the dealer and walked to the cashier window before heading up to his room.

Chapter 31

It was all but over. At least that's what the team thought in the two weeks following the debate. Walters' dismantling of the president that night in West Point left the incumbent reeling. Even the mainstream media had all but declared the election over.

But this president was not a man to be underestimated; especially when his public mouthpiece was none other than William Fredericks.

Fredericks' professional and personal life was in a tailspin since the night of Walters' one man show at Federal Hall. He had verbally assaulted his wife on the platform set next to the stock exchange and followed it up with an on-air rant that resulted in a warning from the FCC. Subsequent shows yielded more of the same until the Monday show.

That was the day that Fredericks opened by stating that through his reliable sources, he had information stating that candidate Walters' cancer, thought to be in remission, had returned. Fredericks reported that the man who led in the polls was weakened by secret chemotherapy treatments. He showed recent pictures of Walters on the campaign trail and compared them to pictures of his original appearance at the Lincoln Memorial. Not willing to attribute Walters' visible weight loss and sunken eyes to the rigors of an aggressive campaign travel schedule, Fredericks pointed to the photographs as evidence of cancer.

The talk show host was doing the president's dirty work and getting results. In only a matter of days, Fredericks accomplished what the president himself had failed to do in the last month, which was to chip away at the candidate's lead in the polls.

Murray and his colleagues were stuck in traffic at the Holland Tunnel. The radio in the limousine delivered the latest polling, revealing their boss's lead shrinking in the last days of the election. The men figured if the president could not beat their man on the issues, he would have to resort to scare tactics, rumors and flat out lies. Unfortunately for them, it was working.

The new founders were nervous and it showed; so much so that their boss scolded them after a rally in Columbus, Ohio. He decided he had heard enough pessimistic talk. Walters told the men to meet with local campaign officials there while he and Pepper flew ahead to New York for a meeting with a conservative PAC group at the Grand Hyatt Hotel near Grand Central Station. The team was to fly back on a commercial jet into Newark the next day. Faulk joked that they had to rough it, not having access to the private accommodations they had become accustomed to.

Murray was concerned. The cancer talk had not let up and it didn't help that the candidate had fallen in the shower, twisting his ankle and walking with a noticeable limp throughout the Midwestern swing. His appearance just fueled the rumors. Now as the car entered the EZ Pass lane, the all news WINS AM radio station reported the story, giving it credence.

Murray hoped Walters would become George Washington once again and answer the allegations with the same forceful zeal he had exuded from the start. The team needed some reassurances and hoped to get some honest answers at dinner that evening.

Pepper set up a private dinner meeting at Fraunces Tavern in downtown Manhattan at Walters' request. The media was not alerted to the event and Ken Rader did not mention the dinner in his daily press briefing. Walters and Pepper arrived in a normal yellow cab as to not draw attention.

The historical significance of Fraunces Tavern was not lost on the new founders. As the limo entered the tunnel, Hahn mentioned that he was a regular there since he began working downtown. He described the history of the restaurant from its establishment as the Queen's Head Tavern to its presence as the site of the Sons of Liberty Tea Party meetings. Hahn said it got its name from its founder, Samuel Fraunces, a free black man born in the West Indies and personal friend of none other than George Washington.

Hahn's tone turned serious when he described in intimate detail the 1975 terrorist bombing at Fraunces that killed four and injured scores of others. He explained that most of his generation unfortunately knew the building as a watering hole instead of an edifice of historical merit. Hahn finished by informing the men that his friend who lost his life on 9/11 in the World Trade Center, first lost his godfather to the lunchtime terrorist act at Fraunces Tavern. He noted with considerable disgust that for cheap politics, a former president granted clemency to the terrorists without them repenting or requesting the pardons.

"Alexander Hamilton wrote in *The Federalist Papers* that 'The dread of being accused of weakness or connivance,' would pretty much guarantee that future presidents wouldn't abuse this power. I guess he never foresaw the modern president."

Hahn's last tidbit silenced the men for the remainder of the car ride. Pepper stood at the doorway of the restaurant as the car pulled up. He greeted the men one by one with the handshake of a man campaigning for political office himself. Everybody thought the gesture peculiar as they had spent most of the last two months together with the man.

Walters was waiting for the men inside when they arrived at the Pearl Street address. As he always did, Hahn noted the music in the Tavern to the team and smiled at the selection of Frank Sinatra's "My Way" playing in the background.

The team believed that after his back to back masterful performances weeks earlier, Walters had the presidency all but sown up. But things had changed since and Josh Anders was the first to bring up the topic.

"George, and I think I speak for all of us, we're concerned with the latest polling. Your numbers are slipping with all this cancer talk and nobody is addressing the issue. We need to tell the press something, even a canned response."

It took a few seconds before the new founders realized that Josh had called the candidate George. At first the men scanned the room to make sure there were no outsiders lingering. Then Murray asked where secret service agent Michelle was, to which Walters curtly responded that she was somewhere else.

The candidate did not seem to notice being called by his real name, nor did he acknowledge Anders' concern. He elaborated on their fantastic journey which brought them to this point. He said almost apologetically that it would soon be ending and, if all went as expected on Tuesday, the team would be faced with the daunting task of governing a nation.

Walters then waved his hand and stated that the presidency was a subject for tomorrow. It might have been a party to the boss, but the new founders all sensed there was more to this dinner than celebration. Walters toasted the team by thanking them for their first class work. Faulk whispered to Steve Anders that the big guy looked as if he had had a few drinks before their arrival. Murray overhead the line and seconded it.

While still holding his wine glass in the air, Walters told of his connection to the old restaurant, telling everybody what Hahn had said less than an hour earlier, that on December 4, 1783, he bid emotional goodbyes to his officers after the Revolutionary War. He waved his hand back and forth, noting that they stood in the very room where the goodbye took place.

Walters explained that each Revolutionary officer had taken a glass of wine and came forward in tears to take his hand. This act of respect was followed by an escort of the General to a boat that took him across the Hudson and on toward his retirement in Mount Vernon.

The new founders were emotional as they listened to their leader's voice crack as he described the glory and sadness of a past life with those he loved but had been gone for hundreds of years.

Walters was the most celebrated man in the country again, yet he was alone. He spoke from the heart.

"My dear friends, those men of 1783 were very special to me, some of the bravest and most honorable men this country has ever seen. I had a world of respect for those men and yet I would take every single one of you over them, one hundred times out of one hundred. There is no doubt about that."

The seriousness of the moment was interrupted by the ringtone of Jack Murray's cell phone. The Virginian excused himself to take the call from his semi-estranged wife. Walters continued to describe his trip back to Virginia following his farewell. He lightened the conversation by joking that he wished he had a private jet and pretty stewardess for the trip instead of a bumpy carriage that took a week to get to its destination. As the men laughed, Murray reentered the room. He looked dejected.

"Everything okay?"

Walters was comfortable enough to ask the question in front of the team. Everybody knew and felt what Murray was going through. They were sympathetic.

"Yeah, everything's good. Todd came out of his coma this afternoon. He's responding well but doesn't remember the accident, which may be a good thing."

The men thought that news would have brought elation from their compatriot and were puzzled by his reaction. Walters thought the same thing, but turned his attention back to his speech. The first president, in barely a whisper, thanked the new founders.

"Gentlemen, in but three days when the election concludes, we will have achieved Providence's calling. You have all done very well. I thank you and our nation thanks you."

Walters sounded sanguine as he concluded.

"I will now take my leave for Virginia as we did in another lifetime."

Murray's attention was fully back in the room. He had been suspicious of Walters' intentions since his first appearance on the Fredericks' show and leaned in to grab Walters' arm.

"What do you mean, sir?"

The General patted Murray's hand as he scanned the room.

"While the other men continue the last few days of the campaign with Mr. Rader, I will ask you and Mr. Hahn to deliver me to my adopted home of Arnold, Maryland. I need to speak with Connor Walters and pay him my respects to his fine father who helped make all of this possible. And lest we forget, I need to cast my vote."

As the men gathered their collective thoughts, they wondered why Hahn and Murray were chosen to go ahead. Before anybody had a chance to ask, their boss added another direction.

"We will then travel back to Mount Vernon and visit my beloved home on the Potomac where I will give thanks to Martha."

The team tried to digest the latest request that sounded like an order. But Walters spoke again, this time sounding again like an eighteenth century man.

"I know not what fate has in store for me but when I am gone, as I have nurtured you, so too should you nurture one another."

Anders had heard enough and jumped in quickly.

"But General, what are you saying? Where are you going? You'll be President-elect on Tuesday!"

Walters managed a smile and told Anders that he was very much like his forefather and that James Madison described John Adams best as always an honest man, often a wise one, but sometimes wholly out of his senses.

"I think we will not want for a qualified president. Do you, Mr. Anders?

Turning to the team yet again, Walters detailed how Providence had pre-ordained that fact, concluding his thoughts by stating that maybe "Mr. Walters" could relapse and expire from his cancer in the same fashion as the real Mr. Walters had met his fate.

"Now, Mr. Murray and Hahn, you will accompany me to Maryland and Virginia. The rest of you gentlemen, I bid a good evening. We will all be together again for our great victory."

Two secret service agents entered the room as Walters finished. He shook hands with the entire team before departing with Hahn and Murray. The streets were desolate as the three men, accompanied by the agents, entered the limo on the brisk autumn evening.

Having departed Fraunces Tavern, the rest of the team stood on the sidewalk and looked at each other, unsure of what had just transpired or what was next.

Chapter 32

The car ride up the west side of Manhattan was uneventful. Rush hour was over and traffic was light as the black limousine made a right turn into the entrance of the Lincoln Tunnel. The occupants had yet to breathe a word since departing downtown and they continued to look at the candidate, waiting for some explanation of what went down earlier in the evening.

Mr. Walters would not be so forthcoming. He stayed silent as the car passed the Mercedes dealership and descended into the tunnel. Hahn could not take it anymore. As the car approached the New Jersey border one hundred feet below the Hudson River, the currency trader cleared his throat. Before he could get a word out, Walters finally spoke.

"Do you think we could stop at a McDonalds before we board our flight? I could really go for a couple of those cheeseburgers and a large chocolate shake."

Hahn and Murray couldn't believe their ears. The burly secret service agents quietly snickered as the driver looked back toward the group through the rearview mirror. Hahn noticed the chauffeur's glance and asked him if there were any on the way.

"Yes, sir, there's one on Route 46 right near the airport."

The candidate nodded in approval as the car came above ground and banked left up the ramp along the New Jersey riverfront. The New York skyline lit up the night sky to the right and Walters peered solemnly across the river, as if to say goodbye to the city of his first inauguration.

Jack Murray observed Frank's odd expression and asked him if he was going to address the rumors about a cancer relapse that were so prevalent in the news. Once again, Walters seemed disinterested in the topic and decided to change the subject.

"Jack, you said Todd was out of his coma before. Why the sour puss, I thought you would be happy to hear that."

Murray hesitated in surprise, not expecting his question to be answered with an unexpected and personal question. He didn't want to talk about it but felt he owed Walters and Hahn an explanation.

"Dot had mentioned that if Todd came out of it, she would join us for election night. When I reminded her, she said there was no way she could leave him at the hospital. I mean, could she leave him in better hands for a few hours than nurses and doctors in a hospital?"

He stopped short, realizing that he sounded a little selfish. Hahn put his hand on Murray's shoulder, reminding him that Todd's health was the most important thing. Their boss looked on approvingly, pleased at Hahn's mature response and kind gesture.

He joked to himself that given their proximity to Weehawken, Hahn would not be challenging Murray to a duel anytime soon. He then asked if they were near the drive thru yet.

"How can you still be hungry after the dinner you ate?"

The diminutive Murray was not a big eater. He marveled at his boss's uncanny ability to stay trim and even lose weight while maintaining a junk food diet. It started at that rest stop in Maryland over July Fourth weekend and it had yet to slow down. He asked the first president for a list of his favorite fast food restaurants and preferred choices. Walters did not hesitate.

"McDonalds has great cheeseburgers and fries. I can eat those every day. White Castles are good, too, but they don't always agree with me. Can't be eating those if I'm going to be flying for a couple hours."

Murray thought if Frank decided to forgo a political career, he could get him booked on the comedy circuit as a stand-up comedian. Johnny Carson would have loved him.

Walters went on to list a host of other establishments, all of which made his top ten. He finished his tally but made sure the group knew he appreciated a finer meal too.

"That filet mignon I had at Bonz in Atlanta was one of the best steaks I have ever tasted. And the veal at Campagnola in Manhattan was incredible. But right now I need a cheeseburger and I see it ahead!"

All heads turned as the golden arches appeared in the near distance. To Hahn and Murray, the scene was surreal. The man next to him could eat in the finest restaurants in America; at any time and for free as they had been comped just about everywhere they went. But all he wanted now was a McDonalds burger. At least he wasn't looking for mutton tonight. Both men shook their heads as they turned into the parking lot.

The Gulfstream jet was wheels up as it climbed and banked left over Bergen County in northern New Jersey. As soon as the plane straightened its turn and started its direct path toward Maryland, Walters unbuckled his seat belt and instructed Murray and Hahn to join him in the private room at the back of the cabin. The men complied and shut the door behind them, leaving the secret service agents to the last of their chicken nuggets and sodas.

Walters sat on the edge of the bed as the others found their seats next to him. Their leader told the new founders that he wanted to speak with them in private, away from nosy eyes and ears of any agents, drivers or pilots. Hahn asked why new agents were assigned to his detail. Walters did not hesitate.

"Twenty-first century ladies may look different and dress differently than eighteenth century women, but they all think alike. And while I was very fond of Michelle, I thought it best not to lead her on in any way. It wouldn't be fair to either of us."

Hahn blurted out that he thought they were an item. He wanted to talk about their rendezvous, but Walters had other ideas.

"She helped me out a great deal. I trusted her with my life. I did not reveal my true identity to her as I did with you and your colleagues. But I believe she suspected it and was attracted to it."

Murray asked specifically how she helped him. Washington was more than happy to elaborate.

"The cancer rumors. I gave her the information detailing the story of the relapse and the secret doctor visits. She made sure the information got to William Fredericks."

Hahn and Murray were flabbergasted. They did not know how to react. Surprise was followed by anger and it was Hahn who was the first to speak.

"You were the source of the rumors? Are you insane? That nut job is reporting it as gospel on every news outlet on television, radio and the internet. Why would you even think of doing something like that? It cut your lead in the polls in half in less than a week. The country is wondering if you're well enough to make it to an inauguration. What do you have to say about that?"

While Hahn ranted, Murray could not help but notice the tranquil look on Walters' face as Hahn's spittle sprayed around him. Murray wanted to say everything his colleague was screaming before the light bulb went on in his head. He finally started to understand the method to Walters' madness that was his presidential campaign. Hahn's raised voice led to a knock at the door, which Walters quickly diffused. The agents appearing at the door left Hahn slightly intimidated. He sat back down and waited for an answer that came after a short pause. Walters dismissed them and they returned to the hallway.

"Gentlemen," Walters' said. "Do you see what that little tidbit of information has done to my adversary, Fredericks? He is slowly disintegrating before us, going mad in front of our eyes. It was preordained; we just sped up the process."

Murray, for one, was not buying the explanation.

"Is that the only reason?"

Walters gave a nod and a wink, confirming that Murray knew better. Murray understood Walters' body language and decided to keep his thoughts to himself. For the first time in a while, he felt good, knowing that he had one up on the rest of the new founders. There could be only one reason why Walters leaked the cancer story to the press and Murray felt he knew why.

He smiled as Hahn changed gears and asked why Republican chairman Dudek had not been on the campaign trail.

"He's taking care of all the Election Night preparations. We have a block of rooms and the ballroom of the Westin Annapolis Hotel. It should be a big gala on Tuesday."

Hahn noted that at least he hadn't set the festivities to take place in one of the many seedy motels near National Airport.

———

In one of those motels sat William Fredericks.

For Fredericks, it was not over. As a matter of fact, his mind was churning faster than ever before. His internal demons would not let go and they no longer cared about the president anymore. He had done all he could to help but the incumbent was destined to lose. Fredericks' attention turned to destroying his nemesis.

As he sat on the motel room floor, propped against the bed with hundreds of pictures and articles scattered on the floor before him, Fredericks wondered how he had not seen it before, had not noticed what was now clear as day. The hand holding his third bottle of gin also gripped a picture of candidate Frank Walters at Federal Hall. He stood next to the statue of George Washington and struck a pose identical to the first president. The talk show host could not believe his eyes.

The photograph revealed the candidate to be the one and only George Washington. His talk, his walk and his mannerisms were all identical to what he had heard and read about the father of America. Even the way he addressed Fredericks on his talk show was eerily familiar. The voices that he referred to as Them told him all along but he was slow to believe it. Now there was no doubt.

Since the humiliation of their last meeting and the public degradation in New York, when Sophia turned on him as she did, the voices focused on unmasking Walters. They knew they had him. Now the demons screamed that Frank Walters was George Washington and demanded Fredericks expose this impostor to the world.

He knew he had to do it, but how? Following his on and off air debacle downtown, Fredericks' already chaotic life had spiraled completely out of control. He stopped eating, barely slept and worst of all, pushed Sophia and his children away. All the while the voices relentlessly pushed Fredericks to unmask Frank Walters and annihilate their enemy.

Fredericks spent most of the last week in the darkness of his motel room, downing bottle after bottle of Beefeater and obsessively pouring over a myriad of newspaper articles, photos, sound bites and internet video of Mr. Walters. The network had had enough and suspended Fredericks, fueling his spiral downward.

Fredericks now had the way to get back into the good graces of his bosses. He pulled out his cell phone and dialed his producer. While he tried to be coherent, measuring his words carefully, the alcohol and the demons would not let him. His producer's first hint of doubt sent Fredericks into a rambling and disjointed rant, demanding that he be let on the air to alert the world of his discovery.

His producer remained calm throughout, but would not relent. He told the suspended host that he had become a liability and that the network had carried him long enough. His loose cannon ways, which had yielded strong ratings in the past, were not working anymore. His show had been displaced by a conservative talk show and there would be more changes coming.

But the producer did extend an olive branch, telling Fredericks that if he sobered up they might give him one last chance in the studio on Election night, to participate on a panel discussion about the election results. He demanded to know where Fredericks was but was met with the sound of a telephone slamming down. It was three days before the election and the demons would not relent. He had to do something but no longer had his pulpit to deliver the message. He had finally had the proof the voices demanded, but Fredericks had no way of delivering it. As he took another swig of gin, the demons told him to kill Walters.

Desperate, Fredericks pleaded with Them.

"Why?? Why him? Why me?"

The voices replied that it was always his destiny and that Fredericks had waited centuries for this moment. They instructed him to fulfill his destiny!

"What does that mean? Who am I?!"

The voices told him to seek Walters out on Election night as he will find him where he goes to die. Fredericks obediently agreed.

Chapter 33

It was usually a day of prayer and rest for Walters. This Sunday he was back at Pohick Episcopal Church in Lorton, near the site of the original Pohick church he attended in the eighteenth century. He preferred the 7:45 service, and this day was no different. Murray accompanied him.

Murray had his first peaceful sleep in over a month. He retired knowing that, Todd was awake and eating. On top of that he finally understood the man for whom he had alienated his family. He thought the long haul might be worth it after all. The history professor had a lot to be thankful for and happily slid into the back seat of the limousine with Walters and the secret service agents.

The men returned to their Mt. Vernon mansion and walked in to the smell of bacon and eggs in the air. They entered the dining room to find Brian Faulk and Anthony Hahn drinking their coffee while reading the Op Ed pages of the *New York Times* and *Washington Post*. Belly laughs followed each editorial line read by the two men. Murray gave Faulk a big hug while one of the staff handed Jack a mug of coffee.

"When did you arrive?"

Faulk flew down on the first shuttle flight out of LaGuardia and came straight from the airport. The campaign itinerary was light and Faulk wanted to join the team for the day.

After dropping Walters off the previous night, Pepper's jet had flown back to New Jersey. Josh and Steve Anders were on their way to Florida for a full day of speeches and handshakes across the state. Josh thought they needed to fully secure the Sunshine state and Walters agreed. They would fly back to Maryland the following morning.

With Faulk back in the fold, Murray figured he had an opening. He knew it was the calm before the storm and there would be a lot of work to do starting Monday, so Murray decided to go out on a limb and ask off the detail for the day.

Walters sat at the table with his coffee and croissant and looked up at his fellow Virginian. Without hesitation Walters agreed, allowing Murray the day off as he reached for the business section of The Times.

Murray pumped his fist and sat down for breakfast. A thousand thoughts went through his head, the first of which was to call Dottie. He thought about driving out to visit her and Todd at the hospital, but a three hour drive each way was not his definition of relaxation. He also wanted to watch the Redskins game at one. The Giants were on the schedule, and after spending more than enough time in New York and New Jersey surrounded by voters dressed in the blue and red of the Super Bowl champs, Murray was anxious for a win.

He dialed Dottie to ask her how Todd was and to let her know that he would be in Mount Vernon for the day. His call went to voicemail and he left a quick message. He then texted her Election Day details and the address of the Westin in Annapolis where the team would hopefully be celebrating on Tuesday night. Murray hoped she would have a change of heart and be able to make it. But for now, his mind focused on breakfast and the sports section.

———

Ken Rader said the day before the election was always busy and the men took his words to heart. Everybody was showered and dressed by seven and anxious to get going. For the first time, the founding fathers waited for their boss.

In no time they were out the door and stuck in rush hour traffic as they headed to Arnold, Maryland to visit Connor. The General was so busy campaigning and touring the country that he had not had the opportunity to get back to Arnold to see his surrogate son. He looked forward to spending some quality time with the grieving young man before a heavy afternoon schedule in DC.

The polling numbers had leveled off and the Republican candidate held a four to five percentage point lead according to Rasmussen and Gallup. Not surprisingly, he trailed in the WNN poll. The cancer rumors had subsided and confidence among the new founders rose once again. This was evident in the jokes and lively conversation among the men in the car. Even the secret service agents broke a smile as Faulk kept them entertained.

Arnold was usually an hour away, but traffic extended the trip. They pulled up to the house a few minutes before nine and were greeted by a couple local television reporters that had staked out the Walters' residence. Cameras caught the candidate gingerly stepping out of the car; but smooth as always, he gave each a few sound bites while he made his way to the front door.

The embrace between the candidate and son would lead the noon news reports. Connor led the General into the house, followed by Murray, Hahn, and Faulk. One secret service agent stepped in as the other stood guard at the entranceway.

Connor Walters still grieved over his father's death a few weeks earlier and broke down in tears once the door shut. To maintain the new founders' secrecy, George quickly ushered Connor into the back bedroom out of earshot from the secret service agents. The new founders stayed in the living room as well, making small talk and looking over family pictures on the bureau. Murray could not help but notice the agent's particular interest in a more recent photograph of the original Mr. Walters. Always very aware of the current situation, Murray interrupted his glance and invited him to the kitchen for a drink. Faulk and Hahn breathed a sigh of relief as the men departed the room.

Once in the study, the General again embraced Connor with an affectionate hug and delivered a line as only the General could.

"I understand your sadness Mr. Walters. Your father was an extraordinary man. The death of near relations always produces awful and affecting emotions, under whatsoever circumstances it may happen."

Connor pulled back, somewhat surprised at the formality of the message. He had watched this man every day on television and identified the gradual erosion of eighteenth century dialect in favor of the more common twenty-first century jargon.

Murray and Faulk entered the room, leaving Hahn to tend to the bodyguard. Murray stood to the side while Faulk reached out to young Mr. Walters.

"I condole with you as we have lost a most dear and valuable relation; but it is the will of God and Nature that these immortal bodies be laid aside when the soul is to enter into real life. We are all spirits, Connor. Our bodies are lent to us, but as you know full well, better than most, our spirits, never die." The General smiled, knowing firsthand how true Faulk's words were. Murray was shocked. He knew the man to be erudite, but Murray was used to a quick-witted storyteller and jokester that kept everybody loose. He realized that Mr. Faulk could deliver a line just as well as the General.

He silently accepted Faulk as Ben Franklin.

Murray explained that they wanted to provide their personal condolences and that the General would vote the following day at Arnold's Severn River Middle School. The men graciously declined Connor's invitation to stay the night and moved to the screened in porch to talk for the rest of the morning. The young man from Maryland reminisced about his childhood, told stories about his father, and showed them the bronze star he won in Vietnam. Hahn and Faulk had switched places, ensuring that the secret service remained out of earshot.

It may have been morning, but Connor and the General indulged in a couple of brandies, much to the chagrin of his advisors. The day was young and a lot lay ahead, but nobody wanted to intrude on the conversation. At that point, and for the first time since they met, Connor spoke in depth about the premature death of his beloved mother who passed away when he was only nine.

Murray listened as the young man's true emotions poured out and filled the porch. Murray related to Connor's lighthearted stories about his father's reaction to his somewhat domineering mother. The looks and good natured smirks he described in reaction to his mother's bossy ways hit home for Murray. He felt very comfortable in Arnold, Maryland.

Faulk had reappeared on the porch at the tail end of the story, sending the agent outside to ready the car for their next stop. Always with humor to spare, Faulk injected a Ben Franklin saying to lighten the conversation:

"Ill thrives that hapless family that shows, a cock that's silent and a hen that crows; I know not which lives more unnatural lives, obeying husbands or commanding wives."

Hahn applauded the rhyme, noting it was very apropos.

The General, who never had a child of his own, was taken by the young Connor. As the men left the house, the General reached into his front pocket and removed a badly damaged brass button wrapped in the red queue that had tied his ponytail when he first appeared in Philadelphia.

The General unwrapped the button, returned the queue to his pocket and, out of view of any onlookers, placed the barely recognizable relic in Connor's palm.

"Take this, young man. I have carried it since the Indian Wars of 1755 when Providence interceded and stopped a musket ball on my behalf. I have cherished it as a giver of life and so I give it to you to remember your father who quite literally gave me his life."

Murray was choked up as he watched Walters and the General embrace again and offer their teary goodbyes.

Sure enough, the lead story on local and cable news outlets was of candidate Frank Walters going home to see his son. The iconic vision of the embrace at the Walters' door did not disappoint an already energized conservative base. As the images shone bright, one man threw up his hands in disgust.

"I could get to Arnold in less than thirty minutes. But he must be gone by now."

William Fredericks was talking out loud to nobody. But the voices in his head were answering.

He said if Walters was in DC, he had to go to the capital to settle his score with him. But the voices intervened, telling him to be patient. They told Fredericks that he would go where they directed him to go and it was not yet the proper time.

"I have to do it before it's too late. I have to seek him out."

Fredericks swilled from the bottle, spilling alcohol on the sweat stained t-shirt he wore. He was adamant about going, but the forces in his head kept him at bay. The voices reminded him that he would be directed to the right place and the right time, where the final confrontation would take place. A sullen Fredericks raised his head and looked to the heavens.

"He will come to me? He will seek me out? Okay, I will wait."

While Fredericks waited, the Walters team descended on Washington DC. The afternoon was a blur as the campaign moved from neighborhood to neighborhood. Rader thought the trip futile as the candidate could never take a traditionally liberal city from the incumbent; and for what, a lousy three electoral votes?

Nevertheless, Walters felt he had to finish strong but did not want to stray too far from his home base in the day before the election. Besides, the Anders boys had done their job down south and the feedback from their eleventh hour visit was all positive.

The last stop of the day was the Willard Hotel, the site where the whole plan was originally hatched. The candidate had made a point to return for a final dinner before the Election Day marathon and the men gladly approved. They pulled to the lobby only to be greeted by more television cameras. Behind the media stood Josh and Steve Anders, campaign manager Rader and RNC chairman Dudek. The new founders in the car mentioned to Walters they were surprised to see that men who were not in on the original plot would join them for dinner at the now historic spot. Walters would hear none of it and responded with a very modern line.

"These men busted their hump for us and left their blood across the whole country. The least we could do is treat them to a first class dinner."

Before exiting the car, the leader reminded the group not to reminisce about the original meeting in front of Rader and Dudek as there would be time for that later. Just then a livery car pulled next to them and out popped Tim Jenson. He had flown to DC after his show to join the campaign team. He was scheduled to broadcast live from the Westin Hotel the following day and wanted to reunite with his colonial brethren.

His appearance enflamed some hurt feelings within Murray. While the original rumors of extramarital affairs had subsided, the thought of Jenson and Dottie together still gnawed at him. He buried the hurt for the moment as he received a big hug and kiss on the cheek from the new national talk show host.

"You son of a bitch, you look great! We have to catch up over dinner. I have a lot to tell you!"

Murray's first reaction was to think "I bet you do." But he quickly realized that anybody who would greet him in that manner could never betray him. The group waved to the cameras as they entered the lobby.

———

Election Day had finally come and the press was entrenched, waiting for Frank Walters at the middle school. Due to the crowds and ominous threat of a severe thunder storm, the candidate and his team pulled up as close to the gymnasium doors as possible. Walters exited the black limousine slowly and deliberately. He looked uncharacteristically feeble as he limped into the school. His ankle was throbbing from constantly being on his feet the day before and the impending storm just made it worse.

In all his wars and battles, Walters could not recall ever spraining his ankle.

Walters made his way past the reporters and cameras thrust in his face. The bright lights blinded him and he stumbled, only to be propped by Murray. A hush fell over the big room as he walked slowly toward the "W – Z" table. He eyed the volunteers manning the registration and leaned into Murray's ear.

"I didn't know my mother's sisters were hired to man the booths."

The candidate stood before the voter ledgers and put both hands on the table, holding himself up.

"Good afternoon, Mr. Walters. It's good to see you again, but you do not seem well. Are you yourself today?"

Murray marveled while Walters kept his composure.

"I am sure, madam, that I am no longer myself anymore. I belong to others. For when a man assumes a public trust, he should consider himself as public property."

Hahn turned to Murray and mouthed the word "Jefferson," correctly noting that their boss had just quoted the third president. Not wanting to press his luck any further, the candidate entered the booth, closed the curtain and voted. As quickly as he could, Walters exited the gym, moving deliberately past the reporters and ambled into the stretch Lincoln without further comment.

"Damn media, I'm glad that's over with. Let us head back to Mount Vernon to feast on mutton and potatoes."

"Okay, General."

Murray's reply reeked of sarcasm. He thought to himself that the father of their country had to be kidding with him. "Just get me through this day," Murray said to himself. "Just one more day and I can go home.

"Where the hell am I going to find mutton around here?" Murray said aloud.

Walters, picking up on Murray's tone, suggested in a very modern fashion that the GPS may have the answer. Less than an hour later, Murray couldn't help but laugh when instead of heading directly to their headquarter mansion, they pulled into the parking lot of a Giant Supermarket to pick up the ingredients for Walters' supper.

William Fredericks was having a different kind of supper that evening. He had just polished off his last bottle of Beefeater as he somehow pulled his car into the lot at the WNN studio on First Street NE. He was originally told to be in the office by eight o'clock and sober and ready to go by ten for the special election night coverage.

He forgot that he had hung up on his producer, who immediately withdrew the offer. Management was not amused as Fredericks barged through security at ten minutes after seven and began babbling nonsense about George Washington winning the election. The producer anticipated the scene and had guards set up to escort Fredericks out.

The president of the network walked out of his office to observe the chaotic scene. He announced that he had had enough and, in front of his staff, engineer and crew, fired his top on-air personality, asking him to leave the premises immediately. As the security team approached him, Fredericks flew into a wild rage, physically attacking an older producer and verbally abusing the staff.

For all his years of instability, no one had seen Fredericks this out of control. His Election Night actions made his diatribe at Federal Hall seem tame by comparison. A guard physically carried him out of the building and happily dropped William in a heap on the asphalt of the parking lot.

The rain poured down. Fredericks lifted himself up and fumbled for his keys as he made his way to his car. Once inside, he realized he did not know what to do or where to go. A thunderclap above brought him a moment of clarity, as if the storm had delivered the answers.

"Fredericks, go! Go to where he goes to die! Go! Now!"

Supper at the Mount Vernon estate was concluding. Walters had insisted on an intimate dinner with just the new founders as his secret service agents sat down the hall watching the initial election returns on television.

He held court over the dining room table, preaching political parables as if it was a scene from the Last Supper with the men as his disciples. They hung on every word and remained silent for better part of the meal.

Jenson was the first to excuse himself, noting that he had a show to do and needed to get to the hotel in Annapolis. Walters rose with right hand extended and, in one motion, shook Jenson's hand and hugged him tight. He wished him a good broadcast and best of luck in the coming weeks, momentarily confusing the men in the room. Jenson bid adieu to the rest of the team and exited the house.

Josh and Steve Anders were the next to leave. They told the group that they had to get to Annapolis to address the media from the lobby of the Westin. Washington's reaction to their exit was the same as with Jenson and the men started out. Faulk rose quickly and told the remaining men that he would hitch a ride with Josh as he had promised to help Pepper and Rader in the ballroom. He motioned to Murray to make sure he did not forget Walters' victory speech for later that night. Jack nodded and Faulk raced out to get his ride.

Three men were left in the dining room. Hahn looked at Murray. "We're staying with Walters, right?"

Murray said yes, and looked to Walters for approval. He agreed and suggested they move to the den to join the agents before they left for the victory party. Hahn joked that he never thought he would live to see a concession speech from the current president and mentioned that he would believe it when he saw it. Murray excused himself for a minute and speed dialed Dottie's cell phone.

He got her voicemail once again and decided not to leave a message.

"Tonight is the boss's night. Tomorrow, I'm Dottie's husband again."

A couple hours passed and Hahn and Murray were getting fidgety. Walters seemed to be settling in on the couch as he watched the eastern states post their results. They knew they should have been at the hotel already. Their cell phones rang incessantly. Text after text poured in, asking where the trio was and when they should be expected. Anders was relentless, calling about every thirty seconds.

The candidate had clammed up. He ignored the pleas from his advisors as he watched Fox News call Ohio and Pennsylvania in his favor. Walters stood and addressed the agents.

"Gentlemen, excuse us for a second."

His security detail waved their hands as if to say no problem. Like the new founders, the secret service agents wondered what they were still doing at the mansion. Murray and Hahn looked as though they were about to fall asleep when Walters motioned for the two founders to follow him.

The men went out the kitchen door and around the house to the back dirt road. A black BMW sat in the driveway, out of view of the television crews camped at the entrance to the estate. Walters told the men to get in as he produced a set of keys and jumped into the driver seat.

He started the car and put it into drive. The car lurched onto the dirt road and started into the woods.

Incredulous and fearing for his life, Hahn reacted, shouting at Walters that he did not know how to drive."

"I'm an excellent driver." The General's reply caught the men off guard. Hahn and Murray just looked at each other and laughed. Walters quickly explained that he had to get away from his protection.

"There's a reason you have bodyguards. Some crazy liberal might want to take a shot at you."

Walters answered Jack's statement in a curt manner, "That won't happen tonight."

The three men looked out the window as their car flew past the gates of the estate and the television personnel. Walters noted the smooth ride, complimenting the Germans for their automotive craftsmanship.

Hahn leaned over the front seat. "Do you know how to get to Annapolis?" he asked Walters.

The General switched on his right turn signal and informed Hahn that the car was equipped with a GPS device. "I've become very familiar with this apparatus. It'll get us there. But I want to make one stop first, before I go."

— ◆ —

The storm raged as the car pulled into the darkness of the lengthy oval driveway. George Washington's Mount Vernon estate had been turned into a national park site many years earlier but still resembled the way it looked in 1789. The sky was pitch-black, save for the flashes of lightning cascading like musket fire across the stately plantation. Power lines had fallen, leaving parts of the estate in near blackness.

The driver side door opened and bottles spilled out, breaking glass across the driveway. Fredericks careened out of the car and stumbled, grinding the larger parts of glass into the pavement. He regained his footing and headed to the dimly lit museum directly in front of him. Cursing and screaming his hatred of George Washington, Fredericks peered through the window at a life-size mannequin of the General, riding his white mount in full Revolutionary War garb.

"You ruined my life, you bastard!"

Fredericks was incensed. A flash of lightning lit up the lawn, knocking the emergency power out. He took advantage of the situation and pulled the largest stone he could find from the muddy earth. He smashed it through the window and crashed into the building, tearing his clothes on the remaining shards of glass.

He looked up at the General Washington statue in the dark and charged, tackling the inanimate figure to the ground. Fredericks pulled the authentic sword from the mannequin's sheath and swung it wildly as he imagined himself in a duel with the first president.

Fredericks wheeled around to the sound of a car coming up the driveway. He made his way to the broken window and peered through the dark rain, straining to see if anybody noticed him. Instead of driving to the main house, the car turned toward Washington's original tomb. It pulled up in front of the small building and the driver door opened.

A man stepped out and stood looking at the door to the tomb. As Fredericks squinted, a flash of lightening left no doubt as to the identity of the stranger in the night.

"It's him, it's him! You were right. I have to fulfill my destiny."

Fredericks stormed out of the building and into the driving rain toward Washington's tomb.

The cell phone lit up for what seemed to be the thousandth time. Both men reached down but only one found it to be his hand-held device.

"It's mine, I got it."

Hahn answered the call from Anders. He told Anders that Walters wanted to make a stop at his original Mt. Vernon estate before heading to the hotel. An exasperated Hahn relayed the fact that their leader had ditched the secret service agents. Anders voice could be heard throughout the entire national park.

"Is he out of his mind? Do they know where you are? I'm calling them right now. Don't panic! They'll be over there in a few minutes."

As he hung up the phone, Hahn shook his head at Anders' condescending and over the top reaction. The speaker function may have been off but the conversation was as clear as day to anybody within fifty feet of the car.

Murray stared at his phone in the palm of his hand. "My cell is dead. Damn it. I forgot to power it after dinner and we ran out of there so fast I forgot the charger. You have anything for a BlackBerry?"

Hahn held up his iPhone and apologized. The apology was hardly out of his mouth before the voice of Tim Jenson caught his attention. The latest election results were being reported on the radio. The two new founders opened the car window and called out to Walters over the roar of the torrent. Walters stood only ten feet away with his back to the car. The men had not realized that Walters had been in the rain for a good five minutes as they were preoccupied with their phones and the results. Without moving his feet, the candidate looked back over his shoulder. The men turned up the volume.

Jenson repeated that all three networks were reporting that Texas was still too close to call. Eighty percent of the precincts were in, yet they could not give the state to Walters.

"How could that be? We won Florida, Ohio and Pennsylvania already but Texas is still up in the air? Maybe we didn't campaign there enough. No. There's no way! They have to be pulling something!"

Hahn looked at the radio console while Murray's gaze stayed on Walters. Jenson's announcement had elicited no reaction from the candidate. Walters virtually ignored the critical news and turned his attention back to the crypt.

Hahn's phone buzzed loudly, diverting Murray's attention back inside the car. The text message came from Dudek, alerting the team that if they won Texas, the president would concede the election. Hahn pumped his fist as Murray looked out the open window, catching a glimpse of his boss disappearing behind the tomb.

"Where the hell is he going?"

Murray was concerned as to why the first president would walk to the back of the tomb in the middle of a driving rain storm. He did not recall anything behind the building except a few trees and the Potomac River. He stayed seated and powered up the window to keep the rain out of the back seat. Hahn stayed focused on Jenson's election report. Murray leaned over the front seat and turned the car off, explaining that they didn't want to drain the battery.

"I'm turning the lights off too. You'll be fine, the radio will stay on."

Hahn was in a trance, hanging on Tim's every word. He did not change expression, even through the commercials. While Hahn kept his head down, Murray looked out the windshield. He saw no sign of Walters and he grew more concerned. A small reflection of light in the rearview mirror made Murray turn around. At the bottom of the long driveway, a pair of headlights appeared.

"Looks like the secret service found us."

One second later, the car made a right turn onto the dirt road that ran behind the garden. Murray thought that the agents must have some kind of tracking device on the candidate to pinpoint his exact location. The road they took would eventually lead behind the tomb. Once the secret service got there, Walters' little adventure would be over. Murray scanned the area in front of the tomb and thought he noticed a shadow.

Thunder roared and lightning flashed as the clock struck midnight on the east coast. The fact that the candidate had yet to leave for the hotel alarmed his team in Annapolis. A barrage of calls and texts found Hahn's phone within seconds. Even the calm, cool and collected Ken Rader incredulously asked Hahn why Murray continued to ignore his calls.

Murray peered out the window through the rain. The shadow he saw a minute earlier did not produce the father of the country. While he did not feel like braving the elements, Murray recalled the vibes from the plane ride home and had a bad feeling about Walters' intentions. He knew it was time to act; he had to go get his boss and bring him back to the car.

"If the agents bring him back here before I do, just yell and let me know."

Hahn nodded as Murray opened the door. A gust of wind blew the cold rain into Hahn's phone. The financial whiz cursed as he wiped his screen with a tissue. The car door slammed shut and Murray was off.

The slight man plodded through the mud with measured steps as he made his way around the tomb and through the cherry trees. Footing was unstable and the ground sloped. He was not about to misstep and end up face-first in the mud. He continued slowly and noticed an opening ahead. At once he stopped.

On the ground before him was a discarded suit jacket, pants, and a white dress shirt that was so saturated it was practically see-through. The discovery confused him. He was about to examine the clothing when lightning struck close by, causing him to jump to the side and stumble into the opening. Once in the clear, he looked up to see Walters kneeling in front of him.

Fredericks took a deep breath and drew his sword.

He inched his way toward his nemesis.

Dressed in his full military uniform, Walters knelt down, facing the banks of the river. It was apparent that he was in deep prayer or reflection. Fredericks paused in admiration of the man; this would be his night of victory and instead of celebrating, he was paying homage to his wife and colonial estate.

The reverence did not last long.

Walters' peaceful reflection was suddenly roused by a primal scream above the din of the storm.

Walters felt the dull impact of Fredericks' boot on his right rib cage. His body twisted from the blow and Walters landed on his back. He looked up to see the wild eyed Englishman spewing threats at him.

"We are going to kill you!"

Walters tried to pull away but could not. He was held down by Frederick's firmly planted left foot dug into his chest. The tip of Fredericks' sword slid across the skin just below Walters' adams apple, but to Fredericks' horror drew no blood. The General was not afraid.

"William, you cannot harm me."

The words enraged the already volatile television host.

"What?? What are you saying? I am sick of your lies. You have ruined us and we will kill you!"

Fredericks took a quick drink from the small flask attached to his belt. He may have been drinking, but his mind could not have been clearer.

"You are not Walters! I know who you are. You are George Washington!"

Walters pulled his head away from the point of the blade. His powerful reply could be heard across the Potomac.

"That's right, William. I am General Washington! You knew that since the beginning. Put down that bottle. It's not helping you. It's killing you."

Washington's unapologetic confirmation further infuriated Fredericks.

"They're not killing me. They led me here tonight. They told me you would be here to seek me out." "

"Who led you, William?"

"The voices, THEM! They always tell me what to do."

Mud flowed around them, down the slope from the hedgerows toward the river. William Fredericks breathed deeply to contemplate his next move. His adrenaline stayed high as Washington pushed the sword away from his throat and scrambled to his feet to face his foe.

"Mr. Fredericks, I know who you are! You are like me. We are not meant to be part of this day and age. We don't fit in. Look deep inside and you know it to be true."

Fredericks burst out in a maniacal laugh. "Then why are you here? And why are you running for President? Your people didn't want you to be president! They betrayed you! That's how I knew of the cancer relapse. Your own people informed on you!"

Washington, now screaming above the storm, fearlessly stepped toward Fredericks and placed his left hand on Fredericks' right shoulder.

"No, you are wrong William. That was me. I knew you would spread the cancer rumors, allowing Mr. Walters to depart without question. At the same time, enough of the populace would believe you insane and still cast their ballot for Mr. Walters. I never meant to be president again."

The inferno within Fredericks raged while George continued.

"I had my chance a long time ago and voluntarily left after two terms. I could have been king of America if I so chose. It's up to twenty-first century Americans to solve twenty-first century problems and Divine Providence has provided us with the right people to do just that. Fredericks, you and I belong in another age and I am going home tonight!"

Fredericks bowed his head and slumped his shoulders. "Then who am I?"

——— — ———

Murray heard the commotion and hurried frantically around the tomb. He felt his way in total darkness through the grove of trees toward the voices.

His second thoughts about staying put in the dry car had vanished. Murray hoped that the agents would not have to use physical force to get him back to the car and wondered why they were talking so loudly. But a third thought crossed his mind as well.

"With the way the results are going, I sure hope he's not facing an assassin."

This last scenario caused Murray to increase his pace.

——— — ———

"You are King George the Third! I knew it since we met. Come with me,

Fredericks."

Fredericks lifted his face and screamed at the first president.

"Nooooo! You lie! That cannot be true! I am going to kill you!"

Fredericks stepped back from the General. He gripped the weapon's handle with both hands and slowly lifted the sword above his head. Washington stood at attention and once again told his assailant that he could not hurt him. Mr. Fredericks would have none of it.

"I will fulfill my destiny!"

Fredericks took one last deep breath, about to bring the foil down upon the defenseless George Washington as he felt a sudden push.

The impact knocked Fredericks off balance and instinctively turned and struck his attacker with the handle of the sword.

Dottie Murray put her hands up to the back of her head as she intuitively rolled away from Fredericks. She kept one hand on her head to quell the flow of blood as she propped herself on the wet grass with the other. A confused William Fredericks quickly surveyed the foreground and deduced that the woman on the ground ten feet from him had just tried to save George Washington's life.

"Your attempt at bravery was futile and you will now pay the same price as Mr. Washington!" Fredericks never saw the blindside hit that came next. As he gloated over the addition of a new potential victim, Fredericks was struck again, this time by Jack Murray. The force of the tackle was much stronger than Dottie's and it knocked the Englishman off his feet and sent the sword flying through the air. Both men crashed to the ground and rolled toward the embankment of the Potomac.

Their momentum and the mudflow sent the combatants tumbling over the river's edge. Dottie scrambled to the sword, picked it up and handed it to a calm Washington before racing to the river to help her husband. The storm only grew stronger as frantic shouts for help cut above the wind and rain.

Dottie made it to the bank to discover the two men hanging on for life. Jack held on to exposed roots in the small cliff while Fredericks grasped a couple of slick rocks jutting from the earth. Jack's heart skipped a beat when he heard his wife call his name through the driving rain. For an instant Murray was not in a life or death struggle over a raging river; he was happy and content knowing his love had risked it all for him.

The immediacy of his dire situation returned when a lightning bolt crashed to earth only a few hundred feet from the cliff. Murray yelled to Dottie to get a stick or a tree limb.

Fredericks, having had the wind knocked out of him a few seconds earlier, tried to catch his breath and ask for help as well. But his energy and strength was sapped by the attack and he pawed at the dirt as he tried to climb the ridge.

Jack held on tight and looked at Fredericks. Both men dangled twenty feet above the water. The ex-pat was no more than three feet away from Fredericks but slightly lower than him. Murray knew that he had a better foothold and would last longer in the elements. He contemplated extending his hand to help his political foe before tasting a drop of blood on his lips.

He looked up to see his wife above. She laid flat on her stomach in the mud and, with her eyes closed and using all of her might, extended a tree branch to her husband. The blood that dripped from her wound through her hair made Jack all but forget about the man to his left. He took the branch in his right hand and worked his way up the embankment as Dottie grasped the base of a small bush. He was near the top when he felt a hand touch his foot. Jack looked back.

Fredericks had lunged for Murray and grabbed on to the weakened root that had supported Jack. He was further down than where the Virginian had been and the footing was unstable. He again reached for Jack's foot but it was out of reach.

One last pull got Jack to the top. He peered over the edge to see Dottie struggling with her grip. He threw his left leg over and crawled to his wife. The release of the weight on the branch made her open her eyes.

Mr. and Mrs. Murray were face-to-face for the first time in months.

She righted herself and embraced Jack with a hurried kiss as she pulled her husband away from the embankment.

Their moment of intimacy was interrupted by the sound of Fredericks' hysterical pleas. The couple grabbed the wet branch and cautiously made their way to the cliff once again. They looked down in the dark to see a manic Fredericks losing his grip. Jack extended the branch as Fredericks screamed for his life.

"Help me!"

A lightning bolt lit the sky, allowing the Murrays to see Fredericks drop into the roaring Potomac.

All at once the rain subsided. The couple stood silent at the top of the ridge. Another minute went by before Jack turned and took his wife in his arms.

"I'm never letting you go again. Now let's go get George."

When the Murrays searched for Washington, he was gone. "I bet I know where he went," said Jack. They plodded their way back past the old tomb and toward their car. As they came around the building, they saw Hahn leaning on the outside of the BMW, with a bottle of scotch in one hand and a full glass in the other. Upon seeing the two figures illuminated in the headlights, he hoisted a toast.

"They called Texas for us and the president conceded. Congratulations Mr. Walters, you are the next President of the United States!"

It took a second for Hahn to realize that the muddy, bleeding, and limping duo was Jack and Dottie Murray. The president-elect was not with them.

"Oh my God! What happened to you? Dottie! What are you doing here? Where's George?

"I think I know!" Jack yelled.

———

The clouds cleared, exposing a full moon over the Potomac. The light of the moon shone brightly on the driveway as Hahn, Jack, and Dottie ambled down a muddy path past the nursery on their right. They finally reached the tomb that had encased the bodies of George and Martha Washington since they were moved from their original tomb in 1831.

A reflection glinted off a shiny object behind the tomb's locked gates. Dottie noticed it first and motioned for the men to walk toward the building. The three stopped short at the entrance and stared at the metallic object inside.

Mrs. Murray said it was the sword Fredericks had when he tried to kill Washington. A wide-eyed Hahn asked her what she was talking about. Jack immediately recognized it as the sword George wore upon their original meeting in Philadelphia four months earlier. The sword was neatly placed on the lid of Washington's sarcophagus.

Murray pulled at the locked gates to see how the saber got in there. He noticed a scrap of parchment tied neatly by Providence's red queue. The words were written in President George Washington's hand:

"With a heart full of love and gratitude, I now take my leave of you. I most devoutly wish that your latter days may be as prosperous and happy as our former ones have been glorious and honorable."

Epilogue

Dottie Murray looked especially beautiful in a new blue coat and hat, her rosy cheeks aglow this Sunday morning. Though the wind and icy rain blew sideways into her face, she didn't flinch as she sat proudly between her men, holding both her husband's and son's hands. The cuts and bruises from the election night events had all but healed and Dottie looked forward to her new life in Washington.

Todd was excited, too. A resilient teenager, he had recently enrolled in a new high school in Alexandria. In only a few weeks, he had made many new friends and looked forward to spring baseball. Although he still didn't remember the fatal bus crash or the weeks leading up to it, Todd had made what amounted to a full and somewhat miraculous recovery.

The events since that fateful July Fourth weekend in Philadelphia seemed like a fantasy now as Josh Anders looked the Chief Justice in the eye, placed his left palm down on the Bible, raised his right hand, and began his oath of office.

"I, Josh Anders, do solemnly swear"

Jack Murray's eyes focused on his friend Tim Jenson, standing to Josh's side. Tim had taken his oath only minutes before.

Jack recalled Jenson's keynote speech at the Republican convention. His Jeffersonian-inspired eloquence in describing the natural inseparability of individual human dignity and liberty moved Jack to tears. It also reminded Jack of the many so-called Republicans who preached individual liberty, but fostered an all encompassing federal bureaucracy.

Jack took one look at the huge audience at the Capitol and realized that most of those politicians were now ex-politicians, having been rejected by a new generation of Tea Party conservatives. Jack hoped these Frank Walters disciples would not give in to the temptations of DC power as so many others had done.

The name Frank Walters reminded Jack of his friend and mentor, George Washington, who insisted as a condition of his nomination that Jenson deliver the convention's keynote address. Jack didn't understand it then, but smiled realizing the General set up this very moment.

"that I will faithfully execute"

Jack looked within. He understood his previous suspicions of Jenson were shamefully unfounded; having mistaken Tim's supportive long distance friendship with Dottie for an affair. Jack was not even sure if the new vice-president was aware of his accusations.

Only six months earlier, Jack Murray was a high school history teacher facing a mid life identity crisis. Now, he was an integral part of a new American revolution as vital to the country's future as the founders themselves. He reflected back on the events that led to his family's prominent status on the steps of the Capitol Building this cold January morning.

Jack had anticipated that his life would slowly get back to normal following Election Day. But nothing was further from the truth. The mayhem and confusion of that night only complicated his life more. At least his family was back together.

"the Office of President of the United States"

Dottie caught Jack's eye and smiled as he drifted back into his quiet recollections.

The irony of Dottie's appearance that stormy night at Mount Vernon was not lost on her husband. As Dolly Madison had once saved Stuart's original portrait of Washington from fire during the War of 1812, so did Dottie Murray rescue the father of our country from attack. Jack recalled her shadowy figure lunge out of nowhere to knock over the crazed William Fredericks as he was about to run his sabre through General Washington.

Jack didn't know at the time that his wife drove the three hours to surprise him on election night. Dottie was an hour from the Annapolis hotel when she contacted Josh Anders, only to be told that Jack was with Washington at Mount Vernon.

As a result, Jack was not even sure Dottie was the mysterious hero until he recognized her screams as Fredericks trained his weapon on her.

"and, will to the best of my ability,"

Jack's thoughts drifted back to George Washington, the real mysterious player in all of this. He was gone now for over two months, but George remained a curiosity. To Jack, he was a hero, boss, teacher, and messiah, but ultimately a trusted friend.

George returned to his time as Jack had suspected he would do since early in the campaign. George Washington rejected a third term in the eighteenth century and exclaimed during the recent campaign that only twenty-first century Americans can pilot a twenty-first century America. Now Jack understood that Divine Providence had brought George back to make sure the right crew manned his ship.

"preserve, protect and defend"

President-elect Walters had a relapse of cancer as Washington had cryptically predicted on his last trip to New York. The media reported his death shortly after winning the election. At his son's request, he was cremated and his ashes spread over the hills of Maryland and Virginia.

While the left continued their daily outcry debating the validity of the president-elect, the Constitution was clear. Vice-President-elect Josh Anders would be sworn in as President and Tim Jenson, both Anders' and Washington's first choice, would assume the vice-presidential slot.

While Anders would miss his mentor George, he saw symmetry in the turn of events and attributed his fate to Providence. Besides, Jack knew that Anders' temperament would not have suited the second spot on the ticket. He also knew that Steve Anders would undoubtedly become a close advisor to the new president, guaranteeing The United States navigate by the winds of traditional conservative principles.

Jack peered over to Hahn seated just on the other side of Todd. Hahn looked forward to his position as Secretary of the Treasury. Jack, despite some misgivings as to Hahn's temperament and trustworthiness, could not think of anybody more intellectually qualified to attack the country's economic woes than Hahn. He would probably begin his new job as soon as the inauguration parties ended.

Brian Faulk tapped Jack Murray on the shoulder. He pointed proudly to the rising sun reflecting off the Washington Monument, undoubtedly a sign from above. Jack turned around and smiled at Faulk and his wife

Deborah. Faulk decided he was too old for a career in Washington DC. He would return to Philadelphia, explaining how he could add more value to the cause through his publishing enterprises.

Jack finally reflected on their nemesis. No one seemed to know what became of William Fredericks and his body had yet to be recovered. Police deduced he had vandalized Mount Vernon in a drunken rage on election night. Even though he was officially listed as a missing person, news reports regarding his disappearance quickly faded away. Even his own network didn't seem too interested in his whereabouts.

"the Constitution of the United States."

Jack closed his eyes as President Anders finished the thirty-nine word oath. Jack Murray was where Providence had delivered him and, as the new Secretary of State, was about to embark on a new adventure.

"So help me God."

Acknowledgements

The authors would like to thank David Dunham and Joel Dunham of Dunham Books for making this project possible. Additionally, a thank you to our friend, Dick Morris, who generously gave of his time and wrote the Foreword to this book; Stan Pottinger, who provided expert advice and pointed us in the right direction; Jerome Corsi, Dave Bossie, Brian Darling, Joe Farah, Joan Romanelli and Tim Sumner, whose belief in two unknowns is very much appreciated; And Walter Duncan and Frank Connor for instilling in their sons the love of family & country and the willingness to fight for our children's future.

Joe
Thank you to my wife Danielle and children Frank and Kathleen, who put up with late nights and self-doubts but believed all the way; my mother Mary, stepfather Gerry and in laws Kathy and Ed, who provided honest feedback throughout.

Mike
I would like to thank my wife Julie, who provided indispensable advice and put up with being awakened at two in the morning on many school nights; Michael and Angelica, my children and daily inspirations; my mother Charlotte and mother-in-law Grace, who are the two best unpaid PR agents we could have; and all my friends, both conservative and liberal, who put their political leanings aside to encourage us throughout the project.

About the Authors

Joseph F. Connor is a husband, father of two, son and brother.

He has testified before the Senate Subcommittee on Foreign Relations regarding President Clinton's 1999 clemency grant to 16 terrorist members who claimed his father's murder, the Senate Judiciary Committee in 2009 during Eric Holder's confirmation hearing and introduced The Pardon Attorney Reform and Integrity Act to Congress in 2000.

Having commuted though the WTC on 9/11/01, Connor eyewitnessed the attacks from his nearby office, losing his cousin among others.

Mr. Connor led the successful 2011 effort to deny parole to the terror leader who refused the Clintons' 1999 clemency grant.

Joe's articles have been published in the *New York Post, Human Events, Los Angeles Times, Newsmax, National Review Online,* and *The Wall Street Journal.* He currently contributes to Breitbart.com (BigPeace) and Redstate.com. Mr. Connor has also appeared on several news shows including: *Hannity & Colmes, Fox & Friends, The NBC Nightly News, Hardball, America Live,* as well as various local and nationally syndicated radio programs including Dennis Miller, Tom Marr, Mark Levin, and Sean Hannity.

Joe had a key role in the Citizens United documentary, *Hillary the Movie,* that was the impetus for the Supreme Court's overturning of the McCain Feingold Campaign Finance law.

Joe is active in the local Tea Party movement and received a 2011 award from the National Conference on Jewish Affairs and The United Liberty Alliance.

A 1988 graduate of Villanova University, Joe is married and lives in the NY metropolitan area with his wife and two children. He works in the financial services industry.

Michael S. Duncan is a husband and father of two. He works in the financial services industry where he is a frequent guest speaker on merger & acquisition industry trends. He is also a regular lecturer of continuing legal education courses to corporate law firms in the U.S.

Mr. Duncan has written numerous articles on shareowner services for trade publications as well as an article on stock options in the Spring 2009 edition of *The Journal of Employee Ownership Law and Finance* published by the National Center for Employee Ownership.

A 1988 graduate of Villanova University, Mike is married and lives in the New York City metropolitan area with his wife and two children. He serves as an officer in The Knights of Columbus and is a member of the local Tea Party. Mike is very active in his church and youth sports as well.